Forget Me Not

Forget Me Not

Dedicated to all the aspiring writers out there.

Don't wait too long to make your dreams come true.

Be bold. Be brave. Be you.

Forget Me Not

Tracey Gramajo

Preface

When I was a young preteen, my older sister started taking American Sign Language as an elective in school. She began fingerspelling words she would hear and see, and I quickly became fascinated by it. Determined that one day my hand would be in constant motion like hers, as soon as my high school schedule allowed for it, I signed up for ASL class too.

At the age of fifteen, I fell in love with American Sign Language. It was everything I had hoped it would be, and more. Though I cannot claim to be an expert, I've spent my life and career as an ASL interpreter, learning and using ASL. It is a beautiful language and a huge part of my life. So, when I set off to write and complete my first novel, I knew I wanted ASL to be involved.

This story is by no means intended to be about the Deaf experience, as I am not qualified to share that. It is a fictional love story. I simply created this story with a mix of hearing and Deaf characters to honor the Deaf community in gratitude for having the pleasure of dipping my toes into their diverse culture. However, before the story begins, I want you, the reader, to have a bit of background knowledge about this language I hold so dear.

American Sign Language is its own language, it is not simply English on the hands. ASL has its own morphemes, phonemes, syntax, and grammatical rules. Because ASL has had immense contact with spoken English, there are some variations that include: Manually Coded English (MCE), Signed Exact English (SEE), Pidgin Signed English (PSE), and Conceptually Accurate Signed English (CASE). These variations can look more like English on the hands because they follow English's grammatical structure and phrasing. Throughout the Deaf community, one can encounter some of these variations.

For the purpose of this book, when characters engage in signed dialogue, it is presented in italics to differentiate between the use of ASL and spoken English. Although the signed dialogue is, for the most part, written in English, I wish for the reader to know that in real life, these conversations would look quite different.

While there are many signs that match perfectly with English words, there are many ASL signs that do not have an English equivalent, and vice versa. Users of American Sign Language use facial expression to intensify words, differentiate between statements and questions, and show size variations. ASL is a visual language that uses space and classifiers to describe details and events. It is a high context language that often requires less "words" in any given interaction because the information is there through context and shared knowledge. Conversely, English is a low context language that requires much more information (words) for the same interactions. I included some descriptions of typical facial expressions surrounding the interactions of the characters, and also threw in some dialogue where the syntax teetered between ASL and English. These elements only touch the surface of the true beauty and uniqueness of American Sign Language.

You might also notice the use of a capitalized "D" with the word "Deaf" in some instances. This is because Deaf, with a capital "D," refers to a cultural identity, whereas deaf, without the capitalization, refers only to the actual hearing loss.

My hope is that through this glimpse into American Sign Language and the Deaf community, readers will find themselves as fascinated by it as I was all those many years ago. For anyone interested in learning more about American Sign Language, I encourage you to find your local Deaf community events and learn from the source. There you will not only find a wealth of knowledge about this beautiful language, but also have the opportunity to learn more about the Deaf community's diverse culture and values.

Part I

Forget Me Not

Chapter 1
Scarlett

The damn key is stuck again. I jiggle it in the lock, trying to finagle it free, and kick my frustrations into the base of the glass door. Mom said she would have the locks changed, yet here I am fighting with this damn door, again. I pause for a moment and wonder if she did have the locks changed and forgot to give out the new keys. The light on the wall of the lobby begins to flash, signaling that the phone is ringing, which I can hear from outside the door. The locked door that won't let me in. I curse under my breath and try twisting the key again. It finally budges. I swing the door open and rush to the receptionist counter, sliding my fingers under the handle of the receiver, pulling it up to my ear.

"All Hands Language Services, how can I help you?" I breathe into the phone, but I'm met with silence. Just missed it. I suppose they will call back and turn to make my way to my office.

"Hey, boss!" Lucy greets me as she walks in the front door. She is always just a few minutes behind me, uber prompt, which is a characteristic I value greatly.

"Hey, Lucy. Looks like I just missed a call, they'll probably be calling back soon." I let her know. She nods and hangs her coat on the rack by the door.

"Never a dull moment," she quips with a smile.

"Certainly not," I agree. "I'll be in my office if you need anything."

All Hands Language Services is a family business that I seemed to inherit. It was never my dream to run an interpreting agency, but I am a legacy. And the business is lucrative. When I say inherit, my Deaf mother, Helen, and her Deaf best friend and business partner, Alana, are still around, and still very much involved in the business. Although, they are in their sixties and should really consider retirement. Mom wanted me to grow up to become an interpreter. Except, I had spent my entire childhood interpreting for her and my father. That is, until he passed away from a heart attack during my freshman year of high school. Over the years, I have come to loathe interpreting. Yet, providing the service is near and dear to me, since I come from a family that relies on it. So, I went off to college and studied business management. By "went off to college," I mean I went forty-five minutes away to North Carolina State University in Raleigh. I could have been a commuter if I had wanted to. I think I needed to get away from the silence for a while. I needed to immerse myself in the hearing world since I had been surrounded by the silence of the Deaf world my entire life.

Of course, after my four years, I found myself back in "Wide Awake" Wilson, business degree in hand, poised and ready to take the reins as business manager of All Hands Language Services. That was the deal, I had to be a part of the business, even if I wasn't an interpreter. The name sounds cliche, "all hands" for a sign language interpreting agency. It made me scoff at first too. In actuality, the letters in the acronym, AHLS, represent the names of my mom, her best friend, and their children. Alana, Helen, Lorenzo, and Scarlett. I'm Scarlett. I'm hearing. Everyone in my life is Deaf. Well, not everyone. Alana's husband, Corbin, he's hearing. She committed a Deaf community faux pas and married an interpreter. Gasp! He was welcomed though, because he is a CODA, like me. Child of Deaf Adults. We are ipso-facto members of the community.

As business manager, I have a pretty nice office all to myself in our strip mall office building. Though, Wilson, North Carolina doesn't offer much in the way of views. There is an excellent Mexican spot next door where we often frequent for lunch or happy hour. Despite the window in my office gracing me with the luxurious view of trees behind the strip mall, I have a modern and sleek looking office. Tucked behind my white desk I have one of those extra wide swivel chairs that allows me to sit "crisscross applesauce" if I want, which I often do. In the corner by the window, I opted for a small, white leather couch that is supported by black iron feet. A small glass coffee table sits in front of it. On the other side, near the door, there's a small round table with two chairs. When you think of an office, often it includes chairs on the opposite side of the desk. Not mine. I don't like the idea of that separation distinguishing me from my team. If ever I am meeting with someone from the team, it's either on the couch, or at the table. I find that when we work together on an equal level, things run much smoother. Sure, my father's life insurance money started this business, but I most certainly don't run it alone.

    As I hang my coat over the hook on the back of my door, I hear the phone ring again and Lucy answers with her sweet, country accent. Despite Wilson being somewhat of a small town, though not as small as it once was, there is a large Deaf population. Probably due to the fact that Eastern North Carolina School for the Deaf, ENCSD, has been long established here. That's where Mom met Alana, where they became lifelong best friends. Our families quite literally do everything together.

    I slide into the mesh-backed chair at my desk and pry my laptop open, starting my day as usual with an email inbox check. Lucy and I are always in before 7:00 am, the other in-house staff typically arrives around 8:00 am. Mom and Alana handle finances and payroll. Lucy, of course, is our receptionist. Emma and Charlotte handle scheduling, which had become so demanding as the business expanded that we had to hire Charlotte a few years ago to keep up with the increasing clientele. Then we have four staff interpreters: Corbin, the lead, Dave, my best friend Macie, and James. Additionally, there are around one hundred independent contractors that take work through most of the northeast side of North Carolina, and even some parts of southern Virginia. Our staff interpreters do mostly local work though.

    Corbin is next to arrive. He taps on my door, juggling a pink bakery box along with his coffee and briefcase. "Good morning, Scar." His hazel eyes glisten as the crow's feet crinkle with his smile. I've always felt close to Corbin, knowing we grew up with similar experiences. After my dad died, he really became like a second father to me.

    "Good morning, Corbin." I nod toward the pink box that looks as though it could topple over at any moment. "You really want me to go up a size before Christmas and have to exchange my dress, don't you?"

"Me?" He feigns offense, "Never! Anyway, one doughnut won't hurt you." He winks.

"One doughnut a week might!" Corbin is one of those men who can eat whatever he wants and never gain a pound. I, on the other hand, must work hard to maintain my size twelve and keep the scale at 170 for my 5'8" frame. Ever and always wishing I could just get down to a size ten. If I do, I'd probably wish for a size eight. Like most women, I'm sure I'd never be satisfied.

"They'll be in the break room when you get a hankering for something sweet." He winks again and makes his way down the hall.

Mom arrives next. Every morning, she stops by my office to give me a hug and chat. I know that she misses me being at home. In reality, I hadn't had much reason to move out, being that it was just Mom and me. We had gotten extremely close when it was just the two of us after Dad died. The idea of leaving her there alone made me a bit sad, so I stayed. It began to be too much, working in the same office all day and living in the same house. On my twenty-fifth birthday I moved out. It was time. Now, after four years living on my own, I cherish these morning chats instead of dreading them.

She flicks the light switch to get my attention. Although this is a culturally acceptable way to get the attention of a Deaf person, she could knock on the door, or even vocalize. But I think sometimes she forgets I'm not Deaf.

Good morning! I sign. My lips purse together as I admire the sight of her. She's short, and getting shorter as she ages, I got my height from my dad. Her once waist-long hair she now keeps in a chin length bob and has fully embraced the shiny gray hue that has taken over. She will always be adorable to me.

She smiles brightly at me and walks over, tucking her arm around my shoulders in a half hug.

Corbin brought doughnuts again. I shrug and roll my eyes to emphasize my frustration.

Mom laughs. She too has a sweet tooth, but she has no interest or care in the size of her jeans. Dad was the love of her life, no need to impress anyone now. It also helps that she's always been naturally thin.

Why so worried about your body? she asks, waving at the air as if to say don't worry about it. *You are beautiful, any size.* She cups a hand over my cheek, then gives it a quick pat.

Thanks, Mom. I force a smile, suddenly being reminded of my lack of love life, which always takes me to this place of hating my body. It's a terrible, endless cycle. *Anyway, I already have my dress for the Christmas party. I can't let it shrink on me.*

My joke is lost on her. *Shrink? Don't wash it before the party.* Ever so literal.

Mom, remember the lock. This morning my key was stuck again. Should I just call a locksmith? I change the subject.

Her mouth curls into a perfect O, indicating that she had forgotten. *I forgot!* she signs slowly and dramatically, gritting her teeth as if sucking in a gulp of air.

I'll call. I wave it off, accepting that it is now my responsibility.

We chat for a bit longer before she makes her way to her office. One by one, everyone arrives, and the workday begins. Business manager sounds like it could entail quite a bit of work. But really, my job is to make sure everyone else is doing their job so that the business runs smoothly. Since I have the most "free time" on my hands around this time of year, my job also entails planning the company Christmas party. This is my favorite responsibility of the job. It's open to all staff, their families, and our independent contractors. I had sent virtual pre-invites to gauge how many people would be attending this year, and today is the deadline for RSVPs. I pull up the e-vite website and see the RSVP total at 75. That's the usual number, as a lot of our contractors live out of town and don't join in. Since Christmas is on a Monday this year, our party is set for the 23rd, which leaves me just over five weeks to get the location set, order the catering with final numbers, and hire a bartender and a DJ.

I'm on the phone with the manager at Tru by Hilton, the newest high-end hotel downtown, when I hear a rap on my open door. I look up to see Lorenzo in the doorway and hold up a finger, asking him to give me a minute.

"Yes, 75 total, we'll need table settings and a dance floor." I listen as the manager jots down notes.

"And you said that is for December 23rd?" she confirms.

"Yes, ma'am. Would your banquet hall be able to accommodate our group?" I question. Lorenzo has moved into the office and taken a seat on the couch. His large frame dwarfs the tiny sofa.

"Absolutely."

The Tru manager explains their rates for the banquet room and reviews their policies with me. Then I reserve a block of rooms for anyone who wants to have a few drinks and not worry about driving home that night. She blocks off the fifth and sixth floors at a discounted rate and informs me that those will be held for bookings until three days before our event.

I place the receiver down and turn to Lorenzo, waving my hand to pull his attention from his phone. *What's up?* I sign.

Lorenzo is Corbin and Alana's son, he's two years older than me. Considering we grew up together, he's practically my big brother, and basically my best friend. He's also Deaf, something Alana is super proud of. Her deafness is hereditary, my mom's was from meningitis when she was a small child, not hereditary. She was so proud of her Deaf child that she refused to try for more in case they might inherit their father's hearing ability.

Nothing. His lips pout in a nonchalant way. *I came to see Mom, wanted to see how you're doing.*

Planning the Christmas party, I just booked that new hotel downtown.

He nods in approval. *Nice.*

There's a moment of us just looking at each other, ready for an exchange. His dark eyes narrow as if he's contemplating something. Alana is half Italian, and Lorenzo had certainly received those genes, dark hair, dark eyes, smooth olive skin. His name was passed down too, from his full Italian grandfather.

Everyone knew he was attractive, hell, I knew he was attractive, I'd just never looked at him in that way.

What's up? I ask again, breaking the "silence."

He shakes his head. *You got a date for the party?* he finally asks.

No, that would require a love life. We both know I don't have that. I let out a laugh, mostly so the reminder of how single I am doesn't hit so hard.

He nods, I can almost see a hint of a smile spread across his lips. *Same.*

How's business? I try to keep the conversation moving, away from our mutually pathetic love lives. Lorenzo never wanted to join the family business, much to his parents' chagrin. He went to college and got an art degree; he sold freelance artwork and graphic designs. Though any real money he made, he always invested into some "get rich quick" scheme, only ever managing to barely get the bills paid. I always thought he had so much potential and wondered what was holding him back.

He shrugs. *Two new contracts this week. Logo designs, nothing too exciting.*

You know, I start to suggest. *We need a web designer on staff here.*

He knows this, I've suggested it on more than one occasion. There's something about that nine-to-five life that Lorenzo can't seem to commit to. *I'll think about it. I'm heading out, happy hour tonight?* He grins at the thought.

Sure.

Happy hour is our unofficial Thursday night team building soiree. Well, at least those of us under forty. James, Macie, Dave, Lucy, and I always go, Lorenzo's been joining us lately as well. Emma will come with her husband sometimes; Charlotte has young kids and very rarely makes an appearance.

I put the final touches on the official e-vite with the venue information and send it out to everyone who had RSVP'd. After

Forget Me Not

gathering my things, I stop to check my reflection in the mirror on the back of my office door. My strawberry blond hair has held up the straight style, avoiding any frizzing throughout the day. I inspect the ends that brush my collarbone and make a mental note to schedule a visit to the salon. The coloring of my hair is where my name came from, Scarlett. That and a little red, heart-shaped birthmark at the top of my forehead. The latter is my reason for always keeping bangs. Mom likes to joke that I was born with a red cap. She gave me the name sign that uses the handshape of the sign SCAR and the location and movement of the sign RED.

This week we decide to try a new bar downtown. The dive bar opened up a while ago, we just have never been. When I arrive at Fire & Ice, there's a Christmas tree already erect in the front entry, even though it's only mid-November. The lights in the bar area are dimmed, but the room is a glow with string lights that twinkle. I spot Macie and Dave, already set up with a high-top table in the middle of the bar area, each with a frozen margarita donning umbrellas in front of them.

"TGIT!" I sing, stepping up from the rung of a stool to lift myself onto it. "Thank god it's Thursday!"

They laugh and raise their glasses. Sure, we have another day in our work week, but who doesn't love a Friday? A tall guy with broad shoulders sidles up to the table, clearly our server. The sleeves of his polo shirt strain at the seams around his thick biceps, and all the hair on his head appears to have relocated to cover his cheeks and chin with a full, black beard. My breath hitches at the sight of him.

"Hey there, beautiful. What can I get you to drink?" he asks, his toothy grin almost glistens in the dim light of the bar. The name tag pinned over his heart reads 'Eli.' My cheeks flush and I have a fleeting feeling that he can sense my immediate attraction to him.

"I, um, a tequila and club soda," I clear my throat, "with lime, please?" I manage to choke out.

His eyebrow cocks, my order obviously an odd request. "Sounds, uh, disgusting." He and my tablemates erupt in laughter at my expense.

"What?" I shrug. "It's my version of a low carb margarita."

Eli's mouth opens, tilting his head back at the explanation. "Oh, I got you. I'll make you my skinny margarita. Anything else for now?"

I look to Dave and Macie. "Go ahead and put in an order of those bacon cheese fries," Dave suggests.

When Eli returns, James has joined us. I bring the straw to my lips and slurp in a sip of my drink while James places his order.

"My god, this is good," I breathe. "There's no way this is low carb."

He gives me that toothy grin again. "Oh, I assure you it is." He winks. "I'm pretty much a magician behind the bar." He brushes the back of his fingers over his chest, and I imagine what his chest feels like. Is it as rock hard as it looks?

"Ooooh, ok!" James sings in his flirtatious voice. "Maybe I'll have what she's having." He winks at Eli and walks his fingers up Eli's beefy bicep.

"Coming right up." Eli sends a wink in James' direction, and I wonder if he's flirting with me or him. Or perhaps he's only angling for a good tip. I convince myself it's the latter. But a girl can dream, right?

"Is this it?" Macie asks as Eli heads off to make James' drink. "I know Lucy said she wasn't coming tonight. She has a date."

James crosses one leg over his knee and leans in. "Ooh, I'm going to need details on this!" James is definitely the gossip in our group. He is also very openly gay, as many male interpreters are, and the biggest flirt I know.

"I don't know any more than that." Macie throws her hands up in surrender. "You'll have to ask her tomorrow." Macie and I go way back. Wilson is a small town; we had been through school together and became best friends over the years. I was fascinated by her curly black hair and creamy brown skin, and she was fascinated by my Deaf parents. We became fast friends and since she spent so much time hanging around my house, she fell in love with ASL. That's why she became an interpreter.

Just then, Lorenzo snakes an arm around my shoulder in a half hug. Having come in from behind me, I'm startled by his touch and let out a gasp. *Hi, Lorenzo.* I sign his name sign, a simple Z to

O in the air. Lorenzo Tate has a large frame in a tall, muscular way, his presence beside me always makes me feel small in comparison. Which I, of course, never mind. Silence fills the atmosphere. Voices turn off and hands go up as we all code switch from English to American Sign Language. James is a particular expert at this transition, being that he is a CODA, same as me.

What are we drinking? Lorenzo points to my drink.

The bartender made it, delicious! And low carb! I explain, grabbing it from the table to offer a sip.

With a heavy arm still draped across my shoulder, Lorenzo sips from my straw, showing no regard for potentially shared germs. We've been sharing everything since I was in diapers, why stop now? His eyebrows shoot up and his lips pout in an expression of surprised approval. *That, I'll take the same.*

Eli returns with James' drink and a plate of cheese fries. "Hey there." He tilts his chin at Lorenzo. "What can I get for you?" His eyes dart between us.

Lorenzo's free hand moves through the air, signing that he wants the same drink I have, and confusion sets in on Eli's face. "He'll have what she's having." James works in the iconic line again.

Eli turns to James and back to Lorenzo. *I'm Deaf.*

"He's Deaf," James voices for Lorenzo again.

It finally registers with Eli, and he nods, darts his eyes back to me, and then heads back to make another drink. I shift a bit in my seat, politely trying to signal that I need my personal bubble clear again. Lorenzo gets the hint and takes a seat next to me.

I saw the e-vite for the Christmas party! Tru downtown? I heard that place is nice, Macie mentions. *Are the rooms expensive?*

Not too bad, I start to explain, *with the group event discount it's $90.*

Why not Uber? Lorenzo jumps in. *We live local, Uber is cheaper.*

Everyone nods in agreement.

I don't know, James adds, *a night in a ritzy hotel after a fancy party? Sounds nice to me.*

Again, everyone nods, each reaching an index finger up to their chins to sign "true."

That was my thought. Plus, some of the contractors who live out of town are coming, I remind them. *They will want to stay if they drink.*

Speaking of drinks, Eli returns with Lorenzo's drink and a fresh one for me. I hadn't even realized that my glass had seemingly emptied right before my eyes. "Thank you." I say and sign at the same time.

Eli brings his hand up to his chin, touching it with his fingers and moving it forward, copying my sign. "Thank you?" he confirms.

Our group erupts in cheers and waves their hands, praising Eli's effort. Everyone except Lorenzo. He narrows his eyes at him, and I can only read his expression as skepticism. When he notices my questioning gaze, he shakes his head and fakes a smile. I know it's fake because I've had twenty-nine years to learn his tells. *Good job,* he signs, then slinks his arm over the back of my stool.

"Anything else I can get for you guys?" Eli offers. James instinctively interprets for Lorenzo.

Deciding that appetizers would suffice for our group, Macie and James put in orders for more appetizers and drinks. Lorenzo holds his glass up and nods, silently asking to keep the drinks coming. Eli gets the hint and snaps a finger in his direction, nodding to acknowledge the order.

What's wrong? I ask Lorenzo. It is blatantly obvious something is bothering him.

His lips twitch and his eyes narrow. *Nothing,* he signs, shaking his head and pressing his pouted lips together, a very "Lorenzo" facial expression that I know all too well.

James catches my eye and cocks his head, subtly questioning our exchange. I just shrug it off and go back to enjoying our evening. Lorenzo's skeptical facial expression stays until we leave the bar.

Chapter 2
Lorenzo

The bed vibrates, jolting me from my sleep. My head is pounding. For a moment, I wonder what day it is, I wonder why I had set an alarm. As a freelance artist, I don't have a rigid schedule or certain time I must wake up. Then I realize the vibration isn't strong like my bed alarm clock. It's the vibration of a phone ringing that's lying on the bed. My hands feel around for my phone in the dusky morning light. It's not on the bed at all, it's on the nightstand plugged into the charger.

The bed vibrates again. When I reach behind me this time, the bed jolts. That's when it hits me that I'm not alone. That's when I remember what happened last night. Well, it wasn't that exciting. Scarlett was too drunk; those drinks that sleazy bartender was feeding her were too strong. So, I wouldn't let her drive, but I didn't want to leave her alone either. So, I brought her here.

Lorenzo? she signs the two letters of my name sign, sitting up in the bed and rubbing her head. *What am I doing here?*

You were drunk last night. Very drunk, I emphasize. *I didn't want you to be alone like that.*

It isn't the first time I've done this. Scarlett means the world to me; I could never let anything happen to her. I've always been here to protect her. Nothing ever happens, much to my disappointment. Absolutely nothing. God, I wish she knew how in love with her I was. Maybe I wish I knew how to tell her. But I can't risk losing her. Like I said, she's special. She's precious to me.

I've been in love with Scarlett Reese since I hit puberty. Well, since she hit puberty.

She nods, unfazed by waking up beside me. I live in a one-bedroom apartment, after all. I couldn't very well let her sleep on that rock hard futon I call a couch. In my twenties, I would have risked it. Once I passed thirty, my body, especially my back, started to betray me.

You have Tylenol? she asks, still rubbing her head.

I hesitate, taking in how beautiful she looks in my ECU t-shirt, she swims in it. The morning light reflecting in the strands of her pale orange hair creates a glow around her. *Yeah, I'll grab it.* As I throw the blanket off and prepare to stand, I realize my morning wood is standing at full attention under my plaid boxer briefs. I panic and quickly throw the blanket back over myself. There's absolutely no way she didn't notice the heat flushing over my cheeks.

What's wrong? she asks. There's genuine concern on her face, assuring me that she hadn't gotten an eye full.

I need a minute. I contort my face, and I can tell by the smirk on hers that she knows exactly what's going on.

I'll get it, where is it? I can tell by the way her lips are turned up and the crinkle around her eyes that she's laughing.

I point toward the attached bathroom. *First drawer.*

When she slides out of the bed, I can't help but notice her long legs, completely bare beneath my t-shirt. I'll never understand why she's always so concerned about her body. I think her body is gorgeous. I imagine her thick thighs wrapped around my waist, her full breasts pressed against my chest, my hands squeezing her round ass. Dammit, now I'm even more turned on than before. If that's even possible. She must be late for work, as much as I want her here in bed with me, I can't wait for her to leave so I can take care of this damn hard-on.

She emerges from the bathroom and starts gathering her clothes. *Fuck,* she signs. *I don't have any clothes here, do I?*

I shake my head, my lips curl into an amused grin. *You should.*

Fuck, she signs again, pulling yesterday's dress pants up over her thick thighs, hopping as she pulls the waist band over her round backside. *And my car? It's at the bar?*

Shit. I have to calm myself down now, I can't just wait for her to leave, I have to drive her home. *I'll drive you.*

You drove last night? You weren't drunk? she questions.

I had two drinks. That asshole bartender kept feeding her drinks. I had to stay sober enough to handle him if I needed to. *No, I only had two. Then I smoked a joint when we got back here.*

She gives me a quick eye roll, knowing I enjoy the occasional joint yet still harboring some disapproval. I shrug, there's no sense in defending it after this long.

She's fully dressed now, and I know I have to get up and get dressed too. I just can't. *Come on!* She points to her watch, letting me know she's already late.

Fuck it. I tell myself, let her see it. Maybe she'll be so turned on by the sight of it, she'll rip those clothes right back off. Yeah, right. *You asked for it,* I sign before I toss the covers off me again and stand.

Not that I can hear it, but I know she shrieks when she sees my hardness stretching the fabric of my boxer briefs because she pulls her hands over her face before turning away from me. Not to sound cocky or anything, but it's a pretty nice dick if you ask me. I take my time fishing for a pair of jeans from the chest of drawers. I can't help but laugh. As I come into her peripheral, she runs out of the bedroom. I guess my fantasy won't come true today. At least not this morning.

Just before leaving the bedroom, I grab my phone from the nightstand. A reflection of the light coming in the window catches my eye. It's Scarlett's phone, she must really be in a rush to have left it sitting here. When I pick it up, the screen lights up and that's when I see it. "New message from Eli."

My head jerks back in surprise. Wasn't that bartender's name Eli? She has facial recognition set up for her lock screen, so I can't "accidentally" read the message. Still, curiosity gets the best of me and I try a couple quick passcodes. Knowing she'll come looking for me soon, I give up and tuck it into my back pocket. She saved his number? When did she get his number?

In the living room, she's waiting at the bar counter that separates the tiny kitchen. *Ready?* She stands as soon as she sees me.

Yeah. Here, you might want this. I pull the phone from my pocket and hand it over to her.

Thanks! She looks at the screen and a smile spreads over her face. Is she blushing? Then she looks up at me and quickly tucks the phone into her purse.

About that web designer position— I start, reaching to pull the door open for her.

Yeah? Her eyes light up.

I'll take it. If it's still available.

I need to stay close to her.

I take her first to her house so she can change. It's closer to my apartment, and the bar is on the way to the agency office. She insists I come inside and wait because she's going to take a shower and she doesn't want me to waste gas just to keep the heat on, not that I'm complaining about being around her.

Wandering around her living room and kitchen, despite having been here many times, I admire the life she's made for herself. She went into the family business I've stubbornly avoided. Looking at it objectively now, she was the one that was able to buy herself a modest house while I live in my cramped little apartment.

The mantle, I think, is my favorite part of her home. It's lined with picture frames that boast "family" photos. Our moms are BFFs, best friends forever. So, her photo collection includes both our families. With pictures of all of us together, I feel at home here too. A familiar longing pangs in my chest, a fleeting hope that one day she'll love me the same way I love her.

The lights flicker and I realize Scar is getting my attention. I turn to see her by the front door. It's casual Friday and she's wearing a pair of dark wash jeans that accentuate her curves. Her heels and the low cut V-neck sweater that hugs her full figure jazz up her casual look. Binx, her black and white cat, circles between her legs. It's hard to avoid the view when she bends down to scratch his head. As she pulls her coat over her shoulders and grabs a scarf from the rack by the door, a fleeting hope that the scarf doesn't cover the bit of cleavage that is peaking through the low neckline of her sweater flushes through me.

Ready? Her eyebrows raise, as is customary for yes or no question in ASL. The expression lights up her face. God, she's beautiful. The fact that she doesn't know it makes her even more beautiful.

I nod, and we head out.

We're a few lights away from the bar, it's almost 9:00 am. She's frantic. She says she's two hours late for work. *Aren't you the boss?* I ask, not sure why she's so concerned with being late. Deaf people are chronically late.

Yes, technically. She holds up air quotes, her sign for 'technically.' *But I'm always there at 7:00 in the morning! People will know something is up.* She emphasizes 'always.'

What is up? Nothing happened. I shrug my shoulders and give her my signature headshake with the corners of my lips turned down.

She lets out a long, exasperated breath, then playfully slaps my leg. *Duh. But they will think something happened.* This time she emphasizes 'think.'

You always care what people think? I know the answer to that question. She knows I know the answer to that question. She rolls her eyes as I park my car next to hers.

Thanks, come by the office? We can talk more about the web designer position.

I nod and she hops out of the car, leaving a trail of her perfume behind her, coconut and vanilla. Hesitating for a moment, I watch her back out of her spot and drive off.

As my eyes trail back to the front door of the bar, Eli comes back to mind. As long as she's been single, there's always been hope that one day she would stop looking at me in a brotherly way. Eli better not come in and ruin that. My gut tells me he will. Which sparks a newfound momentum deep inside me.

Not super motivated to lock in that nine-to-five I'm about to get myself into, I drive around and run a few errands first. There's a new software program I need for my freelance graphic design gigs, and I need to run back home and grab my suit to drop off at the dry cleaners. By the time I'm done with my errands it's almost lunch time, so I swing by Chick-fil-A and pick up Scarlett's favorite salad and a number one combo for me to surprise her at work.

What took you so long? I thought you were coming right behind me, she asks when I tap my knuckle on her open office door. Her door is always open, I close it behind me.

I had some errands to run. I hold out the Chick-Fil-A bag. *Also, I wanted to bring you lunch.*

Her lips spread into a wide smile. *Oh, thank you! I am hungry.* She touches her hand to her belly as if it is rumbling. Maybe it is, I couldn't hear it.

Anyone question why you were late? James and Macie had seen her get into my car. They knew I took her home.

No. James asked if I had a hangover. Macie asked if I was feeling okay. There's not much to do today. I finished setting up everything for the Christmas party. Her face lights up when she mentions the party.

Good. Tell me everything. We both sit down at the little round table, and I distribute the food between us. *Tru hotel, check. Who's the DJ?*

Obviously, it's Mack. Mack is a Deaf DJ in the area. He DJs the party every year. Along with any and all non-conflicting events within our Deaf community here in Wilson.

Obviously. I mimic, she laughs. I love her laugh. I've never heard it, obviously, but she absolutely glows when she laughs. *You book a room? After last night, I imagine you'll need one,* I joke.

She holds a hand over her mouth after shoving a forkful of lettuce inside. Once her mouth closes around the lettuce, she continues. *Right. And I hired the bartender, Eli, so he'll be making those delicious low-carb drinks!* She winks at me.

I'm not amused.

Part of me hopes that was the only reason she saved his number in his phone. Part of me knows that smile on her face this morning tells me otherwise. *Really?* I try, but I know my face is speaking volumes right now.

She cocks her head and furrows her brows, then raises them for her question. *You didn't like him?*

What's not to like? He makes good drinks. He's an attentive bartender, I scoff. *Maybe too attentive.* Shit. I didn't mean to sign that. Maybe she didn't catch that.

She did. Scar's head jerks back and her brows furrow again. This time they stay furrowed for her next question. *What do you mean, 'too attentive?'*

Nothing. My head shakes. *Forget it.* Shit.

She eyes me suspiciously, then shakes her head and takes another bite of her salad. Suddenly, I'm dying for someone to interrupt our lunch. My prayers are answered when I feel the tap on my shoulder just as Scar looks up toward the door. I turn to see my dad behind me. I'm not sure I've gotten enough sleep to handle how happy he will be to see me working here.

Hey, Zo. He pats my shoulder. *Scar tells me you finally decided to take that web designer position.* His face is lit up with pride. My parents have wanted me to join this damn company from the minute it was conceived. I had just graduated from college and moved back home when Helen and Mom secured their first contract. Dad, of course, was the first interpreter covering the assignments.

My lungs fill with air as I take a deep breath to center myself for this interaction. I swallow my last bite and put on the smile. *Yeah, I was thinking maybe it was time for some stability. I'll keep doing my freelance work too.*

Scarlett fans her hand between us and I turn to see what she says. *That's if I hire you.* She's got jokes. I feign a laugh.

I turn back to Dad, he's practically beaming. Fuck. Another deep breath. *I can't tell you how happy I am to see you say that.*

Thanks, Dad.

He shifts his weight for an awkward moment. We've never been that close. I think it was my fault. I think as a kid I resented him because he could hear. Now I've come to not only accept, but also appreciate my deafness. From what I understand, this is a common transitional experience.

Well, I'll leave you two to your lunch. Can't wait to see more of you around here, Zo. My sign name is the same no matter who signs it. But the way Dad's mouth moves when he signs it, and from my years of speech therapy growing up, I know he shortens it to that nickname.

Looking forward to it. I nod along with my pursed smile, and he turns to be on his way.

When I turn back to the table, Scarlett is glaring at me. Fuck. She hasn't forgotten. But she doesn't mention the bartender. I won't say his name. I want to forget his name. *What?* I shrug my shoulders innocently.

Her eyes narrow and she runs them up and down me, keeping her thoughts to herself. *When do you want to start?* Nice change of subject, Scar.

I shrug again, cocking one eyebrow up with my shoulders. *Monday?*

Her lips spread. She's happy. God, those lips. *Want to see your office?* she offers excitedly.

She has an office for me already? Wow. *Is it not right here, with you? We could tuck a desk right there.* I point to the corner adjacent to her desk.

She turns her head in the direction I'm pointing, almost as if she's contemplating the idea. *No, silly. But it is next to mine.*

Her office was the farthest back I've seen. There could be more hidden deep in the back of this strip mall. Honestly, I'm not overly excited to see the office, but I love how excited Scar is. *Let's go.*

She leads me to the next door, this office is a bit smaller, not by much though. Hers is a bit more modernly decorated; I suppose she did the decorating herself. There's a simple black desk with a swivel chair on wheels behind it. It also has a round table with two simple chairs on either side. Instead of a couch, there are two small armchairs opposite the desk. It looks like a typical nine-to-fiver office. Nothing exciting to see.

Scarlett's face is straining to hold back a giddy smile. *You like it?*

Love it, I say by kissing the back of my fist and forcing my eyes to light up. I could get used to the formalities and rigid structured schedules of a "real job." Only if it meant keeping me close to Scarlett. It is more important now than ever. Especially since I now know there are sleazy bartenders out there texting the love of my life.

Chapter 3
Scarlett

Confession? It's possible I've re-read the text from Eli over a hundred times today. It's close to 4:00 pm and I usually dip out of the office early on Fridays. At my desk, I'm scrolling through my phone to kill those last few minutes before I head out for the weekend. My finger hovers over the little green message icon on my main screen. What the heck. I click it open again.

    Eli: I'd love to. Any excuse to see you again. Call me with details.

    Last night he had slipped his phone number to me on a napkin. No one else had noticed. I must confess I was a little giddy at the thought that such an attractive man would be interested in me. But as flattered as I was, I am still very shy. I have no idea how to make the first move. So, I asked him if he would be interested in bartending for our company Christmas party instead. That way if he said yes, I'd have another opportunity to see him.

    Macie taps at my open office door. "Hey, chica. I'm getting ready to head out." She had a few assignments today, but they were all this morning. "Any plans for the weekend?"

    "Not yet." I shake my head but can't hide the grin that remained from reading Eli's text again.

    Macie noticed. "What's that look on your face?" she asks with a knowing brow raise.

    One, somewhat imperative, aspect of American Sign Language is facial expression. It conveys so much meaning. Users of ASL become very well equipped at reading faces. And Macie has had many years to get to know mine. "That guy from the bar last night gave me his number." I cup my hands over my face, attempting to hide the girlish excitement at the confession.

    "Stop it!" She steps in the doorway to get closer for more details. "And?"

"And I asked him if he wanted to be the bartender for our Christmas party," I continue.

She lets out an exasperated breath. "You're kidding me, right? A *hot* guy gives you his number and you solicit him for work?"

My shoulders lift into a shrug. "You know I've never been good at this kind of thing. He did tell me he'd love to and to call him with details." My cheeks start to hurt as the corners of my mouth pull toward my ears. "And something about 'any excuse to see me again.'"

"Girl! You have to call him!" She is practically shrieking.

I press my open palms down in the air, both the sign and a common gesture for *calm down*. "He has my number now too, since I sent him that text. He could call me too," I point out. A feeble attempt and convincing myself the ball is in his court.

"No. I expect you to call him— *tonight*. And then call me with more details," Macie instructs.

The lights flicker and we turn to see Lorenzo in the doorway. He reads our faces. *What's up, why are you two smiling?*

Nothing, I sign. "Don't say anything," I whisper to Macie under my breath.

He notices me using my voice and his face twists even more quizzically. His index finger touches his chin and his brows furrow. *What did you say?*

Call me later, Macie signs to me and moves toward the door. *You two have a good weekend.*

Great. She left me to fend for myself. *Just told her to call me. Sorry, I should have signed.* It is rude to use your voice when a Deaf person is in the room with you and everyone in the room knows sign language. Clearly for good reason.

His narrowed eyes and folded in lips let me know he's skeptical, but he shakes it off. *You have plans tonight? Want to grab a drink?*

As much as I enjoy spending time with Lorenzo, I don't want to bring him back to the bar where Eli works. I also really want to find an excuse to go back to the bar. Maybe I need to follow

Macie's advice and just call him. *Maybe have some wine at the house. Want to help me decorate for Christmas?* I offer.

His face lights up. *Yes. I'll pick up some wine.*

Perfect. I look at my watch and see that it's now just past four o'clock. *I'm going to take off. See you later.*

See you soon, he responds, and we walk out together.

Admiring him as we walk side by side down the hallway, I swell in delight that he is finally joining the business. He notices the smile that has taken over my face and rewards me with the same contented look.

When I open the front door at home, my cat Binx loops his body between my legs and meows up at me. "You hungry, baby kitty?" He's mostly black with white on the tips of his paws and his nose, named after the cat in Hocus Pocus. He meows again, following me through the kitchen where I lay my work bag and jacket on the table before filling his food dish.

The watch on my wrist vibrates against my skin, I pull it up to see a text from Lorenzo letting me know he's running an errand before he comes over. I dig my phone from my purse to respond, I've never liked using the voice to text feature.

With my phone in my hand, I wonder if it's too soon to call Eli. Wasn't there a rule to this calling the next day thing? Fuck it. I open the message chat with him and navigate to his phone number. The 'call' box pops up to confirm and I check yes. It's ringing. My heart is racing. Still ringing. Still ringing. Voicemail. My heart sinks, and yet somehow, I'm relieved.

I leave the phone on the counter and head to my room to shower to get it out of the way before Lorenzo arrives.

My hair is still damp as I pull on a pair of soft, red checkered joggers and a black tank top that I found on TikTok shop that claims to not require a bra. Its claims were accurate, so it quickly became my favorite shirt to wear around the house. I have it in four different colors now. I'm drying my hair with a towel, making my way to the living room in search of my favorite cardigan. Lorenzo steps out of the kitchen, a half-filled wine glass in each hand. The sight of him startles me and I toss the towel in the air as my hands shoot up in fight or flight defense.

I exhale and my hands cup over my heart. *Lorenzo, hi. You scared me.*

His lip curls into a smirk on one side, and he looks me up and down before setting the glasses on the coffee table. *I looked around for you, then smelled your soap. Decided to go ahead and pour the wine.* He winks.

Thank you, I sign. Water drips from my hair and glides down my chest, and I swear I catch Lorenzo's eyes follow the droplet's trail then quickly shift back up to my face. There's a chill in the air that brushes over my arms, leaving runs of goosebumps in its path.

My eyes search the room and land on my cardigan draped over the back of the chair-and-a-half recliner in front of Lorenzo. I take a few strides across the room, as I near him, Lorenzo reaches his arm out for a hug. This is a normal greeting for us, yet somehow this time it feels a little different. He squeezes me tighter or holds the hug a bit longer, I can't put my finger on the difference, but I feel it. My eyes meet his as I back away from the embrace. I feel his hand linger on the small of my back, then slowly he inches his arm back to his side.

Nice pajamas. He winks again.

Thanks, I say before slinking the cardigan around my shoulders. I tie the belt in a loose loop around my waist. *Getting in the Christmas spirit,* I tease.

You should've told me it was a pajama party. I left mine at home. He makes it seem like a joke, but I am sure he's serious. He pulls his glass from the table, tipping it back over his bottom lip to take in a sip, then nods toward my glass, telling me to try it.

Wow, I like that, I sign with my free hand.

My reaction makes him smile. *You hungry? I brought Chinese food.* He angles his head back toward the kitchen letting me know he's left the food in there.

My tummy rumbles and I inhale deeply, just now realizing I can smell the food from the other room. *You're amazing*, I sign, he beams.

Want me to bring it in here? he offers.

I shake my head. *I want to make a plate in the kitchen and bring it here.* It was my way of not overindulging on take-out food. On home-cooked food too, really.

He follows me into the kitchen and opens the brown bag while I fetch paper plates from the panty. That's when my phone rings. Not a text message alert. No. A call is coming in. My heart skips a beat. I step out of my walk-in pantry and close the door behind me.

Lorenzo doesn't seem to notice it vibrating right there on the counter next to him. I dart over and scoop the phone from the counter. I catch a quick glimpse of 'Eli' on the screen and mash my finger on the green button to answer the call.

"Hello?" I practically exhale the word. Lorenzo finally turns toward the physical commotion I'm making. I hold up a finger and quickly sign, *I'm sorry, I have to take this.* He nods.

"Scarlett?" Eli's voice purrs in through the receiver, even sexier than I had remembered.

"Yes, hi, Eli." I feel Lorenzo's gaze on me, so I walk over to the table by the window with my glass of wine and take a seat.

"Hey," I can hear his smile in his voice. "Sorry I missed you before. It was kind of a busy moment at the bar," he explained.

I gasp, almost choking on a sip of wine. "Oh, I didn't even think about it being Friday and that you would probably be working." That was really an oversight for me, I had even thought about going there to see him. I knew he would be at work. Now that he mentions it, I can hear the music and rumble of voices in the background.

"Don't even worry about it. I'm not tending bar tonight," he assures me.

"Oh good, you're not at work then?"

He chuckles. "I am. It's okay, I have a break and I wanted to call you back. I'm so glad you called."

Trying to decide between offering details about the Christmas party and asking how his day has been, my mind goes blank instead. "I, umm, I'm going to need the recipe for that drink you made." I finally manage to spit out, I chase my words with a big gulp of wine.

"No, no. I don't tell my secrets so easily," he banters, then clears his throat. "Though I will share, you know, after I've had a chance to get to know you. Let you in."

My insides flutter. This time his flirting is unmistakable. "I guess I'll just have to watch you next time you make it." I know. I know. My flirting game is out of practice.

"Or we make plans to get to know each other. Then I can begin to trust you with my infamous drink recipes." He doesn't relent.

Leave it to me to have a pang of doubt in my gut, deep down unable to believe someone like Eli could be interested in someone like me. Even though it is quite obvious that he is... interested... in me. I gulp the rest of the wine in front of me, attempting to suppress the nerves rising up inside.

Lorenzo is at the table now, refilling my glass. He sits down opposite of me, refills his own glass, and clears his throat. He knows this is something hearing people do in this situation. I remember him asking me when we were teenagers why everyone was always clearing their throat. He had noticed how often it was in the closed captioning when he watched television.

I nod, acknowledging my rudeness. "We should definitely make plans to get together soon," I agree, trying to rush things along. "But listen—" I start.

"Tomorrow, I'm taking the night off," he offers quickly, as if I'm going to retract my agreement.

I dart my eyes down to the table, shielding my smile at his eagerness. "Sounds perfect."

"It's a date," he confirms.

"Call me in the morning, we'll make plans. I have a friend over right now, I don't want to be rude," I explain.

"I'm sorry, yeah, I'll call in the morning," he apologizes. "Can't wait to see you again."

I smile even harder. "Me either."

Chapter 4
Lorenzo

She's talking to him. She's sitting at the table, just on the other side of the room, drinking her wine, talking to him. Not me. I'm here, talk to me. She can't 'talk' to me.

Maybe that's why we've never left the friend zone after all these years. Maybe she spends so much time in the company of silence, she needs time with auditory stimulation. Mostly, I feel a sense of urgency. If I'm going to make her see me, make her fall in love with me, I'm going to have to act fast. Before this overeager bartender swoops in.

She finally hangs up. She looks up at me, she smiles, embarrassed maybe? *Sorry, Lorenzo.* She juts her chin toward her refilled wine glass. *Thank you,* she signs.

Of course. I feel the corner of my eye squint while she sips from the glass. *Who was on the phone?* I ask bluntly. Deaf people are known for being very upfront, it's a normal question for me to ask. It's a shame I've never been able to channel that Deaf bluntness to tell her how I feel about her. That changes tonight.

She shifts in her chair. I knew it was Eli. I saw his name flash on the screen when she was in the pantry. She thinks I was oblivious to it vibrating, literally right there in front of me. *The bartender, from last night, Eli.* She's honest with me. That's reassuring. We both know I'm a fairly skilled lip reader. Which is probably why she moved over to the table, to change my view of her mouth.

Oh, I see, what did he want? I'm sticking with the Deaf bluntness. At the same time, trying to stay cool, act natural.

Nothing. She throws her hands up quickly to sign that one. *Just confirming the date and info for the Christmas party.* I narrow my eyes at her. She's lying.

Well, I really don't know for sure that she's lying. But from what I caught lip reading, he's calling her back tomorrow to 'make plans.' She also got off the phone out of respect for me. So, there's that. *All set?* I finally ask.

She presses her lips together in a tight smile and nods, then jumps to her feet. *Let's eat.*

I watch her walk to the counter where the little white containers are laid out, ready to serve. She has on these thin plaid joggers that hug her curves. I'm dying to reach out and feel her thigh. To see how soft the fabric is, of course. And oh my god, when she came out of the bedroom in that snug little top, no bra? Fuck me. Am I really that invisible to her? Did she really have no idea that her sexy ass 'Christmas jammies' would turn me on? She didn't put that on just for me? Of course, she didn't. I've been around for so long, every part of her childhood, I might as well be her brother. At least to her. To me, she's everything.

After we fill our plates, I follow her into the living room. I wait as she takes the oversized armchair. Damn. I settle for the corner of the couch closest to her chair. We pull the coffee table in closer for both of us. This is fine, I have a great view of the perfect little line that peeks out from the peak of her neckline. I'm careful not to let her catch me sneaking a glance for a second time tonight.

This is delicious, she signs after a few bites. She mostly has the steamed shrimp and veggies with the Hunan sauce drizzled on top, there's a spring roll and a crab Rangoon on her plate too. I've never understood why she was always so concerned about her weight. It's such a shame that women never know how beautiful they are. In all shapes and sizes. *How did you know I like steamed shrimp with Hunan sauce?* she adds.

Remember when we were at that expo in Raleigh last month? We ate Chinese, you told me that was your favorite. She seems surprised and impressed by my confession. I mentally pat myself on the back and wonder if Eli knows what her favorite Chinese food is.

Mostly we just make small talk while we eat. She asks about some of the commission projects I have going on. I can tell she wants to talk about the web designer job at work, but she doesn't want to talk about work. I also notice each time her eyes glance over at her phone.

So, Christmas decorations? I question, hoping to distract her from that damn bartender. I push my plate away from me on the table and wipe my hands with a napkin.

We don't have to. She waves her hand as if waving away the thought. I see her glance at the phone again.

No, no. I'm here to help. What can I do? I offer persistently. If I'm going to get her to stop thinking about Eli, I have to keep her distracted.

She hesitates, then signs, *Maybe if you could just bring the boxes down from the attic.*

Let's do it.

She leads me down the hall to the spare bedroom that has the attic access ladder. When she reaches up to grasp the string hanging from the pull-down stairs, my hand wraps around hers, like we accidentally reached for it at the same time. Her hand jerks back, *Sorry,* she signs.

Our bodies are inches apart and I stand half a foot taller than her. I flash a grin down at her, *I got it.* I have to admit, I quite enjoy the view from up here.

The ladder stairs unfold easily to the floor. She holds a finger up telling me to wait a minute, then climbs up the rungs, one by one. God dammit, I should not look up. From this angle her voluptuous form taunts me. She's suddenly illuminated when she tugs at the little metal bell at the end of the string that hangs in the opening. Fuck me. I look down at the floor, then back up. She looks around the attic and then tries to explain to me which boxes I need to bring down. I get the gist of it, but act like I don't. I hold my finger up, telling her to wait a minute, then climb up the ladder behind her.

My body engulfs hers, my arms on either side of her shoulders, clutching the top rung, and I'm very aware of her backside resting against my pelvis as I tuck my feet onto the rung just below her feet. I tilt my chin toward the closest box, and she knows I'm asking which boxes she wants. I fight hard to control the blood rushing through me at the feel of her body curved into my hips. She points to three Rubbermaid tubs that have 'Christmas decos' scribbled in Sharpie across the sides, and a box that is obviously a fake tree.

I mouth, *I got you,* and then climb down the ladder, holding it steady for her to climb down too. I'm holding on to one side of the ladder, so her body has to graze mine as she dismounts and steps away from me. God, I'm so fucking turned on. I have to say something tonight. Or I'm afraid I'll regret it for the rest of my life. One by one, I bring the boxes down for her and place them in the corner of the living room. She refills our wine glasses while I'm unloading them, it must be a new bottle by now.

After I unload the last box and bring it back to the living room, she hands me a glass. We clink our glasses and take a sip. She's signing, I honestly have no idea what she's telling me. I'm looking right past her hands, staring deep into her soul, through her deep emerald eyes. I watch as she tilts her head to the side, her eyes squint in confusion.

Hello, Lorenzo? She waves her hand back and forth in front of my eyes.

I snap out of it. *I'm sorry, Scar. I'm distracted,* I confess.

Distracted? she questions, her eyebrows raised in confusion.

I take a deep breath. I'm going for it. I chug down the wine in my glass. *Scar,* I drag her name sign out, slowly pulling the fingertip of my bent index finger down my chin, *I have a confession.*

Her eyes brighten with curiosity. *Really? Tell me,* she questions and commands all at once.

Here goes nothing, or else, everything. *I've been in love with you for... a long ass time.* My hands are moving at sloth speed.

She stares at me blankly. Blinking every few seconds.

I love you, Scar. I've loved you since we were teenagers, I expand on my confession. She still just stands there, blinking at me.

My hand reaches out and cups her cheek. She blinks again, and then her face presses into my hand. She breathes in deeply. I step closer. *Did you see what I said?* I ask. She nods slowly.

I pull her closer to me and step my body into hers. She's trembling. She looks up at me. I can't tell if she's gathering her thoughts or begging me to kiss her. This is a facial expression she's never given me before. My hand is still pressed against her cheek, so I pull her face gently up to mine, bringing our lips millimeters away from each other. I pause, waiting to see if she'll move the last, tiniest little space to bring our lips together. She doesn't, but her eyes are fixed on mine. Fuck. My face dives into hers, my lips part hers, my tongue shoots inside her mouth. It's too much, I pull back and let my lips dance with hers. Her body leans into mine, she's kissing me back. I can't believe she's kissing me back. But much to my disappointment, she pulls back suddenly. Her hand whisks up to cover her mouth, she questions me with her eyes.

Sorry, I sign, boring my eyes into hers. Waiting for some sort of response. Her body is responding loudly. She desperately wants to be touched. She wants her body explored. It's her mind that betrays me. Her body wants me. Her mind is fixed on the compartment she put me in years ago. The friend compartment. Wait, it's worse than that. It's the family compartment.

Lorenzo, she drags the two letters of my name sign out. My heart sinks.

I shake my head. *Don't break my heart. I can't take it.*

Lorenzo, she drags the letters out again, *I just need time. You sort of... caught me off guard.* She smiles kindly, trying to reassure me. *I've never in my life thought of you that way.* The truth fucking hurts. Damn.

Maybe you could, now that you know I think of you that way, I encourage.

She smiles up at me, now her hand cups my cheek. *Lorenzo, I love you very much. Just not that way. I just need to think.*

That's better than no. *Take your time, Scar.* I wait a moment before adding, *But not too much time.*

She laughs at my joke. It's not a joke. Our eyes meet, she sees my face. She knows it's not a joke. Fuck it, I lean in and kiss her again. My hand snakes behind her, pulling her into me from the small of her back. Thankfully, she lets me kiss her again, she's more into it this time. Her body presses against mine and I can feel her nipples harden against my chest. Then, just as before, she pulls herself away, separating our locked lips. Her eyes study mine.

Stay with me? I can't tell if it's a request or a suggestion. *Just hold me?* she asks.

I nod eagerly, and then stand there patiently waiting for her next move. She reaches for my hand and leads me to her bedroom. My arousal is downright painful. Can she see it? My eyes are locked on hers, waiting for my instructions, waiting to learn what I may do next.

Just lay with me, just hold me, she instructs. I nod.

She folds the cardigan down, off her arms, letting it drop to the floor, and climbs in the bed, her side of the bed. I strip down to my undershirt and boxer briefs. There's no hiding how she affects me now. I climb to the other side of the bed and slide my body across the sheets until I find hers. I engulf her with my body again, like I did on the ladder, pressing my hips into her luscious backside.

Her moans pulse between us, the vibrations of her throat palpable. I stiffen more, I press myself forward, harder into her. She reaches back and pulls at my wrist, guiding my arm around her. I breathe her in, and I tuck my hand around her waist. My fingers rest just under her breast, I can feel the fullness resting on my knuckle. My thumb is only inches away from her hard nipple. I slowly graze my thumb up and over her nipple, it puckers under my touch. Her hand swiftly reaches up to cover mine, squeezing it away from her breast. I sign in front of her. *What?*

No sex, she signs in front of her. It's as if our bodies are one. I don't need sex, yet. This closeness is more than I could've asked for. *Just hold me tonight.*

I pull her closer, tucking my supporting arm under her neck. Reaching both arms around her, I manipulate her hand into the letters O and K. Then I kiss the back of her neck, and I can feel the shivers run down her spine. Yes, this is more than enough for now. I close my eyes and breathe in the scent of her hair. I've waited years for this closeness. Even though she didn't jump to confess her feelings back, this is more than I could've imagined.

Chapter 5
Scarlett

I woke up next to Lorenzo two mornings in a row. This time is very different. Yesterday, it was just another day. Like I had had a sleepover with my best friend. This morning, I am keenly aware of how close our bodies are, and how stiff a certain part of him is. Which makes me wonder if his morning wood the previous morning was actually caused by me as well. I can tell from his deep breathing that he's still asleep. His arm that's draped over my rib cage is heavy with confusion. His thumb is so close to my breast if he twitched, it would threaten to harden my nipple. I wiggle under him, he breathes me in, pulling me closer.

My head swirls. Never in my life have I viewed Lorenzo as anything but my adopted big brother. Apparently, he's been viewing me from a different lens for a *very* long time. This could get bad. What if we go for it, what if we see where a relationship between us could lead? What if it doesn't work out? Our moms are still best friends. Now, we work together. Although, I guess he could renege on that anytime. His thumb twitches, my nipple hardens. He's awake. Slowly I feel his thumb and index close in on each other, threatening to pinch my nipple between them.

When he realizes the position he has me in, pulled into his body, my breast in his hand, he breathes my scent in deeply. I allow my body to open, turning my back away from him, opening him up to my side. His hand doesn't leave my breast, fully blanketing it now. My knees flop toward him and he pushes one of his knees between them, tucking it between my thighs. His thigh presses up against my aching core.

Honestly, my confusion doesn't block my arousal. I turn my face toward his, forcing my eyes to meet his. So much is left unsaid as we study each other, trying to answer the questions that hang heavy between us. He leans in, his lips finding mine in a sweet, gentle kiss. Unable to resist, I kiss him back. I would be lying to myself if I said I didn't enjoy his kiss. His body rolls over on top of mine, forcing me onto my back, parting my legs and settling himself between them. He's rock hard, only the thin layer of my joggers separates him from my soaking wet panties, and of course, what made them so wet.

    I'm suddenly very aware of the precarious position we are in. I gently push at his chest, pulling my lips away from his, and shake my head. *Stop, please,* I mouth to him, since our bodies are too close for me to sign. His head hangs, his black hair swooping down and brushing over my chest. *I can't,* I sign when he sits up.

    I can see his heart sink right there in front of me. His lungs exhale all the air they've been holding. His shoulders slump. His hands jolt up to his forehead, brushing his hair back away from his face. *What's wrong?* he finally asks.

    I don't have the words to break his heart. *I'm not ready to see you that way.*

    He nods in understanding. *But maybe you could one day?* he questions bluntly.

    I just need time, time to consider the idea. I cover my face with my hands, taking a break from the conversation. *I never expected this, Lorenzo. I love you... so much. Whatever happens, it has to be guaranteed that I won't lose you.*

    He feels my words, perhaps more than I do. That's why it's taken him this long to make this confession. He bends down and places a light kiss on my forehead, then climbs off me and out of the bed.

    I should go, he signs, then gathers his clothes.

    Now my heart is sunk. I'm overrun with the feeling that I've already lost him, fear that he won't be able to come back from this. I sit up and wave my hand at him to get his attention. His eyes meet mine. *I'm sorry, don't leave like this.*

He swallows hard, then shakes his head. *It's OK, really. Take time to think about it.* He comes back over to the bed and kisses my forehead again. *We're good, really. I promise.*

Thanks for understanding. The doorbell rings causing me to jump up out of the bed. Lorenzo cocks his head at me, questioning why I was startled. *Someone's at the door,* I say, just as confused.

He tosses me my cardigan and I throw it on before heading out to the living room to answer the door. Through the peephole I see James on the other side, holding his tan toy chihuahua and a doggie diaper bag. I fling the door open. "James! Oh my god, you startled me." I'd forgotten that I promised to watch his dog, Bruiser, this weekend while he went out of town. Yes, his dog is named after the chihuahua in Legally Blonde, his favorite movie.

"Did you forget we were coming?" he sang, stepping in the doorway and letting Bruiser down. Bruiser beelines it for Binx's food bowl to scope out any leftovers.

"I did. It's uh, it's been an eventful weekend already." James' face lights up, I know he wants details.

"The bartender?" His voice is mischievous, hopeful for juicy gossip.

My face contorts into an uncontrollable smile. Then incredulousness. "Wait, how did you know about that?" I question. I had told Macie, but no one else.

"Oh, just a sneaky suspicion. I saw him flirting with you. Girl, he is *cute!*" He takes another step in and shuts the door behind him. "Do tell," he presses.

"Well, there's not much to tell yet. Just that we talked last night and—" I'm cut off.

James' gaze slides right past my head, toward the hallway that leads to the bedrooms. "What do we have here?" he asks in a roguish voice.

My gaze follows his to the sight of Lorenzo, bare-chested, wearing a pair of my gender-neutral sweatpants, his bare feet padding the floor as he approaches. He nods at James. *Morning.*

Good morning. James' signs are so drawn out, I can practically hear them. *Or was it a good night?* he adds for dramatic effect.

I could punch him. *He helped me with Christmas decorations last night. We drank wine. He didn't want to drive.* I look at Lorenzo, eye begging him to corroborate my story. It was technically true.

James looks around the room, the tubs and tree that Lorenzo pulled from the attic for me are stacked behind the couch. No decorations are hung, no tree is standing. No evidence to prove my claim. Except for the wine glasses staining the coffee table.

We drank wine, Lorenzo confirms. *And pulled some boxes from the attic.*

I see. James' lips part into a knowing smile. And Lorenzo makes his way to the kitchen. "Looks like you've got yourself a nice little love triangle situation going on, girlfriend," he teases.

"It's not what it looks like!" I playfully slap his shoulder.

"Mm hmm. And I'm not gay." There's no convincing him.

Everyone knows Lorenzo and I are close. They know we grew up together. I've never told them that we sometimes have platonic sleepovers. Well, they used to be platonic, who's to say this one wasn't? "It's kind of like a Dawson's Creek deal."

"Yup, and Dawson was in love with Joey. She was just too blind to see it." Damn, that was spot on. He pulls the bag from his shoulder and holds it out for me. "Anyway, his food and some puppy pads are in here. There's a leash too if you want to walk him, but it's only one night, so don't feel like you have to. Especially if you're," he clears his throat, "otherwise occupied."

"Dammit, James!" He turns on his heel, laughing as he opens the door. "Keep this here, please. Don't say anything at work."

"Not a word!" he calls out from the sidewalk, halfway to his car already.

Lorenzo is in the kitchen making breakfast. He's already started the coffee maker and the aroma of fresh dripping coffee fills my nostrils. He's taken the liberty of pulling a carton of eggs, cheese, and bacon from the fridge.

He's made me breakfast countless times over the years, he's always felt at home here. But this time it's different. He's no longer just my best friend who spends the night when he's had too much to drink. Now he's this very attractive, half-naked man cooking me breakfast after confessing his love for me. Who, I might add, is an *amazing* kisser.

He looks up and sees me in the doorway. *How do you like your eggs?* He knows the answer to this. Scrambled, with cheese and a side of bacon and avocado toast. I purse my lips at him. He laughs. *Just joking. Sit, I'm cooking for you.* He nods his head toward the barstools on the opposite side of the counter where he's slicing a loaf of French bread.

Lorenzo, you don't have to, I try, but I know it's useless.

Knife in one hand, he signs with the other, *I know. I want to. I'm also putting up your tree today.* I shake my head and try to protest, but he holds his finger up at me, refusing to let me object.

Bruiser comes prancing in the kitchen and sits at my feet. He barks, begging for whatever food he thinks I have in front of me. I'm sure he smells the bacon as it starts to release its grease in the pan on the stove. "I don't have any food, Bruiser." I speak for Bruiser and sign for Lorenzo at the same time, so he knows what I'm saying. *I'm going to feed him,* I say before hopping off the stool to fetch the doggie diaper bag James left for him.

It's almost 10:00 am by the time we finish the breakfast that Lorenzo made for us. It's practically gourmet compared to my usual fare. We stay seated at the small table by the window, drinking our coffee and watching the birds gather around the feeder I have set up in the backyard. Binx sits in the window, intently watching the birds along with us.

There's a comfortable silence between us. We're not talking, but it's not awkward. He knows my mind is full, as I'm sure is his. He is watching me though, more than he's watching the birds. Finally, he stands and collects the plates, taking them over to the sink.

A moment later, he returns with the coffee pot in hand, offering to refill my cup. I nod and hold it up for him. *Ok, I'm putting that tree up. Take your time.* He winks and bends down to kiss my forehead again. This seems to be the new thing. I must confess, I kind of like it.

I'll wash dishes and be there in a few minutes.

Of course, as soon as I start the water to wash the dishes, my phone starts ringing. I hear the tune chiming faintly from the other side of the house, still in the bedroom, I'm sure. I run through the living room and down the hall, signing "phone" so Lorenzo knows why I'm running past. Just as my hand reaches to pick it up, the call ends. Not before I saw his name on the screen. Eli. Fuck. Eli. James was right, I do have a nice little, ugly little, love triangle on my hands. Wrapped up with a bright red Christmas bow. I debate for a moment if I should return his call while Lorenzo is still here. As long as I'm in another room, it's not rude, right? It starts ringing again; I don't have to debate anymore.

"Hello?" I answer breathlessly.

"Good morning, beautiful," he sings into the line. "Sorry to call you back-to-back like a creeper. I dropped my phone before and it ended the call."

"No worries, I had left it in the bedroom. You should've seen me running through the house to answer it," I confess. Shit. Is that too eager?

"Mmm," his moan sounds like he's pleased to hear that tidbit of information. "I'm picturing it now," he jokes.

"So, how are you?" I curl up in the round chair I have by the window for reading and attempt to redirect the conversation.

"I'm good now. I've been waiting all morning to call you. Wasn't sure if you were a morning person or not. Now I hear your voice, my day is starting off right." Has he always been this smooth? Is this a line he's used before?

"Usually, I am," I start. "More often than not, I'm up before eight o'clock on the weekends." I can hear his sigh of relief through the phone. "What about you?"

"You know, you would think with my job requiring such late nights that I wouldn't be a morning person. But I just kind of have this philosophy that if you sleep in, you waste so much of your day," he explains.

I couldn't agree more. I've said this many times. "Exactly," I say through my grinning lips.

"So, when can I see you today?" I like that he gets right to the point. "We need to start working on this whole 'get to know you' thing so I can pass along that drink recipe."

"Depends on what you have in mind," I offer coyly.

"I know it's November, and a bit chilly out, but I've been wanting to check out that trail around Lake Wilson," he suggests. "If we go sooner rather than later, it won't be so chilly while the sun is out."

"Sounds nice to me. Actually, I'm dog sitting this weekend, I bet Bruiser would love to go for a walk. Do you mind?"

"Not at all. Meet me there around 12:00?"

"Sure." The smile on my face is practically plastered on. Until I see Lorenzo in the doorway when I click the call off. He sees my smile. He sees how happy I am.

I see his lips pull into a tight, thin line. *Tree is up,* he signs. He looks so defeated and I wonder how long he's been in the doorway. I wonder if he had a chance to read my lips for this conversation. My heart rips at the seam. One side is broken that I've just hurt Lorenzo, the other swooning over the prospect of a sexy stranger being interested in me.

Thank you, Lorenzo. I really appreciate it. I appreciate everything. Thank you. I stand and walk toward him, reaching my arms out to hug him.

He opens his arms and lets me step into him. The breath he takes in, inhaling my scent from the top of my head, is audible. *You're welcome,* he signs after we step away from each other. He pulls his tight lips into a half smile. *I'll take off now. Text me, or FaceTime, either.*

OK, I'll walk you out, I offer. He shakes his head, then kisses my forehead again.

He eyes my lips longingly, reaching a finger out to touch them. *See you soon, I hope.*

See you soon. I give him a demure smile and hold up the ASL sign for 'I love you' that members of the community use for any and all types of love. I've waved this sign at him many times. The intent behind it is the same as it's always been. The meaning, however, may be a bit obscure now. His shoulders slump and he turns to leave. He does stop for a moment, halfway down the hall, and turns back to wave 'I love you' back to me.

Chapter 6
Eli

I'm leaning up against my Jeep Rubicon when Scarlett pulls into the lot by the trailhead. There aren't many other cars here because, well, it's winter. Still, I wanted her to find me easily. She parks her SUV one spot away from mine, her driver's side door directly in front of me.

Her face lights up when she locks her eyes to mine. Until a tiny chihuahua peeks his head up to look through the window, tail wagging wildly waiting for her to open the door. She fumbles with the leash, attempting to hook it to the collar around his wiggly body before her door finally opens.

"Hey, beautiful," I greet her. She blushes. I melt as a warm, red hue flushes over her freckled cheeks. One of the most beautiful characteristics of a woman, I believe, is when they don't know just how beautiful they are. Scarlett has no idea how absolutely radiant she is. Her long, strawberry blonde hair compliments the smattering of freckles across her nose. And though a touch of mascara highlights her emerald eyes, her face is glowing with a natural beauty, not a thick layer of makeup.

The chihuahua runs over and jumps at me, landing his front paws just below my knees. Vying for my attention, scratches, and pets I suppose. "Hey little guy!" I say, bending down to scratch behind his ear. I'm instantly his new best friend.

Scarlett giggles. "This is Bruiser, my friend James' dog."

"Hey, Bruiser, little tough guy, huh?" I straighten up to bring my attention back to Scarlett. "How are you?" I ask, leaning into her and kissing her cheek. I'm half Latino, I grew up watching my dad greet every woman ever with a kiss on the cheek. Plus, the ladies love it.

Heat flushes her cheek at the touch of my lips. "Good." Her voice is soft, almost hushed. She's shy, she doesn't know what to say. It's adorable. "Have you been here before?"

"First time. I've wanted to check it out since I moved here," I confess. "Never had good company to invite along with me." We start walking down the path, Bruiser in front, leading the way. He's a cute ass little dog, but I can't say I'm not relieved he isn't hers. I've never been much of a dog person.

"Since you moved here? How long ago was that?" Her voice has the slightest twang in her accent. Not as strong as most other people around here, which makes me wonder if she's a transplant to the area as well.

"A little over a year. I moved here when I got out of the Marine Corps. I was at Cherry Point for my last station. A buddy of mine was from here. He seemed to love the area so much, I decided to move here and see for myself," I explain.

Her eyes seem to perk up a bit at the mention of the Marine Corps. "Wow, a former Marine? I bet that was interesting. But, why Wilson?" Her expression changes, is it confusion, distaste? I can't tell.

"Honestly, I needed a nice slow pace. After sixteen years in the military and a few tours in Iraq, I was craving a simple life." Her expression changes again, this time signaling understanding. I'd never met anyone with such readable expressions before.

"That actually makes perfect sense," she accepts. "How do you like it here?"

"It has been exactly what I needed. Slow, kind of boring." I chuckle. "Until the other night when the most beautiful woman I've ever seen walked into my bar." I know it's a cheesy ass line, so I turn to see her reaction. She's glowing but trying to hide it. "Now it's a bit," I search for the word, "exciting."

"Is that right?" Her cheeks and voice are both blushing. "Sixteen years in the military? That's a long time. What made you join?" She's getting comfortable, her shyness easing away.

"My dad. He was in the Marine Corps. He retired when I was ten. He was stationed at Quantico in Virginia. After he retired, we stayed in the area, and he got a job working at the Pentagon."

My voice trails off. I swallow the lump in my throat, not ready for her to see my emotional side.

"Following in his footsteps?" She filled the silence that I left.

"I guess." I finally manage after clearing my throat. "He died in 9-11. He was on the side of the Pentagon that was hit. I think I joined more because I wanted to avenge his death," I confess.

"How old were you when he died?" Her voice softens when she asks her question.

"Thirteen, it was the beginning of my freshman year of high school."

She stops in her tracks, her mouth gaping open at me. "What's wrong?" I ask.

"My dad died during my freshman year of high school too." How ironic. "Though, he died of a heart attack, not on 9-11. I was only seven when 9-11 happened." We start walking again.

I did the math in my head. "So, that would make you twenty-nine?" She's six years younger than me. Inwardly, I hope that isn't a deal breaker for her. Really, in the grand scheme of things, when her birthday rolls around, we'll both be in our thirties.

"Yes," she answers sheepishly. "In June I'll be *thirty*." She virtually whispers the word. It's adorable.

I laugh. "It's not as bad as you think. And, you know, since I've already been through it, I can be there to provide moral support." It's my subtle way of letting her know I plan to stick around awhile. If she'll let me. "Sorry to hear about your dad, by the way. I know that must've been hard."

"Thanks. It was. But it was also a long time ago. I do miss him. As I'm sure you miss your dad." We have this thing now, this instant connection over a shared experience. I reach my hand over and loop two of my fingers through two of hers, just to test the waters. She doesn't flinch. In fact, I feel her accepting grip. "Are you close with your mom?"

The deep breath I inhale at her question is telling. "Not really. She was, well, she wasn't around much. I had to go live with her after my dad died. They were divorced. Basically, I was uprooted and transplanted to the other side of the country. She calls sometimes, texts, sends me TikToks she thinks I will find funny. Really, that's about it."

"You don't visit her?" she questions further. I shake my head, pressing my lips together, hoping she picks up on the fact that I don't really want to talk about my mother. "That's sad," she finally says, I think she gets the point. "I see my mom almost every day. We work together."

"What do you do?" I ask, welcoming the change in topic.

"Well, I'm the business manager for the interpreting agency that my mom and her best friend, Alana, started. They started it with my dad's life insurance money." She gives a basic answer before diving into more details. "Really, my mom wanted me to become an interpreter. I just never wanted to because I had spent my whole childhood interpreting for my parents. They're Deaf, by the way." She tacks that last bit on and everything that confused me the other night at the bar finally made sense.

"Ahh," I verbally signal my understanding, "that's why everyone at your table knew sign language the other night."

"Yeah, mostly they are all interpreters that work for the agency. One of the requirements Mom and Alana set for their employees that aren't interpreters is that they must be fluent in ASL," she explains. It sounds like it made perfect sense. Working for a Deaf-owned business, yeah, you should know sign language.

"And the one guy, he is Deaf, right?" I've been wanting to know about this guy. The way he glared at me; it was downright possessive.

It almost feels as though she wants to stop again, I feel her pace hesitate. If there was one thing the military gave me, it was a heightened awareness of subtle cues. "Yeah, Lorenzo. He's Alana's son."

"It seems a silly question to ask, since you're here with me now, he's not your boyfriend?" I eye her from my peripheral for an initial reaction before turning my face to look her in the eyes as we walk.

Her eyes dart up at mine, then quickly back to the path in front of us. "No. We grew up together though. I've known him my whole life. I've honestly never looked at him that way. I would say he's more like family. He may be a bit protective over me, I suppose."

She could very well believe that. He, on the other hand, is very much into her. I keep that thought to myself, just in case she hasn't realized it yet. We come to a clearing on the path that has the most amazing view of Lake Wilson. The calm blue water spans out in front of us, reflecting the sun's rays that pierce through a fluffy white cloud. Water laps onto the sandy edges lined with tall pine and oak trees. There's a small wooden dock that leads out to a covered gazebo in the water. "Let's check it out," I suggest, tugging at her hand to redirect her on the path.

"I feel like this is new." She admires the dock as we walk across the wooden planks. "Although, I haven't been over here in a few years, so maybe not that new."

We get to the end of the dock, I kneel on the wooden bench that lines the outside rails of the gazebo, and resting my arms on the top rail, lean over to look down at the calm water. There are a few ducks paddling toward us from the middle of the lake. "Wish I had brought some bread for the ducks," I muse.

"That would've been cool." She kneels next to me and leans in, our shoulders touching. "Oh well, I guess this date is a total flop now." Her joke makes me chuckle.

"I guess we'll have to have a do-over." I wink. I can feel her shiver next to me, so I wrap my arm around her. "You're cold."

"It's November," she reminds me with a playful smirk. "I'm okay. I'm enjoying myself."

"Me too."

"So, how did you get a Saturday night off from bartending?" she asks.

There was a part of me that hoped to keep this ruse up longer, but since she's asking, I'll be open. "I'm not a bartender," I confess. "I tend bar sometimes, but usually only when I'm short staffed."

Her jaw drops. "Oh my god, I'm so dense! You're the manager?"

"I'm the owner, it's my bar. I opened it when I moved here. I had some money saved up from deployment and had some pretty nice investment returns with the money my dad left me," I explain.

Her face lights up. "Wow, that's really cool. Gosh, what a risk it is to start a business. That's so... brave. I really admire that."

"I never really thought about it being brave. For me, it was being my own boss. I spent sixteen years being told what to do. Now I'm in charge." I smirk at the thought.

The sun creeps out from behind a cloud where it had been hiding since we walked out onto the gazebo. A ray hits her golden strawberry hair so perfectly, it almost glistens. From this angle I notice a spot on her forehead that I hadn't seen before, just behind the bangs she keeps swept to one side. "What's this?" I ask, reaching up to brush the bangs away. There's a small, heart-shaped, red birthmark.

She touches her hand to the birthmark, tucking it behind her bangs. She's embarrassed by it, probably why she keeps her bangs like she does. "Oh, that's my namesake. It's just a birthmark. Mom said that was why she named me Scarlett. And my name sign, it's the sign for 'scar' and 'red' combined."

I study her face, even more intrigued by her and her whole story. "Scarlett, do you know how beautiful you are?" I ask as I reach a hand over to feel the strands of her glistening hair. It's just as soft as I'd imagined.

She blushes, batting her eyes and shying her face away from the compliment. She doesn't know. My hand slides from her hair, back behind her head and guides her face to mine. I leave a soft kiss on her lips, being sure not to linger, suppressing my urge to dive in. Just enough to send her into a desperate rage for more, then slowly back away.

Chapter 7
Scarlett

*M*onday morning rolls around and I'm still reeling from my whirlwind of a weekend. I can't stop thinking about the soft, tease of a kiss Eli gave me while we overlooked Lake Wilson. It was so simple, yet so romantic. He seemed genuine, and very interested in me.

Yet, there is still this tiny voice deep inside me that keeps telling me it was too good to be true. *You're not thin enough, you're not pretty enough, he's too good-looking for you.* These intrusive thoughts swirl around my head along with the positive ones. *This sexy guy is into me, he thinks I'm beautiful, he kissed me!* Why do we do these things to ourselves? Why must we over analyze everything instead of just enjoying the ride? Probably from the multitude of bad experiences and broken hearts.

Then there is Lorenzo. What a confusing mess this is. Why did he wait until the minute an attractive, decent man comes along to profess his love for me? He's loved me since high school? Why did he wait so damn long to say something? It wasn't for lack of opportunity, or availability, that's for damn sure.

Going into work today and facing Lorenzo, going through his onboarding paperwork with him, heck, just seeing his face after this weekend? Oh boy. Load on top of the fact that James saw Lorenzo half naked in my living room. Or coming from my bedroom, I should say. Yeah. Awkward is one word to describe it. Apprehensive is the word to describe how I am feeling this morning.

I take my time getting ready. Sure, I always arrive by 7:00 am, so does Lucy. She has a key. She can handle any calls that might come in before I get there. I'm in no rush this morning. A scalding hot shower always helps me clear my head, so I turn the hot water up and barely turn the cold-water knob, letting the steam creep around the bathroom.

Before the mirror fogs, I study my reflection. I've stared back at this reflection many times over the past twenty-nine years. Each time I find something wrong with it. Something I believe needs to change, never feeling worthy enough to be desired. I search the reflection, looking for that special thing that seems to be so desired now. As the fog closes off my view, I strip down.

With my attention brought down to my nakedness, I'm wishing my thighs were thinner, my stomach was flatter, my breasts— well, I'm actually quite happy with those. Maybe they could stand to be a bit perkier. My mind betrays me again, and I'm left wondering if either of these men that desire me saw me naked, would they still? Desire me?

It's eight o'clock on the dot when I arrive at work. Lucy greets me with her friendly smile. On my way down the hall, I notice a few doors open: Corbin, Dave, Charlotte, and Macie.

"You're later than normal," Macie calls out as I try to sneak past. Fuck. I stop, turn, and give her a fake smile. "How did it go?"

"Huh? How did what go?" I'm not intentionally playing dumb, I'm just that distracted.

"The bartender?" she reminds me.

"Oh, right." I let out a nervous laugh. "We hung out Saturday. It was nice. He actually owns that bar." I give her some quick details, but not too many. I know she is dying for more.

"So, what you're saying is, we need to forgo the Mexican spot next door and always hit up Fire & Ice for our Thursday happy hour?" she suggests, ever so subtly. My cheeks flush. "Oh my god, you're blushing!"

"Who's blushing?" James' sing-song voice breaks through the air behind me as he dips his head between me and the doorway. "Good morning, sunshines!"

"Good morning, James." He had texted me Sunday afternoon to let me know he would be home late and to drop Bruiser off in the evening so he wouldn't disturb my 'beauty sleep.' I haven't seen him since he caught my precarious situation with Lorenzo.

"Are you telling her all about your love triangle?" he blurts. I could punch him again. My fist clenches. I swear he does this shit on purpose.

"Love triangle?" Macie heard it. "She told me about the bartender. Or should I say bar *owner?* No mention of anyone else."

"James!" I shriek. "It's like you completely forgot that I asked you not to mention it to anyone at work." His 'play too much' act is cute sometimes. This is not one of those times.

"She's like your best friend, I didn't think she counted." His demeanor changes. "Sorry, boss." He shrugs and turns to head to his office. "Oh, speak of the devil," he says when he turns around, clearly not done feeding off the drama.

Macie visibly perks up to see who is walking down the hallway, catching on to James' hint. Lorenzo smiles at me as he passes by, headed toward the office I had shown him on Friday. He doesn't stop to chat though.

"Lore..." Macie starts to say his name, then it all hits her and she just nods. "I see."

"It's not like that. I mean... it's... I don't know... it's... complicated." I finally settle on a definition for what's going on between Lorenzo and me. It's complicated. So very, *very* complicated. "I'm going to get to work."

I stop by my office to set down my things and hang up my coat, then I head straight for Lorenzo's door. It's open, he's pulling a few picture frames from a messenger bag he has slung over his shoulder. I flick the light switch to gain his attention.

Can I come in? I ask when he looks up at me.

Of course. He smiles, takes the bag off his shoulder, and places it on the desk. He walks toward me, arms open, ready for a hug. I let him envelop me and he places that kiss on my forehead, that same kiss that's become his new thing with me. Hugs are common in the Deaf community. Kisses are reserved for those that are truly special.

How was the rest of your weekend? I ask when he pulls away from me.

He shrugs his shoulders and makes his signature Lorenzo face, pursed lips and raised brows. *Friday night was the best part.* A twinge of guilt grips my stomach. *You?*

It was nice, very relaxing. I finished my decorations on Sunday. I figure that is a safe answer. I'm not ready to get into a conversation about potential relationships, either with Eli or him.

There's the face again. His nonchalant way of saying nothing and everything all at once. *Good.* He finally smiles. *Can't wait to see them.*

Soon, I assure him. *Anyway, we have to get your paperwork all done today. Get settled in and then come over to my office,* I instruct. I could have his mom or Charlotte go over the paperwork with him, but I'm fairly certain he wouldn't want to do it with Alana. And Charlotte, well, she's pretty busy with the scheduling.

OK. He gives me a thumbs up. *Look.* He then points to one of the picture frames. I walk over to see it's one of us. It was just after my dad died, I was probably fourteen, Lorenzo was sixteen. I had just lost my dad. He had just gotten his license. He took me to the skating rink in town, trying to cheer me up. Looking at the picture now, I see it. I see that sixteen-year-old boy taking care of the girl he was crushing on. Back then, it felt more like my best friend trying to keep my mind off things. It's all over his face. That boy was smitten. How did I not see it?

I pick the frame up out of his hands and pull it in close for a better view. *Wow, this feels like ages ago!* I marvel.

That was the night I realized I loved you, he says bluntly.

How do I respond to that? Where was this bluntness before? *That was, what? Fifteen years ago?*

It looks like he's calculating in his head. *Wow, I guess so.*

There's a moment of 'silence' between us. I stare at the picture a little longer while he stares at me. I know he wants an answer. He wants me to decide if I'm in love with him too. Or at least if I could be one day. The only way to really know that would be to explore 'us.' Finally, I place the frame back on his desk and bring my eyes to his. My lips form into an empathetic smile. *Ready?*

He nods and we head over to my office to get his paperwork done.

It's just before noon when Mom and Alana stop by my office. They each have their purses slung over their shoulders, clearly headed out to lunch. I close my laptop screen and greet them with a smile.

Hi, Mom. Hi, Alana. How are you?

Good! Alana appears to be beaming. *The two of us are going out for lunch. Want to join us?* she offers. *Lorenzo is coming too,* she adds. I tell myself she's beaming because he finally decided to join the family business. Although, the thought that she might know how he feels about me does cross my mind.

I hadn't packed lunch like usual. I'd planned on ordering a salad from Chick-Fil-A on DoorDash. The offer is tempting. I hold my thumb and index fingers up to my chin, appearing to think things over. *Thanks for inviting me, I think I need to stay and get some things done,* I decline.

Mom's face falls and I make a mental note to make time for her. *OK, maybe you'll come for dinner tonight?* she asks.

Sure, that's perfect. I'd love to. Mom gives me a smile then they turn to leave. I wave my hand in the air, trying to catch their eye. Alana sees and turns back to see what I want to say. *Do you mind closing the door, please?*

She flashes me a thumbs up and goes to close the door when Lorenzo appears in the doorway. *Is Scar coming?* I see him ask and Mom shakes her head. He pokes his head in holding the door frame with one hand and signs with the other, *You're not coming for lunch? Come on! The four of us, just like old times.*

Over the years it has always been hard to say no to Lorenzo. He was always the one that would convince me to go out, try this, or do that. Today I take a deep breath, purse my lips, and narrow my eyes at him. And then I say no. *No, thanks, I have some things to catch up on. I'll see you all later.*

There's really not much work for me to do. Like I said, I mostly just make sure everyone else's job is getting done and that business is running smoothly. Lunch hour on a busy day is one of my favorite times. The staff interpreters are usually all out on assignments, Emma and Charlotte often go out to lunch. With everyone gone, the office is fairly quiet, peaceful even. Today, it's only Lucy and I in the building. I'm perusing Christmas decorations on Amazon for the party when the phone on my desk trills.

"Scarlett Reese here," I answer, unsure if it is an intra office call or if Lucy patched in a call.

"Hey, Scarlett, it's Lucy. You have a lunch delivery here." I'm puzzled because I had forgotten to order my DoorDash, so I'm not expecting any deliveries. "Oh, I'm sorry, he says he's a lunch *visitor.*"

"I'll be right up." Now I'm intrigued, but I have a sneaky suspicion of who it might be.

Sure enough, I emerge from the door that separates the back offices from the reception area to find Eli standing a few feet from the reception desk, holding a bag of take out. "Hey, beautiful." He smiles his bright, toothy grin at me.

"Eli!" I don't hide the surprise in my voice, or the delight. "What are you doing here?" We take simultaneous steps closer to each other and he hugs me with his free arm, then places a kiss on my cheek that leaves a flush of heat behind.

When he steps back, he holds the bag up. "It's kind of slow at the bar this afternoon, being Monday and all. So, I made you lunch." *Made* me lunch?

"*Made* me lunch?" I repeat the thought that just went through my head. He gives me his toothy grin along with an enthusiastic nod. "Come on, we can eat in my office."

I guide him down the hall and into my office, closing the door behind us. "It's so quiet around here," he comments, setting the bag of food on the corner table, then looks around the office. "This is nice, Scarlett. I like how you've decorated." There's something about the way he says my name. I can't put my finger on it, but his rustic voice sends heat through me.

"Thanks." I feel my cheeks flush. "I swapped out all that mahogany office-y furniture for a more modern look," I explain, taking a seat at the table. "And no one is here right now. Everyone is out to lunch or on assignment."

"I'm glad you didn't go out to lunch." He takes the seat across from me and pulls two boxes from the bag. "I made you my signature salmon, I hope you like seafood."

"I love seafood, and salmon is actually my favorite fish. I can't wait to try it." I open the box to see a thick piece of pink salmon coated with seasonings and a side of sautéed zucchini and peppers. "This smells amazing." I'm practically drooling over the box.

"It's even better with the Santiago Pinot Grigio we carry at the bar, but I figured I'd save the wine for after hours," he teases.

"I would love to." My inner thoughts escape my lips. He catches on to the fact that the thought was meant to remain just that, a thought. The heat that rushes to my cheeks, I'm sure gives me away. His lips curl into a knowing smile. "Oh, my god! I meant, thank you." I try to cover, but it's a futile effort.

"Add wine date to the queue, check." He winks.

I take a bite of the salmon and outwardly melt. "A bar owner and a chef?"

He's humble, at least his response is. "I don't know about chef, but I do enjoy cooking. And since my bar serves food, I have access to a nice kitchen and an endless supply of ingredients."

"I enjoy cooking sometimes too, although when I'm only cooking for myself, I'm less motivated. I end up doing a lot of take out and girl dinner." Girl dinner is the newest slang term for what women eat when they don't want to cook. My go-to is popcorn and wine.

"Add cook dinner together date to the queue, check." He winks again.

The more time I spend with Eli, the more I like him. He's down to earth, open, and honest. The best part, he's just plain up front with who he is and his intentions. It's such a refreshing change of pace from the men I've dealt with in the past. He's also *really* nice to look at. His height and muscular build make me feel small next to him. When you're uncomfortable with the size of your body, this is a commonly desired feature in a man. He pulls the bald look off well, I'm not sure if it's intentional or necessary, but it's complemented nicely by his full beard. Then there's the tattoos. His right arm is covered in a sleeve, I can only imagine exploring his body to see where else he's tatted.

Enjoying my company for lunch, I've lost track of time. The office starts to bustle, and I know everyone has returned from lunch. "Sounds like lunch hour is over." Eli notices too.

"I guess so." I shrug, not wanting to end our lunch date. "Not sure I'm ready for it to be over," I confess.

"Well, the way I see it, we've got at least three more dates lined up," he says, collecting the trash from lunch and putting it back into the bag.

"Oh really?"

"Yup, there's the wine date, and the cooking together date," he reminds me.

"And the third?"

"Your company Christmas party. I was thinking you should take me as your date instead. I know a bartender or two that would be interested in the work." Well, that is pretty upfront and ballsy. I like it.

There's a faint flutter of butterflies in my tummy, but I decide to be bold too. "That's almost five weeks away. I'm hoping to see you a few more times between now and then. So, the Christmas party, that'll probably be date number six."

"How formal is it? Should I rent a tux? Or just take my suit to the dry cleaner?" he asks. He's standing now, so I stand too.

"Just your suit is perfect." I can't help but smile at him. "Thanks for lunch. This was a really nice surprise."

"Expect it to happen more often." He leans in and kisses my cheek as he had when he arrived.

"I'd like that." My cheeks flush again, sizzling out the boldness that had swept through me only a few minutes ago.

He lingers for a moment, then reaches a hand up to scoop mine in his. He tugs gently, pulling me into him. My body comes alive when it collides with him. Slowly leaning down to me, he softly presses his lips to mine. Our second kiss is longer than our first, he parts his lips, and I follow suit, taking his bottom lip between mine. When he steps back, I hear someone clear their throat. Of course, I'd recognize that sound anywhere. I turn to see Lorenzo in the doorway, holding a bag of take out.

Chapter 8
Lorenzo

What the hell is he doing here? Fuck that. Why the hell is he kissing her? Who the hell does he think he is? That was clearly not a first kiss. My blood is boiling. My heart is crushed. My insides are churning with emotions I just can't process. She had said she was too busy to go out for lunch. So, I brought her lunch. It was the thoughtful thing to do, right? Wrong. If I'm going up against this guy to win her over, it appears the score stands as: Eli – two, Lorenzo – fucking zero.

He steps away from her. I clear my throat. Her eyes meet mine.

Lorenzo. Her jaw drops as she signs the two letters of my name. Her eyes dart to him, and back to me. She closes her jaw.

I brought you lunch, I sign. Part of me relishes the fact that Eli has no idea what's going on. *But,* I motion to the bag in his hand, *looks like you already ate.* Hot tears are waiting behind my eyes. I won't let them fall, but I hope she can see the hurt in my eyes.

Thank you, I can save it for tomorrow. Or dinner tonight. That was very sweet. Her mouth is moving with each word, I can tell she's talking along with her signs. She's making sure he's included, that he knows what's being said. *Have you met Eli?*

Not formally. I watch her lips as she voices for me. I turn my gaze to him, and I can feel my nostrils flare as I jut my chin up to acknowledge him.

He says "wait," I read his lips. Then he fucking signs, *My name is E-L-I.* Are you fucking kidding me? Who taught him that? Did she?

Her face is lit up like a damn Christmas tree. She's impressed. *Nice,* I play nice for her sake. *Where did you learn that?* I watch as she voices for me again. She would be an amazing interpreter, but I get why she doesn't want to do it.

I looked it up after Scarlett told me her mom is Deaf. You know, in case I get to meet her one day, she interprets for him. He flashes a wink and a smile in her direction. This is not the first time they've seen each other since they met at the bar last week. She is positively glowing at his words.

You want to? She's here. Scar's eyes are wide when she voices that for me. I laugh inside, she's not ready for that. She didn't invite him here. That means he surprised her, he just showed up. At least she didn't bail on me for him.

I need to get going. Next time, Scar interprets again, then adds, *I think that's a good idea. Let me walk you out.*

I lay the bag of food I brought for her on the table and step out of the room, allowing them to pass by. Why the fuck did I wait so long to make my move? I watch them walk down the hall, tormented emotions pulsing through me. Honestly, I'm mostly mad at myself. I could have prevented this if I hadn't been such a chicken shit. I go into my office and practically slam the door. I'm half hoping she comes to talk to me after he leaves, half hoping to ride the rest of this day out hiding in here, drowning in my sorrows.

A few minutes go by, I'm just sitting here at my desk looking at the picture of Scar and me at the skating rink, and the light up door-knocker flashes. She's here. I walk over and pull the handle. But when the door swings open, I'm greeted with James' face, not hers.

My brows furrow at him. We're friendly, but not close. *What's up?* I ask, a bit confused as to why he's here.

I want to talk to you about Scar, he says, cutting right to the chase.

I step aside and motion for him to come in. He takes a seat on one of the arms chairs opposite my new desk. My desk that is still not set up, the contents of my messenger bag strewn about it. I sit down across from him. *What's up?*

I see his lungs inhale deeply. My gut clenches, he's about to tell me to back off. *I'm on 'team Lorenzo.'* He sandwiches 'team Lorenzo' between quotation marks in the air. *I've known for a long time that you love her. It's been so obvious.*

Really? That obvious? I'm relieved to know he's on my side. *Clearly not obvious to her. She had no idea when I told her.*

So, have you told her? How you feel?

Friday night. It's why we never got the decorations up. I'm not sure why I'm divulging so much information to him. I guess with this new revelation there's some measure of trust between us. Whatever the reason, I've decided there's no use denying anything. *Nothing happened. Well, I kissed her. She told me she's never thought of me that way and then asked me to spend the night with her. 'Just hold her,' she said.*

She just needs time. James purses his lips and squints his eyes as if he's thinking of something, planning something.

I throw my hands up, signaling defeat. *I don't have time. Eli, that bartender, he's making moves. Calling, texting, surprising her with lunch.*

His expression turns to empathy. *I don't know how, but I'll help. Seeing you two end up together would be like the happiest ending.* A sly smile spreads across his lips. *Like a Hallmark Christmas movie.*

I've never watched one, I confess. Never been interested in watching one. I've always been more of an action junkie, more visual effects and less captioning to read.

Honey, you're in one. And your character always has a happy ending. He winks before standing to leave. He stops at the door. *Just keep showing up. She'll see you.*

I hate waking up alone now. My bed feels so cold without her. Not that she's slept over enough for me to really miss it. But that last night together, at her house, she let me touch her in ways I've never been able to touch her before. And that taste wasn't nearly enough, I'm dying to touch her again. Since that's not an option, I touch myself instead.

My hand slides down my bare abdomen, under the elastic of my sweats, and wraps around my shaft. The image of her in that tiny tight tank top and plush plaid pants that hugged her ass so perfectly is vivid in my mind. I harden immediately. Though not nearly as soft as hers, I imagine my hand is her hand, stroking up and down. My body tenses. I close my eyes tight, now she's sitting on top of me, her long fiery hair dangles down and brushes my chest. She's writhing on top of me, her full breasts punctuated by two perfectly hard nipples in the middle of them. I've never actually seen her naked, but I've imagined it many, *many* times. In my mind, her breasts are bottom heavy with perky nipples, her stomach is soft and fleshy, her ass is full, round, and dimpled. Conjuring the image of her is all I need to coax my release. Dammit, I need that woman.

It's Tuesday, my second day, and I'm late for work. Not exactly late, I could leave right now and make it on time. The extra few minutes I spent in bed this morning, imagining Scar, did put me a bit behind schedule. I have plans, a surprise for Scar. A bouquet of flowers seems a bit cliché, and food, well *he* did that yesterday. I know Scar on a deeper level, though. I know Christmas is her favorite time of the year. After I shower and dress, making a little extra effort in my appearance, I swing by the nursery on Lattice Road. It opens at 8:00 am, but it's not too far away from the office. I'm standing at the door when they open and sure enough, they have exactly what I'm looking for fairly close to the front.

The woman who unlocked the door says something, but I'm too distracted to read her lips, so I throw my hand up in a 'no thanks' gesture. I hope it's not too rude, but I'm on a mission. There's an array of potted poinsettias, red and white, potted and wrapped in shiny green and red paper, respectively. Perfect. I grab two of each color and head for the register. Scar will absolutely love these for her office.

By the time I've paid and loaded my gifts into my car, it's already 8:15 am. I tell myself the surprise will gain me forgiveness for my tardiness. I'm not too late anyway. Mom's still in the parking lot when I get there, so I'm not going to be the last one in, at least. When I catch her eye, I wave her over.

Hi, sweetie. I'm thirty-one years old and she still calls me 'sweetie.' *I'm so glad you decided to join the business.* She wraps her arms around me, her head barely comes up to my chest.

Actually, I was over at Scar's house, looking at old photos. I realized she's doing well. Then I thought about myself, my freelance work and how slow that is. I think I just realized it's time, I explain.

You and Scar are still very close. Her facial expression doesn't indicate that her comment is a question, and for a moment I wonder why she says it. *I think working together will be good for you two.*

I eye her suspiciously. She's never really mentioned my relationship with Scar. It always seemed like she just viewed Scar and Helen as family. *Good for us?*

Yeah, bring you closer. Her lip curls into a knowing smile.

My eyes widen and I give her an expression that lets her know she and I are on the same page. *Can you help me carry these?* I pop the trunk to reveal the poinsettias.

Oh my god, they're beautiful! For the office?

For Scar.

Her eyebrows lift as she catches on. *Smart,* she signs with a wink.

She's at her desk, the door open as usual, when I walk in with loaded arms. God, she looks beautiful today. Her button-down blouse has two buttons open at the top, just a sliver of cleavage peeks through, the button at the top straining with the fabric from the pull of her ripe, ample breasts. Her hair is curled into thick ringlets that frame her face. She stands when she sees me, cornering the desk to help with the plants. Noticing the black, pleated skirt she's wearing, an image of me behind her bent over that desk, her skirt hiked up over her waist, flashes through my mind. Her mouth moves, it looks like she says, 'let me help you.' She places two of the plants on her desk and I set the other two on her little round table. *Lorenzo, I love these! Did you get them for the office?* Her face is glowing.

I got them for you, I say once my hands are finally free. *For your office.*

Her hands cover her gaping mouth. For a moment, I consider snatching her into me and kissing her, but I know it's not the right moment. *I can't believe it.* She can't stop smiling. *I love these, they're so perfect at Christmas.*

I'm glad you like them. I reach an arm around her for a side hug, then place my kiss on the side of her forehead instead of her lips. I wonder if she's thinking about my confession, or if she's too distracted by the bartender. Fuck it, I ask. *Have you thought about what I told you the other night?*

Her shoulders slump. She hasn't. Or maybe she has. Either way, her body language is speaking volumes. And I'm Deaf. *Yes, but—*

But? I question, then hold up my hands. I don't want to know if she's going to break my heart.

I'm just not ready, she says anyway.

Not ready for what? For us? To decide? Discuss? What?

Any of that. I feel my heart clench. *Give me more time,* she adds.

She needs time. She can have time. But not space. I just have to keep showing up. Keep showing her how valuable I am to her life. Keep showing her that I am here for the long haul. After lingering a moment, holding her gaze, I nod and walk away.

Chapter 9
Eli

"You look really nice tonight, boss." Ana is tending bar tonight along with Frankie. I'm more than relieved that they both decided to show up tonight. This way, I won't be distracted when Scarlett comes in with her work friends.

I tug at the collar of my dark purple button-down shirt that I have tucked into my favorite pair of jeans. "This old thing?" She eyes me knowingly. "Try not to need me too much tonight." I wink at her.

"Sure thing, boss."

I make my way around the bar like I do when I'm not covering for someone who called out. I offer to refill drinks and check in on how the customers' night is going. The bar has been open a little over a year, but we already have plenty of regulars. I think this town needed more options, something fresh and new.

Even though I haven't seen Scarlett since I took her lunch on Monday, we've talked on the phone every evening since that first date at the park. She's just so easy to talk to. In the few short days I've known her, I'm already comfortable enough to share some of my experiences overseas that I haven't really talked about with anyone else. She's opened up to me about growing up in such a silent world, expressing how sometimes she craves verbal conversations. But despite that, she wouldn't trade it for the world. I've already made a commitment to myself to learn sign language so I can communicate with her mom. I have the time, or at least I will; I'm interviewing managers this week.

It's just after five o'clock when I notice the receptionist from Scarlett's office and one of the guys that had been with her last week come in and push a couple of the high tops together. My heart seems to beat a little faster at the anticipation of her arriving at any moment. The table slowly fills with familiar faces, and I walk over to greet them.

"Welcome back." I smile, placing drink napkins around the table in front of each of them.

"Thanks, we enjoyed it so much last week that we had to come back," one of the women tells me.

"Love to hear that. Let me get some drinks out for you, what would you like?" I offer.

"Would you make me that skinny margarita you made last week?" the first woman requests.

"Oh, that sounds good," the receptionist exclaims. "I'll take that too." I make a mental note to learn everyone's name.

Scarlett arrives just after I finish jotting down drinks. "Are you bartending tonight?" she asks with a low whisper in my ear. Her warm breath startles me and sends a pleasant shiver down my spine.

Turning to greet her with a kiss on the cheek, I slide my arm around her, squeezing at the flesh on her hip. I like that she's a bit thicker, more to hold onto. She smells amazing, like coconut and vanilla. "Just for you and your friends," I respond for only her to hear, lingering in our embrace. "You look positively gorgeous." I say that last part loud enough for everyone at the table to hear. There was no way to miss the receptionist's smile after I say it.

She's blushing when I pull away. And then *he* comes in right behind her. Lorenzo. I know *his* name. His eyes are boring into me so hard that I can practically feel the holes they're drilling. I nod in his direction to say hello, or at least acknowledge him. He barely cocks an eyebrow back at me.

"Stop it." She playfully pats my shoulder. "You look nice too." She hasn't started signing while she talks yet, for a moment I wonder if she even knows he's behind her. Then she turns her head to check for him. "Come on, sit down," she signs that while she speaks.

He takes the seat on the other side of her, of course he does. His intense need to stay close to her is palpable. And downright annoying. Her silent protector. She doesn't need protection here, except maybe from him. "What can I get you, gorgeous?" I offer her first. The flirty guy that was here last week appears to take on the responsibility of translating for Lorenzo again, signing everything I say.

"Definitely one of those magic skinny drinks you made me last week." How did I know? I smile confidently at her request.

I nod my head in Lorenzo's direction. "And for you?"

He signs something with a smug face, and I hear the flirty guy's voice saying, "No special drinks for me, I'll take a double Jack and Coke."

"Coming right up." I make a point to flash a coy smile at Scarlett before I walk away.

From behind the bar, I watch as he slides an arm to rest on the back of her chair. The table has gone silent, and it appears a few conversations are happening. Lorenzo and the flirty guy are chatting with Scarlett, while the other three seem to have their own conversation happening. Though they do seem to overlap, I find myself quite fascinated by the silent communication passing between them. Two more people arrive, a man and a woman who look to be a couple. Lorenzo takes this opportunity to scoot his chair closer to hers. His legs spread and his knee rests against hers. My gut tells me it is no accident.

"That's why you're dressed so nice today, isn't it, boss?" Ana asks, stepping up next to me to fill a glass with ice from the bin in front of me. "She's beautiful."

"How could you tell?" Am I that conspicuous?

"Please! You're practically drooling over here. That and the way you greeted her when she came in," Ana points out. She reaches her index finger over and pretends to close my gaping jaw. "Also, that guy next to her looks like he wants to kill you."

He absolutely does look like he wants to kill me. I'm not sure if the competition makes me wary or if it makes me even more motivated. I look back at Scarlett's glowing smile and decide on motivated.

"Scarlett, would you introduce me to everyone? I'd love to learn their names," I ask when I set her drink in front of her and then his.

"Of course! I should have done that earlier. Well, now everyone is here, so it's a good time." She smiles, she's happy that I want to get to know her friends. She starts on her left, "You've met

Lorenzo, this is James, Dave, Lucy, Macie, Emma, and her husband Jermaine." She points to each person, signing their name, and they wave as they are pointed at.

"Nice to meet you all." I try to commit each name to memory. It's not too hard since I've always been good with names. I turn to Emma and Jermaine who had just arrived. "Can I get you two something to drink?" Jermaine signs what I say to his wife, and I realize she's Deaf too. I'm pretty sure I catch the sign for 'drink' and decide to try it out. I cup my hand like I'm holding a glass and bring it up to my lips. "Drink?"

Everyone at the table throws their hands up in the air and starts shaking them. Everyone except for Lorenzo; he's eyeing me with a smug look. "Yes! That's perfect." Scarlett is beaming. The fact that I've impressed her thrills me and I flash her a proud grin. "You'll be signing in no time!" she adds.

Jermaine orders for himself and Emma, and a few people order appetizers for the table. When I get behind the bar, I ask Ana to keep an eye on the group and make sure drinks are full. Then I make a loop around the room, checking in with our other guests before pulling a chair up next to Scarlett. Lucy, who was on the other side of her, scoots her chair down to make room, and there's a wave of movement as everyone on the other side of Lucy scoots a few inches too.

"Alright, I'm off the clock," I declare, setting my own drink down on the table. "Let's get this party started."

Scarlett laughs at my joke and then raises her glass to clink against mine. I smile back at her. The back of her chair is still crowded with Lorenzo's arm, so I pat her thigh and let my hand linger there for a moment. She squeezes her knees together at my touch, pulling her leg away from Lorenzo's. He is seething. From my peripheral, I see his jaw clench and his temple throb as his throat rolls, swallowing hard. Game, set, match, mother fucker.

The group does that thing where they talk and sign at the same time. When Emma or Lorenzo contribute to the conversation, James is quick to translate for me. In all honesty, Lorenzo isn't joining in much. "What other signs could we teach Eli?" Scarlett asks the table.

"What's your name?" Macie suggests.

"Oh, I know that one." I'm eager to show off what I learned on my own. I turn my voice off and sign, *My name is E-L-I.*

"Good!" Jermaine appears to voice that for Emma. "But you don't have to sign the word 'is.'" Now it's obvious to me that he is voicing for her, she's signing away and making eye contact with me.

"No?" I had thought sign language was just English with your hands.

"No," Scarlett joins in. She signs for herself while she talks. "Right now we are signing and talking to make sure you, Lorenzo, and Emma are all included in the conversation. So, it looks like the signs match up with the English. But true ASL has a different grammatical structure."

"That's fascinating." I am super intrigued by all of this. Until Scarlett walked into my bar, I'd never met a Deaf person or really seen anyone use sign language for that matter.

"Yeah, and even then, we don't sign the articles," James added. "To ask someone's name in ASL you actually would sign 'your name, what?'"

"That's why it's very cool that you want to learn and made the effort to learn something on your own, but it's best to learn in a class or, even better, from a Deaf person," Macie commends my efforts. "Or Scarlett! She would be a great person to teach you sign!" she adds, excitement fills her voice.

"Scar isn't Deaf." James' tone makes me feel like it didn't come from him. I look over at him and he's pointing to Lorenzo, signaling that he was voicing for him.

Scarlett's smile fades; she's picked up on Lorenzo's negativity. "He wants to learn, there's no harm in that." Her voice is different, defeated maybe? I can't pinpoint it.

Lorenzo's face forms into a scowl. He pulls his arm out from behind Scarlett and signs with both hands. They fly through the air, and even though silent, the emotion behind them is loud and clear. I look to James to interpret. He sits tight lipped with sheepish eyes. My eyes bounce from person to person, asking for a clue as to what just happened when Lorenzo jumps up from the table and storms out. Scarlett throws her hands up, defeated. "I'm so sorry," she says and then follows him out the front door.

"He asked us not to interpret, but that's rude if you ask me," Macie pipes in finally. "He said he's sick and tired of hearing people learning sign language only to benefit themselves. Especially assholes like you who are only doing it to get laid."

Chapter 10
Scarlett

What the hell is your problem? I ask Lorenzo when I catch up to him outside the bar. He's pacing, his hands clenched in his thick brown hair, elbows pointed in opposite directions.

He glares at me, walking back and forth in front of me, taking deep breaths. I've never seen him this pissed before. It's kind of scary, I don't like it. Finally, he pulls his hands down from his head to talk to me. *Do you know how hard it is to watch that? To watch him kiss your cheek and touch your thigh? You know how I feel about you now, but then you flaunt that asshole in front of me?*

It's understandable that he's jealous, but this is intensely jealous. *I told you where we were going. You didn't have to come.*

What? And just step back and let him steal you away? He throws his arms up in the air and they practically slam back down on his thighs. *I told you I've been in love with you for fifteen years. You think I'm going to just sit back and let this nobody you've known for a week rip you away from me?*

I don't like this jealous side of Lorenzo at all. It's the complete opposite of the kind, caring man I know and love. This jealous side scares me. *That's exactly what you're doing. This jealous asshole act you've got going on, that is not the Lorenzo I know. That is not a Lorenzo I am going to fall in love with. You've never acted this way when I dated guys before. Why now?* There had only ever been three others, and none of them lasted very long. Still, he held his feelings back with each of them.

He shakes his head and stops pacing. *I don't know. I guess before I was always trying to hide my feelings. Now that I'm finally*

Forget Me Not

ready, here he comes along. He points to the door where Eli has just walked out. Now he's angry again. *The way I imagined it, I confess my feelings and you immediately confess yours back. That didn't happen. Clearly.*

"Eli, could you give us a minute." I turn to him, signing so Lorenzo knows I've asked him to leave.

"I just wanted to make sure you're okay, considering his temper." He gestures toward Lorenzo, and I can see that adds fuel to Lorenzo's anger. Though I can see it's not only anger, there's sadness hiding in the glassy tears pooling in his eyes.

"I'll be fine. Thank you." I'm trying to make my voice calm and sweet. I want him to know that I do, very much, appreciate his concern for me. "I'll be back inside in a minute," I assure him.

Eli slinks back inside, and I turn to Lorenzo, drawing out the two letters of his name sign. *Lorenzo, I told you I needed time. You've always been here for me, always been in my life. And I love you, so much, but right now that love is family love. Maybe if you had told me your feelings fifteen years ago, things would be different now,* I explain. The emotion in his eyes softens, anger subsiding to leave behind only sadness. I step forward and brush his cheek with my hand. *I'm not saying I could never think of you that way. I really don't know. It's just bad timing, that's all.*

Do you like him?

The pause I take is palpable while my lungs inhale a deep breath. I exhale. *I do, and he didn't need to see someone else interested in me to like me too. I'm sorry, but I feel like I need to see what happens with him. I can't shake this feeling that I met him for a reason.* He throws his hands up again, turns on his heel, and heads off toward his car. This conversation is over. A part of me fears this friendship might soon be over too.

"Let me drive you home," Eli offers when my friends have all cleared out and I'm ready to call it a night. "I only had one drink."

I study his face, debating with the idea of where him driving me home could lead. "I can order a Lyft." I smile, hoping he hasn't been scared away by Lorenzo's behavior.

"You'll need your car in the morning to get to work. Let me drive you, in your car, and I'll take a Lyft back here." He's right. And so thoughtful. Damn.

"Sure, that sounds like a good idea," I agree.

"Come on." He loops his fingers around mine and leads me through the bar. "Ana, can you close up? I'm taking off," he calls to the woman behind the bar.

"Sure thing, boss," she calls back.

We go through a door at the corner of the room that opens up to a staircase. "I just need to grab my keys. Come up with me. I want to show you my place."

I follow him up the stairs to another door that opens up to a spacious studio apartment. There's a kitchen to the right of the door we walked through with all the appliances and an island that adds extra counter space. To the left is another door that I assume is a bathroom. The living space is divided by two Japanese dressing screens. On one side, by the kitchen, he has a small sectional couch facing a big screen TV mounted to the wall. The other side hosts his queen-sized bed, nightstand, and a chest of drawers.

"Wow, this is nice, Eli." His decorative style is tasteful, sleek, and modern. Similar to mine. "I've always loved exposed brick." I run my hand over a red brick on the wall, admiring it.

"Thanks, I was kind of thrilled when I found out this place had the apartment up top. Makes life super easy." He beams proudly.

"I bet it does." The keys are on the island, he reaches for them and turns to go. "I'm sorry, Eli. I'm sorry for the way Lorenzo acted earlier." I stop him.

"You don't have to apologize. You aren't responsible for his actions," he assures me. His tone gives away hints to how he views Lorenzo now though.

"But in some ways, I am." I decide I have to tell Eli why Lorenzo acted the way he did. Not that I want to justify it, but because I want Eli to know everything. I want to be completely honest with him.

"He likes you. A lot," Eli says matter-of-factly. "It's *painfully* obvious." He drags out the word 'painfully.'

My eyes widen, shocked by his perceptiveness. "How can you tell?"

"Are you serious, Scarlett?" His tone isn't anger or frustration, but rather taken aback. "He's physically possessive over you when you two are together. The way he stares at you. The way his demeanor changes when I'm around." He points out a few things, a bit heatedly.

"We've known each other our whole lives. He's always been like a brother to me, like my best friend. I guess I always thought he was protective over me because of that." This is honestly what I had always thought. Until recently, at least. "He did tell me last week that he's been in love with me since high school. Right after I met you."

"And now he wants you to choose?" Wow, he picks up on a lot.

I nod. "Basically. When he told me last week, I said I needed time to think, time to view him in a different way. Then we went on that date to Lake Wilson," I motion between us, "and all I've really thought about since then is you." His face lightens, happy to hear that news. "I just wanted to let you know everything that's been going on. I want to be honest with you, start things off right."

"What are we starting?" His tone is light and flirty. Hopeful. As if all thoughts and talk of Lorenzo never happened. He steps closer to me, taking my hands in his.

"We might need another date or two before we know for sure." I try to match his flirty tone. He reaches his hand up and through my hair, pulling my face to his and my body close to him. His lips are soft, he parts them, taking my bottom lip between his. "And maybe a few more kisses," I add when he steps back.

Eli pulls in my driveway and puts my car in park, though he doesn't turn the engine off right away. I shift in my seat, angling my body in his direction. He does the same. We're silent for a moment, but it's not an awkward silence, per se.

"Despite the bit of jealous rage drama, I enjoyed myself tonight," I finally speak.

He doesn't hesitate. "I always enjoy myself when I'm with you, Scarlett." His eyes soften and he slants his head towards me. I meet him halfway, our lips taste each other, explore each other. This is by far our longest kiss. Not that I've been counting.

His hand grazes the top of my thigh, leaving a trail of goosebumps under the black, lacy tights I'm wearing. I desperately want to invite him in, but I'm not sure I'll have the strength to ask him to wait. If the situation arises, that is. And I'm fairly certain it will. Fuck it. "Want to come in and have that wine date? It's not too late," I suggest.

The engine is off before he speaks, keys in his hand. "Absolutely."

We're inside so fast it makes me hope I can get the bottle open before he attacks me. Then again, maybe I don't. Binx greets us at the door. Of course, ready for his dinner. "This is my cat, Binx," I introduce him, then make my way to get his food.

"I love cats." He bends down to pet him. Binx sniffs his hand, making sure our visitor is acceptable, and then rubs his face against it.

"Wow, he doesn't usually let people pet him the first time he meets them," I comment. "He must like you."

"He's a good judge of character. You should trust his judgment." He winks. "Black cat? What you think, good luck or bad luck?" he asks. I love that he can move a conversation along.

"Definitely good luck. I found this guy by the dumpster when he was a kitten. He couldn't have been more than five weeks old," I explain. "Once I took him home, I got him cleaned up, fed, and snuggled. He fell in love with me."

"Sweet guy?"

"The sweetest." I smile. "Red or white wine?" I ask, holding up two bottles a bottle of pinot noir and a bottle of sauvignon blanc.

"Definitely red wine." There's an impish smile spread across his lips. It makes me think he's playfully copying my word choice. "Where do you keep your glasses?"

My head nods toward the hutch against the kitchen wall behind him. "Just behind you, there."

He fetches two stemless glasses from behind the frosted cabinet door. "You have a beautiful house. Well, really I'm guessing based on the vibe of your kitchen," he says, laughing at himself.

"Thanks, I bought it four years ago. Before that I was living with my mom. Not so much out of necessity, I just didn't want to leave her there alone." I've opened up to him a lot about my dad's passing.

"How's she been doing with that? Living alone, that is," he asks as I finish pouring the wine and hand him a glass.

"I think she's good. She spends a lot of time with Alana. I usually have dinner with her once a week. And she's still working." I hold my glass up to 'toast' his.

"What are we toasting?" he asks, holding his glass up too.

Oh god, what can I say that doesn't sound cheesy or cliché? "Checking these dates off the list."

He touches his glass to mine at that, and we sip. "I'll drink to that."

Chapter 11
Eli

She eyes me over the rim of her wine glass, her nerves evident. As well as her attempts to thwart them. She's wondering where things will go tonight, and if she's ready for that. I silently promise her, and myself, that I will only make my move when she's good and ready. Sex isn't on the table yet. "Want to see more of the house?" she offers.

"Definitely." I give a subtle smile and half wink, showing her that I'm playfully mocking her. Only because I find everything about her absolutely adorable. Right now, the way she says 'definitely' is at the top of the list of my favorite things about Scarlett Reese.

She leads me from the kitchen into a large open living room. It boasts vaulted ceilings and full-length windows on either side of a set of French doors that lead to what appears to be a sunroom, though it's too dark to tell. There's an oversized suede armchair and matching sofa on adjacent sides of a square leather coffee table. Her modern-style flows from one room to the next. Sliding effortlessly between the couch and the coffee table, she pats the cushion next to her, motioning for me to sit.

"You have fine taste, Miss Reese." She blushes, and damn if it's not the cutest thing I've ever seen. I ease back on the sofa, relaxing and allowing my knees to spread. The one closest to hers now rests against her thigh.

Her eyes flit over to where my knee has entered her bubble. Her lip curls into a smile on one side, she likes it. "Thanks." Her voice cracks and she clears her throat. She sips her wine before speaking again. "I've always enjoyed decorating. HGTV is on the regular rotation on my TV." She lets out a nervous laugh along with her confession.

"It shows. So, maybe we could have my first sign language lesson tonight," I suggest. "I need to be ready when I meet your mom." I flash her my flirty grin, but my intentions to meet her mother are *definitely* serious.

She relaxes and shifts her body toward me, pulling one leg up on the couch and tucking her foot under her other knee. The skirt she forgot she is wearing is pleated, so it drapes gracefully over her conspicuously open lap. Now I clear my throat. "That's a great idea," she says excitedly.

We brainstorm some phrases that would come up the first time you meet someone. She teaches me some polite greetings, how to talk about what I do for a living, along with how to ask what someone does, and then we move into the alphabet. "Oh, we should've started with this," I muse.

"Well, technically, you should avoid spelling, you know, once you're fluent. But for now, you might have to use it often," she explains.

"You think I'll be fluent one day?" I beam. The idea makes me think about the long haul.

"Sure! The more you're around Deaf people and using the language, the better you'll get." We practice what she's taught me a few more times to really solidify my learning.

Our glasses sit empty on the coffee table, and it's quickly approaching midnight. I'm tipsy, she's buzzed, which brings us to the end of our sign language lessons for the night. "I should probably order that Lyft," I say, sitting up.

She sighs in agreement. "I do have to work in the morning." I note the disappointment in her voice. Because she doesn't want to end the evening or because she doesn't want me to leave, that I don't know. We linger there, and she stares at me doe eyed.

Fuck me. I lunge into her. My lips devour hers, and she welcomes it. Her foot untucks from under her knee, and she stretches that leg out along the back of the couch, inviting me to scoot closer to her. I gladly accept her invitation. My hand slips around her back, pulling our bodies together. Her free leg lifts to rest on my lap, and now I can feel her heat radiating against my hip. I dive in deeper, kissing her harder. We've gotten ourselves to a precarious point.

I pull back, suddenly overcome by a reminder that I want this to be done right. And sex after a week of knowing each other is not doing it right. It's too soon, no matter how much I want her right now.

"Scarlett, I can't wait for the day that we get to explore each other's bodies," I say breathlessly into her ear, not wanting to separate our bodies just yet. "But I want to do this right, respectfully."

She scoots her body back from mine. Now she's keenly aware of the way our bodies are touching. "Thank you," she whispers. Her hushed tone reminds me of her shyness from our first date, letting me know she's relieved that I've drawn the line.

I nod, and then rest my forehead against hers, exhaling a deep breath. "I'm getting up, give me a minute." She giggles underneath me.

"Technically, you still need to order your Lyft. We could kiss until it gets here," she says coyly.

"Dammit, Scarlett." I exhale, and dive into her lips again.

She lets me kiss her for a minute before she presses her hand against my chest, pushing my lips away from hers. "You have to order the Lyft first, silly," she reminds me.

I pull my phone from the back pocket of my jeans, open up the Lyft app, and confirm my pickup. "It'll be here in 10 minutes, which means we have at least eight more minutes to make out."

When the Corolla that picked me up pulls up in front of Fire & Ice, Ana is just locking up. The timing seems about right. She sees me climb out of the car and waves.

"Hey, boss. Didn't expect to see you back tonight."

"Nah, this one has serious potential. I'm taking things slow with her." Ana has become my sounding board over the past year that we've worked together. "Can I walk you to your car?" I offer.

"Diedre dropped me off. She'll be here in a minute."

"Well, I'll wait with you."

"Hey, so that guy from earlier, the Deaf one, he came back by the bar after you left. He left a note for you," she informs me.

"What did it say?" My mood shifts.

"It was in a sealed envelope. I didn't open it. I just left it on your office desk." Diedre pulls up and stops in front of us on the sidewalk, throwing me a quick wave. "Oh, gotta go. See you tomorrow, boss."

She hops in the passenger seat, and they drive off. I head straight for the bar office. There it is on the desk, a white letter-sized envelope with my name written in a small, all-capped print. With the letter opener, I slice the envelope open and pull out the folded slip of paper. I unfold it to reveal two small words that pack a big punch, *back off*.

Chapter 12
Lorenzo

I'm pissed off when I wake up. The events of last night are still reeling in my head. Deep down, I know I was acting like an asshole. That kind of behavior is not going to make Scar fall in love with me. I know that. I just can't shake this overwhelming contempt for Eli and, I suppose, the situation. But mostly for Eli. We wouldn't be in this situation if he hadn't come into the picture. If it weren't for him, I firmly believe Scar and I would be together by now.

Not ready to face the day, I pull up Instagram and start scrolling, hoping it will help distract me and calm me down before work. A picture of Scar slides over my screen and I stop my scrolling, clicking over to her account. She has a variety of images she likes to share. Naturally, she shares some food pictures, like everyone else. There are other, more subtly artistic pictures of her world. And what Instagram page would be complete without selfies. The selfies are what I'm here for. Seeing her bright smiling face over and over again brings a sense of calm back to me. Though, now instead of anger, I'm filled with arousal. My arousal quickly subsides into guilt and embarrassment remembering the anger in her expression last night.

Cliché as it may be, I stop for flowers on my way in. This time I pick up a bouquet from a grocery store near the office, instead of going to the nursery. I do know she hates red roses, so I pick out the nicest appearing bundle of white roses. There's a shelf by the bouquet bin with a few glass vases. I take a red vase and size it up with the roses. This will work.

Scar's door is open when I get to the office. Shit. I duck into the breakroom before I pass by her door. It's empty, thankfully. I set my messenger bag down and take the flowers over to the sink to arrange them. On the card I'd decided to pick up, I scribble, 'I'm so sorry for being an asshole. Forgive me?' Then place it in the envelope and write Scar's name on the outside. Just as I am headed out the door, I have another idea. I want my gesture to be seen by more than just Scar. So, I opt to set the flowers on the table in the center of the room, and place the card propped up, Scar's name on display. Then I sneak down the hall to my office, careful to walk by her office fast enough that she doesn't notice the movement.

I've been hiding in my office for a few hours before she finally comes to see me. She hits the switch, flickering the lights to gain my attention. She's wearing tight jeans with a red cardigan tucked into them. The cardigan appears to only have a camisole underneath the low cut buttons. Her plump breasts heave over the edge of it with her breath. The mere sight of her evokes conflicting emotions within me. Desperate to get back into her good graces, I stand immediately ready to go to her, hug her, touch her.

Only, I wait for a signal from her. *Good morning, Scar,* I sign, giving her a sheepish smile.

She stands there for a moment, I'm struggling to read her expression. Then she finally lifts her hands. *The flowers from you?*

I nod slowly. *You like them?*

She nods.

Her facial expression is difficult to read, but I decide to move toward her. With my arm outstretched, I cock my eyebrows up to ask permission to hug her. She nods again, standing practically still, waiting for my arm to slink behind her. When I press my lips to her forehead, I can feel her body tense.

You OK? I ask, furrowing my brows in concern. I know she's not, I know she's still mad.

She nods, but then looks away momentarily. *Lorenzo?* I lean my head forward, widening my eyes to welcome the question. *That version of you at the bar last night, I don't like him. I don't want to meet him again.*

It stings. It boils emotions back up inside me. I nod, tight lipped. *I'm sorry, Scar. I really don't know what came over me.* Well, I know what pissed me off. But how much I let that take over, even

I'm concerned about that. *I'm just so overwhelmed with everything. I want to give you time, I do. It's hard because I've waited so long already.* I pout my lips and flash her puppy dog eyes. *Forgive me?*

She stares at me again. Or is it more of a glare? Then she nods again. *Don't act like that again or you'll lose me.* She raises her eyebrows, as if scolding me with her eyes. I nod.

When she opens the door to leave, I decide being in her life in any capacity is better than losing her forever. I just have to wait for this relationship to fail like the others did. In the back of my mind, there's a thought that I may also just have to help that failure along.

Almost three weeks go by, I've been biting my lip, biding my time, and waiting patiently for this asshole bartender to fall through the cracks. He's still very much around, which is why my time with Scar has been incredibly limited. She's been so busy with him. If I hadn't taken this job at the agency, I feel like I would never see her.

Helen is hosting a dinner at her house tonight, of course Mom, Dad, and I are invited. Scar is the last to arrive. I'm two glasses of wine in when the doorbell light flashes. I'm not sure why she knocks on her mother's door, but I realize it could just be to let her know she's here because the door swings open before Helen even stands from her seat on the couch.

Scar walks in, carrying a bottle of wine. She's radiant in her dark wash jeans and cream and black floral cardigan, the usual bit of cleavage ornamenting her chest. And then walks in none other than fucking Eli. Helen lights up.

Who is this? she signs dramatically. Her face is glowing.

Hi, my name is Eli Romero. Of course, he fucking signs it. *It's nice to meet you.*

Mom, this is my boyfriend. I narrow my eyes on her lips. It doesn't look like she's talking with her signs. I'm trying to decide if he understood what was said. I certainly understood it. 'Boyfriend' was very clear. Too clear. Ouch.

So nice to meet you! Helen is downright giddy. The fact that she's so happy to meet this new man in Scar's life crushes me. *Eli, this is my best friend, Alana. Her husband, Corbin.* She motions toward me, and Eli makes eye contact with me. *And her son, Lorenzo.*

Nice to meet you all. His eyes come back to mine. He nods. We eye each other knowingly. Silently daring the other to disturb the peace.

How did you meet? Dad asks. It does appear that he is talking while he signs to accommodate our hearing guest.

It was about four weeks ago. We went to his bar for happy hour. He was bartending that night. We exchanged numbers because I had asked him if he would be interested in bartending for our Christmas party. When I called to talk about details, we hit it off. Scar clearly spoke while she signed so Eli would understand.

Now I'm miffed by his disturbance to our natural language flow. Without him here, there would only be sign language, produced naturally. Not bastardized by the prioritization of spoken English.

You learned all that sign in four weeks? Helen marvels. Scar voices her comment for him.

He nods proudly. *I've been taking a class. Well, Scarlett has been teaching me too.* Fuck him. His signs are clear and produced well. Grammar is off, as it is with most hearing people who sign. I can't stand that he's a natural with *my* language.

Scar's eyes go wide, and the corners of her mouth spread from ear to ear. She had no idea. *You're taking a class?* she asks, pleasantly surprised.

Fucking asshole. He plays dirty. Those other douchebags she's dated never bothered to learn even how to spell their names. They didn't stand a chance. She's barely looked in my direction, and I start to feel like I might as well not even be there. I leave the room in search of more wine. Even though there is a bottle on the coffee table that Scar brought. I need a minute to myself to cool off. That minute is all a get. Because here comes fucking Eli, carrying the other bottle of wine.

He nods to greet me. *Glasses... where?* His sign vocabulary is clearly still limited, but he's getting his point across. His natural ease with my language just pisses me off even more.

I bite my tongue. Literally. *Did you get my letter?* I ask, then pull two glasses from the cabinet for him, setting them on the counter in front of him. It has been three weeks since I left it, but this is the first time he and I have been alone in a room together.

He copies my sign for 'letter,' checking to see if he picked up the right meaning for that sign. He did. *Yes.* He scowls at me. He got it. He closes the distance between us, pointing to his mouth. He wants me to read his lips. "You're not going to bully me away from her."

I swore off my voice years ago, but I make a point to exaggerate my mouth movements when I sign. *Watch me.* I know this is the wrong way to handle it, I know I should come to him man to man. There's just something about him that sets me off.

We're left in a scowl standoff.

Until Scar comes in. He hears the swinging door first. When he turns around, I see her and erase the scowl from my face. I have to play nice. She doesn't like jealous Lorenzo. She likes sweet, kind, caring Lorenzo. That's exactly who I need to be for her. When he faces me again, I can see that he's wiped the scowl off his face as well.

Mom wants a glass too. She is still using her voice. *You two getting along OK?* she adds, eyeing us both skeptically.

It looks like Eli tells her that I helped him find the glasses. He only signed 'glasses.' *I helped him find the glasses.* I add for good measure. See, I'm helpful Lorenzo. I can get along with your 'boyfriend.'

Thank you, Lorenzo. She smiles at me then fishes another glass from the cabinet for Helen. *Shall we?*

Dinner is a mess. Scar spends most of her time trying to keep up interpreting for everyone, though Dad helps out with that too. She's sitting extra close to Eli so she can whisper everything in his ear. He has one hand resting on her thigh the whole time, unless he knows enough to sign part of what he says. Then as soon as he's done, the hand is right back on her damn thigh. There was only one guy in the past that she brought with her to one of these family gatherings. Back when we were in college, she brought her boyfriend at the time home for Thanksgiving. As I recall, he broke up with her shortly after. She told me later it was because he was overwhelmed by all the signing and never felt he would be able to keep up or fit in. She'd been heartbroken and I was there to console her. I'm still here, ready to console her again. I just need Eli to break her heart. Inside, I cringe at the fact that I want her to get heartbroken, but it really is for good reason. It looks like I'll have to grin and bear it for a while though. Especially considering he's passing this test with flying fucking colors.

Lorenzo, you've been fairly quiet tonight. Everything alright? Mom asks me, Scar notices the side conversation. We hold eye contact for the first time this entire evening. I shy my eyes away from hers and give Mom a sweet smile.

Yeah, just... Scar is still watching... *my head is just in another place right now.* Another place and time. A time where asshole bartenders don't exist, and *my* hand is resting on Scar's thigh all night long.

Patience, she signs. She reaches her hand to cup my cheek. *What is meant to be, will be. Just be patient.* Clearly Mom has picked up on my feelings. There's a silent communication between us, for a moment I feel hopeful and not hopeless.

I give her a thankful smile then flit my eyes back over to Scar. She quickly looks away. She saw that. Good. I watch as she places her hand on Eli's hand that rests on her thigh. He turns to her, and they exchange smiles, hers is shaky, his is confident. She speaks, no sign, but it looks as though she's told him it's time to go. He pushes back from his chair and stands to pull hers out for her.

We're going to take off, Scar announces to the group.

Oh, Scar, we still have dessert. It's early, why so soon? Helen stands, protesting Scar's departure.

I'm just really tired. She bends to kiss her cheek. *Dinner was great, thanks, Mom.*

Everything was delicious. Scar must have taught Eli that ahead of time. *Nice to meet you.* He waves at the group.

Helen walks them to the door. If Eli hadn't rudely disrupted our family dinner, I would have walked Scar to the door. It seems futile now. Instead, I watch through the doorway, I can see them at the front door. Scar assures Helen that she will see Eli at the Christmas party. Helen hugs them both and pats Eli's cheek with a huge smile. She likes him. That doesn't bode well for me.

Chapter 13
Scarlett

*M*ariah Carey's voice breaks into my sleep, stirring me to life as she sings about what she wants for Christmas. My alarm is always set to a Pandora Christmas station this time of year. *It's the morning of the party.*

My body jolts up. The party is still twelve hours away, but I am already frantic. Macie is meeting me at the hotel at noon to set everything up, that will allow us time to get showered and ready in our rooms. Everyone in the office booked a room, many of the contractors coming tonight did as well. I want everything to run smoothly. I just can't shake this feeling that it's going to be a mess.

Eli came over last night to help me with wrapping some last-minute gifts for all the employees and contractors. We packed everything in boxes, and he offered to pack them into his car. Before I left work yesterday, I checked in with the caterer to be sure everything was all set for that. My "to-do" list for the party is completely checked off. Every detail meticulously checked and rechecked. The party starts at 6:00 pm, the caterer and Mack, the DJ, are set to arrive by 5:00 pm. Eli took care of securing the bartenders. Every detail is set. I don't know why I'm dead set on the idea that this party is going to be a flop.

My phone buzzes, vibrating the watch on my wrist. I lift my hand to see a text from Lorenzo.

ZO: Anything I can help you with today? To get ready for the party?

Me: I think everything is ready. Do you want to help set up the banquet hall? Meet there at noon?

ZO: I'll be there.

Well, that's helpful. Another pair of hands helping to get the tables set and decorations hung will allow more time for me to get ready. Feeling a bit more relaxed, I get up and make my way around the room packing the things I'll need for tonight. That could be what I'm actually nervous about. Though we haven't discussed it outright, I'm fairly certain that Eli and I will be spending the night together. All night. In a hotel room. Well past our sixth date. We haven't *made love* yet. Well, we haven't said 'I love you' either. Can you make love with someone you haven't said 'I love you' to? Or is it just sex? Either way, we haven't done... that.

Yup, that's why I am extra nervous. I make sure to pack my sexiest matching bra and panty set. My dress for the party is green velvet, strapless with a long slit up one leg. The slit ends dangerously close to where my hip meets my thigh. The bra I've picked out has removable straps, it's black silk lined with lace. The panties are mostly silk as well, with lace trim around the front of the leg holes and along the front line of the waistband.

Feeling satisfied that I have everything I need for hair, make-up, and potential sexy time, I gather my bag and head out. James is going to stop by the house before the party and feed Binx again, but I make sure to fill his bowl before I leave for the day. I pull my phone out of my purse when I get into the car and dial Macie's number.

"Hello?" she answers groggily.

"Macie, good morning. Hey, so I'm going to check in on my mom and then I'm headed to Nail City to get a mani and pedi. Did you want to join me?" I offer.

"What time is it?" She's not as much of a morning person as I am.

"7:15," I say nonchalantly as if that isn't early for a Saturday morning. "They open at 9:00, I figured if I'm first there, then I'll be sure to be done and still be at the hotel by noon."

"Girl, I think we need an eight o'clock rule for Saturdays." She sounds a bit grumpy. "But, yeah, a mani and pedi will be nice. I'll meet you there."

Mom is a morning person, I'm convinced that's where I get it from. My dad's been gone a long time, but I do remember he liked to sleep in on the weekends. Even though I know she's awake when I get there, I always ring the doorbell so the light flashes to let her know I'm here, then turn the key and let myself in. The one time I didn't ring the doorbell, the unexpected sight of me caused her to jump three feet in the air. I couldn't bear the idea of losing both of my parents to a heart attack.

Good morning! She's always so happy to see me. *Ready for tonight?* she asks, then waves her hand for me to follow her into the kitchen.

She pulls two mugs from the cabinet and holds one up to offer me coffee. I nod. *Yes, please, coffee would be great. I guess I'm ready. A little nervous,* I admit.

Why nervous? It's going to be perfect. Everyone will have a great time. She pours coffee into the mugs and slides one across the counter toward me.

I take a sip. Her coffee has always been my favorite. I would take it over Starbucks any day of the week, and twice on Sunday. *The coffee is good, thanks, Mom. Do you need a ride tonight? I'm going early to set up and get ready there. But I could come back for you or send Eli.*

Her face lights up at the mention of Eli. When I brought him to family dinner at her house last week, she seemed to like him a lot. And of course, she was over the moon with the fact that he is learning sign language to be able to communicate with her. *I like Eli. He seems like a nice guy.*

He is a very nice guy. I like him too.

We share a smile, then the Deaf bluntness comes. As it always does. *I always pictured you with a Deaf man. Someone like... Lorenzo. Deaf of Deaf, so maybe I could one day have Deaf grandchildren.*

I practically spew my coffee out all over the counter. I can't believe she said Lorenzo, of all guys. Then it hits me, of course she did. She and Alana have probably been talking about Lorenzo and I being a match made in heaven since the day I was born. I want to tell her that wishing her grandchildren will be Deaf was a horrible thing to wish for. Except that I know where it's coming from.

Within the Deaf community, having your deafness passed down almost ensures an inherent bond.

Mom, Dad was Deaf too. It could already be in the genes. I wink at her, reassuring her that her dreams could still one day come true. *I got my ginger coloring from him.*

That's true. She nods. *Really, I just want you to be happy. Does he make you happy?* she asks.

Very.

Before I head out, she let me know that she'll be riding to the party with Alana and Corbin.

Macie is there in the parking lot when I arrive at Nail City. We walk over to wait outside the door. "You have everything you need for tonight?" she asks, making small talk.

"Yes, I packed my dress, and everything I will need to get ready tonight. Plus, an overnight bag with a change of clothes, and..." I hesitate, "my sexiest bra and panties," I confess with a hushed tone.

She gasps in an overly dramatic way. "You think tonight is the night?"

I can't keep the coy grin from spreading across my lips. "I think so."

She shrieks. "Scarlett! Oh my god. It's perfect," she gushes. "Oh, it's just going to be so romantic!"

I'm happy that she's happy for me. I, on the other hand, am a nervous wreck.

A woman comes and unlocks the door from the inside, pushing it open to welcome us in. "Good morning! What can I do for you ladies?"

"We both want to get mani and pedis," I tell her when we step through the doorway.

"Pick your color," she instructs and then heads back to the pedicure chairs to start running the hot water.

Once we're all set in our chairs, feet dipped into the basin of hot water, Macie and I continue our conversation. "So, this would be the first time?" she inquires.

"Yes. He's been holding back, trying to take things slow."

"How long have you been dating?" she asks, fiddling with the massage chair controller on her arm rest.

"Officially, about four weeks. But our first date was five weeks ago." It didn't seem all that long when I said it out loud. "Wow, that really doesn't seem like a long time."

"Really, you shouldn't measure it by time. Quality, not quantity. How's the connection? That's really what you should be analyzing." When she put it that way, I'd have to say the connection is there. Which in that case, maybe we are ready.

"We talk practically every night. We've opened up to each other about things that we haven't really opened up to anyone else about. There's never an awkward moment between us. The connection is there, for sure." I think out loud. Intense sexual tension is also there.

"Well, I'm team Eli all day. I say go for it. If the situation arises." She gives me a sly smile. "If you get my drift."

We share a laugh, then something she said pings in the back of my mind. "Team Eli?" I question.

She slaps her hands over her mouth. "Oops." Her exclamation is muffled by her hands still covering her mouth.

"Oops?" I sit up so I can look at her directly.

She slowly uncovers her mouth. "I wasn't supposed to say anything."

"Macie! Spill it!" She's supposed to be my best friend and yet here she is holding a secret that revolves around my relationship.

"James started this interoffice bet. If you will. Except, there's no money involved. Guess... it's more of a guess. No, that's not right—"

"Macie!"

"You remember when Twilight was all the rage? And everyone was either hashtag team Edward or hashtag team Jacob?" I nod, slowly, still waiting for the rest of the story. "Well," she continues, "James started saying hashtag team Lorenzo. And the rest of us, well, we just kind of started to respond with 'hashtag team Lorenzo or team Eli.'"

"Team Lorenzo? How is that even a thing?! We've never even dated." I'm not sure if I should be embarrassed or pissed off. I'm leaning toward being pissed off.

"Scar, it's completely obvious that Lorenzo is in love with you. Everyone sees it, has seen it, for years. Except for you," she points out. "And frankly, since Eli came into the picture, Lorenzo's heart has been on his sleeve." She's right, it is obvious, yet somehow, I have been blind to it.

"Everyone, like *everyone?* Mom, Corbin, Alana?" She nods. Now I'm leaning toward embarrassment. The entire office has had this thing going on for weeks now behind my back.

"Your mom, Alana, and Corbin, they didn't know about the hashtag thing until like two days ago." She is trying to make me feel better about it. I don't.

"Oh my god! Now I have to face everyone tonight at the Christmas party knowing they've been team Eli or team Lorenzo this whole time? Why are you just telling me about this?" I'm in full on panic mode now.

Two ladies come over to start our pedicures now that our feet have soaked. "I thought it was harmless. I'm sorry, Scar. I should have told you sooner. If it makes you feel better, almost everyone is team Eli."

"Who is team Lorenzo?" I ask, but I know the answer.

"James, Corbin, Alana, and..." she hesitates, not wanting to tell me the last one. "Your mom."

"Of course."

Chapter 14
Lorenzo

*T*he lobby at the hotel is pretty busy when I arrive. No sign of Scar yet. I scan the room, noting that it's very modern for a hotel lobby. There are a few sleek high-top tables surrounded by yellow or neon green barstools, a black leather sectional couch, and a few pairs of white leather armchairs on either side of a glass coffee table. The mural on the back wall that reads 'Wilson' is a nice touch, it makes it feel less stark like many hotels I'm used to seeing. The artist in me is pleased. There's also the convenience of a round snack station, manned by a self-check-out register, filled with drinks, chips, snacks, and candy. A nice step up from vending machines. The place is impressive. Although, I wouldn't doubt it with Scar in charge of planning.

Taking a seat on the black leather couch with a view of the front doors, I watch as the line of people at the front desk clears. One by one, they check out, grab their bags, and head home. Or to their next destination, I suppose. It's too early for check in, but I decide to walk up and see if I can anyway.

A young woman behind the counter with her dark auburn hair pulled into a bun smiles and says something to me. Looks like she asked how she can help me. I point to my ear and shake my head, mouthing *I'm Deaf.*

Her face lights up. *Wait... I know sign language.* Her signs are slow and rigid, she's clearly new to the language. I give her an A for effort anyway, letting my charismatic smile take over my face.

Very cool. How do you know sign? I keep my signs slow and clear, not wanting to overwhelm her.

I went to Barton College. I had a friend that knew sign, she made me join the ASL club with her. She spoke slowly, signing the words she knew while she talked. I read her lips to fill in the holes. Barton is a local college that has a Deaf Education and Interpreting program. Many of the students do internships at the Deaf school in town.

I reach my hand up to my throat, fisted like it's holding a key, and then turn it, telling her to turn her voice off. *Not bad, practice without your voice, you'll get even better.*

Thanks for the... "advice?" She doesn't know the sign for advice, so I feed it to her. *Advice. Thanks!* She is beaming at the opportunity to use and show off her sign skills. Though, I'm not sure skill is the right word yet.

You're welcome. I'm here for the Christmas party tonight. Is it possible to check in early? I finally ask what I came up here to ask.

She holds a finger up and says, "Let me check," giving up on the signing for a moment. *What's your name?*

L-O-R-E-N-Z-O T-A-T-E. I spell for her at turtle speed. I watch her mind work as she reads each letter of my name. She's kind of cute, actually. Way too young for a relationship, and way too hearing. But I start to think maybe she could be a fun distraction if and when I need one.

Yes! she signs, then spews out a full sentence that's a little hard to follow. Something about an early check-in list. I guess Scar put me on that list. She types a few things on the computer keyboard, then holds her finger up again and walks behind a doorway out of sight.

I wait there for her to return with my room key. There's a tap on my shoulder, and I turn to see Scar behind me with Macie at her side. *Hey.* I smile and hug Macie first and then Scar, placing my kiss on her forehead. She smiles sheepishly at me. God, that smile does something to me.

You checking in? she asks. She's so fucking beautiful. Even in her t-shirt and leggings. Tight leggings that don't leave much to the imagination, I might add.

I quickly bring my eyes back up to hers, hoping she didn't notice how long they lingered elsewhere. *Yeah, I thought I would see if I could.* I shrug.

The clerk comes back, and I make a point to check her name tag, Kendra, when she hands me my key. *Sixth floor, room 624.*

You sign? Scar asks, excited to see that. *Looks like I picked the right hotel!* She's signing too fast for Kendra, not realizing her skills are still fairly novice.

There will be more Deaf people coming, you'll have plenty of opportunities to practice. I wink at her. She looks a little overwhelmed, her eyes darting between Scar and Macie. When she nods in understanding, I assume Macie interpreted for her.

I'm going to check in and take my things upstairs, then come down and start getting the banquet room ready. Scar directs that to Macie and me.

I nod and scoop my bag and suit bag from the floor beside me. *Ok, see you in a few minutes.*

Upstairs, I find my room and am pleased to see it's a Deaf friendly room. There's a doorbell that connects to a flashing light inside the room. The fire alarms are also fitted with strobe lights. Many hotels have started adding this, but I wonder if Scar set that up or Kendra. Either way, it was thoughtful. I hang the suit in the closet and toss my bag on the bed, then check my reflection. I've been growing my beard out, the black hair finally starting to fill out over my face. I've always been a clean-shaven kind of guy, but it seems beards are in these days. Scar certainly seems to like them. I'm not shaving my fucking head, though. Quite the opposite, actually, I've been growing my hair out and keeping it tied back in a man bun. Content with how I look, I make my way out to the hall. We open our doors at the same time, her room is right across from mine. I wonder where *his* room will be.

She looks surprised to see me. *Hey,* she signs it nervously. *Wow, your room is right here?*

Did she not see Kendra sign my room number? Looks like it. Is that okay?

Yeah... it's fine. She checks her watch, but not just for the time, she got a text message. It makes her smile. *Ready to set up?* I nod and follow her down the hall to the elevator.

The large banquet room is an elegant blank canvas ready for Scar's vision to come to life. One side of the room has floor to ceiling windows that look out into a courtyard. In one corner there is a Christmas tree, decorated with warm white twinkling lights and round, gold ornaments. Red bows are placed sporadically around it, and it's topped with one very large matching red bow. There are fake presents under the tree, wrapped with red, green, and white striped paper. On the opposite end of the room, a portable bar has been set up, and in front of it, two large carts with round tables waiting to be placed around the room.

Want me to start with the tables? I offer.

Yes, here. She pulls a piece of paper from her cleavage, since she doesn't have any pockets. *This is how I want it set up.*

A hint of her scent wafts up as I unfold the paper. *Where will the DJ be?* I ask after looking over the sketch.

She points to the center of the wall of windows. *With the dance floor in front.* She turns around to point to the wall where people will enter. *The food will be set up over there. There are long rectangle tables for that.*

Ok, sounds good. I smile at her, holding her gaze for a moment. Without Eli around, it feels like old times, like we're connecting again. My heart swells with hope that she feels it too.

She bats her eyes down before turning away to get to work.

We've gotten all the tables set up, and Macie found the chairs with a dolly in a corner closet. We're pulling those out, one stack at a time, when Eli walks in. Only two hours after us. Scar stops what she's doing and walks over to him, throwing her arms around his neck, then locking lips with him. She doesn't even seem upset that he's so late. My lungs inhale a deep, frustrated breath as his hands reach behind her and squeeze her ass. I swear he's watching me from the corner of his eye, taunting me on purpose. She's oblivious to the way he dangles her in front of me. There's no way he could misinterpret the glare that I send his way, clearly he wasn't fazed by my note.

Scar turns to me and signs, *I'm going to help him unload his car. Be right back.*

Macie and I keep setting out the chairs, ten each around the eight round tables. Once we've finished, Scar and Eli have a pile of boxes stacked near the bar. There are quite a few boxes of booze, and some that look to be filled with gift bags. I watch him for a moment, hoping that he's too busy helping out with the bar to be glued to her side the entire evening.

Macie walks up to me, her back to Scar. *Careful with your facial expressions, you're looking very jealous right now.*

My head jerks back as I scrunch my nose and squint my eyes at her. Did she really just say that? *You serious?*

She's with Eli now. And it's really good for her, please don't ruin it. Macie's been hanging around with Scar since we were kids, so I give her the benefit of the doubt. I understand she's just trying to look out for Scar. It doesn't change the fact that she just pissed me the hell off. How could she take Eli's side over mine?

I know you're looking out for your friend. But we don't even know this guy. I'm just looking out for her too. I look over Macie's shoulder where Scar is busy talking to Eli. *We both want what's best for her, maybe you have a different idea of what that means.*

What that means is she is happy. And she is very happy. Just let her be happy. Her facial expression is stern without scolding.

Macie doesn't give me a chance to respond. She turns and walks away, leaving me in direct line of sight to see Eli tug at Scar's hand, pulling her in for another kiss. This time, there's no question that he is glaring at me. When she steps back from his embrace, he makes direct eye contact with me, with a smug ass fucking smile spread over his lips. I want to be kind, caring, helpful Lorenzo, but this jerk makes that beyond difficult.

It's almost 4:00 pm by the time we've finished setting up the room. Scar did such a great job planning this event, the room looks beautiful. I'm in awe of how Scar's vision transformed this generic banquet hall into an exquisite Christmas wonderland.

She thanks us for helping and releases us to go relax and get ready in our rooms. We all take the elevator up, tired from working to organize and decorate. When we exit the elevator I hold my breath, waiting to see which direction Eli goes, if he follows Scar to her room. Thankfully, he and Macie turn right, while Scar and I go left. I'm so relieved to know that the asshole bartender has his own room. That's a good sign, and good news for me.

Just outside our doors, I tug at Scars hand, stopping her from going into her room. I glance down the hall to see if Eli has gone inside his room yet. He has, though I'm surprised he's not watching us. I guess he trusts her. Thankful for the moment, I take the time to connect with her.

You've done such a beautiful job organizing this whole event, Scar. Our moms will be so happy. I'm laying on the sweet, caring Lorenzo charm nice and thick. It isn't hard when it's just Scar and me around. It's actually quite natural, as if she brings it out of me.

Thanks, it's my favorite part of the job. I do it every year. She's blushing. She holds my gaze for a moment, seeing if I had something else to say. *I'm going to shower and get ready. See you at the party,* she finally says.

Sure. Wait...

What's up?

Will you save a dance for me? I ask with my puppy dog eyes.

Sure.

There's a moment where for the first time in twenty-nine years, I can't read her expression.

Chapter 15
Eli

Scarlett told me to meet her downstairs, outside of the banquet hall. She hasn't seemed to wrap her head around the fact that I'm old school. I have a corsage stashed in the mini fridge in my room and I plan to knock on her room door, pin it to her, and escort her to the party. None of that new age 'meet me there' mess.

I shoot a text to Ana making sure that she's arrived and has everything she needs to tend bar. She and her girlfriend Diedre had jumped on the opportunity to make some side money, and I was glad to have them so I could stay focused on Scarlett tonight.

Ana: All set, boss. Enjoy your evening. Can't wait to see you in that suit. She adds a wink emoji.

I check my outfit one last time in the full-length mirror. I am rocking this suit, that's for damn sure. I tuck a green pocket scarf in the jacket pocket and loosen my red and green striped tie, so it's not choking me, then spritz a bit of cologne in the air to walk through.

As I make my way down the hall, I spot Lorenzo coming from his room. He stops and stares at the door across from him. His hand reaches up like he's about to knock, but he looks down the hall before he does, locking in on me. Are you fucking kidding me? His room is right across from Scarlett's. That's the exact moment I decide she will be spending the night in *my* room. I'm glad I went ahead and booked a room, even though I knew Scarlett and I wouldn't need two between the two of us.

He glares at me, his eyes shifting to the corsage in my hand as I get closer to him. *You're not working?* he signs at me, mouthing each word to make sure I understand.

"The party?" I ask. "No, I'm not working." I sign what few signs I know to help him understand. Even though I don't like or trust this guy, I can at least show him that much respect. When I'm right up next to him, I point to myself, sign Scarlett's name sign that she showed me, and say, "I'm Scarlett's date." *Asshole.* I learned that sign just for him.

He grits his teeth and bucks up at me. *I thought I told you to back off.* He makes his lips very clear for me, then adds a sign that looks like his middle finger where the sign for 'mother' is, his mouth clearly saying, 'mother fucker.'

I'm about to lay into him with words when Scarlett's door swings open. She's shocked by the sight of us, now both smiling as if nothing has happened between us. "Oh, what's going on here?" she asks, signing while she talks. She's absolutely stunning. Her green velvet dress skims the floor, and her modest gold pumps peek out from underneath. One long leg is exposed damn near up to her waist from the sexy ass slit. The dress is strapless, highlighting her collarbone adorned with a gold chain necklace, the pendant dipping down into her perfect cleavage. The green of her dress compliments her pale orange hair that she took the time to curl into thick ringlets.

"I don't know about this dude." I motion toward Lorenzo, who is practically drooling over my girlfriend. "But I'm here to pick up my gorgeous girlfriend for our date tonight." I hold out the corsage, a white rose accented with a green sprig of pine and a red ribbon.

"Oh my god, Eli, it's perfect!" She doesn't sign. Lorenzo doesn't exist in this moment. She leans in and kisses my cheek. Fuck that. I wrap my hand around to the small of her back and pull her in for a real kiss, parting her lips with my tongue.

You look beautiful, Scar, Lorenzo signs when Scarlett steps back from our kiss.

Her lips press together, turning up slightly at the corners. There's empathy in her smile, like she feels bad for being so happy in front of him. I sure don't.

See you at the party, he says, his face sullen as he makes his way down the hall.

Her eyes trail after him for a quick moment, there's a hint of sadness in them. But when she turns her attention back to me, she takes a deep breath and her face lights up again. I take my time pinning the corsage, grazing Scarlett's exposed breast with my knuckles, ensuring that we have our elevator ride in private. In the elevator alone, it takes everything in me not to press her up against the wall with my body and ravage her lips on the way down.

All eyes are on us as we walk into the banquet room. Her arm slinks over my elbow, and I escort her straight to the bar. Ana is pouring a drink as we approach.

"Looking good, boss." She shoots her hand out toward Scarlett. "Good to see you again, Scarlett. You look beautiful!" she compliments. They've met a few times at the bar, but only small talk so far. "This guy won't stop talking about you."

"Thank you." Her cheeks flush, and she takes Ana's hand to shake. "I hope it's been all good things you've heard." I just want to pull her close to me.

"Of course, only great things." Scarlett glances at me with curiosity. "What can I get for you?" Ana offers, though she's already mixing my favorite drink, Captain and pineapple juice.

"Oh, I think I should stick with red wine tonight." Scarlett plays it safe, which is probably a wise decision. The thought makes me do a quick once over of the room to see where Lorenzo might be lurking.

"I brought over the Cougar Run pinot noir, get her that one," I instruct. It's a local North Carolina wine, and I know that pinot noir is her favorite varietal. Ana nods with a wink, knowing I've made a good choice.

Scarlett squeezes my hand and leans her body into me, a giddy grin on her face. She's pleased. Ana finishes pouring the wine and hands it to her. She takes sips. "This is perfect." She's beaming.

Ana hands me my Captain and pineapple. "Thanks, Ana." I hold my glass up in salute.

We turn to scan the room, then Scarlett loops her fingers in mine and leads me to a table not too far from the dance floor. Her mother is there with Lorenzo's parents. I take note that he's not at the table even though he came down before us. My years in the military trained me to keep good stock of the room, especially in larger crowds. Especially when there's someone you don't trust lurking around. And I don't trust Lorenzo.

Hello! Helen stands to greet me with a hug. *Nice to see you again.* Scarlett looks over at me, checking to see if I need her to interpret for me.

Nice to see you too. After I left Scarlett's house last night, I stayed up half the night practicing for today. I turn to Alana and Corbin to greet them as well. They both smile nicely at me, but don't stand.

Scar, this is wonderful! Helen exclaims, she hugs her too. *Wow, you look beautiful.*

Not as beautiful as you, Mom, Scarlett returns the compliment, not even acknowledging her own beauty. Her humility makes me fall deeper in... love? Maybe, though I wouldn't dare say it yet. I don't want to scare her off.

We sit down around the table. Even though I helped to decorate, I can't help but admire the work Scarlett put in. The white tablecloth is lined with a green table runner, and in the middle sits a glass bowl with red floating candles. Despite being disposable, the tableware is a sturdy white plastic with gold trim.

Alana begins to sign. I think she's asking Scarlett if she has seen Lorenzo.

"Need an interpreter?" The snarky voice comes from behind me, I turn to see James' smug smile. I tilt my head and narrow my eyes, studying him for a moment. He has always seemed so helpful. Right now? I'm getting a bit of a different vibe.

"I only started learning a few weeks ago, so I wouldn't mind the help." I try to ignore the vibe and respond with a light and friendly tone.

"He was just upstairs before Eli and I came down," Scarlett tells her, using her voice with her signs for my sake. "I thought he came down here before we did."

Oh, there he is. Alana's face now lights up at the sight of her son.

He cleans up nicely in his well-tailored suit, I'll give him that. When he approaches the table, the tension between us is palpable, but he somehow pulls off a friendly smile. He hugs his mom, then Helen. Then he makes his way around the table to

Scarlett. She doesn't stand to greet him, but he bends down and wraps his arm around her bare shoulders. She gives him a meek smile, and he kisses her forehead. I cringe. I am trying incredibly hard not to let this rivalry escalate. He's making it equally difficult.

Scar, wow, you did an amazing job organizing this. Everything turned out beautiful, almost as beautiful as you, James voices for him with almost a whisper in my ear. It sends a shiver down my spine. I'm overrun with this feeling that the night will end with my fist in Lorenzo's face.

Thank you, she responds with a tight-lipped smile. I can sense her unease.

I reach my hand over and place it on her thigh, letting her know I'm there if and when she needs me. Her head turns down toward my lap. Nothing is spoken, but I know she's thanking me for being there. The table slowly fills, as does the room. Looking around, there are pockets of groups using sign language and other pockets where they are only using spoken language. Our little pocket, I realize, would only be signing if I was not at the table. Except for Macie's date, who also appears to need her to interpret for him. From what Scarlett has told me about her previous relationships, this type of situation scared them off. Not me. For me, it's just an obstacle to overcome. A challenge to conquer. And I vow that this time next year, sitting at this table, I will be able to communicate fully with Helen and the rest of Scarlett's extended family.

Will you announce when everyone can get dinner? Helen asks Scarlett. James' voice fills in the holes for me.

"Yes." She pulls her phone from her gold clutch purse to check the time. "Actually, I should do that now." She stands, then turns to Macie. "Would you mind interpreting for me?"

Macie nods and follows her to the DJ booth.

"Welcome, everyone!" Damn, she is gorgeous. "Thank you all for joining us for our fifth annual Christmas party. On behalf of everyone at All Hands, we want to thank you for everything you do to make this agency run smoothly. We wouldn't be able to do it without our staff members and each and every one of our contractors. We have the space until midnight, and there's an open bar and plenty of food! It's buffet style, so please feel free to come up and eat. Before you leave, there are gift bags with just a small token of our appreciation." She clears her throat, then remembers one more thing. "Oh, and drink responsibly! If you haven't pre booked a room, I heard they still have a few available. Enjoy yourselves, and merry Christmas!"

She hands the mic back to the DJ. She's absolutely glowing, I can't take my eyes off her as she makes her way back to our table. Before she has a chance to sit down, I stand and pull her in for a kiss. I don't even care that there's a whole table full of people behind me, watching my tongue slip between her lips.

She only lets me kiss her for a moment before pulling back. "What was that for?" Her face is plastered with euphoria.

"Just because you're you and I couldn't resist." I give her hand a squeeze. "Shall we eat?"

"We shall."

Chapter 16
Scarlett

*T*o say I am a bit uncomfortable would be an understatement.

Looking around the table, I am quite aware of who is team Eli and who is team Lorenzo after the conversation with Macie at the salon this morning. Team Eli is seriously outnumbered. I shake my head at the thought, knowing it doesn't mean anything, and try to enjoy dinner. The food is amazing; baked chicken, mini crab cakes, greens, and macaroni and cheese. There's a nice leafy green salad and rolls as well.

The food is delicious. Mom seems to be having a great time. Everything is amazing, delicious, and beautiful. And her smile, it's priceless. I love seeing her so happy.

"Glad you like it, Mom." Even though Eli's sign vocabulary is rapidly expanding, I make sure to include him by talking while I sign.

You're not eating very much, Lorenzo points out that my plate is considerably less full than everyone else's.

I've trained myself over the years to not overindulge in buffet situations. I am also wearing a very tight dress. That, and my stomach is aflutter with butterflies. I couldn't eat much if I wanted to. *I'm not very hungry.*

Eli's hand finds its place on my thigh. "You okay, beautiful?" His words are whispered, meant for me and only me. The feel of his hot breath combined with the pressure of his hand sends a current through me, disturbing the butterflies.

"Yes, I'm just not hungry," I assure him. "I would love another glass of wine, though."

I push my chair back to head over to the bar, he stops me. "I'll get it." He turns to the rest of the table. "Would anyone else like a drink?" He signs 'drink,' but James interprets for him anyway.

Everyone declines, except James' date, Dante. He joins Eli on the trip to the bar.

As soon as his back is turned, Lorenzo scoots over to Eli's seat. *You sure you're okay? You barely touched your food.*

I'm fine, Lorenzo. I can feel all eyes at the table on us. I can feel Lorenzo's eyes on me. I wish I had included a shawl in my wardrobe to wrap myself in, a coping mechanism to hide when I feel too seen. Really, I appreciate Lorenzo's concern, I do. The fact that everyone at the table is rooting for him over Eli is causing my unease.

Alana taps the table to get our attention. *I just want to say, it makes me so happy to see you two still such good friends.* She smiles proudly at Lorenzo and me.

I always thought... hoped you two would end up together, Mom adds.

That was always their dream. Corbin motions between Mom and Alana. *Mine too, if I'm being honest.*

If I'm being honest, this conversation is wildly inappropriate and it's making me very uncomfortable. I take a stab at the Deaf bluntness myself. *I'm sorry, I'm with Eli and he's here tonight. And this conversation, well, it's just kind of rude.*

I agree, Macie chimes in. *You all are being very disrespectful to Eli.*

Who cares? Lorenzo's face is scrunched to add emphasis. *He's here right now, but for how long? I'm not going anywhere, Scar. I've waited fifteen years for you, can't you see that?* His signs are rigid with contempt, but I can see in his eyes that his intent is more vulnerable.

Eli is at the bar, he says something to Ana, then turns around to smile at me. He doesn't like the sight of Lorenzo in his seat. I can see the fire rise up in his face, his jaw clenches and his shoulders stiffen. The whole love triangle has hit me, it's come to a head, a very uncomfortable head. *Excuse me,* I sign, then get up from my chair to join Eli at the bar, putting distance between hashtag team Lorenzo and me.

The closer I get to Eli, the more his face softens and the tension in his shoulders eases. He's relieved to see me walk away from the table. "Hey, gorgeous." He hands me the glass of wine Ana had just poured, then rests his hand at the small of my back. Another electrifying touch. He must feel my own tension. "You okay? You seem... annoyed."

"I'm sorry it's so awkward." I get straight to it. "I hope he gets over it soon."

Eli lets out a deep sigh. "You think he will? Cause I'm not so sure."

Honestly, I'm not so sure either. Especially now that I know my entire family needs to get over it too. "I don't know." I give him an empathetic smile. "But what I do know is that you have made me the happiest woman since I met you. I won't let him get in the way of that." The rest of my thoughts, I keep to myself. Despite how much it might hurt, I'm preparing myself to walk away from Lorenzo to strengthen my relationship with Eli.

The smile that spreads across his face lets me know he's pleased with my answer. "Want to dance?" he asks, slurping the rest of his drink down with the straw.

I follow suit, taking a long deep gulp of my wine. "Sure. Let me put my glass on the table."

He follows me over to our table with one hand on the small of my back, sending little fires through me. After setting my glass down and purposefully avoiding eye contact with everyone aside from Macie, I take Eli's outstretched hand and he leads me to the dance floor. "Can you dance?" I ask through nervous giggles.

"The question is, can *you* dance?" His sly wink tells me he knows what he's doing on the dance floor, and I'm about to be schooled.

He spins me around gracefully, then pulls me into his body. One hand is on my hip, the other holding my hand out in the proper ballroom dance position. I cock my eyebrows up at him, impressed so far. "Ok, I see you." I laugh and he rocks me back and forth, not yet showing off his moves.

"I've taken a lesson or two over the years. I can do a few different styles, mostly Latin dances. But I've got a decent Rumba too," he explains. "Want to learn a basic step."

"Absolutely." I step back so he can show me. We practice the basic Rumba box step a few times, then he leads me through it until the song ends.

"You're a natural, Scarlett." He kisses my cheek. "We could take lessons if you want to learn more. By next Christmas, we'll be blowing the socks off everyone."

"Next Christmas?" My mouth gapes open at his comment. He just caught me off guard. Yet, it sends a hopeful wave through me.

He winks at me as he takes a finger and slowly lifts my chin to close my mouth. "Yeah, a year from now. I can see us tearing this dance floor up." There's a playful confidence in his voice. Another song starts and he opens his arms back into the dance position, I settle right into him.

Unable to hold the smile on my face back, I look up at him and ask, "What else do you see for next Christmas?" He pulls me in closer to him. His hand on my hip slides dangerously close to my behind.

"I'll be fluently signing, so you won't have to interpret for me anymore." His words are coupled with an optimistic grin.

"Oh really?" My face hurts from the permanent smile he's left there. "That's a big goal."

His grin turns mischievous. "It will be worth every effort put into it." He steps back, lifts his hand and I instinctively know he's leading me into a twirl. When he pulls me back to his body, we are pressed against each other, and our faces are cheek to cheek. "I'm not going anywhere, Scarlett." He breathes the words in my ear. My body is on fire.

Macie and her date, Brent, join us on the dance floor. "Those are some nice moves!" she compliments Eli.

"Thanks, I've kind of been into dancing for a long time. Scarlett said she wants to take lessons with me." He winks at me again, knowing I haven't officially agreed to it yet. It's fine because I am totally into the idea.

"Is there a place around here that does lessons?" Macie asks. "That actually sounds like fun."

"We'll have to look it up, you two should join us!" I suggest, noting that Brent has Macie in the typical sway back and forth dance that most of us have been doing since middle school.

She turns to Brent, who looks a bit overwhelmed by the idea. "I'll try anything once," he says nervously. Brent is fairly new in the picture, though she has been seeing him for a few months now.

"Sounds like a double date. I'll get everything set up," Eli offers.

We dance for a few more songs, and when the DJ shifts to some hip-hop music, we make our way back over to the table. My glass of wine is right where I left it. Thirsty from all the dancing, I gulp down what's left.

Eli excuses himself back to the bar for another round. I stand by my chair, waiting for Eli to return, as a few people stop by to thank me for throwing such a great party. By the time he returns, and I take a sip of my wine, I'm feeling a little woozy. I bring my hand to my forehead and let out a long, controlled breath.

"Scarlett? What's wrong?" Eli's face immediately twists into concern. "You're pale, come here, sit down." He pulls my chair out and helps guide me down to it.

"All of a sudden I just felt dizzy, a little light-headed." I'm sitting now, he's kneeling in front of me with his hands holding onto to either side of my waist. I take a deep breath. "I think I'm okay now."

"Scarlett, you're worrying me. You hardly ate, maybe you need something. A roll?" he suggests.

"Yeah, I'll try that," I agree, knowing he's probably right. I had barely eaten anything, all day for that matter.

He trots over to the buffet and returns with a plate of bread. I take a roll and eat it slowly, pulling small pieces off it one by one. "Maybe we hold off on this wine for now." He takes the glass from the table.

Mom, Alana, and Corbin are walking back to the table from mingling. I take a quick look around for Lorenzo, and I'm a bit relieved when I don't see him. Mom notices my facial expression immediately and can tell something is wrong.

Scar, are you okay? Mom asks when I sit down.

I just got a little dizzy. I think from the wine and dancing and not enough food today. I give a quick explanation.

Mom pushes her plate toward me. There's still some chicken and macaroni left. *Eat,* she instructs with her motherly, yet firm, expression. I obey, I've never been able to say no to that look.

Eli sits beside me, his hand rubbing up and down my back, soothing me. After I finish the bit of food Mom gave me, I am starting to feel better. "I think I'm good now." I use both languages.

"You look better," Eli remarks. "Just rest for a minute." His hand is still rubbing my back, it feels quite amazing.

Mom smiles lovingly at Eli. She may be 'team Lorenzo,' but she can see that he cares for me. She can see that he makes me happy. And that makes her happy too. *Thank you, Eli. You're so sweet to my baby.*

You're welcome. He knows that sign. The next sentence comes out slowly, yet clearly practiced. *I think I might love her. Shh, don't tell her yet.*

Mom's hands fly to her face, she's gushing at the revelation. I'm speechless. He's wearing a sly smile, intentionally not looking at me. Then Mom smiles and signs, *Your secret is safe with me.*

Chapter 17
Lorenzo

The sight of Eli parading my Scar around on the dance floor made me sick to my stomach, so I had to leave the room for a while. I swear he is literally dangling her in front of my face. The more I see him, the more I resent him. And truthfully, I want to punch him in the fucking face. Instead, I take a walk around the block to try and cool off my steamy emotions in the cold winter air. I'm glad I brought a small joint with me, because I need something to calm me down. It's not something I do often, but it helps mellow me out when I need it. Deep down, I know if I cause a scene in front of Scar, that won't help my situation. Eli brings out an ugly, jealous side of me that I know she doesn't like. Hell, I don't even like that side of me. She worked so hard to make this night magical, I don't want to ruin everything by confronting that asshole.

I have a nice buzz going, starting to feel that elated high and less pissed off. So, I head back into the party. Walking down the hall to the banquet room, Eli passes by me, his cell phone to his ear. He looks a little frantic. I realize I finally have an opportunity for a moment alone with her. I step a little faster. Once inside, I search the room. She's there at the table where we ate, sipping on a new glass of wine. My strides are long and I'm across the room, taking the seat next to her.

How's your night going? I ask, trying to be nonchalant. I look around the table for my glass of wine, but it seems I must've finished it already.

Hey, Lorenzo. It's good, I'm really enjoying myself. She smiles hesitantly. She's still bothered by the group ganging up on her earlier. I hadn't asked them to do that, but I certainly didn't mind their show of support. Still, I know it bothered her, and I feel bad for that.

Sorry about earlier, Scar. I didn't ask them to do that. I reach a hand over and place it on hers.

She meets my gaze and gives me a meek smile, then slides her hand away quickly, probably anxious about Eli walking in to see it. Her head tilts to one side, and her eyes search mine. *Lorenzo—* she starts, but I cut her off.

Where's Eli? Deaf bluntness. I can ask anything I want.

The bartender he left in charge at the bar called. He had to take it. Must've been some kind of emergency. I press my lips together to keep myself from smiling at the relief of him having to leave the party.

Why call him? Why not the manager?

She giggles. *He owns the bar.*

Wow, I didn't know that. She's beaming with pride, and I hope one day she could be that proud of me. *Well, since your date is busy, how about that dance you promised me?*

Her expression changes, apprehension maybe. Her chest inflates with a deep breath, heaving her breasts over the seam of her dress. The image sends a rush of heat through me, causing me to shift in my chair. *I don't know, Lorenzo.* She tries to decline. I won't let her. I need to hold her, even if it's only for one dance. I need a chance to connect, to show her we're meant to be together.

I put on my puppy dog face and touch my hand on her thigh. *You promised.*

Her perfect breasts heave out another sigh. *One dance,* she insists. She's attempting a stern face, but all I see is how adorable she is. I nod.

Standing, I hold my hand out to help her up from her seat. She wobbles a bit as she rises to her feet. I catch her behind her back, supporting her with my open hand. The velvet of her dress is soft, and I can't wait to hold her closer on the dance floor. *You okay?* I ask once she's got her footing.

A little drunk, I guess. Her signs are slow and relaxed.

Forget Me Not

It's hard to chat and slow dance when you use your hands to talk. With one hand tucked behind her waist, I hold her other hand, though not outstretched, close to us. I hold her gaze and smile at her, trying to communicate my feelings without words. Our bodies are close, I haven't held her this way since her senior prom. Memories of how I felt that night rush through my mind, sending a warmth straight to my heart. Her eyes are glassy, she's starting to look a bit dazed. I take a deep breath, breathing in her scent and pull her closer to me. For a moment, she nestles her face into my neck, relaxing against me as I sway her back and forth. Then, almost as quickly as her head rests against me, she steps back and studies me with questioning eyes.

She pulls her hand from mine to sign, *Lorenzo, can we talk?*

What's up? I sign with my now free hand.

Not here. She looks toward the door that leads to the front hallway and nods her head in that direction. *Let's step outside.*

Her gait is wobbly as we make our way across the dance floor, I don't think I've ever seen her this drunk before. I step up next to her and hold out my arm for support. She accepts and the heat of her hand sends electric shocks through me. Just as we step outside the door, her body falls into mine. I steady my feet to keep us from hitting the wall and look down at her in surprise. She's looking up at me, the corners of her eyes crinkle the way they always do when she giggles. Our eyes lock and her giggles fade away into a look of contemplation. The mix of emotions flowing through me are dominated by my desire, and for an instant, I think she feels it too. My mouth crashes into hers. She doesn't pull away, she relaxes, and I think maybe... yes, she kisses me back. Just as my tongue parts her lips, she's ripped away from me and a thick, hairy-knuckled fist slams into my nose, knocking me down to the floor.

Scar is on the floor too. She lost her balance, thankfully she appears to be fine. In an instant, all love and lust inside me subsides, and every ounce of contempt for my rival boils up from my gut. I'm up on my feet now. Squaring off with Eli, both our fists clenched and poised in the air. He looks as though he's battling every part of him not to pummel my face in. I glare at him through clenched teeth, daring him to hit me again. I'm fighting a battle too. Right now, I am the one who hasn't been violent yet. Right now, he's the jealous one, the violent one. He steps forward, lowers his fist, and again points to his mouth. "Don't you *ever* touch my girlfriend again. You understand me, mother fucker?" He uses the sign for mother fucker, I know he learned it from me.

He runs to Scar and helps her up from the floor. She's crying. If he had just stayed gone longer, I could've shown her. I know she was feeling it too, it was all over her face. For a moment, I wish his emergency had been serious enough to make him leave the party and not come back. Fuck. This is torture. I hate what it's doing to me, who I am becoming.

Scar! I'm sorry. I try to sign to her. She doesn't see me as he ushers her away. "Scar!" My voice has been turned off since the day I graduated high school, thirteen years, but that is the one name I can dig deep inside of myself to voice.

That gets her attention. She stops, pats his arm, and turns to look at me. *Lorenzo, I care about you a lot, but I need space right now.*

She looks like she's going to pass out, her face is pale, her cheeks wet with tears. *I love you, Scar. We're meant to be together. Don't you see that?*

She inhales a deep breath, then signs slowly, *No, Lorenzo, I don't believe we are.* She loses her balance and begins to slide to the floor again. Then it hits me, she must've drunk the rest of my wine. The wine I had put some CBD oil in to relax myself for the evening. Fuck. Somehow, I know this is all going to come back on me. Eli catches her. Then he turns her body, guiding her away from me. Stealing her away from me. Walking her away from me. My Scar.

Chapter 18
Eli

I could fucking kill him. Scarlett looks a mess. Physically and emotionally. God, what would've happened if I had left to tend to the dumpster fire at the bar? Literal dumpster fire. The bar is just around the corner, I wouldn't have been gone long. But from the looks of things, it would've been long enough.

    Scarlett can barely walk. I'm practically carrying her to the elevator. Something is off here, she only had started a third glass of wine, I've seen her drink more at home and still be able to carry herself. My instincts tell me he put something in her drink. I wouldn't put it past him. The way he was fondling her, kissing her where anyone could walk by and see. Who the hell does he think he is? I'm seething mad, but I won't let Scarlett see that. She saw me punch him. Once. Just enough to protect her. From where I stood, her body language looked like she was screaming for help. But she doesn't need to see my angry side.

    "Baby, I'm worried about you." She's leaning up against the corner of the elevator, I'm holding her steady. "You didn't drink that much."

    "It's weird, my body just feels so relaxed, like I can't hold myself up. I'm not that drunk though." She is fairly self-aware, that's a good sign. "I'm sorry, Eli," she says after a moment of silence. "I should not have danced with him. I shouldn't have gone out into the hall with him either."

    My lungs inhale deeply, and I let the air gush out of me. "Why did you?"

    "I had promised him one dance. I tried to decline, but he insisted. Then, he had this look on his face, and I don't know, I wanted to go talk to him to make sure he understood where we stand." I don't want her to see how mad I am. I'm not mad at her, though I am a little frustrated that she hasn't figured out who he is yet. He is not a nice guy, if you ask me. "I've known him my whole life, Eli. I didn't think he would do anything to hurt me. I laughed when he caught me, maybe he misread signals."

The elevator dings, signaling that we've arrived on our floor. She looks as though she wants to head down the hall to her room. "No ma'am, you're staying with me tonight." That wasn't a request. Though, the reason has changed. There will be no sex tonight. "I'm fairly certain he put something in your drink. I want to keep an eye on you."

Her eyes widen in fear and disbelief. Her hand reaches up to cover her mouth. "Really?" She shakes her head. "No, no, he wouldn't do that."

"Why else would you lose so much control over your body? Don't you see, Scarlett? He was going to take advantage of you if I hadn't come back when I did." At this point, I can hear the stiffness in my tone. I'm done hiding my suspicions about him. I do not like Lorenzo Tate, and I intend to make that known from here on out. If Scarlett and I are going to be together, he will need to be out of the picture.

We get to my door, and I tap the key card to the reader, turning the handle when the green light flashes. She's silent, aside from slow, controlled sniffles. She sits on the edge of the bed and lets her head drop into her hands, while tears just start flowing out of her. I let her cry for a few minutes, sitting beside her and rubbing her back soothingly. After a while, she sits her head up and wipes her cheeks with the back of her hand. They're still covered with black streaks of mascara. "I just can't believe he would do that," she finally says.

"I can," I confess brusquely. "Scarlett, I don't trust him, at all. And I can't very well tell you I don't want you to see him anymore because I know that in a way, he's your family." I hesitate before I say the next part. "But I really would feel a lot better if you didn't. See him. I know that's not possible, just be careful around him. Don't be alone with him, don't let your guard down around him."

A heavy sob heaves out of her. She's crying again. I stand and go into the bathroom to retrieve tissues, wetting one with a bit of water. When I come back to the bed, I use the wet tissue to wipe the black streaks from her cheeks. I hand her the other to dry her eyes and blow her nose. "Do you know how hard it is going to be to avoid him?" She shakes her head. She stifles another sob, taking a deep breath and blowing it out slowly. "He's such a huge part of my life."

Now it's my turn to take a deep, calming breath. Every part of me wants to forbid her from seeing him again. I know I can't ask that of her though. "Scarlett, I really care about you. This thing we have is special, and I want it to work. He made a move on you tonight, despite all the times you've told him we're together. He doesn't respect you, and he damn sure doesn't respect me. I don't want to see anything come between us, but my gut tells me if you don't set boundaries with him, this will continue to happen."

Her eyes shift from her hands fidgeting in her lap to meet mine. "I will try my best to avoid him, at least being alone with him."

A sigh of relief escapes me. I'm so glad to hear her say that. "Where's your room key? I'll go get your clothes so you can get comfortable," I offer.

She pats the bed around her. "Shit, it's in my clutch. It's downstairs, probably at the table where we ate."

"No worries, I'll be back in a few minutes." I kiss her cheek before getting up to retrieve her clutch.

When the elevator doors open, Macie is frantic on the other side of them. "Oh, Eli! Is Scarlett okay?" she asks, her voice in panic.

"She's a little shaken up, a little heartbroken." I'm honest with her. "She left her clutch in the banquet room. I'm headed down to get it."

"No need." She holds up the little gold clutch, "I brought it up for her," she says, handing it to me. "What on earth happened down there?"

"I got a phone call from my bartender, Frankie, he said the dumpster out back was on fire. So, I left the party to talk to him outside. When I came back in, Lorenzo had his fucking hands all over her, his lips on her. As far as I could see, she was fighting to get away." I don't hold back my anger with Macie. "It took everything in me not to pulverize him."

"That's crazy, I saw them dancing, then they were gone. Next thing I heard was you screaming at him in the hall. What came over him?" I'm not sure why she's asking me questions about his motive. But I know the answer.

"Jealousy, obsession. To name a few," I say through gritted teeth. "Macie, I think he set the fire at my bar, it's literally a short walk from here. And I think he drugged her, put something in her drink. I think he was going to try something. I think he was going to take advantage of her." Saying it out loud makes my blood boil.

"Oh my god." She gasps. "Lorenzo? I can't believe he would do that. No, there has to be some other explanation. I know he's in love with her, but he... no, he wouldn't do that."

Man, this guy has everyone around him blind to who he truly is. "Obviously, I don't have proof. But, Macie, you should see her."

"Wow. I just hope she's OK." She exhales. "Take good care of her, Eli. Tell her I'll call her tomorrow, let me know if there's anything I can do to help."

"Thanks, Macie."

I make my way down the hall to Scarlett's room and let myself in. There's a duffel bag on the bed, so I grab that, then take a look around to see if there's anything else she might need. Her toothbrush is on the counter in the bathroom. I toss that and her hairbrush into the duffel bag. Satisfied that I have everything she needs, I open the door to make my way back down the hallway. Lorenzo is standing there, hand poised to knock. This asshole just doesn't get it.

"I thought I told you to stay *the fuck* away from my girlfriend." I exaggerate my mouth movements for him, but I don't bother to sign any of the words I know. He doesn't deserve my respect in this moment.

He steps back, jaw and fists clenched. I'm pretty sure he says something about how he told me to back off. *Scar is mine.* That part I understand.

No, mother fucker, she's not. I push past him, practicing some serious self-discipline not to punch his fucking face in, and make my way down the hallway.

I'm barely two doors down when I feel a tug at the collar of my suit jacket. He pulls me back, I stumble, but quickly regain my footing. "Not today, mother fucker," I say. He wants to fight, but I won't give him the fucking satisfaction. I keep walking, even though I feel him on my heels. He pulls at my collar again.

This time I turn around and back him up against the fucking wall. Shoving my finger in his face. "Leave me and Scarlett the fuck alone." I slam the palm of my hand against the wall next to his head, careful not to hit him, but hard and fast enough to make him flinch. "Touch me again, and I'm calling the fucking cops." I guess he decides to save the fight for another day after that.

Inside my room, Scarlett is laying down on the bed, asleep. She's still in her dress, though her slit is open, exposing both of her bare legs. I don't want to wake her, but I can't very well let her sleep like that. Under different circumstances, I would be making love to her right now. Not tonight though, our first time can't be poisoned by Lorenzo's shitty actions. Neither one of us is in the right headspace for this step in our relationship tonight. That's fine.

There's an intense need deep inside me for her to be safe and happy, and it seems to trump everything else. It kept me from beating some respect into Lorenzo. Now it's keeping me from taking the next step with Scarlett. Yes, that can wait at least one more night.

Crossing over to the bed in two long strides, I bend down and kiss the top of her head, right where her birthmark hides under her bangs. She stirs. "Scarlett, I have your clothes. Let's get you more comfortable." I laugh inside at the unintentional reference to the cliché line women use to not so subtly say they are changing into lingerie. Although, the hope is still there that lingerie is all she brought.

"Eli?" She says my name groggily, not yet opening her eyes.

"Yes, baby, I'm here." I fling my suit jacket off and toss it on the chair by the bed, then slide down next to her, tucking my arm behind her neck.

"Thank you." She nuzzles her face into my chest and curls her body closer to me. "For protecting me, for taking care of me."

"Of course, I will always protect you. I love you, Scarlett." I had hinted at it earlier when we were chatting with her mom. It may be too soon according to dating advice, but I don't care. I've always been one to speak my mind. Really, five weeks doesn't feel too soon to me.

Her eyes flutter open, and she looks up at me. "I love you too, Eli."

My mouth finds hers. Despite my body telling me it's time, my mind is still racing. I kiss her softly, tenderly, holding back the passion that's boiling inside of me. After a few moments, I pull back. "I just want to hold you all night. Let's get you out of this dress."

"I think that would be perfect," she agrees.

She slides down the bed and tries to stand, but her body is still over-relaxed and she stumbles. I rush to her and help her to sit on the edge of the bed. "Let me help you, baby." I reach for the duffle bag and set it down next to her. "Did you bring something to sleep in?"

An impish grin spreads across her face. "No." She curls her lips into her mouth, pressing them together. "I figured I probably wouldn't need anything," she confesses.

Her confession sends a rush of blood through me, hardening me instantly. I take a deep breath, willing myself to relax. "I have a t-shirt you can wear."

I walk to the closet where my overnight bag is and pull a t-shirt from it. When I turn around, Scarlett has her dress unzipped, she's trying to stand on her own again, with no luck. She plops back down on the bed, the top of her dress is now loose and falls to her lap. I have to fight off the urges as her perfect breasts taunt me from behind the black lace bra. "Here, let's get this off," I say, tugging the dress down. She lays back so I can slide it down past her full hips, revealing the matching panties she's wearing. Oh, god. I'm certainly hard now, and it won't be easily relaxed at this point. "Hands up," I instruct as I hold my t-shirt out to help her into it.

Once the shirt is covering her, I pull the dress away and toss it over the chair with my suit jacket. "Can you help me?" she asks, trying to reach behind her back to unsnap her bra.

Fuck me. "I got you," I say. I sit down next to her and slip one hand up the back of the t-shirt, effortlessly unsnapping the bra and pulling it out. Her nipples are hard, the pink showing through the thin white fabric of my shirt. This is going to be a long night. I stand again, pulling back the covers and helping her slide under them. Then I ease myself in behind her, settling in as the big spoon. After turning off the bedside lamp, I pull her close to me, certain she can feel my stiffness. "Good night, gorgeous," I whisper in her ear.

Chapter 19
Scarlett

There's a stream of light shining in from a slit between the curtains, shining right into my eyes. I squint one eye open, but my head is pounding. I roll to my back and pat the bed next to me, it's empty. My body jolts up, the events of last night swirling around in my head. What room am I in? Is this my room? No, the window was on the other side of the room. It must be Eli's room, but where is he?

Bit by bit, everything that went down the night before is coming into my mind. It's all unfolding, from dinner and dancing to Eli and Lorenzo fighting. Why did they fight? Oh god, because Lorenzo kissed me. Then I remember what Eli said, why I had so much trouble walking and holding myself up. He thought Lorenzo drugged me. My hands reach up and run through my hair, I'm stressed just thinking about it. Everything makes it look like this man I've known my whole life has done a complete one eighty on me over the past five weeks. It's like I don't even know who he is anymore. I shake my head at the thought, there has to be an explanation. Lorenzo wouldn't do that, would he?

The door opens and Eli walks in. He's sweaty, like he's just come in from a run. "Good morning, gorgeous." He smiles at me. "Did you sleep okay?"

"Maybe too well. Did you go for a run?"

"Yeah, I just needed to clear my head, forget some things that went down," he says, wiping the sweat from his forehead.

"I'm trying to remember everything from last night," I say, rubbing my head.

He pulls his bag from the closet, reaches in and gets a bottle of Tylenol, then tosses it to me. "You should forget most everything that happened last night." His smile has faded. "Literal dumpster fire."

"What?" I ask, popping two Tylenol in my mouth and downing them with a swig from the water bottle on the bedside table next to me.

He shakes his head. "Let's forget all the parts of last night that aren't the part where I told you I loved you and you said it back."

He's next to me now. I can see the sweat gliding down his temple. He kisses me, softly. "So that part wasn't a dream?" I ask when he sits up, rolling onto my side and propping my head with my elbow.

"Definitely not." He winks. "I'm going to shower, you need anything?"

I can feel the smile spread across my face. "No, thanks. I should probably take a shower too." I quickly realize that it sounds like I want to shower with him. "When you're done, of course."

His face contorts into an impish grin. "We should conserve water." He winks again.

Does he really think I'm going to strip down naked with him in the shower? We haven't gone *there* yet. How in the world am I supposed to bare my whole body to him? "You're silly." I laugh it off.

"I am one hundred percent serious." He reaches for my hand, trying to guide me out of the bed.

My head shakes rapidly. "I'd be too embarrassed," I admit.

"Embarrassed by what? Scarlett, you are beautiful. Your body is perfect." His eyes slice into mine when he speaks. "Plus, I practically saw you naked last night when I helped you change out of your dress. So, you have nothing to hide now."

Heat rushes to my cheeks and a lump forms in my throat. I look down at the white T-shirt I'm wearing and images of me attempting and failing to change come to mind. "Oh, god."

"Yup. Might as well," he teases. "Seriously though, I would love to shower with you, but if you aren't comfortable with it, you don't have to join me."

There it is right there. This man in front of me loves me. He respects me. He protects me. Why should I be embarrassed to open myself fully to him? I smile demurely at him, then pull the covers off me and stand. "OK."

He's up, he's standing, he's ripping the sweaty shirt off his body. Now I get a glimpse of him sans clothes. His body is absolutely divine. I'm struggling to find an ounce of fat on him. By the time we're in the bathroom, he's completely naked. His long legs are thick and muscular, his butt round, defined muscles ripple over his back. I'm standing in the doorway, watching him start the water, waiting for him to turn around. I haven't removed anything. The fact that my body is much squishier than his is the prominent thought in my mind.

He peeks over his shoulder. "What are you waiting for? You going to shower with that T-shirt on?"

I step inside and close the door behind me, as if someone could walk in and see us. He turns around, only now giving me a full frontal view. My eyes widen as my gaze travels from his face, down his chest, his six-pack abs, to his... *gulp*. He's long and thick and half hard. The mere sight of it chokes me up. I clear my throat with a single cough.

He follows my gaze and looks down at it too, a cocky smile takes over his lips. "Don't be scared, Scarlett." He steps over to me and grips the bottom hem of my shirt, pulling it slowly over my head. There's steam coming from behind the shower curtain, but still a chill in the air. My now exposed breasts shiver, hardening my nipples.

It's his eyes' turn to widen at the sight of them, he fully erects. I eye him, wondering exactly how all of him will fit inside me. It's been so long since I've been with anyone, and I can feel all the pent-up tension pooling at my core. His fingers dig into the elastic band of my panties, and he slides them down to the floor, his face stopping right in front of my pelvis and I'm glad I decided to do some trimming yesterday.

He smiles up at me as I step out of the panties. We're both completely naked. Raw and exposed. He keeps his eyes locked on mine, placing quick soft kisses up my abdomen, between my breasts, my neck, my lips. I'm not even sure we'll make it into the shower at this rate. My hands slide over his bald head, pulling us firmly together as our lips part and he sucks on my bottom lip. He reaches around behind me and pulls me closer to him by grabbing onto my ass. The hard length of him slides between my thighs when our bodies meet. A deep moan escapes from his lungs at the touch.

"Oh god, Scarlett," he breathes the words into my mouth. "I can't tell you how badly I want you." He bends his head down and laps one of my nipples into his hot wet mouth. My head falls back, now I am the one moaning. Both of his hands reach around, squeezing my ass, then gliding down to the back of my thighs. He lifts me effortlessly and sets me on the bathroom counter. The hot running water has the room full of steam, there is no water being conserved today.

With me on the countertop, he settles himself between my legs, gripping onto my fleshy hips, kissing my neck. He is dangerously close to sliding inside me. I clear my throat. "Do you have anything?" I ask.

"No," he says breathlessly, "I'm clean."

I giggle. "That's good to know, I meant a condom," I clarify.

"Oh, right." He laughs at himself, then slides the drawer next to my leg open and pulls out a box of magnums. He came prepared. I watch wide-eyed as he rips the foil and glides the thin rubber over the length of him.

His eyes meet mine in a silent request for permission. I nod. Slowly, inch by inch, he presses himself inside me. "Oh god, Scarlett." He's breathless already.

The thickness inside me takes all the tense pain away, and I wrap my arms around his neck, pulling him closer to me, pushing him deeper. I release a moan in his ear, causing him to move his body quicker and harder. I let my body fall back, my head now resting against the mirror, my nakedness fully exposed in front of him.

He dives in, licking his tongue around one nipple, then the other. Then he stops, pulls out of me, and kneels down. His face poised between my legs, his lips kiss on the folds of my lips, his tongue starts flicking against my sensitive bundle of nerves. My hands slap against the counter, gaining the stability to press myself harder into his face, causing his nails to dig into the flesh of my hips.

"Eli, oh shit! That's... oh my god... I'm coming!" My entire body tenses before every ounce of me releases. I shudder on his tongue, but he grips tightly to me, not letting me wriggle away. "I need you inside me again, Eli," I beg breathlessly.

He delivers, standing to position himself between my legs again. Now that I am soaking wet, he slides effortlessly inside, deeper this time. His hands move from my hips, under my ass, and he lifts me again. I'm backed up against the door, supported by his hands. My arms grip tight around his neck. The pressure of his thickness inside me is enough to send me into a second orgasm. My head knocks against the door as he hammers in and out. Sweat trickles down his head and his body tenses, his hands squeeze tight, then he cries out. After he finishes, he lets my legs drop, one by one to the floor, and his forehead rests against mine.

"Damn, baby. That was incredible." His words come out with a groan.

"Yeah," I sigh back. "I don't think we conserved any water though."

"Oh, shit!" We burst into laughter. Then take our time showering together.

We book the room for another night and spend the rest of the weekend together. We make love in every corner of that room. With take out and Uber-Eats, we don't have to leave at all. In love and full of passion, we let everything out that weekend. Eli had set the bar to be closed for Christmas Eve and Christmas Day, so he wouldn't have to worry about that. I texted Macie and offered her a week of paid vacation if she would take care of gathering things from the banquet hall and check in on Binx. She happily obliged and cheered me on.

Monday morning came, Christmas morning. I had promised Mom I would come over for Christmas brunch. We also go to the Tate's every year for Christmas dinner, though I may have to sit that out this year. "Do we have to leave our little love bubble?" I ask Eli, nuzzling my face into his chest.

"Unfortunately." He sighs, wrapping his arms tighter around me.

"Do you have plans for Christmas?" I ask, remembering our first date when he didn't seem to want to talk about his mother. It made me realize he probably didn't have anything planned for today.

"Not really, actually." He laughs nonchalantly. "I might call my mom. I might wait for her to call me." I want to ask more questions about that relationship but put it on hold for now.

Sitting up and turning to him, I grin. "Come with me," I offer. Of course he agrees.

I say a quick prayer that Mom hasn't invited the Tates for Christmas brunch, and that she won't be offended if I sit out from dinner. I'm hoping that I can at least avoid Lorenzo until I go back to work.

As soon as we're back in the office, I know I will have to face him. And everyone else for that matter. I had barely checked my phone all weekend, focusing all of my attention on Eli, and meshing our bodies together. Once I finally accept that our blissful weekend is over, I check my messages. There are twenty messages from Lorenzo. And just like that, reality slaps me in the face.

Chapter 20
Lorenzo

She hasn't answer me all weekend. She hasn't even looked at the messages. There are no read receipts, only delivered. I'm terrified something happened to her. Really, I'm terrified that I've lost her. My head is spinning. Is she mad at me? Did she see Eli punch me in the face? Does she know that asshole damn near broke my nose? The idea that I could lose her forever tortures me. She's always been there. I can't even begin to fathom my world without her in it.

It's Christmas morning and I'm spending the day with my parents. Mom always does a big Christmas dinner with turkey, mashed potatoes, and the works. Usually Scar and her mom join us. As much as I need to see her, I'm afraid she will bring *him*. And I *really* don't want to see him. Outside of my parents' door, I take a deep breath to rein in my emotions and brace myself for the day.

Inside, Dad is in the living room sipping on a mug of coffee. *Hey, Zo,* he greets me, standing to hug me. I hug him with my free hand. *Here, let's put those under the tree.* He takes the bag of gifts from my other hand.

Merry Christmas, Dad. Where's Mom? I ask. I feel bad for immediately asking for Mom, but I just feel like I need her right now. I guess deep down I'm a mama's boy at heart.

In the kitchen. She's preparing the turkey. He doesn't seem fazed by it. He's used to me going to her for support. And I'm sure word about what happened at the party got around, so he knows I need her right now.

Thanks. I'm going to say hi.

I make my way into the kitchen and find Mom behind the counter with a turkey baster in one hand and a glass of wine in the other. *Little early for wine, no?*

Lorenzo, Merry Christmas! She puts both items down and wraps me in a hug. Her face changes to concern. *How are you?*

I'm fine, Mom. She grabs my chin and inspects either side of my bruised nose. *I'm fine,* I insist.

She cocks both eyebrows up and purses her lips, then subtly shakes her head. *What happened the other night?*

Mom, it's Christmas, I don't want to talk about it. That's not entirely true. I know my parents want to see Scar and I end up together. There's a part of me that wants to ask her about that now. Ask for advice on how to make it happen. I let out a deep sigh. *Do you think I've lost her forever?*

She reaches for her glass and takes a sip of her wine. *Not forever.* She shakes her head. *For now, maybe. But not forever,* she assures me with a sympathetic smile.

I fucked up. Mom gives me a glare over the curse word. Seriously? I'm thirty-one. I guess in her eyes I'm still sixteen. I pour myself a glass of wine and then plop down on a chair at the little round table in their breakfast nook. *Are they coming today? Scar and Helen?*

I invited them. Helen said she would check with Scar this morning. She's finished putting the turkey in the oven and is toting her glass of wine over to join me at the table. *We all want to see you two together, but she's not available right now. You can't force your way in.*

Why are moms always right? *I know. It all happened at the same time. I told her how I feel, and she met him. Then she chose him. It's just frustrating.* I open up to her, just as I have every time I've needed her in the past. *And he's an asshole. He just gets under my skin.*

Really? Her eyebrows raise in confusion. *He seems so nice to me.*

Who's side are you on, Mom? I can't believe what I'm seeing. *You just said you want to see Scar and me together. Now you're defending him?*

I do. That doesn't change that he seems to be perfectly nice. In my opinion at least. She throws her hands up in surrender, not wanting to take blame for her comment. *Maybe your view is colored by your emotions.*

I huff. *Well, maybe that's because you aren't a threat to him like I am.*

Maybe. She eyes me suspiciously, deciding whether to respond further. *Let's go open gifts,* she suggests, changing the subject.

With a long, frustrated swig, I finish the wine in my glass and pour another. On some level, I know she's right. It's just hard to accept when my heart is so deeply shattered. *Sure.*

With just the three of us, there aren't too many gifts to open. I help Dad clear the ripped paper from the floor and stuff it into a trash bag. *Oh, there's one more,* Dad says, pulling the box from the bag I had put under the tree.

It's for Scar, I say. *If she doesn't come, maybe Helen can give it to her for me.*

Dad gives me a sympathetic smile. *We'll make sure she gets it.* He sets it back under the tree and pats me on the back. *Just be patient, Zo. If it's meant to be, it will be.*

I hate that fucking phrase right now. And the patronizing expression on his face just riles up my torturous emotions. I give a curt smile and nod. *I guess so.*

Chapter 21
Eli

Walking on cloud nine from the weekend I've spent with Scarlett, I happily follow her into her mom's house. She rings the doorbell, but then just walks right in. Helen emerges from the kitchen to meet us at the door.

Good morning! Merry Christmas! Her face is glowing as she hugs us both. Scarlett had taught me 'Merry Christmas' in the car on the way over.

Merry Christmas, Mom, Scarlett says. *I hope it's okay, I brought Eli for brunch.*

Of course! Happy to have you. Helen smiles and pats my cheek. Scarlett voices for her to be sure I understand.

Scarlett and I have been together about a month now, so I picked out a gift for Helen and brought it along this morning. *Thanks for having me. Merry Christmas.* I extend my hand out with the gift bag dangling from my fingers.

Oh, Eli, you shouldn't have! she exclaims. I peek over at Scarlett and see that her face is lit with joy. *Thank you. I was just fixing sangria for brunch. Would you like a glass?*

Scarlett interprets for me, and we both say, *Yes, please,* at the same time.

After we've finished eating, we gather around the tree and exchange a few gifts. *Eli, you aren't spending Christmas with your family this year?* Helen asks.

I glance over at Scarlett, hesitant to divulge everything. "Can you interpret, please?" I ask, and she nods, of course. "My father passed away when I was young, early high school. He was in the Pentagon on 9-11 when the attack happened. My mother... she's another story." It's not the worst backstory one could give, I just don't like talking about it much. I also haven't really told Scarlett yet. Mostly because I'm embarrassed by my mother's story.

Oh, I'm so sorry to hear that. Scar lost her dad around the same time too. Helen's face is filled with empathy, Scarlett's voice is meek. It's been fifteen years for her and twenty-two years for me, but these special holiday times are still hard. *You don't visit your mom?*

I take a deep breath and decide it's fine to just go ahead and share. I only wish Scarlett didn't have to interpret when I tell her. "My mom is a drug addict. She got involved with the wrong guy at work, while my dad was stationed in California. He showed her a life she couldn't resist, I guess. When my dad was reassigned to Quantico, she decided she would rather stay and get high than be a mom and wife." I've spent the last twenty-five years holding a grudge against her for choosing drugs over me. Even when I was forced to go live with her for those last four years, I barely spoke to her.

"Oh, Eli," Scarlett exhales the words with a sigh. "It must have been so hard to go live with her after your dad died." She signs while she talks, once finished, she reaches over and places her hand on my thigh, squeezing sympathetically.

A tear has welled up in Helen's eye, and I watch as it slides down her cheek. *You poor thing,* Scarlett voices for her, *I can't even imagine what that was like.* She stands from her seat and walks over to hug me, placing a motherly kiss on the top of my head before sitting again.

"It's been a long time. Of course, I am still bothered by it, and I don't have much of a relationship with her. But at the same time, I've come to grips with it. I've learned to rely on myself, ever since I was fourteen years old," I say, hoping to avoid too much sympathy or damper the mood of the day.

We chat a little while longer, then Helen turns on How the Grinch Stole Christmas, a family tradition, so she tells me. It's not long before she doses off. Scarlett is nuzzled under my arm, her head on my chest, and she peeks up at me. "You want to see my old room?" Her face is plastered with mischievousness.

"Absolutely, yes, I do." I'm on my feet, taking the hint.

The house is a craftsman bungalow, the main bedroom is on the first floor with two smaller rooms and a bathroom at the top of the stairs that lead up from just behind the front door. It's adorable, nonetheless.

At the top of the steps, Scarlett turns right into the bedroom door on the opposite side as the living room, what I assume is above the main bedroom downstairs. There's a small couch at the back of the room, and a desk that looks out over the backyard by the one window.

"Since I was an only child, I basically had both of these rooms. After college, this became like my office space," she tells me.

"Mm hmm, this is nice." I nod, going through the motions until we get across the landing to her actual bedroom.

She turns and leads me through the doorway. "Private bathroom, of course," she says through a smile. "And here's my room. Wow, it doesn't look like Mom has changed it since I've moved out," she muses.

It does look as though Scarlett did some updating from what her childhood bedroom would have been like. Though, it still has a young woman charm to it. Pale blush painted walls with a floral bedspread over the full-size bed, white matching nightstands and vanity, and there's a lone armchair next to the window in this room.

We step inside. "Nice." I turn toward the door and begin to push it closed. I really have no interest in how the room looks. "What's behind here?" I ask playfully, latching the door shut before I spin back around. My hand grasps hers and I pull her into me, my lips finding hers.

"Eli!" she shrieks, surprised as if she hadn't invited me up here for exactly this reason. "My mom is downstairs."

I reach behind me and turn the lock on the knob, studying her face for any sign of her lack of desire. All I see is her coy smile. "Then I guess we'll have to be quiet." I wink.

She erupts with laughter at my joke. With a swift whip of my hand, I spin her around and backed her up against the door. One hand reaches behind her back, the other traces the lace pattern on her stockings, creeping up behind the fabric of her skirt. I love the fact that she always wears skirts. I can't wait for warmer weather when the stockings will stay in her dresser. Her head thrashes back as my fingers find her core, she lets a moan escape from deep inside of her.

"Oh, Eli." Her words come out hot and breathy in my ear. "Looks like you're on the naughty list today."

The joke might be corny, but I don't fucking care, it still turns me on. I pull the fabric of her skirt up, then find the top of those damn tights and yank them down. She still has her boots on, and honestly, I don't even think she'll need to take them off.

I kiss her lips again, pressing my body against hers, tracing my fingers around the elastic of her panties on the back side. My lips leave hers, trailing down her neck and into the plunging neckline of her sweater. She writhes beneath me. I rip the damn sweater off and over her head, then dive my face back between her plump breasts. Her body quivers with anticipation, so I leave a path of quick, hot kisses down her abdomen until I reach her hot, silky center.

God, she's fucking soaked. My tongue slides between her lips, and she grasps my head, crying out in pleasure. I lick her sweet juices until I feel her body tense and release.

"Oh, god, Eli!" She practically screams as she orgasms.

Fuck. I realize I don't have any condoms with me. "Shit," I curse under my breath.

"What's wrong?"

"I don't have a condom," I confess.

She doesn't slump in defeat. Instead, she lets her body slide down to the floor, her face now poised in front of my cock that's anxiously waiting for her next move. Her soft hands reach up and unbutton my pants, and my stiffness falls forward as she peels my jeans away.

My arms thrust out, slamming my hands against the door behind her. I lean my head forward to watch her perfect, pink lips kiss the tip of me. The contrasting colors turn me on, causing the air inside me to gush out in a loud moan. I watch wide-eyed as her lips slowly take in the head. She suckles on it and I'm throbbing.

Her tongue glides from the base all the way back to the head, then she takes me in her warm mouth. My entire body shudders and I reach one hand down, clutching the crown of her head. My hips move in rhythm with her, back and forth, as her mouth eases up and down my shaft. Fuck. It feels incredible. As I am just about to explode, she pulls back and slowly slides her body back up to a standing position.

Her mouth comes to my ear and her warm breath whispers, "I'm on the pill."

Fuck me. I whip her around so fast, bend her over and slide myself deep inside her. She cries out as my hips slam into her luscious round ass. She's supporting us, her hands pressed against the door, and my hands cup her dangling breasts. It doesn't take long for me to climax in this position, afterward, my body slumps onto her back.

"That was fucking amazing." I manage to gasp out.

"Merry Christmas." I can hear the smile in her words. My naughty little imp.

Chapter 22
Scarlett

The office is literally the last place I want to be right now. Unfortunately, I can't keep hiding in the love bubble with Eli. I have to face reality. The holiday gave me a couple extra days to avoid coworkers who may have seen the love triangle drama unfold at the Christmas party, but it's time to face the music. Honestly, I feel like a toddler being told she has to clean up her toys, I don't wanna! I really want to scream.

Ah, but c'est la vie. At least I took off enough days to make it a two-day work week. The agency really can function just fine without me most days. That revelation just adds to my reluctance to go into the office. When I arrive, Lucy is already at her place behind the reception desk. She greets me with her usual friendly smile.

"Good morning, Scarlett, how was your holiday?" she asks.

"It was very low-key. Something I really needed. How about you?"

"It was nice, I really enjoyed the time with my family." There's a look on her face, curiosity I believe; she wants to ask more questions. It appears she's smart enough to hold her tongue though.

"That's good, welcome back. I'll be in my office, hoping to finish out the week pretty low-key as well," I hint, not so subtly, that I don't want to talk about the Christmas party.

Thankfully, I'm able to hide out in my office most of the day. Mom and Alana both know I want to lay low at work this week and promised not to interrupt my day. Most of the staff interpreters have assignments out of the office all day. Which keeps the place fairly empty. By lunch time, I still haven't seen Lorenzo. Despite the fact that I typically keep my door open, I've kept it closed today, perhaps he got the hint. Of course, I couldn't go the entire day undisturbed. As if on cue, there's a knock on my door.

Macie steps inside, she has a couple hours between assignments and came for lunch. "Hey, Scar, how was your Christmas?" she asks.

I motion for her to come in and close the door behind her. "It was really good. How about you?" I say, joining her on the couch.

"You know, the usual. Went to see the fam, did the whole Christmas thing." She giggles at her quick rundown. Then she raises her eyebrows, questioning me without words. "Umm, are you not going to tell me about your weekend in the hotel with Eli?"

A sigh of relief streams out of me. "Oh, right, um... I forgot you knew about that." I giggle to myself at the thought of remembering the weekend. "It was undeniably the best weekend of my life." The confession gushes out of me.

"Girl, I need details." She scoots forward in her seat, sitting up and resting her elbows on her knees in anticipation. "How was he?"

"The best." I flash her a sly smile. Macie has always wanted details about each and every bit of these types of things. She also likes to overshare from her own experiences. I, on the other hand, usually prefer to keep things a little more discreet.

"That's it? That's all you're going to tell me? How long have we been friends?" she asks, gripping her chest in mock offense.

I take a deep breath, then start to go into more detail. "Nothing happened after the party. Eli told me later he didn't want our first time to be tainted by what had happened. That, and he thinks Lorenzo put something in my drink." I frown, realizing I've moved away from the fun details, but I only want to focus on the fun details.

"Oh my god, he did mention that," she remembers. "We need to talk about that too." Her face twists into a questioning expression. "Do you really think he would do that?"

My lips purse and I look down to my hands that are fidgeting with each other in my lap. "I don't know, Macie. No? Yes? I doubt it? All I know is that I'd rather forget that part," I admit. "Anyway, Eli went for a run Sunday morning. When he came back, we were going to shower together, but we didn't make it into the shower." A devilish grin takes over my face.

"Stop it! I mean, don't stop, tell me more!" She laughs at herself.

Without divulging too much, I give her a few juicy tidbits about the weekend, making sure not to leave out our stealthy rendezvous in my childhood bedroom with Mom downstairs. "So, have you seen Lorenzo?" She leads the conversation back to him.

"Not yet." I shake my head, wringing my fingers together. "I'm hoping to avoid him for the next century." I know that's not possible, but I can't deal with the idea of having that conversation right now.

"Well, that's impossible. But I guess he's giving you a little space. He is here, he was here yesterday too." She places her hand on my shoulder, offering support. "I know it's hard and awkward now. I hope for both of you that you can find your way back to being friends."

My gaze falls to my hands resting in my lap, I'm studying my fingers like there's a final exam on each wrinkle and crease. "Honestly, Macie, I think that's going to be very hard. He's different around Eli. His jealousy and insecurities are on his sleeve now. It feels hard to be around. And the thing is, I *really* like Eli. And he basically wants me—"

I'm about to tell her that Eli wants me to stop seeing Lorenzo when I'm interrupted by a sound at the door, not a knock, but the crank of the doorknob turning.

"Speak of the devil," Macie says as both of our heads turn to the noise and see Lorenzo step in. She turns back to me, inhaling and exhaling a deep sigh. "We'll talk more later."

Much to my dismay, Macie pats her knees, stands, and heads out of the room. As she passes by, Lorenzo steps deeper in to make room for her. My gaze flicks back to my hands, avoiding eye contact with him, essentially avoiding conversation with him.

Hesitantly, he strides over and eases into the spot Macie just vacated, reaching a hand over, covering mine to stop their fidgeting. My reflexes are quick, and I pull my hands back, looking up to see what he has to say.

The eye contact is discomforting at best, setting my nerves on fire. He finally lifts his hands. *Scar, I'm sorry.* The conflicting emotions I feel are too much for me. I shake my head and look away. I don't want an apology right now. It won't help me make sense of this mess.

Ever so slowly, his hand moves to touch my thigh, again entering the view of my averted eyes. The touch sends a mix of fire and ice through me, I jolt from my seat, I'm on my feet, backing away from him. *Please don't touch me.* My signs are rigid, and I refuse to make eye contact with him. I do stare at his chest to see what he's going to say, though.

Scar, my behavior the other night was unacceptable. I'm so sorry. Honestly, for a moment I thought you were feeling it too. I was a total jackass, it's only because I was afraid that I would lose you forever. He steps closer, I step back. *Please, I hope you can forgive me, and we can continue being friends.*

Did you drug me? Anger and confusion rile up inside me, lifting my eyes to his. My brows rise up and I press my lips firmly together.

His nostrils flare as he takes in a deep breath. Then a look of realization takes over, his brows lifting and his mouth forming a knowing 'o.' *Shit, Scar. I think you drank my wine.*

What are you talking about? I press.

I had put CBD in my wine so I could relax. I noticed it was gone, I thought I had finished it. His expression seems genuine. *You must have drunk it by mistake. I'm so sorry, Scar.*

Still, I'm left confused.

Lorenzo! You brought drugs to a company Christmas party? I'm livid. *You work here now, this is our family legacy, and you disrespect it like that?*

Scar, you know I use it sometimes, that's not news, he protests, attempting to justify his actions.

Before responding, I take a deep breath, exhaling it out slowly. *It's one thing to do it on your own time. I can't even believe I have to explain this to you.*

I'm sorry, Scar. I'll keep apologizing until all of this goes away. He motions between us to show that he's talking about the tension and awkwardness.

Before, I told you I needed time to figure things out. You refused to give it to me. I take another deep breath. *Well, now, I'm asking for space. You can continue to work here, if you can promise me that you will only see me in a professional way, talk to me about professional matters, and do not, under any circumstances, touch me.* I say my peace, then walk to the open door, inviting him to leave, poised to close it behind him.

He nods, catching on to the fact that there won't be any convincing me otherwise in this moment. It takes him only a few long strides to cross the room. As soon as he steps over the threshold, I close the door and rest my back up against it. My hands cover my face and I weep, mourning the loss of a lifelong friendship. That was quite possibly the hardest thing I've ever done.

Forget Me Not

Part II

Forget Me Not

Chapter 23
Eli

June might be my favorite month of the year. The outside world is beautiful, painted with full green foliage. The temperature is mild, warm, but not yet hot and muggy. Also, it's Scarlett's birthday month. She's turning thirty and I have a big surprise planned for her. Huge, really. What am I hoping to add to this list of reasons I love June? I'm hoping it will be the month Scarlett agrees to marry me. Her birthday is on a Thursday this year, thirty on Thursday. It's so perfect because she'll be going to happy hour with her work friends, as usual, at my bar. What she doesn't know is that we've planned a huge surprise party for her, cake, decorations, the works. And of course, what great thirtieth birthday surprise would be complete without a little black box holding promises of the future? Although, I'm the only one in on that secret.

 Macie took the day off. She gave an excuse of having some doctor appointments in Raleigh and wanted to make sure she was back in time for Scarlett's birthday happy hour. That's all Scarlett thinks is happening; happy hour. Macie is actually running errands and decoy for me. Helen has also left work a little early to help me decorate. She told Scarlett that she didn't feel well, and she wanted to get a nap in before any birthday celebrations. Speaking of Helen, it's been just over six months since I met Scarlett and vowed to learn sign language. I'm practically fluent. Sure, there are words here and there I need to spell, but I'm always fed the sign when I do and commit it to memory. It helps that Helen has welcomed me into the family and I join their family dinner every week. I'm still a fairly slow signer, though no one seems to mind.

 It has been the best seven months of my life. I never imagined I would find someone who made me as happy as Scarlett has. Never before have I felt so strong and secure with women I've dated in the past. And I certainly have never had any inkling of proposing marriage. Scarlett is different. Deep down I know she came into my life for a reason. I know she's the one.

Fire & Ice is set to close at 4:00 pm today for a "private event." I probably could've kept it open to the public. I just don't want to be distracted by business. Of course, Ana is working the bar, my number one bartender and second in command. She's happy to get the extra hours and be there for the big moment.

"You nervous, boss?" she asks as I help her clean up from the last guests to leave.

"Nervous about what?" Macie is here helping set up the birthday decorations. "Pulling off the surprise? She has no idea. It will work," she assures me.

"You think she'll say yes?" Ana asks Macie. Macie cocks her head in confusion, then the light goes off and her eyes light up.

"Are you going to propose?!" she practically screams. The streamers she's holding fly out of her hands, trailing a colorful tail across the room. She runs over to hug me. "Oh my god, Eli! That's so exciting! Of course, she'll say yes!"

If Scarlett is half as excited as Macie, it will make my night. "You think so?" I am a little nervous and trying desperately not to second guess myself.

"One thousand times, yes!" Macie's grin stretches from ear to ear. "She'll say it just like that."

The party guests start arriving around 5:00, knowing Scarlett will be there at 5:30. Helen is one of the first to arrive, she comes straight over to me for a hug. I'm learning that hugging is a huge part of Deaf culture. Despite being one who doesn't care much for hugging, it's growing on me.

Thank you so much for doing this. She is absolutely beaming. *Scar will be so surprised.*

I love her very much, Helen. I'm thrilled to be able to do this for her.

She gives me a warm smile and pats my cheek. *She's lucky to have you. Your signing is getting very good,* she comments.

I've been working very hard. Being able to communicate with you was moved to the top of my goal list when I met Scarlett. A few other people from the agency arrive and I look at my watch. *Oh, I need to run upstairs and change. Be back down in a minute.*

I bound up the stairs to my apartment where I've laid out a nice button-down shirt with black slacks. The outfit I had laid out on my bed also had a tie, but I opt to forgo that. Once satisfied with my reflection, I fish the little black box with the rose gold ring from the top drawer of my dresser. Carefully, I open the box and check the ring one last time. The rose gold matches the luster of Scarlett's hair, and the pea-sized diamond catches the light, sparkling up at me. A shiver runs through me. Not a shiver of fear, a shiver of anxiousness and excitement. This is it. This is happening. I clasp the velvet box shut and shove it deep in the pocket of my slacks, checking my watch. Scarlett would be walking in at any minute.

Back downstairs, the bar is full and lively with Scarlett's close friends and adopted family. Helen is at a table chatting with Alana and Corbin, which doesn't surprise me. James and his boyfriend are chatting with Macie and her boyfriend. She's still with Brent, we've double dated quite a few times over the past seven months. Brent surprised us all and turned out to be a natural in the dance classes we took earlier this year. I wave at Emma and her husband Jermaine, who are sitting with Dave and his wife. Lucy and her girlfriend are sitting at the bar chatting with Ana. Ana looks up and gives me two thumbs up with her supportive grin. The sight around my bar brings a contented smile to my face. Here we go.

"Scarlett just texted me! She's on her way! Let's turn the lights down and hide," Macie suggests, signing while she talks.

"Good idea!" I agree, crossing over to the switch on the wall.

Everyone crouches down under the tables where they are sitting, and I flick the switch. It feels too soon, but the front door opens, we all jump up and shout or sign "Surprise!" When the lights flick back on, it isn't Scarlett standing in the doorway, it's Lorenzo. Are you fucking kidding me? What the hell is he doing here? He better not ruin this night for me.

Forget Me Not

"Come on! Come on! She'll be here soon!" Macie waves Lorenzo over to her table, and he crouches down with everyone else.

Of course, Lorenzo is here. He's been a thorn in my side since I met Scarlett. Not so secretly competing with me from day one. He fucked up big time, and she chose me, although I'm not sure there was much of a debate for her. As much as I wanted her to let him go completely, she couldn't. We both knew that. I had asked her to avoid any social situations with him, which she has respected. But they work together, mutual heirs to their family business, unofficial cousins, the list really does go on. We've run into him a time or two, and he was seeing a chick that he'd met at the hotel the night of the Christmas party. But I notice he's alone tonight and wonder if that fling is over.

"Eli, the lights!" Macie calls out, pulling me from my reflective reverie.

With my eyes trained on Lorenzo, saying a quick prayer he doesn't try anything stupid tonight, I flick the switch to dim the lights again. It's about five minutes before the door creaks open again, and this time it is Scarlett. I throw the lights, and everyone jumps up to shout "Surprise!" again. Her face is radiant.

"You guys!" She's blushing. "You really got me!" Her eyes scan the room and land on mine. They glisten as she gives me a thankful smile, knowing I was the one behind this.

As we begin to cross the room toward each other, Lorenzo steps forward and pulls her in for a hug. *Happy birthday, Scar.* I see him sign when he pulls back from her, then he kisses her forehead. Now my blood is boiling.

Her eyes meet mine again, clearly caught off guard by his gesture. *Thanks,* she signs to him, then keeps walking toward me. A deep breath inhales through my nose, and I breathe it out slowly from my parted lips. A calming mechanism I've used since my days in the military. When we reach each other, she throws her arms around my neck. "Thank you for this, sexy." She plants a kiss right on my lips. The feel of her body against mine instantly calms me. She loves me, she won't let him come between us. Deep down, I know this. In fact, I very confidently know this.

"It's a big birthday, I had to." I wink. "Thirty on Thursday." She giggles at my joke. I knew she would like it.

"Did you close the place down?" she asks, looking around the room and only seeing people she knows.

"Yup. Just for you." I kiss her again.

"I can't believe it! You're so amazing!" She turns around to thank the room as well, using both voice and sign. "Thank you all so much for this! You got me for sure!"

Everyone cheers and shouts, "Happy birthday!"

"Drinks are on me tonight!" I shout, signing as I do. A few people immediately jump up and make their way to the bar. "Go ahead, mingle," I encourage Scarlett. "I'm right here with you."

Her bright smile is complimented by a glistening in her eyes. She kisses me again, and as she walks over to greet Helen, I watch her, admiring every little thing about her. I'm taken over by this overwhelming emotion of pure happiness, a feeling that confirms I am making the right decision.

After filling drinks for everyone, Ana sidles up and nudges me with her elbow. "You ready, boss?"

My gaze shifts to her. "One thousand times, yes," I respond. "Get the champagne ready."

"Sure thing, boss." The grin on her face is infectious. Though maybe it was my grin that infected her.

Scarlett is chatting with Macie and Brent as I make my way over to their table. Macie's eyes meet mine and there is that infectious grin again. Scarlett must have noticed her face because she turns to see me striding over.

"Hey, you." She smiles, wrapping an arm around my waist and kissing my cheek. "I still can't believe you did all this."

"Macie was a big help, and so was your mom." I nod at Ana, letting her know it's time. "Macie, would you mind interpreting for me?"

"Absolutely." She beams.

Scarlett's face twists into curiosity as she studies mine. I grab her hand and lead her over to the bar, a more central location. Ana flickers the lights, the room hushes as all conversations stop and heads look around to see who is seeking their attention.

"What's going on?" Scarlett whispers as I guide her into a seated position on one of the barstools. I kneel down in front of her, my hand scrambling in my pocket for the velvet box. "Oh my god!" she shrieks, her hands covering her face.

"Scarlett, the first time I saw you walk into my bar, I knew you were special. Not only were you the most gorgeous woman I'd ever laid eyes on, but your smile also lit up the room, warming it with your beautiful personality. It didn't take me long to fall in love with you, and each day I think I fall deeper in love with you. If that's even possible." I pull the box out, open it up, and present it to her. "I truly believe I'm meant to spend the rest of my life with you, and I hope you feel the same. Scarlett Reese, would you make me the happiest man on earth and become Mrs. Scarlett Romero?"

"Yes! One thousand times, yes!" She pulls me to my feet and our lips lock, our bodies embrace. "This is the best birthday ever," she whispers in my ear and giggles.

I step back and slide the ring on her finger. My heart feels so full as she admires it before waving her hand in the air to show it off. I'm so focused on her that it takes a few minutes for my mind to register the cheers and applause from around the room.

Helen rushes over to inspect the ring. She hugs Scarlett first. *Congratulations.* Her smile is so huge I can tell that she is genuinely happy for us. *Eli, I'm so happy for you to become my son-in-law.* She pats my cheek, holding my gaze for a moment.

I'm more than happy to be your son-in-law. We embrace.

I reach over, taking Scarlett's hand in mine to squeeze it. Everyone in the room has left their chairs and is surrounding us, each one wanting to hug and congratulate us. Everyone except for Lorenzo, of course. He is still seated, his eyes dark and dead set on me. His chest heaves up and down with deep controlled breathing. The feeling I get can only be described as eerie unease. This man is positively seething. And I am clearly the subject of his indignation.

Chapter 24
Scarlett

As women, I think we fear the big 3-0. Right now, I can't fathom why. This is by far the best birthday of my life. I can't stop twisting the diamond back and forth against my ring finger with my thumb, feeling the weight of it, the cool metal against my skin. Eli hasn't left my side since he slid it on my finger, and I haven't let go of his hand for more than to communicate with signs.

"Let me see, let me see!" Macie reaches for my hand, pulling it up close to see the ring. "Oh my god! It is absolutely gorgeous!" She turns to Eli. "Nice taste, Eli."

"Thanks." He blushes and kisses my cheek. "It's almost as beautiful as Scarlett."

Now I blush. "Stop it." I slap his chest playfully.

"When are we thinking? Summer, Christmas, Fall?" Macie is ready to plan the details already.

"I would elope with her tomorrow if she let me," Eli cuts in.

Macie laughs. "Seriously, I'm ready to plan this whole thing with you."

"Well, I'm sure we will have to chat about it. I guess I've always dreamt of a beach wedding." My lip curls into a smile at the thought. "Something small, not too lavish." I can see Eli nodding next to me. We seem to be on the same page.

"So, that gives us either a month or two to plan, or a year," Macie jokes, although her point is quite valid.

"Like I said, I would elope tomorrow if you wanted." Eli squeezes my hand and kisses my cheek.

"Absolutely not." Macie's tone is firm. "And miss my opportunity to be the maid of honor? I think not." We share a laugh.

"Yes, of course you will be my maid of honor," I assure her. "And, as fun as eloping would be, it would break mom's heart," I say to Eli, or should I say, my fiancé.

Brent, Macie's boyfriend, makes his way over after finishing up a conversation. He slinks his arm around her waist. "Congratulations, guys. This is exciting." He turns to Eli, "You're setting the bar pretty high, man."

Eli lets out a guttural laugh. "Well, sorry if I put you in a spot, man. But I love this woman." He pulls me in close to him. "I have to make it official so she can't sneak away from me," he jokes.

Macie's eyes light up at the thought of being the next bride to be, and she bats her eyes at Brent. "Don't get any ideas," he says, jabbing his finger playfully in her abdomen. "For real though, I'm happy for you two."

The guys shake hands and Brent gives me a friendly hug, then he and Macie make way for the next person to congratulate us. It's James and his current boyfriend, Stephan.

"Congratulations you two." His smile is wide, and he hugs us both, then turns to address Eli. "I have to admit, I wasn't sure if you would make it. But you have really shown your dedication to this woman, and we all love you for it."

"I had no doubt in my mind we would get to this day." Eli's tone is firm, yet friendly. I think he caught on to James being 'team Lorenzo' a while ago, though it seems now that James is really 'team Scarlett.'

"Scar." He turns to me. "My beauty, I am so happy for you. You have to let me help you with planning, and of course, cake tasting," he jokes.

"Sure thing, James." The smile on my face isn't going anywhere.

It goes on like this, one by one, everyone has congratulated us. Everyone except Lorenzo. As much as it pains me to see him sitting alone at his table, I don't have it in me to walk over there. I'm very aware that Eli had asked me not to socialize with him, and I can sense his unease at Lorenzo's presence. That last time Lorenzo and I were in my office, and I told him he had to give me space, was the last time we were alone together. It was six months ago, and I've only seen him a handful of times outside of work since then. Each time, Eli was with me.

Everyone has moved back to their tables, refocusing their evening back on whatever conversations were happening before the big moment. I can't help but to keep looking over at Lorenzo. There's a tug at my heart, wishing things had gone differently when Eli came into the picture, and we could still be friends. I actually do miss him.

Eli squeezes my hand. He must've read my face. "He'll be fine," he says curtly.

A deep sigh eases out of me as I meet Eli's eyes with mine, then flit them away and purse my lips. "Maybe," I concede. "Do you mind if I go talk to him?"

We both know I don't need his permission. We also both know that we respect each other. He nods but doesn't let go of my hand until I've stepped out of reach.

Hey, Lorenzo, I greet him. His eyes are full of sadness.

Congratulations, he signs quickly with zero expression. That's not entirely true, his expression is sad, mismatched from a congratulatory sentiment.

Thanks, I hope you can find a way to be happy for me. I tilt my head to get his eyes to meet mine.

Maybe one day. He shrugs. *I still believe we are meant to be together, Scar.*

I know you do. Maybe in another lifetime. I'm not sure what else to say. *What happened with Kendra?* I'd noticed he had been seeing her occasionally since the Christmas party.

He flicks the corner of his nose up and shakes his head. *She's too young, and too hearing. She's a nice girl, but I don't see long term potential there.*

You know I'm hearing, right? I point out.

That's different... you're different. He's referring to me being a CODA and growing up with his language. *There's no future with her. But with you... with you I can see forever.*

There could be if you opened your mind up to it. Stop focusing on me, take this as your final answer. You've been released from this trap of waiting, I try to encourage him. His body tenses, and I think I've only made him more upset.

Right, because it's that easy? Wow. Thanks for the great advice, Scar. He stands abruptly from the table and his chair topples to the ground with a loud crash. All the hearing people in the room turn to see the commotion, and before I can react, Eli is at my side.

Everything OK here? he asks, using sign out of respect for Lorenzo.

Everything is fine. Lorenzo's eyes glisten, wet with fresh tears. *I was just leaving. Happy birthday, Scar.* His gaze holds mine for a moment before he leaves the bar, not bothering to right the stool he'd turned over.

"You okay?" Eli asks after the door closes behind Lorenzo.

"Yes, I guess." The whole thing saddens me. I hate the thought of losing Lorenzo for good. And I hate that he is hurting so much because of my happiness. "I just hope he can find peace one day."

Eli's hand rubs up and down my back. "I know you do."

With the majority of us having to work the next day, the party dies down before 10:00 pm and everyone is off and headed home. The bar quiets as it empties, Macie and Brent are the last to leave before Ana.

"You want some help cleaning up?" Macie offers Eli.

"No, I've got it, thanks for everything." They hug, then Macie hugs me.

"Have a good night, you two." She winks at us as they head out.

"Ana, go ahead and take off," Eli instructs once the door is closed.

"I can help clean up," she offers. She's used to working much later.

Eli walks around behind the bar and shuffles her to the door. "I'll add the extra hours to your time clock. Let's call it a night."

Her face twists into a knowing smile. "Sure thing, boss." She hugs me when she reaches the front door where I am still standing. "Congratulations, you're going to make a beautiful bride."

"Thanks." I blush.

Eli is on her heels, and once the door closes behind her, he turns the deadbolt. Now we're alone. "Let me see." He reaches for my left hand to admire the ring he placed there a few hours ago. "It looks quite nice on you."

"It's absolutely perfect." My cheeks hurt from how much I've been smiling all night. Yet here I am, still smiling as I admire my new ring. I'm not sure I'll ever get tired of how it sparkles in the light.

He curls his fingers together with mine and presses me up against the door, kissing me softly. My free hand reaches up to hold his smooth, bald head, and his free hand wraps around me. He pulls back. "I'm so glad you said yes."

"I'm so glad you asked." I notice the room behind him where there are still plates of food and half full glasses on the tables. "Let's clean up just a little," I offer. "You don't want to wake up to fruit flies tomorrow."

"The guys in the kitchen are gone already. I think the dishwasher has already been shut down. It's okay, Scarlett. I just want to make love to my new fiancée." He waves his hand as if waving the sight of the bar in disarray behind him away, then kisses me again.

The food is bothering me. "It won't take long," I say playfully and push him back, stepping away from him. The exasperated sigh he lets out is intentionally over exaggerated. It makes me giggle as I walk away.

I quickly move around the room and gather the plates of food, taking them back into the kitchen. I've been in it a time or two and know my way around. I scrape the leftover food into a trash bin and then wash the plates by hand in a large metal sink. He hadn't followed me, so I go back to find him collecting drink glasses and bringing them behind the bar. I gather the few he had left behind and follow him. Together we wash the glasses in the triple sink behind the bar, his hand wittingly brushing past mine each chance he gets. We lay the glasses upside down on the mat to dry. Once all the glasses are washed, he pulls the lever to empty the sink.

"Toss me that rag," I instruct, pointing to one of the rags hanging from a hook behind the bar, then find a bottle of cleaning solution and start spraying down the bar top. Peeking over my shoulder at him seductively.

"Okay, that's kind of sexy," he muses, watching me clean.

"Hey! Get on those tables out there." I motion to the high-top tables on the other side of the bar.

"They'll be fine until tomorrow," he assures me. He sidles up behind me, grabbing hold of my hips. "I think the bar is clean enough."

His voice is low and breathy. He spins me around and makes eye contact, cocking his eyebrow up with a single nod, telling me it's time to stop cleaning. "We don't need this anymore." He takes the bottle and rag from my hands and places them on the counter behind the bar.

"Yes, sir," I tease.

"That's more like it," he teases back.

Before I can say another word, his lips are devouring mine. Since we started dating, I've wondered what it would be like to make love in his bar. Tonight, I get to find out. There's no question in his eye, there's no time to make our way upstairs. There's only time for raw desire. His hands paw at my clothes, pulling my skirt up and over my hips. I rip his shirt up and over his head. We separate long enough for the fabric to pass over his face, then we lock lips again. His fingers work one by one to free the buttons of my shirt before he pulls it off my shoulders and down my arms. His body is pressed up against me and I cock one leg up, hooking it around his waist. I can feel his arousal pressing against me through the thin fabric of his slacks. With one hand still holding the small of my back, his other hand fumbles with the fly of his pants, then he wriggles them down to a puddle around his ankles and steps his feet out. He stands there only in his boxers.

"God, I love you, Scarlett," he breathes out the words, taking in the sight of me.

"I love you, too, Eli." We lock our eyes momentarily, then his lips meet mine again and he hoists me onto the bar.

He tugs at the waistband of my panties and slides them down off my feet, tossing them into the growing pile of our clothes. I reach my hands behind me, unsnap my bra, and toss it into the pile too. His hands take hold of my naked breasts, sending a shiver down to my core.

"Fuck," he says under his breath, then hoists himself onto the bar, lowering me to my back and situating himself between my legs.

Sliding effortlessly into my soaking wet core, we make love on the bar top. It's hard and cold, but we don't care. Our bodies are only desperate for each other, desperate to consummate our new life together.

Chapter 25
Lorenzo

What the fuck just happened? Did he seriously just propose to her? What's worse, she said yes. I've lost my chance. I've lost my soulmate. My emotions are so raw and ragged I can't decipher if I'm hurt, pissed, or just plain devastated. The walk from Eli's bar to the Tru hotel is not nearly enough to clear my head. I hadn't really planned on walking here, but the closer I get, the stronger the urge is to see if Kendra is working. The sight of her behind the front desk brings me some relief, but there's still turmoil in my chest.

I pace back and forth in the lobby while I wait for her to finish checking in a couple. I fear if I sit down, my emotions will pour out of me.

Kendra sees me and waves me over. *Hi, how are you?* She flashes me her sweet smile. Her signing has improved considerably since we've been spending so much time together over the past few months.

Hey. I try to smile. *What time you get off?*

Are you OK? I can tell by her concerned facial expression that my effort to smile didn't work and she's picked up on my mood.

My lips draw into a tight line as I take a deep breath in through my nostrils and shake my head. *Not really*, I answer honestly. Not really OK is a mild way to put it.

Her head cocks to one side as empathy takes over her face. She wants to help, though I'm not sure she'll be thrilled to find out why I am so bothered. *I'm off in about ten minutes, what do you need? How can I help?* A rueful smile spreads over her lips. It's the same look she gives me whenever she's feeling a little frisky.

A momentary thought flashes through my mind, contemplating whether that would help distract me. As quickly as the thought flashes, it fades. *Maybe we could take a walk when you get off, go for a drink or something?* I offer instead.

Sure. She holds a finger up and dips into the office next to the front desk. A moment later she's back with her purse slung over her shoulder. *Let's go. Have you ever been to Fire & Ice? I've been wanting to check it out.*

Anywhere but there. Of course, she would suggest that place.

OK, my cousin Katelyn owns a wine bar down the street. It's pretty cool, we could go there, she suggests instead.

Perfect.

We turn in the opposite direction of Eli's bar and walk about three blocks. Inside, there are self-serve wine dispensers along the side walls. Straight ahead, there's a counter separating the main area from what looks like a kitchen. A tall woman with caramel toned skin and long black braids spots Kendra, she circles from behind the counter to give her a hug. I check out, taking in the room while they greet each other.

Kendra taps my shoulder. *This is Katelyn, my cousin.* She turns to Katelyn. *This is Lorenzo, my um… friend.* Her signs are slow as she makes the introductions with both languages.

I press my lips together, attempting to smile, and nod to acknowledge the introduction. *Nice place you have here. How does it work?*

I watch as Kendra attempts to interpret Katelyn's explanation, but ultimately, I have to rely on my lip reading skills. We load money on a card, slip it into the wine dispensers, and pick what size pour we want. Seems simple enough. Even though I know Kendra is trying her best, I can't help but think how much more natural this would be with Scar.

After tasting a few wines, we settle on one we each like before we find a table in the corner. Kendra eyes me over the rim of her glass as she takes a sip. *So, what's wrong?* she asks after a moment.

I take a sip, delaying my response. *It's nothing really.* Only, it's actually everything. I immediately regret coming to find Kendra. She doesn't need to know that my whole world just ripped apart because my soulmate got engaged to someone else.

She reaches a hand over and places it on mine, her eyes soften as she studies my face. *Lorenzo, you're clearly bothered by something. I wish you would let me in. Let me help you.*

I watch her mouth more than her hands, reading her lips and studying her face. Guilt wrenches my gut knowing that I've spent the past few months using her as a rebound. Can you rebound from someone you weren't even in a relationship with? Either way, Kendra deserves better. I swallow and clear the emotion from my face. *I just had a bad day, that's all. I'll be alright.*

She gives me a suspicious side eye, then shakes her head. *I know there's more to it than that.*

You remember Scar? She nods. *She got engaged.*

An unspoken understanding passes between us, and we enjoy each other's company for the evening, knowing that whatever this thing we have going, isn't going anywhere past tonight.

When Kendra and I part ways for the night, I remember my car is still parked by Eli's bar. Reluctantly, I head back over there, hoping the party has ended so I don't have to see the happy couple through the window as I pass by. No such luck. Well, really, the party has ended. I'm here just in time to catch a great view of the happy couple making out behind the bar. Did they seriously not realize anyone walking by could see them? He has her on display for anyone on the damn street. Well, not exactly on display. The blinds are pulled shut, I am at a precarious angle, viewing between the lettering etched over the frosted front door.

For just a moment, I watch as they strip each other down naked. Scarlett's naked body, that I've waited so many years to see, is right here in front of me, separated only by this two-inch door.

And that asshole bartender. He helps her up onto the bar and lowers his body onto hers. Every ounce inside of me is on fire with conflicted emotion. Fiery rage watching another man take advantage of Scar's supple, open body. Also, fiery desire at the sight of her. I can't take my eyes away from her. Blocking out Eli, I zone in on Scar, wishing that one day this nightmare will be over. Wishing that one day she'll wake up and come to me.

    I force myself to look away, I can't watch this. All I can do is find my car and get the hell out of here. It's parked down the street, on the opposite side of the road. Just before I get to the crosswalk, I notice Eli's Jeep. Everything about this asshole sends unbearable, intense rage through me. As fumed as I am with him, deep down, I know it's my own fault for waiting so many years to tell Scar how I feel, not Eli's.

    Agonizing emotions pulse through me. Images of the events that have happened to pull Scar farther and farther away from me flood my mind. Unable to handle what's happening in my heart, the tears finally heave out of me. I pace back and forth, frantically looking for something to ease the pain, then stop in front of the stone wall behind me and slam my fist into it. I punch it again. And again. Then my hand hurts, my knuckles sore from the blows. I look down at my hand, clenching my fist. Blood starts to seep from my prominent knuckle. The sight of it makes me realize this won't help me, it's only hurting me more. Taking a deep breath, I give up for now and cross the street to my car.

Chapter 26
Eli

Waking up next to Scarlett, my soon-to-be wife, is my favorite thing in the world now. Honestly, it was my favorite thing in the world before I put that ring on her finger too. It just feels even better now. She's still asleep, she'll wake naturally in about thirty minutes. We both pride ourselves in being morning people, but I still have her beat. She's the little spoon, draped over my arm. With my free hand, I fiddle with the ring, twisting it back and forth. She stirs at the disturbance.

I nuzzle my face up to hers, kissing the soft skin just in front of her ear. She moans. "Good morning, my gorgeous fiancée," I whisper softly in her ear.

With her eyes still closed, she smiles at the sound of my voice, squeezing my hand into her, tightening my hold on her. "Good morning, sexy." She practically moans the words.

It's enough to harden me, and I press myself against her plump backside. I wasn't sure I would have any energy left after the night we had. I made love to her on the bar, behind the bar, on the stairwell up to my apartment, in the shower... pretty much all night long.

She stretches for a minute then snaps awake. "What time is it?" she asks frantically. "Did I oversleep?"

"Take the day off. Spend it with me. Let's celebrate," I urge, not relenting from my tight hold around her.

"That does sound nice, doesn't it." She rolls her body to face me, kissing my lips and then resting her forehead against them.

"It sounds amazing," I encourage the idea.

"I actually have a couple important contract meetings. One to renew and a new one. I wish I could take off." Her voice sounds just as disappointed as I feel. "But!" She sits up. "I could totally take off Monday and we could sneak away for a three-day weekend," she offers.

"Sold." I don't hesitate at that idea.

Scarlett has settled into our relationship quite comfortably, she keeps enough things here now, with her very own drawer and hangers, that we don't have to worry about her going home before work. This means I have time to make love to her one more time before she has to leave for work. Well, two more times. I can't help it, I'm just so fucking happy.

She's ready to go. I have to fight the urges that come over me when she stands at the foot of the bed dressed for work. She's wearing her skinny jeans that might as well be leggings with a loose, silky blouse, untucked. The top two buttons are open, and I imagine ripping the rest of them open, pulling her back into the bed with me.

"God you're fucking gorgeous," I say, admiring her.

"Wish I could stay right there in that bed with you." She corners the bed and bends down to kiss me.

"Love you, my beautiful bride-to-be, I'll plan our getaway trip while you're gone," I offer.

"That would be amazing. I'll get everything set for Monday so I can turn my phone off for the entire weekend." Her keys jingle in her hand as she makes her way to the door.

"Oh, Scarlett, take my Jeep. I'll take your car in for that inspection. You said it was about to expire, right?" Look at me, already playing the part of the dutiful husband.

"Oh, Eli, that would be amazing, thank you!" she gushes, then swaps her keys out for mine. "Love you, my sexy future husband."

Not even five minutes after she leaves, I'm up. My military trained brain won't let me stay in bed and waste time. Well, if Scarlett had stayed, I would have stayed in bed with her, hands down. But I wouldn't call that time wasted. I take a quick shower and make my way down to the bar to finish cleaning up. I'm actually quite relieved that we hadn't left the food sitting overnight. I make a note to thank Scarlett for that later. I just have to wipe down the tables and sweep, which takes me all of twenty minutes or so. I still have plenty of time before the place opens to run Scarlett's car over to my buddy's shop for inspection. I send her a quick text message on my way out the door.

    Me: Thanks for making me clean last night, it was a good idea. Have a good day, gorgeous. See you soon.

George's garage is only a few minutes away. He's about to open up when I arrive.

He looks up from the computer when the bell above the door rings as I step in. "Hey, Eli, what brings you in today?"

"My lady needs an inspection, I brought her car in. You got time for that?" I ask, laying the keys on the counter.

"Sure thing. I'll have you out of here in a few minutes." He taps a few more times at the keyboard, finishing up whatever he had been doing when I came in. "How's business?"

"It's real good, man. I'm glad I went for it. Being a bar owner seems to be working out great for me."

He picks up the keys and motions for me to follow him into the shop. "That's awesome. I'm going to pull her in right here." He pushes a button on the wall and the garage door glides up.

While he pulls Scarlett's car in, I check my phone. She must be at work by now. I'm starting to get a bit concerned that she hasn't responded to my text yet. I shake it off and shove my phone back in my pocket. George chats with me while he looks over the car.

"You're all set, man. The car looks good. You might want to get those brakes changed in a couple of months, but it's not super dire." He hands me over the keys.

"Thanks, I appreciate it." I fish my wallet from the back pocket of my jeans.

He waves his hand. "Not necessary, just have a drink for me next time I come in."

I nod in agreement, and we shake hands, pulling each other in for a 'bro hug,' before I hop in the car and head back to the bar. The fact that Scarlett still hasn't texted me back is eating at me, so instead of turning off to head back downtown, I keep straight toward her office.

That's when I see it. My heart breaks instantly at the sight of my Jeep crushed into a tree on the side of Ward Blvd, surrounded by emergency vehicles. I barely check the lane next to me when I swerve across to the right lane and pull up behind the accident scene. My hand fumbles with the door, I can't get out of the car fast enough, literally running up the shoulder toward the fire truck blocking my view.

"Hey, hey! Get back in your car. We've got this covered!" An officer posted by the flares set up around the scene holds his hands up to stop me.

"That's my Jeep! That's my fiancée!" I shout, not stopping.

He steps out of my path, letting me whip past him. But I'm brought to a halt on the other side of the firetruck. The Jeep is a mess, all the airbags have all been deployed. The front end is smashed in so deep the engine must be in the driver's seat. I can only pray that Scarlett was thrown from it, otherwise she would've been crushed in that mess. It's for sure totaled. I don't give a fuck about the damn Jeep. I need to see Scarlett. I need to see that she's okay. Frantic, I scan the area. There are no other cars involved, no stretchers in sight.

"Where is she?" I scream my question.

Another fireman trots over to me. "You can't be here, man. Come on. Let's go." He tries to usher me back to Scarlett's car.

"That's my Jeep, my fucking fiancée was driving it. I'm not going anywhere." I move quickly around him and keep searching the area. "Where is she?"

"The driver?" he asks, insensitive prick.

"Yes, the driver!" Hot tears are pricking my eyes, and I can feel my words choke in my throat.

"We got her in the ambulance already. Looks like they've already headed off to the hospital."

I'm halfway to Scarlett's car before he finishes his sentence. I know I have to let Helen know, so I send her a voice-to-text as I speed off down the road, pulling off an illegal U-turn right in front of the officer I'd blown past. It's a good ten-minute drive to the hospital, but I run every yellow light and push the speed limit to get there in seven minutes.

The sliding doors open as I run through them, my sneakers squeak against the waxed floor when I run up to the check-in desk in the emergency room. The woman behind the desk doesn't look up right away.

"Scarlett Reese," I say through ragged breaths.

"I'm sorry?" she asks, not turning away from the computer screen in front of her.

Her nonchalant attitude and zero sense of urgency don't seem to fit for an emergency department. "I'm here for Scarlett Reese, she would've been brought in an ambulance not too long ago."

"Let me check, just a minute." She pushes the glasses sliding down her nose up and taps at her computer. "No Scarlett Reese in the system yet. Have a seat and I'll call you up when I know more."

I let out a frustrated breath. "Are you serious? She was in a car accident, thrown from a Jeep. Please, I need to be with her, now!" I'm trying so hard not to shout.

"Sir, there's nothing I can do or tell you until she shows up in my system. Have a seat, I'll call you when I know more."

"What the fuck?" My attempts at keeping my tone down are beginning to fail.

"Sir, watch your language, please," she scolds me. I deserve it, none of this is her fault.

Taking a deep breath, I apologize before I start begging. "I'm sorry, it's just... you didn't see the car. Please, I need to see her, now," I insist.

She inhales a calming breath. "I understand you are worried about your—"

"Fiancée."

"Fiancée," she continues, "but I really can't do anything for you yet. Please have a seat."

Defeated, I scan the room for the closest seat to her desk. Just as I stride over to a chair, the doors to the back slide open and in an instant, I decide to run through them instead of sitting down. Trying to get through as many as I can before I get caught, I look around every curtain I can, but I don't see her anywhere.

"Sir!" A tall guy in scrubs calls after me. "You can't be back here!"

My feet move quicker, trying to continue my search before he catches up to me. It's futile, he grabs my arm and stops me. "I have to find my fiancée," I plead. Tears are welling in my eyes now, one trails down my cheek, opening the floodgates. "She was in an accident, on Ward Blvd."

"I'll help you find her." He takes pity on me after seeing the tears stream down my face. "But you can't invade these people's privacy. Come on." He leads me to a chair by the nurse's station. "Sit here."

I obey. "Her name is Scarlett Reese."

He taps at the keyboard of the computer behind that desk. "She's not checked in yet." Of course, she isn't. "Was she brought in an ambulance?"

"Yes, it couldn't have been that long ago."

"Kind of strawberry blonde hair?" His face lights up as if he knows exactly who she is.

"Yes! That's her!" I literally jump to my feet.

"Hold on." He pulls a walkie from the desk up to his mouth. "Can I get info on that car accident that came in a few minutes ago? Do we know where she is?"

I hold my breath and strain my ears to hear the response. It's kind of staticky, but I hear plain as day. "They took her straight to surgery."

The man looks at me sympathetically. "She's in surgery."

I'm already slumped back in the chair, my hands clutching my head. "I heard."

"What's your name, man?" he asks.

"Eli Romero. We literally just got engaged last night on her birthday." I give him some details, as if knowing that information would make everyone work harder to keep her alive.

"Come on, Eli, let's get you back to the waiting room. I'll make sure the doctor with her comes to update you as soon as possible." He pats my back to encourage me to stand.

I nod, defeated. They certainly aren't going to let me into the operating room.

Back in the lobby, Helen rushes through the sliding doors, followed by Alana and Lorenzo. He would fucking show up. I take a deep breath, reminding myself that he does care about her too. Even if he does it out of his lane. I wave Helen over.

Oh my god, Eli, what happened? She hugs me and I can feel her entire body shaking.

I don't know anything yet. Just that she is in surgery. I give her the little bit of detail I do know.

What happened? she signs again. She's in shock and doesn't know what else to say.

She had an accident, I saw the car, but I don't know what happened.

Her car is out front, Lorenzo says, joining the conversation.

She drove mine today. I took hers to get inspected. He eyes me suspiciously.

She wrecked your car? he finally asks. His jaw clenches and his eyes narrow at me as if somehow the fact that she was in my car makes this all my fault.

Chapter 27
Lorenzo

Fuck, fuck, fuck. How the hell did this happen? I had texted Scar this morning, asking her if we could chat when she got to work. She responded with one word, 'sure.' Then she never showed up at work. I can't help but wonder if my text is what distracted her, causing the accident. If I lose her because of this, I will never forgive myself. My head is slung between my knees and the tears just start flowing. Mom and Helen sit on either side of me, rubbing my back. I should be comforting Helen right now, not crying because this is all my fault. Fuck me.

Eli keeps eyeing me suspiciously. He hasn't trusted me from the first day we met. If I'm being honest, I never trusted him either. I eye him right back, even though I know it's not helping anything.

Helen waves her hand at Eli, trying to get his attention. He turns to see what she wants to say. *Can you call for an interpreter, please. You should not do it. And not Macie either. Call Lucy and ask for a contractor.*

Sure, he says quickly, then pulls his phone from his pocket and starts dialing. *She's sending someone,* he tells her after hanging up the phone.

Have the hospital call, Mom suggests. *They should provide one.*

Helen shakes her head. *It's always a hassle when it's not for the patient.* She's right. Plus, by calling our own agency, we can make sure there's no conflict of interest.

I wish Eli would sit the fuck down. He's pacing back and forth so much that *my* feet are starting to hurt. It's very distracting. *How are you?* I ask Helen, trying to ignore Eli's pacing.

I'm so scared, she signs, her hands are shaky and her eyes are swollen with tears. *I can't lose my daughter. I've already lost my husband.*

You won't lose her. I won't let that happen, Eli jumps in.

Fuck him. I fucking hate him. None of this would have happened if he had just minded his own damn business seven months ago. If there's anyone to blame, it's him. He catches me glaring at him and we hold eye contact for a beat too long. Long enough for me to see his eyes narrow, still filled with suspicion. He must hear something because his head whips around suddenly and he rushes over to a man in blue scrubs that had just stepped out of the sliding doors to the back. I jump to my feet to follow him.

I'm struggling to read his lips behind his thick mustache and goatee. *What's he saying?* I demand. Eli doesn't even turn to see my signs. I stomp my foot. *What's he saying?* I demand again. Still nothing. "Hey!" I finally turn on my voice and shout to get his attention.

He turns to me, clearly agitated. *Wait,* he insists, then turns back to the man to finish their conversation. Fucking asshole.

The man takes Eli's hands and apologizes, then slips back through the sliding doors. Eli's shoulders visibly slump.

What the fuck happened? I ask again when he finally turns around.

I don't know how to sign it all. She's out of surgery, not awake yet, he tries, but I know there's more information to share than that. Where is the god damn interpreter?

Helen and Mom have made their way over now too. *What did he say?* Helen asks, her face darkened with concern.

He shrugs. *The surgery is done, she's still asleep.* His chest heaves a sigh of relief when my dad walks through the front door.

Dad trots over to us. *Where is she, what's going on?*

Can you interpret for me, until the interpreter gets here, please? Eli asks.

Dad nods. *Of course.* Eli starts talking and I watch as Dad lets some information process before he starts interpreting. *She has a few broken ribs, and a dislocated shoulder. One of the ribs punctured her liver. The surgery was successful, and there's no more internal bleeding. But the worst part is her head. She has a cracked skull and bleeding in her brain. They also did surgery to relieve the swelling from that and induced a coma to let her rest and heal.*

Oh my god, Helen gasps. *How long will she be in a coma?*

Hopefully not more than a few days, Eli says, signing for himself.

When can we see her? Helen asks.

As soon as the doctor comes back, he said we could go in one at a time. He lets Dad interpret that for him. He and Helen hold each other's gaze, silently deciding who will go first.

Eli's mouth starts moving again, and Dad signs. *He said she was lucky she was thrown from the car. If not, she would have been D-O-A.*

What does that mean? D-O-A? Helen asks frantically.

I know what it means. *Dead on arrival,* I sign with slow, rigid movements.

The man with the thick mustache comes back. Eli turns to hear what he says. *One at a time, she can have visitors now,* Dad interprets.

Eli nods at Helen, letting her go first. *Please, go first,* he signs, *she's your daughter.*

Can I have an interpreter with me? she asks the man, and Dad voices for her. He nods. *Corbin, I know it's not appropriate, do you mind?*

Of course not, he agrees and follows Helen through the doors.

That was really nice of you, Mom says to Eli as the three of us sit down to wait our turns.

It's all I can do to keep from punching my fist through the wall. Tormenting emotions rush through me. Fear, anger, guilt. Eli is pacing again, his physical agitation is starting to agitate my anger.

Can you sit the fuck down, please. It's not so much a request as it is a demand.

He stops long enough to glare at me, then continues pacing. Now I'm pissed that he wouldn't respond to me. I'm up on my feet, I'm in his face. *Sit... the... fuck... down.* I produce my signs slowly and firmly.

He squares his body up to mine. His jaw clenches, moving back and forth. He holds eye contact with me but refuses to sign.

You got a problem? I know I should drop it. I know I should sit my ass down and ignore him. I know this isn't the time or the place. But the hatred I hold deep inside me for this man is coming to a head. If I can't punch a hole in the wall, I'm going to punch a hole in his fucking face.

Clearly, you are the one with the problem. The fact that his sign skills have gotten this good pisses me off even more.

You, walking back and forth, back and forth, it's driving me crazy. I can feel my own jaw clench.

Then don't fucking watch me. His shoulder slams into mine as he pushes past me and continues pacing.

My reflexes cause me to reach out and grab his shoulder. I'm not thinking, I know this is stupid. With the look on his face when he spins around, I'm surprised he doesn't knock my teeth out. I can feel my own fists clenching at my sides, my chest filling with air as I puff myself up.

Lorenzo, if you care about Scarlett, you will leave me alone. He's done and walks to another area to put more distance between us.

I take the seat next to Mom again. She waves her hand in front of me to get my attention. *What's wrong?* Frustrated with her question, I shake my head and look away. She gets my attention again. *I know this is hard for you, for all of us. But picking a fight with Eli right now will not fix anything.*

I know, I concede. She's right. I take a few deep breaths and try to calm myself down.

About a half an hour goes by before Helen and Dad return from the sliding doors. Of course, Eli gets to go next. She's his fiancée now. Mom would probably be satisfied just to be moral support for Helen. I need my turn to see Scar, he better understand that much.

I flag down my dad before Eli has disappeared behind the doors. *Tell him to remember the rest of us want a turn too.* I watch Dad's lips move, then turn to see if Eli has acknowledged it just in time to see the sliding doors close behind him. Fucking asshole.

Chapter 28
Eli

The sight of her brings tears to my eyes. I run over and snatch her bruised hand in mine. Her head is wrapped in gauze, a single tube sticking out from the back where the excess blood is being drained. Her face looks as if she lost a fist fight with black and blue circles around one eye and red swollen lips. One arm is in a navy-blue sling from where they put her shoulder back in place.

"Oh god, Scarlett." I press her hand against my tear-stained face. "Please get through this." I'm sobbing again. There's a huge part of me that's happy to have this time alone with her, happy that no one else is allowed back here.

Letting Helen go first was a no-brainer. But now that I'm back here, I'm not leaving, unless it's for Helen. Lorenzo can fucking wait until they allow more than one visitor for all I care. My instincts tell me he had something to do with this. I don't know how, I don't know what happened, but best believe I'll be following up on that police report.

A nurse comes in, not bothering to knock on the door. She's startled by my presence. "Oh, hello," she greets me. "I'm here to check her vitals, are you family?"

"She's my fiancée," I say firmly. Even if she tried to kick me out, she wouldn't have any luck with that.

"Well, that definitely counts." She's friendly, thank god. She gives me a sympathetic smile. Her kind voice and choice of words reminds me of something that Scarlett would say, causing me to choke up.

I watch as she checks the beeping box next to the bed that has wires and tubes extending from the back of it to Scarlett's bed. She squeezes the IV bag, checking to make sure the drip is working. "Since we don't know how much pain she could be in, there's a bit of morphine in there along with the medicine that keeps her asleep."

I'm relieved to know they're making sure she's comfortable. "Do you know how long they'll keep her in a coma?"

"We can't know for sure. Usually, the swelling goes down after a day or two and then we can stop the drip, allowing her to wake up on her own," she explains. "Each case is different, of course."

"Of course," I agree. I look back at Scarlett for a moment before lifting my head to ask, "Would I be able to stay here? I can't leave her like this."

"Not here in the ICU. If we get her into a regular room, then you can stay." Her face is empathetic, knowing that the answer she gave me was not the one I wanted.

"I won't even be noticed. I promise. I'll be right here in this chair, out of the way." I'm practically begging.

"Off the record, if I was the overnight nurse, I would let you stay." She gives me a sad smile. "I'll try to see if the nurse switching out with me will be as open to it." She smiles again and then heads back out of the room.

The room is eerily quiet outside of the beeping of the heart monitor. Scarlett is still, too still, except for the slow rise and fall of her chest as she breathes. Left alone in the quiet with her, everything hits me at once and a loud sob heaves out of me. I let go, allowing my head to rest on her chest and let all of my emotion pour over her. I'm terrified of losing her. "You can't leave me, Scarlett," I whisper. "We've only just begun."

After a few minutes, there's a knock at the door. I turn to see Dr. Harris in the doorway, the doctor who had performed her surgery. "Sorry to bother you." He clears his throat. "There's a man out in the waiting room who is insistent that he come back to visit her."

"I'm not going anywhere." I know who he's referring to, and there's no way I'm leaving her side for Lorenzo to take my place. No way in fucking hell.

He nods in understanding. "We won't be having any problems here, will we?"

"Not as long as you keep him out of here." I know my tone is gruff. I know it isn't Dr. Harris' fault. I know Lorenzo thinks he has some claim to come visit her. Maybe he does. But I'm not going anywhere. "I'm sorry, Dr. Harris. As long as she's only allowed one visitor, it will be me or her mother. That's it."

He steps into the room and looks over her monitors, same as the nurse had not too long ago. "Her heart rate looks good, as well as her oxygen levels. If she maintains these vitals for a few hours, I'll get her moved to a more private space."

"Thank you, Dr. Harris. Thank you so much." I'm conflicted with his statement. On the one hand, it means I could stay with her all night. On the other, it means she could have multiple visitors. Which would put Lorenzo and I in tight quarters together. That's a volcano waiting to erupt.

"I'll check back before shift change. Keep your spirits up, I find positive energy is one of the best medicines in these types of situations." He flashes me a supportive wink then heads back out of the room.

Once alone again, I pull my phone from my pocket and dial Ana's number. She picks up after a couple rings. "Hey, boss. What's up?"

"Ana, I need a huge favor. I'm at the hospital, and it looks like I'm going to be here for a few days—" I start, she interrupts me with a gasp.

"Everything okay? Are you okay?" Her voice is frantic.

"I am okay, physically at least. Scarlett was in an accident this morning. A very bad accident. She's in a medically induced coma and I'm not going anywhere at least until she wakes up," I explain.

"Holy shit. Yeah, I would do the same. Don't even worry about the bar. I've got it under control," she offers without hesitation.

"Thanks. Would you also mind packing a bag for me and bringing it to the hospital? I know that's a lot to ask. There's a spare key to my apartment in the safe in the office." She has keys to the bar, but my personal space I've always kept separate.

"Sure thing, boss. I'll head over now. Anything specific you want me to grab?" she asks.

"Just some t-shirts, sweats, a couple of boxers, my phone charger by the bed, and my toothbrush and deodorant. They're both on the bathroom counter. That should be plenty." I run through a list of basics.

"I'll have it over to you shortly, boss. Hang in there, she has to come out of it. She's your soulmate." Her words are hard to hear and choke me up again.

Another sob heaves out of me, but I try to quickly regain myself. "Thanks, Ana. I appreciate you."

As if on cue, Dr. Harris returns around 5:00 pm. I haven't moved from my seat, and my hand is still holding on to hers. "Let's see," he says, checking her numbers again. I've been watching them the whole time. From what I see, they haven't changed much at all, which makes me feel hopeful.

"What you say, doc?" I ask, trying to keep my tone light and positive.

"I say let's get her to a private room down the hall. She'll still technically be in intensive care, but this way she can have more people around. I truly do believe it helps."

"Oh, thank you." I breathe a sigh of relief.

"It'll be just a few minutes. But listen," he begins to warn me, "positive energy. You understand? Any problems or fighting, and I'll limit her visitation immediately."

"Got it."

I pull my phone out again and send Helen a text.

Me: They're moving her to a private room, you'll be able to come back and sit with her. I'll text you when she's moved and I have a room number.

She responds almost immediately.

Helen: Thank you!

Barely five minutes after I text Helen with the room number, Lorenzo is through the door. Followed immediately by his parents, Helen, and a woman I have never met before. I can only assume she's the interpreter.

Lorenzo is by Scarlett's side, taking her hand into his. He bends down and kisses her bandaged forehead and I cringe. My body tenses at the sight. It can't be good for her swelling. And frankly, I can't stand the sight of it. But I'm ruminating over the doctor's warning. Lorenzo may be a hot head, I won't be. I need to keep the peace for Scarlett's sake.

I'm so sorry, Scar, I watch him sign. It seems ridiculous to me, perhaps she could hear people talking while she's sleeping, but she certainly can't see anything. Though, maybe it's more cathartic for him than anything else.

Helen waves to get my attention and I refocus my attention on her, keeping one eye on Lorenzo. *Any news from the doctor?* The interpreter looks at me to see if I understand.

Not really. He said keep the environment positive. I cut my eyes over to Lorenzo to see if he saw the message. His eyes are focused on Scarlett. I wave at him to make sure he gets the message. His eyes slice into me. *Did you see that? The doctor said to keep things positive.*

He nods with a clenched jaw. *You know this is all your fault, right?*

Please don't start. Here we go.

She was driving your car. Why was she driving your car? This would have never happened if she had never met you. We'd all be better off if she had never met you. His signs got bigger and more rigid as he signed.

I turn away from him and make eye contact with the woman I don't know. "You're an interpreter?" I ask.

"Yes, hi, I'm Bonnie." She extends her hand to shake mine, stepping closer to the chair where I'm seated next to the bed.

"Eli, nice to meet you. Would you mind interpreting for me, please? I've only been signing for about seven months, and I need this to be super clear."

She's already interpreting my words as I make my request. "That's what I'm here for." She tries to give a friendly smile, but the tension in the room is palpable.

"Thanks." I turn back to Lorenzo, making him look up again. "The doctor said we need to keep a positive environment around her. It will help her heal faster. You can be pissed with me all you want. You can be pissed with this situation, as well as the fact that she chose me over you. What you can't do is disrespect me in front of her. I am her fiancé now. You see that ring on her finger? I put it there, and she accepted it. Which means I'm in charge here. So, you'll keep the peace, or you'll get out."

I say my peace and don't give him an opportunity to respond back.

Three days go by. Lorenzo and I have barely left her side, ignoring one another entirely. And she finally wakes up.

Chapter 29
Scarlett

Beep. Beep. Beep. This high-pitched sound keeps penetrating my brain. My eyes twitch with each repeated beat. My head is pounding, my abdomen is sore, and my shoulder freaking hurts. Everything hurts. I reach my hand up to rub my forehead.

"Scarlett! Scarlett, baby, oh my god, you're awake!" I hear a man's voice, though I haven't opened my eyes.

I want to open my eyes, but I can't. Two pairs of warm hands grab hold of mine, one pair holding each hand. "Scarlett, baby, I'm here." I hear the man's voice again. I feel soft lips on the hand closest to his voice. "Open your eyes, baby. Oh my god, I can't believe you're finally awake."

I begin to wonder how long I've been asleep. Finally, I will my eyes to open, they flutter open to see two men, one on either side of me, both of them with tearful eyes and huge, hopeful smiles.

One of the men speaks. "Scarlett, oh baby, I love you so much." He stands over me and kisses my lips. I flinch at the touch.

The other starts moving his hands in the air. Sign language, I suppose. The odd thing is, I can understand him just fine. *I'm so happy you're awake.* He stands and kisses my forehead.

My eyes dart back and forth between the two of them. My heart is racing, causing the beeping noise to speed up. "I'm sorry, who are you?" I ask, somehow producing signs along with my words.

The two men look at each other in confusion and then back at me. "Scarlett, I'm your fiancé, Eli."

Fiancé? I look down to my hands, sure enough there's a ring with a fat diamond decorating my left hand. "I'm sorry... I... I don't know who you are."

What are you saying? The other man signs. He produces a sign on his chin that I think means 'scar,' then continues with, *it's me Z-O.*

Who is Z-O? And how do I know sign language?

"Do you know who you are?" the man who says he is Eli asks. I think for a minute and then shake my head. "Shit." His smile fades away.

He jumps up and runs to the door. "Help! She's awake, where's Dr. Harris?" he shouts before disappearing out into the hallway.

The one who signs gives me an empathetic smile. *This is your name sign.* He produces the same sign from before. *S-C-A-R-L-E-T-T,* he spells. *I'm L-O-R-E-N-Z-O.*

Nice to meet you, I respond. *Though, I think we've met before.* There's something about him. Right now, I have no idea who he is. I have no idea who I am. But there's something about Lorenzo that feels comfortable and familiar to me.

We've known each other for a very long time, Scarlett.

I'm sorry, I don't know you, or him. Or myself, I guess. Do you know what happened? For some reason, I feel like I can trust this man.

You were in an accident. A bad one. Hopefully the doctor will be here soon. He can explain things to you. A woman steps in the doorway and signs to Lorenzo, asking if he needs an interpreter. He shakes his head. *Not until the doctor comes, thanks.*

The woman smiles at me, and I wonder if she knows me too.

Eli is back, he rushes over to me, scooping my hand up in his. "The doctor is coming, baby." There is zero familiarity with him. He may as well be a perfect stranger. The touch of his hand leaves me uneasy.

You know sign language. You could show some respect and sign for me. Lorenzo's smile fades when he looks at Eli to say that.

The two men exchange dirty looks, they clearly do not like each other. And clearly both of them like me very much. "My head hurts," I complain, pulling my hand away from Eli to rub my head. He seems to slump from my retraction.

"I'll get Dr. Harris to get you something for your head, baby," Eli assures me.

Moments later a man with a thick mustache in blue scrubs comes into the room. "Miss Scarlett, you're awake." He has a wide, friendly smile. He strides across the room and checks my vitals on the machine next to the bed, then touches my forehead. He pulls a pen from his pocket and holds it up in front of my face. "Follow this with your eyes," he instructs, moving it left, right, up, and down in front of me. Then he uses the same pen to jot down some notes on his clipboard.

"Well?" Eli questions. There's a mix of hope and concern behind his lifted brows and wide eyes.

The woman has come back in the room, she signs everything for Lorenzo. An interpreter, I guess. Dr. Harris is silent for a moment, reading over his notes. "Scarlett, do you know where you are?"

I look around the room. "Well, I'm in a hospital." Eli smiles, the doctor frowns.

"Do you know which hospital? What city, or state even?" I think for a moment before I shake my head. "Do you know your name?"

"Everyone keeps calling me Scarlett," I point out. "But I couldn't tell you any more than that."

The doctor turns to Eli. "She's signing." He turns to me. "You're signing."

"That makes sense, it's her first language," Lorenzo signs but it's the woman's voice the rest of us hear. Dr. Harris turns to Lorenzo, pressing the pen up to his lips in contemplation, then nods in agreement.

"Yes, that does make sense," Dr. Harris confirms. "Memories and language are housed in different parts of the brain."

Sign is my first language? I ask Lorenzo, the woman puts my signs into words.

Yes, your parents are Deaf. You've been signing your whole life. He seems to light up at the opportunity to help me work through my loss of memories.

"Doc, what's going on?" Eli asks.

"She appears to be experiencing retrograde amnesia. Most likely there's been damage to her hippocampus or thalamus. We'll have to run some tests and scans to be sure," he explains. "There doesn't appear to be any other damage, only memory loss. Though, the tests will tell us more."

Eli looks devastated. Lorenzo looks hopeful. I'm just confused.

"Will I be able to get my memories back?" I ask Dr. Harris.

His lips press together as if he doesn't want to answer. "In most cases, it comes back after a few months or so. But I caution you not to get your hopes up, because in some cases, it never comes back."

"Is there a way to help it along?" Eli asks. He looks positively heartbroken.

"She'll need to stay here for at least a few more days," he starts, then addresses me. "Once you are released, you'll need to get back into your old routine as much as possible." He turns back to Eli. "Share pictures and stories as much as you can, it will help."

We'll help you through it, Scar, Lorenzo signs, then reaches over to hold my hand. I give him a thankful smile.

"We're all here for you, baby." Eli steps back close to me and grabs hold of my other hand. I give him a pursed smile.

My eyes dart back and forth between the two men. I feel trapped, smothered even, with both hands enclosed in theirs. I'm suddenly overwhelmed with the news, surrounded by people I don't know. Tears well in my eyes, and then stream down my cheeks.

"Don't cry, baby, we're going to get through this," Eli tries to console me, squeezing my hand tighter.

I pull my hands away from both of them to sign while I speak. "Can I have a few minutes alone, please?" Eli's lips turn down into a heartbroken frown. "I'm sorry," I say to him. "I know you only want to help me. I just... I'm just very overwhelmed right now."

Lorenzo fans his hand to get my attention. *We will be just outside, I'll text your mom and have her come too.*

Thank you.

Chapter 30
Lorenzo

Scar losing her memory should be sad, it should be devastating. For me, it might be a blessing. It could be a fresh start, a new opportunity to gain her trust and eventually her heart. At the very least, a chance to have my best friend back. I have to be exactly what she needs right now. I have to wait patiently for her to be ready to open up to me. The doctor said show her pictures, share memories, get her back into a routine. Guess who a big part of those things is. Yours truly.

Eli is pacing again. We're both out in the hall, trying to give her the space she asked for, but not too far away either. His pacing three days ago drove me nuts. Today, it amuses me. He's in panic mode, and I'm at ease. Scar is going to be okay. Even if she never regains her memory, she's alive and well. She's a blank slate, and I'm ready to write all over that blank slate.

He stops pacing and glares at me, then speaks. Bonnie is close by and immediately interprets for me. *Why the fuck do you look so happy?*

Scar is alive. She's going to be OK. I shrug my shoulders. *That doesn't make you happy?*

She doesn't know who I am, of course I'm not happy. He's still speaking.

After Bonnie finishes interpreting, I look back over at him to see his eyes narrow at me suspiciously. *She will remember. Just be patient and help her through it.* Being the supportive, positive force in Scar's life should start right now. I take a deep breath and decide right here and now that Eli is no longer my enemy.

He inhales deeply and blows it out. An attempt to relax, maybe. *Did you text Helen?* He signs for himself this time, changing the subject.

I nod. *She will be here soon.*

Thanks. His response is short and simple.

The fact that he's signing to me instead of using Bonnie tells me he's decided I'm not his enemy anymore either. Or at least not right now. Honestly, in an alternate universe where he and I aren't fighting over the same woman, I could see myself being friends with him. I shake the thought because I know it will never happen. The damage between us is too deep to mend.

When Helen arrives, she runs down the hallway, stopping short when she sees Eli and me outside of the room. Her face is scrunched in confusion, looking back and forth between us.

Why are you out here? What's wrong? Her signs are fast and frantic.

Scar is awake, but she's lost her memory. She doesn't know us, or herself, I explain. Saying it to Helen seems to upset Eli again, he chokes up and starts pacing. Again.

Helen's hands cover her mouth in shock. *I have to see her. Maybe she will know me.*

My lips purse, I know she won't recognize Helen, she hadn't even known her parents were Deaf. I just don't have the heart to tell her right now. *She asked us to leave because she was overwhelmed earlier. It's been a while, maybe she's feeling better,* I say instead.

Let's go. Helen is on a mission. She's not about to wait around.

I'm closest to the door, so I step in the doorway and knock to get her attention. *Your mom is here,* I sign when she looks over. *Is it alright if she comes in?*

She nods, giving an uneasy smile. *Sure.*

Scar, my sweet Scar. Helen's eyes fill up with tears when she sees Scar's eyes open for the first time in days. She still looks a mess, with her bandaged head and bruised face. I cringe at the sight, knowing my text could be responsible for it. But I push that thought to the back of my mind.

Hi, she signs, not sure what else to say. *You're my mom?*

Yes. She steps closer to the bed and holds her hands out, asking if she can hug her. Scar nods. *Oh sweetie, I'm so glad you're awake. How do you feel?*

My head hurts. She shrugs. *And I'm very confused, it's a little scary not knowing who I am.* She's honest with us.

I'm sure it's very scary, I say from the foot of the bed, trying to give her a supportive smile.

Her eyes move over to the door, and I turn to see Eli standing in the doorway, hovering. I purse my lips and nod my head at him to acknowledge him. *We're okay, let's not overwhelm her.* I try to keep my face friendly, not wanting him to get pissed and affect the energy in the room.

Thanks, Scar signs. Then she says something to Eli without signing. Bonnie is on it. She interprets from behind Eli in the doorway. Scar asked him to wait a few minutes, saying she would visit with him next.

My soul is beaming right now. She's more comfortable in the silence with her mom... and me.

Helen settles into a chair next to Scar's bed. She holds eye contact with her for a beat, just smiling from ear to ear. Scar seems uncomfortable with the exchange, but willing to try for Helen's sake.

Do you know what happened to me? Scar finally asks, breaking the 'silence.' *I know you said an accident. Do you know what happened, exactly?*

Yeah, I'm afraid you read a text message I sent you while driving and it distracted you, causing you to drive into a tree. I don't say that, instead I let a heavy sigh heave out of me. *We don't know for sure until we get the police report. But an officer came by the other day, he said most likely distracted driving. For some reason, you swerved off the road and slammed into a tree.*

She's pensive for a moment, as if she's trying to remember it.

You had surgery when they brought you in, and then the doctors put you in a coma to let the swelling in your brain come down, Helen adds. *Eli and Lorenzo stayed with you for three days, they never left your side.*

She turns to me and asks, *You're Lorenzo?* I nod. She points to the empty doorway. *He's Eli?*

Yes, you and Eli just got engaged. He asked you last Thursday, the night before the accident. It was your birthday, Helen explains. *It was so sweet. He's so sweet. You know he learned sign language to communicate with me.* My eye twitches seeing Helen so proud of Eli. I take a deep breath.

How are we connected? Scar asks me.

Our moms are best friends. We grew up together. You could say we are best friends too. Best friends really is the best way to put it. I know she's thought of me like a brother before, but I have never once thought of her as my sister.

Yes, you two are best friends, that's for sure, Helen adds with a proud smile.

Scar turns back to me and studies my face. *There is something about you, I don't know how to describe it...* she looks down at her hands, a look of awe takes over her expression. *It's so crazy that I know this language, it's instinctual. It's your language,* she says to Helen before turning to me. *And yours.*

And yours, Helen interrupts.

Scar contemplates that response for a moment. *I guess so,* she signs, then turns back to me again. *You said my parents are Deaf, where is my dad?*

Helen and I exchange sorrowful glances. This poor woman has woken up to the news that she doesn't even know who she is, now we have to tell her again that her father died. *Sweetie, he died sixteen years ago. He had a heart attack when you were just a teenager.*

Oh. Surprisingly, she doesn't seem too sad from the news. It must be a lot to take in. *The doctor said to share pictures with me.*

Helen pulls a small album from her purse. *Lorenzo asked me to bring some. We have many more at home, these were quick to find.* She hands the album over to Scar. *Keep it as long as you need.*

Thanks. Scar runs her fingers over the cloth cover of the album. It's a light blue and white checkered fabric with white embroidered letters that read 'family.'

I immediately recognize the album. Helen keeps it on a side table by the couch in her living room. I've looked through it many times. Inside, Scar will find pictures of her and her parents, my parents, me with my parents, and many pictures of her and I as kids. On the third page she looks up. *This is my dad?*

Helen and I both nod. Scar's dad was a ginger, like her, though the red hue of his hair was more pronounced than the faint orange of Scar's. *You look like him in many ways.* Helen smiles to herself at the thought. It's a sad smile, remembering the love of her life.

Scar's eyes squint, then it looks as if she let out a light giggle. Even with the bruised face and bandaged head, I can see the beauty that takes over when she laughs. *What's funny?* I ask, my expression reflecting my own amusement.

I just realized I don't even know what I look like.

The three of us share a laugh.

I can feel his presence in the doorway again. There's no doubt he heard our laughter and came to see what we could find so amusing under these circumstances. Scar looks over at him, her smile fades and she closes the photo album. *Would you give us a few minutes,* she asks Helen and me.

I muster up the most understanding expression I can pull from deep inside me and sign, *Of course, anything you need.* We share a moment of unspoken thanks. Then Helen and I leave to make way for Eli.

Chapter 31
Scarlett

"Hey, you," Eli says timidly once Lorenzo and Helen have left the room.

"Hey." The awkwardness is palpable. I fiddle with the ring on my finger while I study his face. He looks as though he's waiting for me to say something. "Sit down," I finally offer.

His long legs carry him across the room in a few slow strides and he takes a seat next to my bed. "How are you feeling?" he asks. His hands fidget in his lap like he's straining not to reach out and touch me.

"I would say I've felt better, but that would be cliché. Also, it's weird because right now, I can't remember feeling any other way." A hint of a smirk graces his lips as he catches on to my intended humor. "Honestly, everything hurts, yes, but the worst part is the confusion. It's very overwhelming."

"I can imagine," he says, giving me an empathetic smile. "I certainly don't want to overwhelm you. I love you very much, I only want to help you get better."

His dark eyes are sad. I take a moment to study him again. He's very attractive, I can see why whoever I was before I woke up would be attracted to him. He seems like a very nice man, sweet and caring. Maybe a little protective and overbearing. Right now, though, he's a complete stranger calling me 'baby' and telling me he loves me. "So, you're my fiancé?" I ask after a moment.

He nods, trying to smile. "Yes, the night before your accident I threw you a surprise birthday party for your thirtieth birthday. Thirty on Thursday, we said. You answered, 'one thousand times yes,' just like your best friend, Macie, said you would," he explains. "We were so happy that night." He closes his eyes and takes a deep breath. "We made love all night." His last sentence is almost a whisper.

My cheeks flush with his last comment, embarrassed by the idea of being intimate with this gorgeous stranger. Then I suddenly become aware of how awful I must look. From the few pictures I saw, I could see how he might find me attractive. However, the way my head throbs, I'm certain I am not attractive now. "I'm sorry I can't remember. I'm sure it was beautiful."

"It was very beautiful. The best night of my life." He seems to begin relaxing and reaches out to hold my hand. I let him interlace his fingers with mine, and he twists my ring back and forth between them.

"Do we live together?" I'm nervous at the idea of leaving this hospital to live with a man that I hardly know.

He shakes his head. "Not yet. You have your own house. I own a bar and live in the apartment above it." He owns a bar? That sounds cool. "We met at my bar. You came in with your coworkers for happy hour. I was instantly attracted to you, and I'm pretty sure you felt the same." He chuckles to himself. "You ordered the worst drink I had ever heard of. I made you my skinny margarita instead, and you were hooked."

His story makes me giggle a bit too. "What did I order?"

He inhales, visibly searching his brain for the rest of that memory. "Like tequila with club soda and lime. It sounded awful. You said it was your version of a low-carb margarita."

This is what the doctor ordered, sharing stories and memories. I'm quiet for a moment, trying to search my brain for that memory, but only hitting a brick wall. It washes sadness over me.

"That must be fun, owning a bar," I finally say after my failed attempt at recall.

"It can be. It can also be a lot of work. I have a really great bartender slash manager though, Ana, she's been taking care of the place for me since your accident."

"You haven't been home?" I ask. The thought shows how much he cares about me.

"Nope. I couldn't leave you. I practically begged the ICU nurse to let me stay there with you before they moved you into this room." He pulls my hand up to his lips and kisses the back of it. "You're my world, Scarlett."

My lips purse at his sweet words, though they make me a little uncomfortable. "How long have we been together?"

Half expecting him to say two years or more, he says, "Seven months. We started dating right before Christmas. We kind of fell hard and fast for each other." He chuckles a bit at the memory again. "I'm hoping I can make you fall in love with me again. That or remember how much you love me."

His hopefulness is endearing, so I smirk at him. Though, I'm not feeling quite as hopeful. "That sounds like a whirlwind romance," I say, attempting a joke.

"It was. And we had some battles to fight in the beginning." As soon as he finishes his comment, his lips fold inward as if he didn't mean to say it out loud.

"What do you mean? What battles?" I question.

He shakes his head. "I shouldn't have said that." His words are short and clipped.

"Well, you did. So…" My eyebrows cock up, silently requiring him to say more.

Inhaling slowly, he sits up and adjusts himself in the chair. "Lorenzo is in love with you too," he says through his exhaled breath.

There's more to the story, I can tell. "I see," is all I say.

Dr. Harris taps on the door, interrupting right on time. "How are we doing, Miss Scarlett?" he asks, walking over to check the numbers on the beeping machine by my bed again.

I have to admit, I'm a touch relieved by the interruption. "A bit overwhelmed, honestly. And everything hurts," I confess.

He turns his wrist, checking the time. "Well, I know you just woke up from a long nap, but perhaps some rest would do you good." He clears his throat and turns to Eli.

Eli doesn't take the hint. Dr. Harris cocks his eyebrows up at him, encouraging him to get the point. "I am kind of tired," I add. The irony isn't lost on me, being tired after a three-day nap. The truth is, I am tired, I also just really need to be alone with my thoughts for a while.

Eli's eyes dart between Dr. Harris and me. He finally gets it. "You're asking me to leave?" he asks Dr. Harris. The doctor nods and Eli turns to me. "Do you want me to leave?"

What an awful situation to be put in. I do, actually, want him to leave. However, I don't want to be the one to say it. "I'm kind of tired," I say once more, hoping that answer suffices, and I don't have to admit that out loud.

"I can assure you, she is out of the danger zone. We have an excellent nursing staff here who will take good care of her. You should go home, recharge and refresh. She'll be right here tomorrow," Dr. Harris suggests.

Eli looks absolutely heartbroken. "I can't leave her," he says to Dr. Harris, then turns to me. "I can't leave you." His voice is desperate, and his face is confused as if the idea is preposterous.

"Eli, I'll be okay. I just need some time to myself right now. Come back tomorrow, and we'll talk more," I offer. "Bring some things that could help with my memory of us. I would love to see them."

Letting out a disappointed sigh, he slaps his hands on his knees, then rises to his feet. "Okay, baby. If that's what you want." His words are heavy with heartbreak. "I get it, I do. It's just so hard."

"I know. Please, come back tomorrow." I attempt to give him a reassuring smile.

He nods, and before he turns to leave, he bends down and kisses my forehead. "I love you so much, Scarlett." His face lingers close to mine as if he wants to kiss my lips, he lets his head hang instead. Then lifts it back up and says, "I'll be back first thing in the morning."

"Thank you, Eli." I smile at him again. "Will you tell my mom and Lorenzo that I'm resting, and I'll see them tomorrow as well, please?" He nods, then slips out the door.

Chapter 32
Eli

Scarlett's awake. I should be over the moon happy. She's alive, she will be just fine. Except her memory is gone. Like I've been completely erased from her brain. It's killing me; eating me alive. I can't touch her, hold her, kiss her. I can't do anything to physically show her love, because to her, I'm a complete stranger.

It's still early afternoon, and I can't think straight. Going to the bar or even just up to my apartment would drive me insane with the questions and unease pulsing through me. Instead, I drive to the police station. It's the first time I've left the hospital since Scarlett was brought here in an ambulance. I've talked with the insurance company over the phone. My Jeep is at the shop, though I already know it will be declared totaled. I need to see if there's anything in that report that would help me to understand how Scarlett and my Jeep ended up wrapped around that tree. The longer I spent in that hospital room cooped up with Lorenzo, the more this suspicious feeling about him eats away at me. I have to shake the thought, there's no way he had anything sinister to do with this.

"Hi there, how can I help you?" The woman behind the plate glass window greets me with her friendly southern accent.

"My fiancée was in an accident last Friday on Ward Blvd. She's been in a coma in the hospital, and she just woke up today. This is the first time I've left since then." I feel like I'm babbling. She really didn't need to know all that information. "Anyway, I haven't seen the police report, and well, she was driving my Jeep, so I was hoping I could take a look at it."

"Oh, my goodness, I'm so sorry to hear that. Let me see what I can find out." She seems genuinely apologetic. "Do you have the vin number?"

I pull my wallet from my back pocket where I keep an extra copy of my registration and insurance cards. I rattle off the vin number while she taps at her keyboard.

"Thank you." She hums while her eyes scan over the screen in front of her. "Mm hmm. We have one right here. Are you Elijah Romero?"

"Yes, ma'am, that's me." I pull my driver's license from my wallet before she can ask for it to verify and slide it through the open tray at the bottom of the window.

"Thank you, sir." She looks over the ID then prints off the report. "Give me just a minute, I'll go get that for you."

The woman stands from her chair and makes her way to a large printer at the back of the room she's in and waits for the pages to finish printing. Then she shuffles back over to her seat in front of the window. "Oh dear," she says, looking over the first page of the report.

"What? What's wrong?" My heart races in anticipation, expecting to hear the worst news.

"This looks like it was quite an accident. Also, there's a note here," she starts to explain. "It appears there was a witness that stopped at the scene."

A witness? Most people just keep on driving when an accident happens. There's a part of me that is relieved to hear that one stopped. "What did the witness say?"

"Let me see." She runs her eyes over the document, then begins to read. "Ah, here we go. The witness stated that another vehicle had cut off someone in front of the Jeep and that the driver of the Jeep had plenty of time and room to brake safely, but that it appeared they did not brake until the last minute and swerved off the road to avoid collision."

"Why wouldn't she brake?" Though my question was meant to be for myself more than for her, she answers me anyway.

"Most likely distracted driving." She taps the small stack of papers back in line with each other before sliding them through the window tray.

"Thank you," I say, pulling them up quickly, anxious to read the report for myself.

"Sure, thing. I hope your fiancée recovers quickly. Is there anything else I can do for you today?" she offers kindly.

I shake my head. "No, ma'am. This is what I came for, have a good day."

I can't get back to Scarlett's car fast enough to read the report, though I don't find much more inclination of what happened outside of the witness statement. Another note on the last page catches my eye. Likely cause: distracted driving. Then it hit me, I had sent her that text message. Could it have been my text that took her eyes off the road? A sudden wave of guilt soars through me.

According to the report, my Jeep was taken to a shop downtown. Caliber Collisions is on my way home, so I throw the car in drive and head that way.

There's another friendly receptionist with that strong southern accent seated behind a desk to greet me when I arrive. "Hey there, how are you doing today?" She smiles up at me, smacking a wad of gum between her teeth.

"I've been better." I'm honest. "Listen, my Jeep was brought in here over the weekend after my fiancée was in an accident this past Friday. I just wanted to touch base with you all. I rushed to the hospital to be with her, it was towed in by the police department," I explain.

She takes some information from me and pulls up the file on her laptop. "I have a 2020 Jeep Rubicon, smoke gray." She gives me the make and model before tacking on the plate number.

"Yes, that's it." My hands support me on the counter as I instinctively attempt to lean forward to see the laptop screen. I don't have a good enough view to make out any pertinent information.

"Well, you know it's totaled, right? Has insurance contacted you?" she says matter-of-factly. Her index finger reaches up and tucks into her mouth, stringing out the gum and circling it around her finger.

"No, they have not, and yes, I know. All the airbags deployed."

"We've valued the damage—"

"I'm not worried about that, I'll call the insurance company and work that out with them. I'm curious though..." I pause because I know it sounds crazy. "Was there anything to suggest faulty equipment?"

"Oh, that would require a diagnostics report, insurance doesn't cover that." Her tone goes a bit flat. "It takes a few weeks, do you want that as well?"

Conspiracy theories run through my mind. I know I'm clutching at anything that could suggest that it wasn't my text message that distracted her. That it wasn't my fault. "What's the cost of that?"

Her head shakes. "It's a bit expensive." She shoves the gum back in her mouth and taps at the keyboard in front of her. "Fifteen hundred."

I let out a frustrated sigh. I could swing it, sure. But I think deep down I know it would be money wasted. "Thanks anyway," I say, defeated. Then I turn to head back home, my heart aching with the fear that this is all my fault.

The bar is fairly busy for a Monday evening when I arrive. Ana is helping Frankie behind the bar, though she has really slid well into the manager role recently. She stops what she's doing when she sees me come in the front door.

"Hey, boss. You're back!" She tries to sound happy, but her smile fades when she reads my body language. "What happened? Is Scarlett okay?"

Ana crosses the room and meets me halfway. I take one look at her concerned expression and every emotion inside of me pours out, a loud sob escaping my lungs. I'm completely unable to speak yet, only sob as the tears seep from my eyes.

"Hey... no... boss... come here." She pulls me in for a hug. I try to ignore the fact that some patrons have noticed and are starting to stare at our exchange. Ana notices too. "Come on, let's go to the office."

I nod and follow her across the room to the hallway that leads between the bar area and the kitchen. She opens the door to the small office tucked in the hallway, there's barely enough room for two people to sit. She guides me into my chair, then pulls the extra chair up so we are sitting knee to knee. "What's going on?"

Wiping my face with my hands, I take a deep breath to control my sobs. "She doesn't know who I am," I finally manage.

Ana gasps, her eyes wide with shock. "What? How?"

"She woke up this morning. She didn't know who anyone was, even herself. The doctor said retrograde amnesia, most likely from damage to the hippocampus or thalamus," I explain. I had read up on it when Scarlett sent Lorenzo and I to the hallway too.

"Oh, Eli," Ana breathes empathetically. "What's the prognosis?"

There's a clench in my chest, forcing me to take a deep breath before I speak again. "He said to share memories and photos, have her get back into a routine when she leaves the hospital. He warned us that in some cases, these patients never regain their memories." Saying those words out loud, reminding myself that she may never remember the best six months of my life, hits me like a bus. My head hangs between my knees, and I sob again. "And what's worse, I think I caused her accident with a text message I sent to her." Speaking that confession out loud breaks me to my core.

Ana reaches over and rubs my back, consoling me. "Shit, boss. That's hard." She lets me cry it out for a few moments, before speaking again. "Listen, I've got this place under control. You do what you need to do, I got you."

"Thanks, Ana. I appreciate you."

Chapter 33
Lorenzo

Scar is being released today. She's been at the hospital a full week since she woke up. The doctor finally cleared her to go home. He cautioned us not to let her do too much, that she would still be weak from the surgery and broken ribs. When I say us, I mean Helen, Eli, and I. We were all there for her discharge.

Eli wanted her to go home with him, of course. She wasn't comfortable with that. I can't even describe how elated I was when she told him no. The doctor said she should not be home alone yet either. So, she agreed to stay with her mom. I am over the moon. Helen might as well be my auntie, so I can and will be around as much as possible. If she had gone to Eli's apartment, I wouldn't have been able to see her at all. If she had gone home, Eli would have kept me from being there too. At Helen's, I'm family.

My web designer position at the agency is a pretty flexible gig, so I took the day off for Scarlett's discharge. Honestly, I've spent so much time at the hospital with her over the past week, they may as well have given me a bed. The doctor had said to show her pictures and share memories. I did just that. Every photo I have, every album I could collect from Helen's. I even have a box of mementos that I've collected over our lifetime together that remind me of her. Movie tickets, the corsage she wore the year I escorted her to prom, the playbill from the one musical she participated in her senior year, her charm bracelet. She may have left that one at my apartment and I never told her. Looking back, I remember when she was frantically looking for it.

When I arrived at the hospital, of course, Eli was already there. We've learned to tolerate each other's presence this week. He has accepted the fact that I hold more memories with Scar, and sharing those memories will only help her. The fact that it drives him absolutely insane isn't lost on me.

Scar still doesn't know any of us, but she's most comfortable with Helen, perhaps because she's female and motherly. Or maybe, like me, she's familiar from having been in her life for so long. Since Helen rode with me, Scar is riding with me back to Helen's house. Eli is following behind us.

We're here. I find her eyes in the rearview mirror and sign to her with a smile.

She looks out the window at the little bungalow that she spent the first twenty-four years of her life in. Her expression is sad, as if she's searching deep in her mind and just can't find where this house fits. She purses her lips and nods slowly. *It's cute.*

Helen tries to smile, but she has been weighed down by Scar's loss of memory. Her precious baby girl can't remember her. Scar is all Helen has in this world, outside of my family. I reach over and pat her knee reassuringly. *She will remember, she will.*

Helen's eyes glisten with wetness, though no tears fall. She smiles at me, thanking me for being here for her, for both of them. As if I would be anywhere else.

None of us make a move to get out of the car.

Eli parks behind us in the driveway and does not hesitate. He walks up and opens the trunk, pulling her bag out. Then he makes his way to the side of the car Scar is on and opens the door for her. He doesn't sign, but his lips read, "You ready?"

I'm watching in the mirror, Scar looks nervous. She reaches a shaky hand to take hold of Eli's outstretched hand and allows him to help her out of the car. Helen and I follow suit. As he supports her with an extended elbow toward the front door, I try to hold back the resentment that the sight stirs inside of me as I follow them up the walkway.

This is where I grew up? Scar asks once inside, taking in the sight of Helen's perfectly preserved living room. It's barely changed over the years. Scar and I spent many nights watching movies on this couch or doing homework at this coffee table together. Even though we went to different schools and had different classes.

Yes, your whole life until you bought your house a few years ago. Helen's expression is forced, an attempt to comfort while hiding her own sorrow. She doesn't even realize how strong she is in this moment.

Eli, still holding Scar's bag, points toward the stairs. *I'll take this up to your room,* he offers and then trots up the stairs when Scar nods.

Can I get you something? Helen offers. *Some coffee? You always loved my coffee.*

Coffee sounds nice, Scar accepts with a smile. Then her face contorts into an expression of utter embarrassment. Her hands cover her mouth for a moment, then she signs. *I'm sorry, is that rude? To say it 'sounds' nice?*

Helen and I exchange glances. She's signing just as she always has, that part of her brain is perfectly intact. Though she's asked questions and said a few things that let us know she's lost her knowledge of Deaf culture. We both laugh, not a hard laugh, just an amused chuckle. *It's fine, really. Deaf people say it all the time, but some would be offended. Not us,* I assure her. Helen excuses herself to the kitchen to fix the coffee.

She looks relieved. *It's so weird how I can sign and understand it,* she marvels. She's been baffled by it since she woke from the coma.

I give her my signature pursed lips and shake my head. *Not really, it makes sense. The doctor said the part of your brain that controls language is fine. ASL is your first language.* My shoulders pull back with pride as I sign that last part.

Scar's lips purse too and her eyes look up as she nods, expressing her agreement with what I said. *Makes sense, I guess.* Her eyes look over to the couch, and she looks exhausted already.

Here, come here, sit down. I hold my hand out for her and guide her over to the couch. She winces as I help her to a seated position. *Did I hurt you?*

No, no. I'm just still very sore. She smiles up at me. *Thanks.*

Neither one of us signs, I simply eye the spot on the couch next to her, tilt my head forward and raise an eyebrow. She understands I'm asking permission to sit next to her, she nods and pats the cushion. I take a seat just as Eli trots back down the stairs. His expression somber when he sees me seated beside Scar. I don't budge. We make eye contact, and he glares at me. I give him an innocent smile and twitch my brows up subtly. He knows we have to be on our best behavior for Scar. Not that I've been keeping score, but right now it feels like Eli – 0, Lorenzo – 3. At least.

Can I get you something, baby? It looks like he uses his voice when he talks since some of his signs are missing.

Scar shakes her head, she uses her voice too, but it's easy to read her lips when she says, 'No, thank you.' Her eyes dart back and forth between us. She's anxious. I don't slide away from her, but I do lean back on the couch to soften my presence next to her. It's difficult to resist the urge to stretch my arm across the back of the couch behind her.

Helen returns from the kitchen with a tray holding four mugs of coffee, a small carafe of creamer, and a cup of sugar. She sets it down on the coffee table, then prepares Scar's coffee the way she's always taken it. *This is how you liked your coffee before. I hope you still like it this way,* she says after handing the mug over to Scar.

Helen takes her usual seat in the armchair next to the couch as Scar sips the coffee. We all wait for her response. *It's perfect,* she signs with one hand. She finally relaxes and sits back on the couch too, now shoulder to shoulder with me.

Excitement rushes through me at the touch. As much as I want to stay here, shoulder to shoulder with her, I know she needs space. I slide over just an inch, then lean forward, and prepare my own coffee. Eli glares at me as he scoops two spoonfuls of sugar into his cup, then he takes the armchair on the other side of Helen.

There are a few moments where no one says anything. We just sit here in each other's presence sipping coffee. Scar sets her cup down.

I think maybe I should rest for a bit. Please don't feel like you have to put your lives on hold for me.

Glances bounce around the room. She's right, though, being here like this is only creating ever-present awkwardness. It's forced, unnatural even. It's like we're suspended here waiting for her memories to come rushing back at any moment. Eli's face morphs into heartbreak, his chest fills with a long, deep sigh. Before he has a chance to exhale and speak, I turn to Scar. *Let me help you upstairs to rest.* She smiles at me agreeably.

Eli's on his feet. *I'll help her,* he insists.

Scar's eyes pan over to Eli, and her smile fades. The competition between us is evident, and clearly disturbing her. *I appreciate both of you trying to help me, really I do. I think it would be best if I spend time with you both separately. This thing between you,* she motions her finger between us, *it makes me very uncomfortable.* Her signing cadence is very English, making it obvious she's using her voice for Eli.

I suppress my annoyance and smile supportively at her. *That's probably a good idea,* I agree, knowing that keeping the peace is what's best for her right now.

Eli says something, but I don't bother to read his lips. The two of them have a quick spoken exchange. *I'm sorry, Eli, thank you for understanding,* Scar signs. He stands, a defeated look on his face, and makes his way to the door. Helen follows him over to see him out.

Now I wish I had read their lips. I'm dying to ask her what happened, but I don't want to be an overbearing presence. I want to make sure she continues to be comfortable around me. Once the door closes behind Eli, I turn to Scar. *Want me to help you up the stairs?* I offer again, praying she says yes.

Her lips flatten into a tight smile, and she nods. Mentally, I add another point to my scorecard. I stand, offering a hand for her to hold as I help her to her feet. She takes hold of my elbow and I guide her up the stairs. When I open her old bedroom door, she stops there for a moment and takes in the sight of it. I remember helping her paint the room this pale rose color in high school, I hope to help her remember it too.

This was my room? she asks, though her question seems to be more rhetorical.

Yes, I helped you paint it when we were teenagers. You asked your mom if you could paint because you didn't like the yellow color it was before. She said if you did the work, that was fine. I share a bit of the memory and Scar's eyes trail around the room, then back to me. *You were so excited, you practically begged me to help you. Really, you didn't have to beg. I was always willing to do any and everything for you.*

She smiles, then steps forward, heading toward the bed. I guide her over and help her sit down. *You've been in my life a long time,* she muses. It's not a question, more of an observation.

Your whole life, Scar.

I'm sorry I can't remember. Her eyes hold my gaze for a beat, then flicker down to her hands fidgeting in her lap. She looks up at me again. *There is something very familiar about you though. It's almost like my mind doesn't remember you, but...* She pauses mid sign, her hands held hesitantly in position.

But what?

Slowly, she allows her hands to continue. *But my soul does.*

My heart flutters at her words. I take the seat next to her and our bodies turn to face each other, her knee touching mine. Everything inside of me is on fire. *That makes me so happy to know, Scar. I want to help you remember everything. Soul and mind.* I do want to help her. But I also know that if and when she remembers everything, she'll remember when she cut me out of her life. I have to make her fall in love with me before that happens. Maybe then it will be easier for her to forgive.

I study her green eyes for a moment, desperate to kiss her. She holds my gaze, setting my insides on fire. Scar's still in there. Her memories are gone, but everything I love about her, it's in there. Even through her timid unease, her beautiful personality is seeping out. God, I want to kiss her so badly. Touch her. Hold her. Right now, I have to push what I want to the side and focus on her needs. Smothering her won't help her get through this.

I pat my hands on my knees and stand to my feet. *I should go, let you rest.*

Her lips curl into a thankful smile. *Thank you for everything,* she signs. When I reach the doorway, I turn and make eye contact with her again, allowing space for any final words. She picks her hands up. *Come back tomorrow, I'd love for you to tell me more stories about growing up.*

You don't even have to ask. I wink before I trot down the stairs with an extra pep in my step.

Chapter 34
Scarlett

Helen is possibly the sweetest woman on the planet. I can see she is trying to give me space, understanding that I don't know her as my mom right now. Yet, she has this innate need to nurture me. Coming home from the hospital last night had been incredibly uncomfortable for all of us. I'm sure I'll hear all about how Eli and Lorenzo started vying for me eventually, but right now, no one wants to talk about it and it's just so painful to be around.

The only word to describe Eli's face when I asked him to leave is devastated. It's quite obvious he loves me deeply. I can see that. It's also quite obvious that Lorenzo loves me. He seems to be showing more patience than Eli, though. It's like he's waiting for me to allow him to care for me. Eli wants me to care for him right this moment.

With Helen, though, it's so much easier to be around her. Sure, she loves me as much as any mother would love her daughter, but that feeling is almost comforting. Not suffocating.

Before I go downstairs, I turn the hot water on in the shower, letting the tiny bathroom steam up. I stare at my reflection in the mirror. My face still has fading bruises around one eye that tint the skin around it a greenish yellow color. My pale orange hair is greasy and matted against my head. The entire week I was in the hospital I hadn't been allowed to wash it. The doctor said I could finally wash it today. This woman in the reflection, I can see that she is quite pretty, when she doesn't look like she barely survived a car wreck. Perhaps a little heavier than the models on the magazine covers the nurse had brought me in the hospital, but still beautiful.

I wish I knew her. I wish I knew who Scarlett Reese, Scar as Lorenzo calls me, was. I wish I knew who she is. The steam circling the air fogs the mirror and my reverie disappears along with my reflection. I step into the hot water and let it engulf me. There's a set of shampoo and conditioner on the wire rack that hangs from the shower head. I open the bottle of shampoo and breathe in the scent. Coconut and vanilla. I close my eyes and breathe it in again, hoping to unlock memories with my senses, though it doesn't seem to work. Reaching up to wash my hair is painful, my ribs are still terribly sore, but the soapy suds in my hair combined with the hot water feels absolutely amazing.

Feeling refreshed from my shower, I find a pair of leggings and an oversized hoodie in the chest of drawers. Helen had gone to my house and gathered some things for me to have while I stay here with her. I make a note to ask to go see my house, even if I don't go to stay there for a while.

As my bare feet pad down the stairs, I can smell bacon frying on the stove. In the kitchen, I find Helen bouncing back and forth between slathering butter on toast and tending to the pans of frying food. Not wanting to startle her, I wait awkwardly in the doorway. She catches a glimpse of me from the corner of her eye, and as I expected, is startled to see me.

She clutches at her chest. *Scar, you scared me. Good morning.*

I'm sorry, I wasn't sure how to let you know I was here, I apologize. *The food smells amazing.*

She waves her hand through the air in a humble gesture, like she's brushing away the compliment. *You can flick the lights next time. It's a common way to get attention from across the room. One that I would expect and not be surprised by.* She pulls the pan of eggs from the burner and holds it up, raising her eyebrows.

Yes, please. I take a seat at the little round table tucked up next to a bay window. Helen divvies up the food, then takes a seat across from me. *I have a lot to learn, or remember, I guess.*

She waves the thought off with her hand again. *You will,* she simply says, no doubt in her mind. *What would you like to do today?* She takes a bite of her eggs, which prompts me to try mine. They're delicious. At this moment in time, the best I've ever had.

My shoulders slink up and shrug. *Really, I don't know. What would Scar usually do?*

Today is Tuesday, she would go to work. Helen checks her watch. *She would have been at work a couple of hours already.* She smiles to herself, it's a look of pride knowing her daughter is punctual. Then she looks up at me, an idea hidden behind her eyes, but she shakes her head. *The agency would be too overwhelming. We'll save that for another day.*

Yes, I agree. I'm not ready to see all those people who will know me, and I won't know them. But I would like to go see my house, I suggest instead.

That is a good idea. After breakfast?

Sure.

My house is about a ten-minute drive from Helen's. It's a brick rambler, a bit longer than Helen's bungalow, with a wide driveway shaded by a tall oak tree. The outside of the house speaks to me. Honestly, I don't remember what my style is, but this feels like it fits. And I haven't even seen the inside. There is a car in the driveway, and I wonder if it's mine.

Macie is here. She's your best friend, Helen says after pointing to the sedan. *She's been taking care of your cat.*

I have a cat? And a best friend. *I think I would like to meet my best friend.* The idea of meeting one person, who isn't in love with me, but has known me a very long time soothes me.

Helen is encouraged by my receptive response. *Good, dear. Let's go.*

Inside, a black cat trots over to us by the door. He circles between my legs and meows at me. His throat is rumbling from his loud purrs as he presses his head against my calves. "Hi, sweet kitty," I say out loud to him. My voice seems to encourage his welcoming greeting.

"Scarlett?" A woman with a milk chocolate complexion and curly black hair rushes out of an archway to the right of us. "Scarlett, you're home?" She looks as though she could run across the room to hug me, though she is clearly restraining herself.

I use my voice to talk to her but find my hands moving along with the signs as well. It makes me wonder if this was an innate response and something Scar did often. "I'm not home exactly, I'm out of the hospital, but staying with Helen for now," I explain. "She said you're Macie, my best friend?"

She nods feverishly. "We've been friends since we were kids. Like first grade, I think. I mean, we're practically sisters." Her face twists from a bright, excited smile, to a disquieting frown. "They said you've lost your memory?" I notice she's signing while she talks too.

"It seems so." I'm not sure what else to say.

We will help her get it back, Helen says to Macie and then turns to me. *Macie can share many memories with you. She would be a good person to spend time with,* she suggests.

Giving Macie a quick once over, I decide that Helen is right. The idea of spending time with Macie is encouraging. She could help share memories with me but not be vying for my affection at the same time. Sounds like just what the doctor ordered.

You understand sign pretty well. Macie turns her voice off to gauge my comprehension of her signs.

I nod. *It's kind of mind-blowing, really.* I give her a demure smile. *I would like that, spending time with you to help get my memory back.*

I would love to help! Her signs are big and enthusiastic, much like the glowing smile that takes over her face.

You're not working today? Helen asks.

I had a break between assignments, so I came by to check on Binx. My schedule is empty after 2:00 today, she explains.

There was one sign I hadn't recognized, but she pointed to the cat when she signed it. *Is this my cat's name?* I ask, producing the sign as well.

Yes, his name sign. Macie smiles, she signs it again and then spells, *B-I-N-X.*

"Binx." I speak the name to hear how it sounds. *Cute name.*

You picked it, Helen says, and we all share a laugh.

When I'm done for the day, why don't we meet up here and spend the afternoon together? Macie suggests.

Great idea. Then I can go into the office and get a few things done, Helen agrees.

Sounds like a plan. For the first time since I woke up in the hospital, I realize I am looking forward to something.

Chapter 35
Scarlett

Spending time with Macie is exactly what I need. Being around her is so easy, it's almost relaxing. There is zero pressure. She does seem to hesitate in our interactions, waiting for me to give some sort of approval. It only helps me to feel at ease though, as if she's trying not to overwhelm me.

We're sitting on my couch looking through high school yearbooks. From what she told me, we went all the way through school together, graduating from Fike High School. We weren't in the 'A' crowd, but also not in the 'loser' crowd, as she called it, either.

"Oh, this yearbook has a picture of you on stage when we did that musical, *Grease*. You were picked to play Frenchie since you were the only natural redhead," Macie reminisces, flipping through the pages to find the picture.

The pages whip by until she lands on the one she's looking for. There I am in a knee-length pencil skirt with a pink, silk jacket, my orange hair curled and pinned. "Oh wow." I pull the book closer to my face to get a better look. "Was that the only time I did a play at school?"

"Yeah, you joined the drama club freshman year as part of the stage crew. They practically begged you to audition for *Grease* because Mr. Hardy heard you singing while you were cleaning up the stage after club one day. And, you know, the red hair," Macie explains.

"Were you in the drama club?"

She laughs heartily. "Yes, stage crew with you. I was no actress." Her lips purse as her eyes look up toward her furrowed brow. "It's funny, now as an interpreter I feel like I have to channel the inner actress I never thought I could be."

"Really? Interpreting requires acting?" I question, I really don't know a thing about interpreting and am a bit curious.

"Well, when you voice for someone, you have to add the inflection and intended affect. Even when you take spoken words and put them into sign language. Oftentimes, there aren't exact signs for a concept, you really just act it out," she explains. "You don't think about it when you talk for yourself, but when you are talking for someone else, you have to intentionally include their affect. It's a lot like acting."

"That's pretty interesting," I say. "I wonder why I didn't become an interpreter. I'm fluent in sign, right?"

Macie's laugh reverberates through the room. "Because you spent your whole life interpreting for your parents. At least that's the reason you gave me. By the time you graduated from high school and went off to college, you hated the idea of becoming an interpreter."

My shoulders shrug as I contemplate the reasoning. "That makes sense," I concede. There's a short lull in the conversation, so my eyes avert hers and look at the pages of the yearbook still open in my lap. "Did Lorenzo go to school with us?"

She shakes her head. "No, he went to ENCSD just like your moms. He's lucky that he grew up here and didn't have to live on campus."

"ENCSD?" I question, having never heard the abbreviation before.

"Oh, duh, I'm sorry." She slaps her hand on her forehead. "Eastern North Carolina School for the Deaf. It's here in town. Helen and Alana, Lorenzo's mom, they met there as kids," she expands.

"But he grew up with me? Like, we spent a lot of time together as kids?" I've been wanting to find out more about that relationship without talking to him directly.

"You guys were basically inseparable. I mean, your moms are inseparable. Your families did everything together." She stands from the couch and crosses the room, retrieving a photo album from a bookshelf near the fireplace. "Here, this has pictures from every family vacation you all had growing up."

Forget Me Not

The binder is thick with the word 'family' stitched on the cover. I open it to the first page of photos and see a very young Helen with the ginger man from the other album. The little girl who I assume is me couldn't be more than two years old. The three of us are standing, feet in the sand, with a backdrop of puffy white clouds over a turquoise ocean. The second page has more people. The other man and woman look like younger versions of Alana and Corbin, Lorenzo's parents who I met at the hospital last week. The little boy, only a couple years older than me, with a mop of dark brown hair and tanned skin has Lorenzo's eyes. Eyes that seem to look right through me, deep into my soul. Even from this picture. As the pages turn, the people in the photos age before my eyes. The backdrops change, but the people remain the same six people. Until there are only five. I close the album, having had too much stimulation.

Macie touches my arm. "I know, it's sad when you get to the years after your dad passed."

Although I am sure it is sad for Scarlett to see photos of her family after her dad passed. Physically, I am Scarlett, I just don't have her memories yet. I give Macie an empathetic smile. "We were basically inseparable, but never dated?" I inquire further.

Her head shakes. "Nope. He took you to senior prom because you wanted to go but didn't want to go without a date. You always viewed him as an older brother of sorts, honestly." She gets quiet and her smile fades. "Scar, you were very much in love with Eli. *Are* very much in love with Eli." She corrects her tense. It's as if she can read my mind.

My lips press together, and I cover my face with my hands, almost groaning into them. "I just don't know him, like at all," I finally say. "I know he cares for me; it's written all over his face. But he's treating me... I don't know, too intimately... but for me, he's a perfect stranger."

"Aren't we all strangers right now?" she points out. It's a valid point, I suppose.

"Yes and no." She eyes me quizzically. "I don't know how to describe it. There's something... very familiar... and almost comforting about Lorenzo. I think it's in his eyes." My words come out slowly. "Being around Eli makes me... it's like...it's like he wants me to be someone I'm not. At least not right now."

Macie's eyes are sad. "I'm sure that's very confusing," she reassures me, validating my feelings. "Might I make a suggestion?" I nod without a verbal response. "What if you express that to Eli, maybe take things back to the 'get to know you' phase. He is a very respectful man, if you tell him how you're feeling, he'll back off and take things slow with you."

"You think so?"

Her head nods rapidly. "I know so."

"Would you do me a favor?" I ask after a moment of thought. She nods. "Would you take me to see Eli before you take me back to Helen's house?"

Chapter 36
Eli

*T*uesday evenings are never too busy at the bar. After what Scarlett said to me last night, I'm not sure I even want to go downstairs and open up. Ana has been a huge help since the accident, and she doesn't seem to mind at all, but I do feel a little guilty taking advantage of her willingness. It's just after three o'clock in the afternoon and the bar opens in an hour, so I need to get myself downstairs to set up.

Carlos and Jim are in the kitchen already opening up the line when I finally get my ass down to the bar. Frankie is here too, and the sight of him tempts me to head back up and hide in my apartment for another night.

"Hey, boss," he greets me. "How you holding up?"

I grunt at him. I open up to Ana often, she's like a sister to me. Frankie and I, on the other hand, never really got that close. "I've been better." I decide to add as I start pulling chairs down from their perch on the tables.

"How's Scarlett?" he asks cautiously.

A lump forms in my throat, causing my eyes to sting with tears. "She still has no idea who I am, and I don't want to talk about it." I know it's not Frankie's fault, and he doesn't deserve my tone. Not that I can control my tone right now anyway.

Frankie takes the hint, and we finish opening up in silence. Just like clockwork, when I turn the deadbolt to unlock the front door, I can see Scarlett's fiery hair on the other side of the frosted glass. My mind immediately fills with images of my memories of the last time she was in this bar with me. The night she agreed to marry me, and I made love to her on top of the bar. The lump in my throat grows heavier knowing she has no recollection of that very intimate moment between us. I push the door open and breathe in her scent as she slides past me through the doorway.

When she's only two feet inside the door, she turns back to face me. "Hi."

"Hey, you." Clearly, I was making her uncomfortable before, so I choose my words carefully now. "I'm glad you're here, how are you?" The urge to pull her into me and wrap my arms around her is unbearable. Instead, I stand there with my hands shoved deep in my pockets, shifting my weight awkwardly between my legs.

"Helen took me to see my house today, and I met Macie. I'm told she's my best friend," she tells me. There's a hint of a smile on her face as she speaks. "I spent most of the day there and she shared some memories from when we were kids," she explains.

"That's great." I try not to sound too enthusiastic. "Macie is really sweet. I'm sure she was glad to spend that time with you."

"It was nice," she concedes.

We stare at each other for a moment before her eyes shy away from me. It's obvious that she's still uncomfortable around me. "Would you like to come in and sit down?" I offer, motioning toward a booth not too far from the door.

"Sure." She follows me over to the booth and slides into the side that faces the door. Usually, I prefer to sit facing the door, but in this moment, I know she needs it more than I do.

"So, what's up?" I know there's a reason she's here, even though she hasn't expressed it yet. "Can I get you something? Water, food, anything?"

Her head shakes immediately. "No, thank you." I watch as her hands fidget with each other, wringing her fingers together like knots. "I... um... I wanted to see your bar, where we met," she finally spits out. "I asked Macie to bring me by before she takes me back over to Helen's." Her eyes wander around the room, taking in the scenery, they squint as she digs deep into her brain to find the folder that holds these memories.

"Does it look familiar?" I ask hopefully, though I already know the answer.

Her head shakes again. "Eli, I'm sorry about last night," she blurts out. "I think I was a little harsh."

"No, no, you don't need to apologize." Her words are burned into my brain because they reminded me so much of the note that Lorenzo had left me shortly after we met. *I need you to back off a little.* Boy did that sting. "I know this is all very overwhelming for you. I do. I get it." I want to reach out and touch her hand, but I don't. Taking a deep breath, I debate with my next words before spitting them out. "It's hard for me too."

She nods solemnly. "I know it's hard for you too. I get it. In your mind we just got engaged and are very much in love. For me, it's like I'm meeting you for the first time. I asked Macie to bring me here because she had made a suggestion, and I think it would be very helpful for me."

"I'm all ears." I know Macie has my back, so I am very curious to hear what she suggested. Whatever it is, I trust she has my best interest in mind.

"When you call me 'baby' and say you love me, I know you're feeling that in your heart. For me... it's like you're a stranger talking to me in an intimate way... it really... makes me feel... uncomfortable."

Her words stab at my heart, but I'm glad she's opening up. "I'll do whatever you need me to, Scarlett. I–" I start to say, 'I love you,' but swallow my words. "What do you need from me?"

Her hands are still wringing on the table, flipping the ring around her finger, and she stares at them, then brings her eyes up to meet mine. "Can we start over? Like we just met?" Her words rush out like a quick exhale of air she'd been holding in.

It takes everything in me to swallow that heavy lump in my throat. I made her fall in love with me once. In fact, it was easy for us to fall in love with each other. I can do it again. "Sure, Scarlett, anything you need." I muster the friendliest smile I can, though I'm sure it's filled with fear.

"Thanks, Eli." The next part shatters my heart. She slowly slides the ring off her finger and places it on the table between us. "Please hold on to this until we get back to that place."

My lungs hold all the air inside me, refusing to breathe as she stands from the table. Stinging tears threaten to slide down my cheeks, and I will myself to be strong in front of her. Slowly, I let the air out of me and stand to walk her to the door. "Can I give you a hug?"

She shakes her head. "Not yet." She pauses at the door with her hand poised to push through it. "Where did we go on our first date?"

"We went on a walk around Lake Wilson." Vivid memories of that day flood my mind, and I'm crushed knowing hers is still blank.

"Take me there again? This weekend?" she suggests.

"It would be my pleasure." I try to smile through the pain of restraining myself from touching her.

A slight smile spreads over her lips. It's the first smile she's given me since she woke up. With it, I have a renewed sense of hope that she'll be back in my arms soon. Though, not soon enough.

Chapter 37
Lorenzo

At Scar's request, I went back to work. She asked us not to put our lives on hold for her. Considering I'd taken a lot of time off over the past couple of weeks while she was in the hospital, I am a bit backed up at work. Who knew a web designer job would actually entail a lot of work. Well, day to day, it doesn't. When I slack, it adds up. That and the freelance gigs I still do on the side. Needless to say, going into the office this morning makes me realize just how much I need to be here.

James is the first to come check on me, or Scar really, I think. He flicks the switch on the wall, flashing the lights to grab my attention. *Hey, you're back at work.*

My eyes squint at him, not sure why he's pointing out the obvious. *Yeah, Scar went home last night. She encouraged us to get back to our normal routine.*

How is she? he asks, stepping through the doorway and taking a seat across from my desk.

My shoulders shrug and I scrunch my nose. *She still doesn't remember anything.* I don't mean for it to happen, but I feel the smile that takes over my lips.

James notices it too. *What's that smile for?* He's very intuitive, also because he grew up with Deaf parents, he's quite skilled at reading body language and facial expression.

Before I started working here, I knew James on an acquaintance level. He had interpreted for me a few times over the years. I would never have pegged us as friends though, considering we didn't have much in common and we've never really bonded over the years. Since I started working here, I've come to trust James more than I thought I would. Especially since he's been rooting for me all along. *There's something promising, but I don't know how to describe it. It's kind of like she's more comfortable around me and she doesn't want Eli around.*

James' eyebrow cocks, his interest piqued. *That is interesting.* His signs are slow and drawn out, something I've noticed he does often for dramatic effect. *How is Eli taking that?*

My chest tightens, empathy for what Eli is going through flashing through me, along with a touch of guilt for my own hopeful feeling. *It's driving him insane.*

You know, she will get her memories back, right?

He had to let his realist side out and ruin the moment. I shrug one shoulder. *Maybe. The doctor said sometimes they never come back.*

All amusement leaves his face. *Bless her heart. I hope she does get them back eventually. And you should too.*

His words hit me like a brick in the face. He's right, and now I feel like a total asshole. Hoping that she never remembers when she cut me out of her life isn't fair to her. It's selfish. I know that. *I just have to get her to fall in love with me before that happens.*

True. You could certainly try. His stoic face dons an unreadable expression. He stands and walks toward the door, turning back to me before he leaves. *When she's ready to see people, please let me know.*

I will.

Around lunchtime, Dad comes into the office. Working with him was one of the pulls to not join the family business, but since he is an interpreter, he's hardly ever in the office. Because of that, I've actually come to enjoy seeing him when he is around.

Hey, Zo. He waves his arm from the doorway. *Glad to have you back in the office.*

Thanks, it's good to be back. There is some truth to that. The nine to five life I had dreaded so much has grown on me.

I saw Helen in her office, that must mean Scar is doing well. My head jerks back at the news. I would have thought Helen would stay home a few more days with Scar.

Scar did say last night that she didn't want us to put our lives on hold for her. Maybe she convinced Helen to come to work. This is what I tell myself. I believe it. Scar doesn't want to be babied.

She invited us to dinner tonight, said Scar approved.

A smile spreads across my lips. *Can't wait.*

With a bottle of wine in one hand and a bouquet of white roses tucked into the crook of my elbow, I ring Helen's doorbell a few minutes after six o'clock. My parents' car is already in the driveway, so I know I am the last to arrive. Only a few seconds pass before the door swings open and there stands Scar. The bright smile on her face and the visible sigh of relief that escapes her lungs makes me swoon, almost bringing me to my knees.

You're here! Thankfully, she's more excited to see me than she has been in a long time. I can't help but take a once over, her legs are bare under a pair of loose linen shorts, her perfect breasts peek out over the rim of her tank, but her shoulders are covered by an oversized cardigan. She looks so casual and comfy, just like the Scar I've spent many movie nights with over the years. No matter how hard I try, the sight of her still warms me, every time.

I point to the flowers with my free hand before signing, *For you.*

For me? Her face lights up and she takes them from my arm, then steps back from the doorway. *They're beautiful, thank you! Come in, come in.*

Did they start without me? I ask after she closes the door behind me.

She shakes her head. *Only wine. Everyone is out back on the patio. Come on.* She leads me through the living room and into the kitchen. *I'm glad you're here. I kind of felt out of place with just the parents. They are all very nice though.* She finds a vase in one of the cabinets and arranges the flowers in it.

Once her attention is back on me, I circle my index finger toward the back door to reference my parents and Helen sitting outside. *They all love you, Scar. Like family.* There's an open bottle of wine on the counter, so I pull two glasses from the cabinet and hold one up to ask if Scar would like a glass.

I have one out back, thank you. I realize this is the first time she's probably had wine since she woke up without memories, which would explain why she's less timid and more outgoing. More like the Scar I know and love. The thought brings a smile to my face, and I can feel myself relaxing more.

Mom shuffles in the back door as I'm pouring myself a glass of wine. *Zo! You're here!* She's at least on her third glass based on the smile that occupies her face. She corners the island to hug me. *We've been sharing stories with Scar from when you were kids. Oh, how I enjoy reminiscing.*

Nothing embarrassing, I hope. I can feel my brows pinch together as I eye my mother. She's clearly intoxicated enough to share any and all of the embarrassing stories of our childhood.

Scar's face erupts with laughter. God, I miss that face. *She did tell me about the one Halloween where I insisted on being Little Red Riding Hood and made you go as the wolf but dressed in the grandma's clothes.*

I'm glad you find that funny. That memory actually is funny, not embarrassing, I don't mind that it was shared at all. *Does she have pictures too?*

Mom nods. *You know I do. Come on.*

We file out through the back door and find Dad and Helen seated at the large round wooden table. The string lights that cross over the patio are on, and it smells as though the charcoal grill is fired up, ready for whatever Helen has planned to cook. Helen is the first to stand and hug me, Dad waves from the other side of the table.

Can I help with anything? I offer Helen after she pulls away from the hug.

Her eyes widen as her eyebrows pull up with revelation. *How are your grilling skills?*

Champ, I sign with a cocky grin.

Good, you can grill the steaks!

Being grill master really only means standing over the grill and occasionally flipping the steaks. Scar joins me a few minutes after our parents shift back into their conversation. We each have our glasses of wine set on the deck railing next to the grill, a beautiful sunset paints the sky behind them. From my point of view, I can 'eye drop' on the conversation happening around the table, while Scar's attention is turned toward me. This scene right now is like my dream come true.

How do you like your steak? I ask Scar. My question is more of a formality, I know she likes her steak medium. Then it occurs to me, maybe Scar doesn't know how she likes her steak at all.

She laughs, clearly feeling at ease from the wine. *Actually, I don't know. I don't remember eating steak,* she confesses.

My lips curl into a confident smile. *Don't worry, I know how you like your steak.*

Do you? She's intrigued.

Yup. Scar, I know almost everything about you. I can't help but notice how relaxed she is with me right now, and I am absolutely eating it up.

She smiles over the rim of her wine glass that she lifts to her lips to take a sip. This is the first time I notice it. Her left hand is bare, there's no ring. I feel my brows clench together, giving away the fact that something caught my eye. *What's up?*

Damn, she still has the innate ability to read facial expressions so well. I shake my head and purse my lips. *Nothing.* She eyes me, demanding an answer. Demanding is too harsh a word because she's absolutely fucking adorable right now. *I just noticed your ring is gone.*

Oh. Her eyes trail down to her hand, and she rubs her ring finger with her right hand for a moment. *I felt awkward with it on. I don't know who I am, or who Eli is, yet I'm wearing an engagement ring?*

Makes sense. I nod in agreement. *Where is the ring?* My curiosity presses for more information.

She exhales a long, slow breath before responding. *I gave it back to Eli.*

I've never heard angels sing. I've never heard anyone sing for that matter. But there is a choir of angels sounding off in my brain right this very moment. *You called off the engagement?*

Not exactly. Her eyes shy away from me, gazing down at her flip-flopped feet.

Bending over slightly, I wave my hand in her line of sight to get her to look back up at me. *It's okay, you don't have to talk about it.*

Her lips press into a thankful smile. *I just told him it felt awkward to be engaged when I have no memories of our relationship. So, I asked him to start over with me.*

I see. She hasn't given up on him completely. That's fine, I'm already two steps ahead of him. I'm here now. Where is he? Yep, that's fine. She can start over with him while I make her fall in love with me. At least this time around she's giving me an equal shot.

Chapter 38
Scarlett

*E*ach day it gets a little easier. Not knowing who I am, or my previous life experiences is still daunting. What makes it easier is the people I have in my life. I am surrounded by amazing, kind hearted, supportive people. After spending the evening with Helen's best friend, Alana, and her husband, Corbin, I can see how they became such good friends. Sure, the wine helped to ease my nerves, but really it only helped me to open up and see just how amazing these people are.

I'm staying here alone today for Helen's first full day back at the office. Before she leaves, I get up early to make breakfast for her. She's been so sweet to me. I want to do something for her. Yes, I know she's my mother, but I still feel like a guest in her home. Her gasp at the kitchen doorway lets me know that she's startled to see me standing over the stove.

Losing your memory is an intriguing experience. The connections each face once held in your memories disappear, yet things as complex as full languages remain intact. At one point in time, I'm sure I learned how to cook, studied and memorized recipes. Having no memories, I would think I'd forgotten how to make French toast. Yet, here I stand, instinctively preparing food that in my current head space, I've never prepared before.

Good morning, Helen. I turn around when I hear her gasp, a big smile spread across my face.

You startled me. Good morning. She mimics my smile and shuffles over to sit at the round table by the window. *You're up early.*

I wanted to cook for you. You've been so sweet to me, I explain. The French toast looks like it's done, so I scoop a couple of slices onto two plates and carry them over to the table. *Who knew I could make French toast?*

Pride beams from her eyes. *I knew. You've always been a good cook, Scar. Breakfast is one of your favorite meals to cook.*

I look down at my plate, staring through the egg-battered bread and into my brain wishing I could find this image, or a similar one, hidden in there somewhere. Nothing comes to mind.

Instinct now, I guess, she says after taking a bite. *It's delicious, thank you.*

My pleasure. I take a bite too and see for myself that I am, instinctively, a good cook. After a few bites, I place my fork down. *I think I would like to go to the office today. I think I'm ready to meet more people.*

Her eyes widen, full of excitement, letting me know she's happy with my news. *That would be wonderful. Everyone would love to see you.*

Even though Eli brought my car over to the house the day before, Helen and I ride together. She still doesn't like the idea of me driving with my head injury. Not that I want to admit it, knowing how bad an accident I was in, I don't want to drive either. We're greeted at the door by a petite woman with platinum blonde hair.

"Scarlett! You're back!" She jumps up from her seat behind a tall desk and corners it, arms outstretched for a hug.

"I'm just here to visit," I speak and sign. Since the woman didn't use sign, I'm not sure if she understands it. "Can you remind me of your name please?"

"Oh, I'm so sorry. Yes, I'm Lucy. I'm the receptionist here." She follows suit, signing while she speaks as well.

Now that I know she can sign, I turn my voice off because it feels more natural. *Nice to meet you.*

She says she's ready to meet more people and see the office, Helen chimes in. *Still doesn't remember, though.*

Lucy nods, disappointment now replacing the smile. *Oh, I do hope you remember soon. It's good to see you.* She tries to force a sympathetic smile, unsure of how to respond to the news.

Helen takes me around the office building to see who has arrived. I meet a brunette woman named Emma with long curly hair who is Deaf and does the scheduling work. Alana and Corbin are in their offices, though I am already quite familiar with them. There is another man here whose dark brown skin glistens on top of his bald head. His name is James, he seems very friendly and says we were close before the accident. Then Helen takes me to my office.

There is something alluring about the space. I can see myself sitting in this office. There's a desk in one corner of the room that allows sightline to the door without closing off the space. Straight ahead, there is a small couch with a coffee table, and a round table with a few chairs at the opposite corner. It feels welcoming and homey, not stark and stiff like some of the others I saw walking through the building.

This is my office?

Helen nods. I walk over to the desk and sit down in the oversized white leather chair. It's eerie to see my things there, waiting for me to return. My eyes are drawn to a framed photograph. It's Eli and me. The Scarlett in this picture looks so happy, and so in love with Eli. His lips are pressed to her cheek, both arms around her waist. Her head is back, eyes closed, and mouth open in unabated laughter. A pang of guilt pulls at my heart. Taking note that there aren't any pictures on my desk of Lorenzo, I wonder what exactly happened. He seems so involved in Scarlett's life, my life. There's a photo of me with my parents, I couldn't have been more than thirteen. Another picture of Helen and me. None of Lorenzo.

I turn to Helen. *I think I might hang out here today. Obviously, I don't know what kind of work I can do, but if you want to work, I'm okay hanging out here in my office.*

Are you sure? Her eyes light up, expressing how much she wants to be here too.

I nod. *Yes, I'm okay. I think being here will be good, maybe I can get into Scar's head.*

Sitting at my desk, I read through emails from the laptop. My laptop, I suppose. There are mostly work emails, and I'd be lying if I said they weren't kind of boring. It appears that most of my day consists of directing people to other people. There are emails requesting interpreting services which I pass along to Emma and Charlotte. There are emails asking about compensation, and I pass those along to Helen and Alana. It does look as though I do interviews and recruiting. Scrolling through the myriad of saved emails, one from Lorenzo Tate catches my eye. Just as I click the hyperlink name to open the email, Macie knocks on my door.

"Scar! I'm so glad to see you sitting at your desk today!" She crosses the room without hesitation and gives me a half hug. "How are you feeling?"

Macie and I have been fast friends since I 'met' her at my house earlier this week. She texts me often to check in. There is no question in my mind how she and I have remained friends for so many years. "I'm doing really well today. I told Helen I wanted to come see the office. Once I got here, I just kind of felt a pull to stick around today," I explain.

She takes a seat on the small white sofa. "That's so great, Scar. Anything ringing a bell?"

My head shakes. "Not really. I've been reading through old emails." I nod my head toward the open laptop on my desk. "But it's all quite boring."

Her laugh comes out as an adorable giggle. "Your job is kind of boring, I'm not going to lie. You do usually plan the company parties at Christmas and July 4th though, that might be the fun part."

"Isn't that soon? July 4th?" There's a calendar on the desktop. I find 'my birthday' written on June 13th and try to count the days since I woke up in the hospital.

Macie answers before my math catches up. "Yes, it's next Thursday. Alana has the party covered this year." Her eyes light up. "Today is Thursday!"

My eyes widen in response to hers. "What's exciting about Thursday?"

Her hands clap together in giddy excitement. "Happy hour. We go almost every week, it's kind of like our office team building meeting. Since you're here, you should totally come with us tonight!"

Unease takes over my body. "I don't know—" I start to protest, but Macie won't have it.

"I'm not taking no for an answer. Plus, you said you told Eli you wanted to start over, right? Well, we can go to Fire & Ice, just like we did the night you met him." Her hands clap together again. "It's perfect!"

Part of me regrets telling her what happened when she brought me to see Eli the other day. "It might be too much, no?" I try to protest again.

"No, I don't think so." She's on her feet, sporting a seriously infectious smile. "I have a couple of assignments after lunch, but I will be back here to pick you up right at 5:00 pm. Don't you dare skip out on me."

I stand along with her and motion over my outfit. "I'm not dressed for happy hour."

"First of all, you're gorgeous, as always. Second of all, I'll run by your house and grab you an outfit." She winks and heads out the door, removing any chance I had to protest again.

As Macie slides through the doorway, Lorenzo appears, sliding past her on his way into my office. I'm still standing, and we instinctively cross the room to hug. I've noticed this is something Deaf people do when they greet each other. He holds our hug a beat longer than I expect, squeezing me into his thick chest. There's a familiar comfort about our embrace, so I don't seem to mind that he holds it longer for me.

I just saw James. He said you were here today. The smile he's wearing lights up his dark brown eyes.

Yeah, just hanging out, reading old emails. I scrunch my nose up. *My work is boring.*

Lorenzo's genuine laugh is deep and hearty. It vibrates through me. *Your work* is *very boring... and kind of unnecessary.* He holds a finger up to his lips in a 'shush' gesture. *I won't tell anyone this place runs just fine without you.*

Thanks. I can feel my cheeks flush alongside my bashful smile.

We linger there for a moment, eyes locked, waiting for the other to say something. *I'm glad you're back, Scar. Maybe we can go get lunch together later today.*

Sure. I hadn't planned on staying today, so I don't have lunch with me.

There's another moment of us staring at each other, this time both with awkward smiles. He nods and turns to walk toward the door, stopping in the doorway to look back at me. *I'll pick you up at 12:00.* He winks and then dips out into the hallway.

Chapter 39
Lorenzo

*E*verything about our lunch date feels like just that... a date. I 'pick her up' from her office, drive her to this Mexican spot downtown, opening all the doors for her. We're tucked into a booth at the back of the restaurant, and I swear she hasn't stopped smiling since we left the office. She is so relaxed and happy around me now. If it's even possible, she looks more gorgeous than ever wearing that smile knowing that I put it on her face.

So, what's my favorite thing to eat at a Mexican restaurant? she asks after thumbing through the menu.

I don't need to look at the menu to answer her question. All of Scar's favorite things are filed into my brain. *Shrimp fajitas with corn tortillas.*

That was a quick response. Her eyebrows shoot up, she's impressed. Then they twist into skepticism. *Wasn't there a Mexican place by the agency?*

Yeah, but that place is trash. This is your favorite.

She smiles coyly at me, sending a rush of shivers through me. I'm glad we're seated, and the table is hiding any sign of the blood that might rush south at the sight of her glowing face. A waiter walks up to the table, it looks like he asks what we want to drink.

Scar signs while she orders a glass of water with lemon, then turns to me. *What do you want to drink?*

She's so fucking considerate of me. She always has been. It's one of the things that made me fall in love with her in the first place. *Same, please. And you love guacamole.*

Her face lights up and I watch as she orders my water and the guacamole. The waiter leaves and she turns back to me. *How do you know so much about me?*

I've spent my whole life learning what you love, Scar. When your dad passed away, I spent every minute we weren't in school with you for a week. My mom finally told me I had to come home and let you and Helen grieve on your own.

Her eyes widen with shock and her mouth forms into a perfect 'o.' *You stayed with me a whole week? Wasn't I like fourteen?*

Nothing like that happened. We spent the night with each other many times. Many, many *times.* I really emphasize the sign for 'many.' *Nothing ever happened. You let me hold you, hug you, comfort you. And even though I've been in love with you since I was sixteen, you never saw me that way.* Shit, did I really just say that? Am I trying to sabotage myself?

She looks disappointed. She's pouting and her eyes are sad, maybe a little confused. *I don't know how I never fell in love with you.*

Wait. What did *she* just say? I eye her quizzically, trying to find the words to ask her to elaborate. At the same time, I feel like a hunter who has just stumbled on his prize buck, too scared to move for fear of scaring her off.

Thankfully, I don't have to. The waiter returns with our drinks and dip. Now there are cups and chips and bowls between us. The atmosphere and the conversation interrupted, but not forgotten.

Scar signs while she speaks. *He says I love shrimp fajitas, so I'll take that.* She turns to me again. *What about you?*

Super burrito. I'm too stunned to say anything else. I'm too stunned to move my eyes away from her. Folding my menu closed, I hand it to the waiter, eyes still glued on Scar, waiting for her to finish giving my order.

When her eyes finally trail back to mine, I ask, *What do you mean?*

About what? Is she actually confused or is she playing dumb for effect? Either way, the look on her face is so fucking cute.

Scar. My head leans forward, and I push my brows up, insisting she answer me.

She giggles her adorable fucking giggle and dunks a chip in the guacamole, shoveling the whole thing in her mouth. She points to her mouth, as if telling me she can't talk because her mouth is full.

That's one of the beautiful things about sign, Scar. You can sign while you eat and still keep your mouth closed. I scold her with my brows again, silently insisting she answer me.

She lets out a gasp of air she's been holding in. *I don't know... I just feel something when I'm with you. There's something... I don't know how to describe it... like we're somehow deeply connected. Look, I don't remember anything, but you, you are more familiar to me than anyone else I've met since I woke up.* Her eyes shy away from me, but I wave my hand under them to get her to keep going. *Right now, after learning about our history, I don't know how I never fell in love with you before.*

You never let yourself. You never gave us the chance. Her eyes shy away from me again. I tap the table. Her green eyes are wet as if tears threaten to fall. *I waited too long too. Maybe if I had told you how I felt sooner, you would have opened your mind sooner.*

Why did you wait? There is a tear, it topples over the lower lid of her eye and glides slowly down her cheek.

Because you are my favorite person, Scar. If I lost you, I would be lost, broken. I take a deep breath. *The night you met Eli, I saw his interest in you immediately. I knew if I didn't tell you how I felt then, he would swoop in and steal you away. So, I tried. You said it wasn't how you viewed me, and you needed time. But you didn't give it time, you fell fast for Eli; just jumped right in. You told me it was because he didn't need to see someone else interested in you to like you.* Why am I telling her all of this right now? I make myself slow down. I force myself to end there. The ugly details could wait for her memories to return. *But it took me so long because I couldn't bear the thought of losing you, not because I didn't like you. Hell, I love you.*

  She turns her head toward the kitchen doors. My gaze follows hers as I smell the steamy trail from her fajita plate. The waiter crosses the room and places our food in front of us. He asks Scar if we need anything. She shakes her head and thanks him. Her eyes fall to the hot plate of food in front of her. *I'm not hungry anymore.* She pouts.

  My own eyes fall to the giant burrito in front of me. *Me either.*

  She reaches her hands across the table, asking for my hands. I oblige and place my hands in hers. We sit there for a moment, just like that, hand in hand. She can't say anything to me with our hands clasped like this. If anyone in the restaurant saw us, maybe they would think we were praying over the food, except that our eyes are open and locked in on each other. Then she mouths the words, *I'm sorry.*

  Her hands have become electric shocks, sending waves through mine, up my arms, and down into my soul. She doesn't remember any of this. How valid is her apology? What does all of this mean? Fuck me.

  She pulls her hands back. *I'm going to do it differently this time. I'm going to give you each an equal chance... if you want it.*

  I hate the idea of competing with Eli. Last time I went up against him, he somehow took me out before I even had a shot. At the same time, I'm beyond grateful that she's giving me a chance. I also feel like I have a head start in the race this time around. *How does Eli feel about that?*

I haven't asked him. He's taking me to Lake Wilson this weekend, like our first date. I'll talk to him about it then. She's sitting there, waiting with a hopeful smile for my response.

There's a small part of me that feels bad for Eli. A very small part. He's about to be blindsided. Two weeks ago, he got engaged to the most beautiful, sweet, caring woman. Now, she wants to see where things could go with someone else— with me. I try to put myself in his shoes, then I remember, I was in his shoes seven months ago. There's this nagging feeling in my gut telling me that all this happened for a reason, that destiny intervened. *I've been in love with you for damn near sixteen years, Scar. Of course, I would love for you to give me a chance, even if you're giving that same chance to Eli.*

Her lips are parted by a wide smile. She's pleased. She grabs a fork and starts filling a tortilla with the shrimp and peppers from her plate. Her appetite has returned.

When we arrive back at the office, I walk behind her down the hallway and into her office. With my foot, I kick the door closed behind us. She turns and smiles at me. *Thanks for lunch.*

Anything for you, Scar.

This silent stare between us has happened so many times today, it has to be a sign. She's standing there, her eyes zoned in on mine, her lips parted, her eyebrows cocked up. I take one long stride to close the gap between us, hook my arm around her waist and pull her into me. She stands on her tiptoes to bring her face closer to mine and closes her eyes. She wants my lips on hers just as badly as I want hers on mine. I oblige, devouring the creamy coconut lip balm she applied on the car ride back here. I part her lips with my tongue but hold myself back. She wants a soft, tender kiss. A romantic kiss. I'll have to save the passion for later.

I could stay here and kiss her all day long. If I thought we could go uninterrupted, I would. Instead, I pull away and step back to allow signing space. *So, when's our next date?* I ask, allowing the flirtatiousness of my smile to seep through.

Chapter 40
Eli

It's Thursday. Exactly two weeks ago my bar was filled with happiness and anticipation. Two weeks ago, we celebrated Scarlett's birthday, we got engaged, and we made love in practically every inch of this building. Exactly two weeks ago, I was the happiest I've ever been. Now I feel like everything that's ever meant anything special to me has been ripped away from me.

Ana is working tonight. She's behind the bar getting everything set up. "Hey, boss," she greets me when I come down from the apartment. "How you holding up?"

She knows Scarlett gave me the ring back. She knows I have to start over with her. I let out a sigh from deep inside me. "I've been better." There's no use in hiding my feelings from Ana, she always gets them out of me.

"Look, boss, you got her to fall in love with you before. Pretty fast, I might add. She'll fall in love with you again. Just be yourself like you were when you met." Her advice is legit. I'm just not in the right headspace for positive advice.

"Thanks for your vote of confidence." I start lowering the chairs from their tabletops to help her get things set up.

"When are you seeing her again?" Ana asks from behind the bar.

"Tomorrow, I'm taking her to Lake Wilson where we went on our first date." I don't mean to be gruff with Ana, but I can hear it come out in my tone.

She's not offended. "That sounds like a good plan. Maybe it will help with the memories."

"Maybe."

Ana catches on to the fact that I don't feel much like talking and we continue to open the bar in silence. She rounds the

Forget Me Not

bar and walks over to the jukebox to get some music going before unlocking the doors. With that, we are open for business. It's not long before our regular Thursday patrons start arriving. We do have a great Thursday happy hour special, probably why Scarlett and her friends happened upon the bar all those months ago.

Sure enough, shortly after 5:00 pm, some of Scarlett's coworkers file in the front door. I take a deep breath and muster everything I have inside of me to put on a happy face and walk over to greet them. So far, it's only Lucy, Dave, and James, so I don't have to sign yet. "Hey, how are you guys?"

"Probably much better than you." James tilts his head with a pouty face. I suppose he's trying to be sympathetic. I'm not sure I dig it. "How are you?"

My shoulders shrug. I'm not a huge James fan, I don't want to say too much to him. "It's hard. I'm not going to lie. But I just have to keep a positive attitude and be patient."

Lucy rubs my shoulder. "She'll come back around."

"Thanks, Lucy." Lucy's empathy seems much more genuine. "What can I get for you guys tonight?"

They go around and place drink orders, then I help them pull over another table to accommodate their growing group as Macie and her boyfriend arrive. Once they've settled, I make the drinks myself and then bring them back to the table. That's when an all too familiar scene plays out right in front of my eyes. Scarlett walks in, and on her heels, Lorenzo.

Scarlett looks absolutely radiant. Her face is glowing with delight as if she'd recently been laughing. She's dressed casually in leggings with a flowy tunic, not her usual post-work happy hour attire. Though I suppose she hasn't returned to work yet. Lorenzo looks positively arrogant. He stands taller than before, and is he... puffing out his chest? Scarlett's eyes meet mine, and her fading smile crushes my heart yet again. The mere sight of me drains the happiness right out of her.

"Pretend like this is the first time you're meeting her," Macie leans over and whispers in my ear. I turn my attention to her and give her a skeptical look. She nods. "Trust me."

As they always do, the group falls silent and transitions from speaking to using sign language once their Deaf compadre arrives. Scarlett and Lorenzo make their way across the bar to the group, and I step aside from the empty chair next to Macie to make room.

Scarlett slides into the chair. "Hey." She gives me a weak smile.

Remembering that this is one of the reasons Scarlett fell in love with me, I make sure to sign as much as I can while I speak. "Hi there, beautiful. Welcome to Fire & Ice, what can I get for you?" It's a stretch, but I take Macie's advice and act as though this is the first time we met.

Scarlett eyes me quizzically for a beat. "What do I like to drink?" she whispers to Macie.

Lorenzo has taken the seat behind Scarlett, and in true possessive Lorenzo fashion, he drapes an arm over the back of her chair. "What's that low carb drink you make?" Macie asks me before answering Scarlett.

"Oh, you mean my famous low-carb margarita?" I lay on the charm and wink as I smile. Scarlett looks intrigued.

"Do I like low-carb drinks?" She has lost all of her memories of insecurities, though I can see she is still shy and humble.

"All women do," Lucy chimes in. The ladies around the table laugh.

You're always watching what you eat and drink, Scar. You never liked your body. James takes on his usual role as Lorenzo's voice, despite knowing that I understand him just fine these days. *I never understood why, I think you're beautiful.*

Scarlett lights up again. This mother fucker. He's going to make this a challenge for me. It takes everything in me not to call him out. "You will love it, beautiful." Calling her baby when she woke up bothered her. But when I first met her, I called her beautiful all night long and she ate it up. I hope she loves it tonight.

"Then I have to try it." She keeps her glowing smile when she talks to me. That's promising.

I let the rest of the evening run much like it did the first night we met. I don't intrude into their group, even though up until two weeks ago, I had become a part of the group. I let her interact with her friends and coworkers, only coming around to refill drinks and drop a few flirtatious lines. I bite my tongue every time Lorenzo gets too physically close to her, waiting for her to react the same way she had before. She doesn't though. She allows him to touch her without discomfort or unease. She welcomes him into her personal space. Deep down, I fear if she never gets her memories back, I'll never get her back. A few people begin to gather their things to head out for the night. They flag me down to bring their checks.

"No, no. It's on me tonight," I say, waving them off. "Just don't get used to it," I quip. As Dave and Lucy head out, I turn to Scarlett. "So, how did you like the drinks?" I served her at least three and I can see that she is tipsy, but not drunk. Knowing that she came in with Lorenzo, I feel fairly certain that he is driving her home, so I made her drinks a little bit on the weak side.

"They were delicious, thank you." She smiles at me. "I can officially say, that's my favorite drink."

"Well, if you want the recipe, I only share that with my close friends." I remember our first phone conversation. She was so nervous that she didn't know what to say. She asked for my recipe instead.

"Then I suppose we need to be close friends." She winks at me. This is promising.

Pulling a pen from my pocket, I grab a napkin and write my number on it just as I had the first night we met. "Call me, we can start to work on becoming close friends." I wink back at her.

She giggles and folds the napkin, tucking it into her purse. I know she has my phone number. She knows she has my phone number. Macie is a genius, because this little role play, and these few drinks have helped to ease her discomfort around me. When no one notices, I look to Macie and mouth the words 'Thank you.' She nods and gives me a knowing smile.

After the bar dies down, I leave Ana to close up and head back up to my apartment. It's lonelier than it was before I met Scarlett. Even with the evening's events and a newfound hope, I can sense that she's missing. Her toothbrush hangs on the rack next to mine. Her hairbrush, deodorant, and mascara sit in the basket I set for her things. The throw blanket she brought over because she said my place was too chilly is draped over the back of the couch. There are pieces of her all over the small studio space, yet she's not here. I sit on the couch and cover myself with the throw, resting in the silence. Not even a minute after I sit there with my eyes closed, deep breathing, my phone chirps, signaling that a text has come in.

Scarlett: Are we still on for tomorrow?

I text back immediately.

Me: I wouldn't miss it for the world.

The three dots appear, and I know she's typing. Then the message appears along with my hope.

Scarlett: I'm looking forward to it. Thanks for tonight, I needed to "re-meet" you.

Me: Can't wait to become close friends with you. ;)

On our first date, I met Scarlett at the lake. I waited for her outside of my Jeep in the parking lot. She brought James' little pocket piranha. We had our first kiss. I remember it like it was yesterday. It was one of the best days of my life. Today, no one is comfortable with her driving yet, so I pick her up from Helen's house in my rental car. I know my Jeep is totaled, but the shop has yet to declare it, so I'm enjoying my free Charger rental while I wait.

Scarlett answers the door almost immediately after I ring the bell. "Well, hello there, beautiful." I greet her with a smile before she can say a thing. She's chosen a pair of capri leggings and a workout tank to wear on our hike around Lake Wilson. "You look ready for a summer hike."

She looks down at her outfit and kicks out one of her Reebok clad feet. "When you say 'hike,' how hike-y are we talking?" She seems anxious about what we have in store.

"Not very hike-y." I put air quotes around the adorable word she invented. "Although, you do love hiking." I bite my tongue. I had promised myself not to tell what she likes unless she asks. "Really, it's a couple of miles around a big lake. There's a trail, and it's pretty flat. But the views are nice."

She seems relieved after my explanation. "Ok, let's go." She pulls the door shut behind her and throws a string bag over her shoulder, then stops when I step out of the way. "Woah, nice car."

We start down the walkway toward the Charger idling in the driveway behind her car. "It's a rental. Mine is still in the shop, I'm just waiting for them to tell the insurance company that it's totaled so I can get my check and buy a new Jeep."

When we reach the passenger side door, I open it for her and gesture over the window for her to sit down. "My lady."

She smiles at my gesture, then frowns. "Your car is totaled because of me, isn't it?"

"Don't even think about that." I give her a reassuring smile and close the door once her legs are tucked in. There's a huge part of me that still believes something fishy happened with my Jeep, but I don't have anything to prove it yet. I decide to keep that to myself.

"Do you know what happened?" she asks me once I'm behind the wheel. Her words are slow and cautious as if she doesn't want the answer to her question.

I put the car in reverse and back down the driveway. "Honestly, I don't know for sure. I stopped by the police station and got the report, they said a witness reported that a car in front of you was cut off. And that you had plenty of room to stop but waited too long to brake and swerved off the road to avoid collision." I decide it's better not to tell her they suspect distracted driving. That would make her feel more guilty. It would also remind me that it could have been my text that distracted her.

She's quiet for a moment, taking in what I've said. "I'm sorry I totaled your car."

The situation isn't funny, but her apology makes me chuckle. "I don't think it was your fault." We're at a stop sign leaving Helen's neighborhood so I turn to wink at her.

She holds eye contact with me for a beat before turning to look out the window and growing quiet again. I continue driving in silence and let her marinate with her thoughts. After a few minutes, I can hear the sniffle she tries to hide. She brushes the back of her hand across her nose and takes a deep breath. "Ok, back to our date, sir," she tries to joke, but I can hear the suppressed emotions behind her voice.

"Yes, I'm glad you said yes to coming out with me today. Ever since I saw you walk into my bar, I haven't been able to stop thinking about you." I shift back into role play.

"Thanks for the invite." She smiles and turns her body inward, her knees now pointing toward the gear shift. "Tell me about yourself, how long have you lived here?"

It dawns on me that she really doesn't know much about me at all. Since she woke up, I've been mostly concerned with her and her well-being. We haven't shared much of our past experiences, well, mine at least. "I moved here about a year and a half ago when I got out of the Marine Corps."

"You were in the Marine Corps?" She seems fascinated. "How long?"

"Sixteen years, I joined right after high school. My dad was a marine. I wanted to follow in his footsteps." I give her a shorter explanation, leaving space for her to ask more questions.

"Was he proud of you for joining?" Thatta girl.

"I like to think he would have been. He died when I was a freshman in high school." Before I start to retell the story of my dad's passing, I realize Scarlett wouldn't even remember 9-11, so I take a moment to explain that to her. "In 2001 there was a terrorist attack. They took over four planes. Two flew into the Twin Towers in New York City, one crashed in a field in Pennsylvania, and the fourth crashed into the Pentagon in Washington, DC."

"Oh my god," Scarlett gasps.

"Yeah, it was very tragic, many people died that morning. My dad worked in the Pentagon after he retired from the Marines. He died that day. We all refer to it as 9-11 because it happened on September eleventh." We're pulling into the parking lot at Lake Wilson as I finish, choking up on the last few words. "It's been over twenty years, and it still gets me."

She reaches a hand over and pats my knee in consolation. "I'm sorry you went through that. I don't remember it, but I'm told my dad died when I was about the same age."

"I remember. It was kind of something we bonded over when we first met."

She holds my gaze for a moment, empathy painted on her face. Then she shakes her head as if shaking away the sad thoughts. "Looks like we're here?"

"Yup, let's go." I climb out and circle around the car to open her door. She takes my outstretched hand to pull herself up and out of the car.

"This place is beautiful," she muses, looking around the park in front of us.

"You haven't even seen the best part." I take her hand and guide her along the trail.

She lets me keep hold of her hand as she continues the conversation. "You were signing last night at the bar. Did you know sign language before you met me?"

"Nope. I'd never even seen anyone use it before I met you. After our first date, I went home and searched the internet all night about ASL. I learned how to say, 'My name is Eli,' before we met again." I'm happy to tell her these details that, even if she had her memories, I haven't shared with her yet.

"You did that for me?"

"Yes, well, for your mom. Once you told me your mom was Deaf, I knew I wanted to be able to communicate with her. I didn't want you to have to interpret between us. Because, I mean, I had decided after that first date that I wanted to spend as much time with you as possible. I knew I would be meeting your mom one day." We've veered into memory sharing and not starting over. "We're supposed to be starting over, remember?" I remind her.

"Oh, you're right." She covers her lips with her free hand as she giggles at herself. "Although, I do appreciate this insight. I'm quite impressed that you learned sign for my mom... and me." The smile on her face is audible in the last two words she adds.

"Your mom was impressed too. She took a liking to me immediately after that." I grin at her confidently.

"And you own Fire & Ice?" Seems an odd topic change, but I roll with it.

"I do. When my dad passed, he had put me as his beneficiary for his life insurance. But because I was under eighteen it went into a trust. I just left it there while I was in the military, I didn't need it. So, I combined that with my own money I had saved and bought the bar."

"What about your mom?"

I knew this question would come up. My lungs inhale a deep breath before I answer, bracing myself for the topic. "She's in California somewhere, last I heard."

Scarlett can hear the shift in my tone. "You're not close with her." It's not so much of a question as it is a realization.

"Not at all. She calls on occasion, usually asking for money." I pause my feet along with my words, pulling Scarlett to a halt with me. "My mom was a drug addict. *Is* a drug addict. She left my dad for her dealer. When he and I moved to Virginia, she stayed in California. After he passed, I had to go live with her. It was the worst four years of my life. I couldn't wait to leave for the military."

"Oh, Eli, that's terrible." She wants to ask more, but she visibly bites her lip instead. That's new, and it's positively sexy as hell.

"It was a long time ago. I think that's why I've been mostly alone my whole adult life. Watching what that did to my dad, I didn't want to go through that with someone. And then to see the person she had become?" My voice cracks again as I realize that Scarlett is all I have in the world outside of my bar. And I feel like she's slipping away from me.

Her eyes fill with tears for my tears. She reaches an arm up, wiping her soft hand on my cheek. "Thank you for sharing that with me, Eli. I can't imagine that it was easy."

I nod, then compose myself. She takes my hand back into hers and we head back down the trail. We find the wooden dock that leads to the gazebo on the lake. There is a mother and her young daughter feeding the ducks, but we walk down to the gazebo anyway. I don't mind waiting it out for privacy.

Scarlett kneels on one of the wooden benches that line the edges of the gazebo and pulls the string bag from her back. "I looked up Lake Wilson last night after I texted you. Something told me I should bring this." She opens the bag and pulls out a loaf of bread. The one thing we were missing from our first date.

The little girl and her mom run out of bread. The mother looks over at us and smiles, then encourages her daughter to head back down the dock, leaving Scarlett and I alone in the gazebo. Scarlett starts tearing pieces of bread and tossing it into the water. The flock of ducks that had been surrounding the girl paddle over to our side to continue eating their treats. I watch Scarlett's face illuminate as she admires the ducks below. Just as it had before, her glowing orange hair glistens in the sun's light.

She notices me watching her. "What are you doing?" she asks coyly.

"Just enjoying the view."

Her pale face flushes red with the heat of embarrassment. "Watch the ducks, they're cuter," she teases.

"I assure you, they are not." My voice is firm, yet breathy.

Slowly, she starts tearing a piece of bread again and tossing the pieces into the water. I scoot closer to her so that we are shoulder to shoulder, then I obey and move my gaze to the ducks below. Images of our first kiss right here in this gazebo flood my mind and I'm saddened knowing that the same image is eluding her mind. I wish desperately to pull our memories back to the forefront for her. I can feel her look over her shoulder at me, but I force myself to keep my gaze down on the water, allowing her the space to study me. Of course, I can only take it for so long before I turn my eyes to meet her eyes.

"We had our first kiss right here. Just like this," I tell her suggestively.

She keeps her eyes trained on mine. "Oh, did we?"

"We did."

"How was it?" She's being coy. It's fucking adorable.

"It was soft, sweet, and short." That's exactly how it was.

"Short?" She seems intrigued.

"Yeah, I wanted to leave you wanting more," I confess.

Her eyes fall from mine, but only down to study my lips. I slip my tongue across my bottom lip, moistening it.

"Show me," she whispers.

Chapter 41
Scarlett

*D*ammit, I have myself in a pickle. Eli just dropped me off at Helen's house after recreating our first date. Complete with recreating our first kiss. He did exactly as I asked; he started over with me. He backed off and gave me the space I needed to meet him, get my feet wet before diving in. And now I'm conflicted. I've had two amazing kisses with two very attractive men. Both of whom are madly in love with me. Both of whom I can see myself falling madly in love with. Dammit.

It's after 5:00 pm, so I'm hoping Macie is off when I dial her number on my phone. She picks up after two rings. "Hey, chica! How was the date with Eli?"

"I'm in trouble," I groan into the phone. "I think I need a girl's night."

"Brent's here tonight. Do you want me to come to Helen's?" Macie offers.

As sweet as Helen is, I don't want to tell her about my love triangle drama. "What about my house?" I suggest.

"Perfect, I'll pick you up in about an hour."

Helen isn't home yet, so I send her a text message to let her know where I will be and that I may stay the night there with Macie. Then I run up to my room and pack an overnight bag. Although, it strikes me that I probably have everything I need over there since it is my house.

Macie arrives right on time. "I brought snacks and wine," she says when I climb into her car.

"Good thinking." My smile turns into a frown. "Brent is okay with you ditching him at the last minute?" I ask, remembering that she told me she and Brent had been together for a while but didn't live together yet.

"He's been spending the night pretty much every night for the past two months. I think he'll be okay for one night," she assures me as she backs down the driveway.

When we arrive at my house, Binx greets us at the door. Macie has been feeding him and checking in on him daily. He circles between my legs, clearly missing my presence in the house and I immediately feel a twinge of guilt.

"Poor Binx, I should take him back to Helen's with me," I say, bending down to pet him. He lets me scoop him up and hold him like a baby.

"Your mom is not too keen on cats. She doesn't mind him when she visits, but she never let you have a cat growing up. I guess we could ask, though," Macie explains. "I really don't mind checking in on him every day."

"How could she not like cats?" I almost shriek. "He seems like the sweetest creature on earth!"

Macie laughs. "You have always loved cats."

I nuzzle my nose against Binx's nose, then he wriggles out of my arms and runs to the kitchen. Macie and I follow him and find him circling his bowl on the floor. I scan near the bowl for any sign of his food, not sure where I keep it. Macie points to a door, I open it to find a walk-in pantry where the bag of food is on the floor.

"So, how was your date?" Macie asks as she uncorks a bottle of red wine.

"Well, I kind of had two dates. Yesterday, Lorenzo took me out to lunch. When we got back to the office, he came into my office and kissed the hell out of me," I start.

Macie's jaw drops to the floor. "Lorenzo kissed you?" Her eyes blink repeatedly as she stares at me. "How the hell did that come about? Wait, Scar, you're engaged to Eli."

I suck in a deep breath of air and let it out. "Not right now, I'm not. I gave him the ring back, remember?"

"Yeah, but—" she starts to protest, but I wave my hand. "Okay, so how did it get to you and Lorenzo kissing?" She saves her opinions and lets me continue unfolding my love triangle.

"I don't know, I just feel something around him. I'm completely at ease in his presence, he feels so comforting and familiar to me. He was telling me how he's spent our whole lives learning about me and everything I love. He told me how he fell in love with me when we were kids. And I was just taken over with this question of how I never fell in love with him too," I explain. Macie listens with wide eyes. She motions for me to go on and pours the wine. "He said it's because I never gave him the chance. So, I told him I would give him a chance this time. I don't know, I feel like he deserves it."

"Woah, woah, woah. Scar, I'm not so sure he deserves it." We each take a sip from our glasses then move over to the table by the window.

"Why do you say that?"

"Well, first of all, he waited fifteen years to tell you he was in love with you. How many opportunities did he have? And he waits until a good man comes into your life and then tries to sabotage that?"

"How did he try to sabotage it?" I cock my head at her with furrowed brows.

She lets out a deep sigh, unsure if she wants to give me the bad memories. "The night of the Christmas party, it was going to be your first time with Eli. Eli had to leave to tend to a dumpster fire at his bar. When he left, Lorenzo got you on the dance floor, somehow convinced you to go in the hall, and then kissed you, even though he knew you had come with Eli. And… Eli believed Lorenzo drugged you, although Lorenzo claims you drank his wine that he laced with CBD oil." She says it quickly, practically in one breath as if she's been holding it in for days. I suppose she has been. "I'm not sure I believe that he drugged you on purpose, but you were upset that he brought CBD to a company party."

I'm in utter shock. "Really?" My head shakes at the thought. "He doesn't seem like he could do that. He seems like such a sweet and caring man."

"Well, he did. At least the part where he kissed you. Love makes people do crazy things sometimes I guess." She shrugs her shoulders and takes a sip of her wine.

I take a moment to let her words sink in. She's probably right, love can make people do crazy things. If I wasn't conflicted before, I'm definitely conflicted now. We sit silently for a few minutes, sipping our wine. My head spins with the new information Macie just shared with me.

"What are your thoughts on Eli?" I finally ask. I know I've asked this before, but it feels weird to change the subject by going straight into the details of our date from earlier today.

"Scarlett, he's amazing," she says bluntly. "He learned sign language for your mom. He takes you to dance lessons. He took the time to get to know your friends. He's always there for you when you need him." She lists a few things before adding, "I mean look at him now, he's heartbroken. His fiancée was in an accident, and she doesn't know who he is, so he backed off and respected her wishes of starting fresh."

Her tone has shifted, it's become sterner. Not as if she's mad, but rather disappointed. I can't think of any response, so I hang my head.

"And now she's kissing and falling for the man that tried to single-handedly destroy their relationship before it even had a chance. I guess he's doing that again."

Damn. Truth hurts. "Wow, when you put it like that, I kind of feel like a dirtbag."

Her lips press together, and she sucks in another long breath, blowing it out slowly before speaking. "Scar, I don't mean to make you feel bad. I really only want to help you find yourself. But the Scar I know? She wouldn't lead on two guys. Honestly, that's why you never gave Lorenzo a chance."

"What do you mean?"

"Lorenzo told you how he felt about you after he knew Eli was interested in you. You told him you needed time to see him in that way, but you already had a date set with Eli. I think you fell in love with Eli after that first date, because you told Lorenzo you had to see where that relationship would go. You never gave him a chance because you weren't the type of person to date two guys at the same time."

Her words sink deep into my mind, and I let them marinate there for a minute. "Thanks," I finally whisper meekly.

"Thanks for what?" she asks.

"Thanks for helping me remember the kind of person I was. The kind of person I am. I want to be her. I want to remember her. Lorenzo and Eli, they can both share their views of the person I am, they can share their memories of me and with me. But I think their perspectives are tainted, biased. Your opinion means a lot to me because you can share it more objectively with me," I elaborate.

"That's what best friends are for." She lets a smile take over her lips then holds her wine glass up. We clink our glasses together. "Now, tell me about your date with Eli."

"He kissed me too," I say meekly, my cheeks hot with embarrassment.

"Well, I'm team Eli, I have been from jump." We share a laugh. "Seriously though, maybe you need to take a break from both of them until you get your memories back."

"Maybe you're right."

I pull my phone out and send two texts. One to Eli and one to Lorenzo asking them both to meet me at my house tomorrow morning.

Eli and Lorenzo both arrive on time. I watch from the front window as they eye each other, confused as to why they are both here. They file up the walkway to the front door, Eli leading the way, and I open it before he has the chance to ring the doorbell.

"Scarlett?" His voice is breathless. "What's going on?"

Lorenzo taps his shoulder to grab his attention. *You know sign; please use it.*

Sorry. Eli throws his fisted hand to his chest to produce the sign hurriedly, as if he's annoyed by the request.

"Stop, you two," I sign and speak at the same time, wanting everyone to be included. "Come in, I want to talk to both of you."

Stepping back, I pull the door open wider and allow them to pass by me into the living room. Binx runs over and circles between Lorenzo's legs first, then Eli's. I gesture toward the couch and they both take a seat on opposite ends.

"Thank you for coming." I take a long, deep breath, gathering my words before expressing them. "These past couple of weeks have been hard on all three of us. I know I'm not the only one affected by my memory loss." They nod in agreement. "Even without having memories of either of you, of my relationships with either of you, I've come to care for you both."

"You were never in a relationship with him." Eli is using his voice, though he does throw in the signs for 'never' and 'relationship' before pointing to Lorenzo.

"I'm using the word to encompass many types of relationships, not only romantic relationships," I clarify. "Please, let me say what I need to say."

Eli nods, his face sinking in defeat as his body sinks back into the couch.

"It's not fair to either one of you for me to spend time with both of you, developing relationships and stirring feelings. So, I've decided that I need to be alone. Whether my memories come back or not, I need to spend some time getting to know me and who I am now in case they never do."

Scar, how can—

I wave my hand, cutting off the rest of Lorenzo's signs. *I won't be back at the agency for a while.* I turn off my voice as I address Lorenzo directly. *I'm going to explore some other opportunities.* I turn my voice back on to address them both. "I'm going to move back in here. Macie will stay with me for a while, at least until I've been cleared to drive."

My eyes shift over to Eli to gauge his reaction. He's utterly stoic, speechless. After a few moments of silence, he stands and swipes a hand over his bald head. "If that's what you want–" His voice cracks and he clears his throat, taking a deep breath before continuing, "I guess we have to respect it."

With that, he strides over to the door and leaves without another word. The finality of the door latching shut behind him sends a stab of guilt straight to my heart. Lorenzo stands, striding slowly over to me. He holds his hands out and raises his eyebrows, asking for my hands to clasp his. I hesitate, but let my hands drape over his, we stand there momentarily, communicating only with our eyes. He's telling me that he understands why I'm making this decision. He's telling me that he has faith that one day we will be with each other again, even if only as friends.

He pulls his hands away from mine so he can put words to our unspoken thoughts. *I'll always be here for you, Scar. All you have to do is come find me.* One arm reaches out asking for a half hug. I give him a full hug allowing my head to settle in against his chest for a beat. His breath is warm on top of my head as he places a gentle kiss there before withdrawing from our embrace.

Thank you, Lorenzo.

His lips purse together and one corner flinches up into a disheartened smile before he slips past me to follow Eli's path out the front door. He stops with one hand on the handle and turns back to me, his free hand holding up his thumb, index, and pinky, a combination of the ASL letters for I, L, and Y. *I love you.*

I love you, too, I reciprocate the sign.

Forget Me Not

Part III

Forget Me Not

Chapter 42
Eli

It's been almost a year since I met the love of my life. It's been almost six months since she was ripped away from me, ripping my heart right out of my chest along with her. The first two months were the hardest. But, as I eased back into life on my own, back into my old ways and my old habits, I found solace in my life of solitude. Macie came by to get all of Scarlett's things from my apartment. I couldn't take seeing her toothbrush next to mine, the throw blanket on the couch, or her drawer full of clothes any longer. Scarlett's work friends went back to their old happy hour spot, no longer gracing my bar with their torturous reminders of her. Once all traces of Scarlett were gone, I was finally able to move past my heartache, move past my grief. And that's exactly what it was, grief.

When the insurance company finally approved the totaling of my Jeep, I gave up on the notion that something sinister had caused the accident. The police report came back and said it was concluded that the accident had been caused by distracted driving. After looking at the phone records, she had received two text messages that morning that could have been around the time of the accident. She had also responded to one of the messages. Deep down I knew that one of them was the text message I had sent her. The other, I'm sure, came from Lorenzo. The thought that she responded to his message tortured me for months.

There's still a fleeting feeling deep inside me that pops its head every now and again, a feeling that one day she'll walk through the front door of Fire & Ice, run up to me, wrap her arms around my neck, kiss me, and tell me she remembers everything. Every day that passes, every week that passes, the feeling becomes less prevalent and more fleeting. Still, I can't help but think of her now. It's near the end of November, right around the time when she first walked into my bar. Every time a gush of cold air comes in with a patron, I look to the door hoping this is the day she walks back into my life. Every time I look over and don't see her fiery orange hair, my heart breaks a little more. I'm starting to wonder if there are any pieces of it not yet broken.

"Hey, boss." Ana breaks my reverie. She's early for her shift, ready to get things set up for the night. I give her a warm and thankful smile. I never had a sister, but I can imagine what it would be like with Ana.

"Hey, Ana." She can hear the dejection in my voice. It's hard to miss these days.

She gives me an empathetic smile, then snaps her fingers in my face. "Listen, Eli. It's time to move on. It really sucks that Scarlett came into your life and then was snatched away. I know you loved her deeply—"

"Love." I correct her tense because it feels like I am still very much in love with Scarlett Reese. I know I need to get over her, and I'm sure I will. One day.

Ana gives me an exaggerated eye roll playfully. "Love her." She adds quotes to the word 'love' as if discounting it. I let it slide and let her continue lecturing me. "Anyway, it's been almost six months. It's time. Open yourself up to meeting someone new, that will help you get past your feelings."

I know she's right. I hate when she's right. Chuffing air, I move past her and corner the bar to start setting up the tables. "What would you do if you lost Diedre?"

She gasps at the question and then ponders her answer for a moment. "I would curl up in the fetal position in bed and stay there for the rest of my life."

Letting the stool in my hands steady on the floor, I turn my body toward her with my hands folded over my chest. My face, I'm sure, reads 'I told you so.' "Therein lies my point."

She scoffs, her tone playful. "That's different, you're stronger than me. You're stronger than this. If you could survive two tours in Iraq, you can survive this."

She's wrong. Military service, war, witnessing people get blown up right in front of me? None of that compares to finding your soul mate and having her ripped away from you. "I would do two more tours in Iraq if it would get my soulmate back."

There's a moment of silence, and then Ana speaks. "What if she's not your soul mate?" Ana poses the question causing me to stop in my tracks to ponder the notion. Maybe she's right. I don't dare concede that to her though, I keep that thought to myself. In this moment, and for the foreseeable future, I can't fathom the thought of anyone else.

The rest of the night is uneventful, business as usual. Until it isn't. I'm delivering drinks for Ana at one of the tables closest to the door. The cold air from outside rushes in as a group of people walk in. That fleeting feeling sweeps over me, and I can't help but turn in their direction, hoping to be greeted with Scarlett's smile. It isn't Scarlett, but the people in the group are signing. I don't immediately recognize any of them. Intrigued, I walk over to the group as they scan the room for a table large enough to accommodate them.

Welcome, I sign. *Let me help you get a table. How many?*

A man at the front of the group cocks his head back, his face signifying that he's impressed with my signing. *You know sign?* he asks.

Kind of, but I could use some practice.

A smile takes over his face and he throws his hand through the air as if brushing my humility away. *I'm impressed.* A few others in the group nod in agreement. He does a head count before answering my question. *I think we have three more coming, nine total.*

I will get you set up. Without hesitation, I move to the high-top tables in the center of the room where Scarlett and her friends used to always sit. After pushing three tables together, I wave the group over to take their seats.

Thank you, a few of them sign to me as they sit.

What can I get you to drink? I offer.

The man who seems to be the head of the group orders first, followed by who I am assuming is his wife or girlfriend. After all three couples have ordered, I head off to make the drinks.

"Putting those signing skills to good use, I see," Ana comments as I grab a bottle of rum from the well in front of her. "If nothing else, you walked away from that relationship with a new skill."

"I didn't walk away from anything," I remind her gruffly.

"You know what I mean." She jabs her elbow in my side.

I punch the drinks into the point of sales system and add an order of cheese fries to get them cooking in the kitchen, then comp them from the bill. When I get back to the table with the first round of drinks, another couple joins the table.

The man signs something that I don't recognize, but it appears he's telling the group that another person is parking the car. That's when the cold air rushes in again. That's when I turn my head and see fiery red hair draped past the shoulders of a woman. My heart races waiting for her face to turn to mine, waiting for Scarlett's pink pouty lips to smile at me. She turns, I sink. She smiles and makes her way straight toward me, straight toward the empty chair at the table with her friends. Her eyes meet mine, and she gives me a friendly smile. I step back to allow her space to mount the high barstool.

Hi, she mouths, taking a seat.

Hi, I sign slowly. I'm almost frozen there. Maybe it's shock, I'm not sure. It isn't Scarlett. Now that I see her up close, I can see her hair is more strawberry than blonde. Scarlett's hair is more blonde than strawberry. She stands a couple inches shorter than Scarlett, her frame somewhat more petite, yet still full. Her lips are fuller, pinker, and more freckles scatter across her face. I'm not sure if it's the hair or the sign language, but she reminds me of her. She doesn't even really look like Scarlett. Maybe it's just the feeling I got in her presence. Either way, my lungs seem to seize up, not wanting to release a breath.

The man that just joined the group moments before waves his hand in my line of sight, pulling me back to reality. *You sign?* he asks when I turn to him. I nod. *Can we get two glasses of merlot, please?* He motions between him and the woman that walked in with him.

Sure. I turn to the redhead. *What would you like?*

Her thumb and index finger slide through the air so gracefully, rubbing her chin between them as she ponders. *Cosmopolitan.* She spells the word slowly for me, and I wonder if there is a sign for that.

Good choice. I curl the side of my lips up into a smile and give her a wink.

Her eyes narrow in on me, trying to read into my expression. After a moment, she bats her eyes and signs, *Thank you.*

I continue to tend to the table full of our new Deaf patrons, determined to bring them on as regular customers. Especially the redhead. There's something about her. At first, it felt like a connection to Scarlett. But the more I watch her from behind the bar, the more my heart races, and when I approach the table, the more I realize it is a pull. A pull to her, a connection *like* the one I had with Scarlett. Only different. The group stays a couple of hours, and it's nearing closing time. Some of them have left, leaving only a few still at the table. I decide it's time to make my move. I need to at least know her name.

Any last call drinks? I offer from the corner closest to the redhead.

She turns to me and smiles, clearly tipsy. *I think I'm good on drinks, thanks.* She turns her attention to the two couples still at the table with her. *Want anything?*

They all wave their hands in the air, a 'no, thanks,' gesture. Since they had already established how to separate the checks, I have them in my pocket. On the back of the redhead's check, I had written my phone number with a little note encouraging her to text me. After everyone finishes with payment, they all head toward the door. The redhead lingers for a moment, looking back at me behind the bar. Our eyes meet momentarily, then she waves at her friends, telling them she would order an Uber. She crosses over to the bar and hoists herself up on the stool across from where I am washing glasses.

E-L-I. She reads my nametag, spelling it out slowly. *That's your name?* The nod of my head matches the pace of my name spelled slowly from her fingers. *My name is R-O-S-E.* She spells it out first and then taps the 'R' handshape on one side of her nose, then the other. *That's my name sign,* she explains.

Nice to meet you, Rose. I produce her name sign with intention. *I don't have a name sign.*

She eyes me quizzically, cocking her head to one side. *How do you know sign? Clearly, you're not Deaf.*

No, I'm not. A quiet chuckle escapes me, admiring her blunt mannerisms. *My ex-girlfriend, her mom is Deaf. I learned so I could communicate with her.*

Rose's eyebrows shoot up, her pink lips pout, awe seeping from her expression. *That's impressive. You must have loved her very much.*

I hesitate, eyeing her for any inclination of how I should respond. There's a feeling deep inside me that is pulling me to her. I don't want to scare her away. Deciding on honesty, I finally answer her question honestly. *I did. Very much.*

What happened? Wow. The bluntness of the Deaf community that Scarlett had mentioned before is ever present in Rose. Most people wouldn't ask these questions on a first date. Then I remember this isn't a date at all, we literally just met.

It's a long story. I'd love to tell you about it one day. I attempt to open us up to a first date, and hopefully subsequent dates after that. I need to see more of this woman.

She reaches across the bar toward my chest, pulling a pen from my shirt pocket and then grabbing a napkin from the nearby caddy. Her delicate hand scribbles down her phone number on the napkin and slides it over the glossy bar top to me. *You can text me, but I prefer FaceTime.*

With that, she winks and stands from her perch on the stool. We hold eye contact for a beat as her lips curl into a wide smile that mimics my own. *I think I prefer FaceTime too,* I finally find the words.

She nods and turns to head to the door, her fiery hair whirling around as she turns. The scent of her shampoo or perfume eases into my nostrils, and they flare trying to breathe her scent in deeply. Apples and... roses?

Chapter 43
Lorenzo

When Scar told me she was going to spend some time alone, trying to find herself in her new headspace, I thought it would be impossible for us to avoid seeing each other. It's been almost six months, and somehow, I haven't seen her. Wilson is a small town, and the Deaf community even smaller. From what Helen has said, she comes over for dinner weekly and their relationship is developing in a new way. Helen has had to learn how to mother her without actually mothering her. I see Macie at work. She is the only other person that Scar has been socializing with since she walked away. She tells me Scar is good but won't give me any more details.

    It's been interesting to see myself grow in this time. I spent quite some time loving Scar in silence, waiting for the perfect time to share my feelings in hopes that she would reciprocate them. Looking back, I picked the absolute worst time to share my feelings. That's clear to me now. I still love Scar, very much. I still believe we will be together one day. My stubbornness to open myself to love someone else has allowed me to focus on myself in the absence of the object of my affection. One of the first things I did was sit down with Kendra and break things off officially. It wasn't fair to her that I knew our relationship wasn't going anywhere. Scar's decision to take some time for herself had inspired me to do the same. When she comes back to me, I'm certain I will have matured, ready to be the man she needs. You know what I've realized in this time of focusing on myself? I really like working full-time. I've come to not only appreciate the stability and structure of my schedule, but I also actually look forward to it. Though I haven't let go of my side gigs either.

    It's Thursday afternoon in late November. The weekly happy hour moved back to the Mexican spot next door to the office. Macie had suggested it, saying it was hard on Eli to see us there as a reminder of Scar. Most everyone agreed. I agreed to moving it, but really only because I didn't want to see Eli anymore. I wanted him to be far away, out of my life forever. Before happy hour, I'm heading out to ENCSD, they commissioned me to do a new logo design, wanting to revamp their online presence. This afternoon, I will be meeting with their digital communications coordinator.

The lights in my office flicker as I'm packing my messenger bag for the day. I turn to see my dad in the doorway. *Hey, Dad, what's up?*

Just checking in with you, how are things? In the past year that I've been working at the agency, Mom and Dad have allowed me my space, trying not to hover. Mom and I have lunch together once a week, and Dad tries to check in weekly instead of daily.

I give him my signature face, raised brows and pouted lips. *Good, I'm leaving for ENCSD, I have a meeting over there this afternoon.*

He makes a face that I can't quite read. Surprise maybe, but there's more to it. *Meeting? At ENCSD?*

Yeah, they want a new logo design. They wanted a Deaf artist to do the job, and since I graduated from there, they reached out to me, I say as a quick explanation.

Dad's lips curl into a sly smile, his eyes twinkling behind the apples of his cheeks. I cock my head at him, knowing there's something going on behind his questioning. *Sounds like you're the perfect man for the job.*

You could say that. Still on for family dinner this weekend? I ask before throwing my messenger bag over my shoulder, ready to head out.

Yep, Saturday at 7:00 pm. He's still sporting his mischievous smile. *Good luck today.*

My shoulder shrugs nonchalantly. The gig is already mine. I don't need luck. I guess it's the 'dad' thing to say. *Thanks, see you later.*

He waves and turns to leave the office. Following behind him, I close my office door before heading out to the front.

Campus hasn't changed much in the fourteen years since I graduated. I'd heard they had renovated some of the dorms and classrooms, though it isn't evident from the outside. I smile to myself as I watch some upper-level kids gathered around a tree with books open in their laps, remembering when I was that age studying around these same old oak trees. Deaf schools all around the country have been closing as more and more kids are sent into mainstream schools, their parents not wanting to ship them off to a boarding school. The fact that ENCSD is still going strong makes me happy. Even though I never lived on campus, since my family lived in town, it still gives me a sense of home, a feeling of belonging. I make my way to Woodard Hall, the administrative building in the center of campus. Once inside, I look around and see that not much has changed.

A receptionist greets me, using both voice and sign. *Hello, how can I help you, sir?*

I'm pleasantly surprised to see her signing since many of the people that worked in the administration building when I went to school here did not. *I have a meeting with Andy Davidson.*

Ok, I will let him know you're here. She motions to a chair on the opposite side of the room. *Have a seat, he'll come meet you when he's ready.*

Thanks.

From my seat I can see down the hallway of office doors. I'll be able to see him coming before the receptionist. Above each door there is a name plate that extends out from the wall. That's when I see it a few doors down: Executive Assistant to the School Director – Scarlett Reese. She works here now? Helen had told me she had found a new job but didn't want her to share it with everyone. She said Scar wanted to keep to herself as much as possible, and maybe she just didn't want to run into me. Clearly, Mom and Dad knew, or at least Dad. That was the secret hiding behind his smile earlier. I stare at the nameplate, then trail my eyes down to the door. It's open. Scar always keeps her office door open. The sight brings a smile to my lips, and I wait there, willing her to come out and see me. I look away momentarily to scan the name plates for Andy Davidson's office, it's right across from hers.

Unfortunately, while I wait for Scar to emerge from her office, Andy emerges from his first. He waves at me from down the hall. *Mr. Tate?* I can't tell if he's voicing while he signs, but it looks as if he is.

I stand and angle my body toward him, flinging my bag over my shoulder. *Yes, Lorenzo.* I spell my name first, then show him my name sign.

He stops where he is. *Great, come on back,* he signs, waiting for me to meet him in the hallway. *How are you today?* he asks once I've closed the distance between us.

We are just outside of Scar's door, and it takes everything inside me not to turn my head and look inside. *Great, ready for the weekend. How are you?* I purposefully ask my question without entering his office yet, hoping my presence is noticed.

Quite well, thanks. Mr. Davidson motions toward his office doorway and I'm forced to move inside, out of Scar's potential sightline. *Thanks for coming in. Our graphic designer recently retired and we're in the process of looking for a new one. But we didn't want to postpone this project.*

They're hiring a new graphic designer? To work in the same building as Scar? The idea of applying is heavy in my mind, though I know I can't desert the agency at this point. *Well, I'm glad you contacted me. Tell me about what you're looking for in the new logo,* I cut right to the chase.

You were a student here, yes? I nod. *I don't want to set any boundaries. Obviously, incorporate our mascot, but otherwise, feel free to make the project your own.*

My favorite kind of project, my own. *Sounds perfect. I think you'll be happy with what I can do.* I give him my most charismatic smile.

Also, if you know any talented graphic designers that are looking for a career opportunity, send them our way. His eye glistens as he winks at me, his expression giving way to his subtle hint that I should apply.

No leads yet?

He shakes his head. *No, though, we've only recently put out the job posting.*

I'm the only graphic designer I know, unfortunately. I think AHLS would be sad to see me go, since I am one of the heirs to the company.

His eyes widen at the realization of who I am. *AHLS, oh I can't believe I didn't connect it sooner. You're Alana and Corbin Tate's son?*

The one and only. I allow myself to laugh, relaxing more now that he's made the connection.

We work a lot with your agency, your dad interprets here often. He really shouldn't have said the last part, but I guess he assumes I know where the interpreters work. Except as web designer, I don't work much with interpreters. *I imagine there could be room for the graphic designer position to be part time.* He throws his hands up in surrender. *Only if you're interested.*

I'll consider it. So, when would you want that logo design submitted? I attempt to turn the discussion back to the reason I am actually here.

I would love for it to be ready before the new year, would that work for you? he asks.

My lips pout, pursing out as I nod. *Perfect.*

We both stand, realizing there isn't much left to discuss. He reaches his hand out for me to shake. *Nice to meet you, Lorenzo.*

I'm looking forward to seeing what you come up with. Shall I walk you out?

My head shakes almost immediately. *No, thanks. I'm going to say hi to a friend.*

When I open the door to the hallway, Scar's door is still open. She is sitting at her desk, eyes trained on her laptop screen. I suppose the door sounded as I closed it behind me, because she looks up from the screen and our eyes meet. Her lips part as the corners pull apart into a wide smile. She's happy to see me.

Lorenzo? What are you doing here? She stands, crossing the room as she signs to me.

I take the two steps from one doorway to the other and open my arms for her to fall into my welcoming hug. Her head rests on my chest as we embrace and I inhale, breathing her in deeply. Coconut and vanilla. I squeeze her tighter into me at the familiar scent. She squeezes me tighter too, then steps away from the embrace so we can talk. *You're working here?*

She nods, the grin still plastered on her face. *Yes, I've been here for about five months now. Sorry, I asked Helen not to share it with anyone.*

She didn't. I was surprised to see your name on the door when I came in, I admit. *You like it here?*

Love it. She steps back and allows me the space to fully enter her office. There's a couch on the wall next to the door, she motions to it for me to sit down. *Everyone here is very friendly. What are you doing here? Did you interview for the graphic designer position?*

No. Not yet at least. The idea is growing on me, that's for sure. *They commissioned me to do a logo redesign. I didn't even know they were looking for a graphic designer.*

I think it's recent. If you apply, put me down as a reference.

Will do.

We share a smile and then a moment of 'silence.' So many questions linger in the air between us. I wonder if she's regained her memories, or if she thinks of me as often as I think of her. I wonder if she's seeing anyone, or if she wonders that about me. *You should come by the agency sometime,* I finally suggest, holding off on my questions for now. *Everyone there would love to see you.*

She gives me a tight-lipped smile and then hangs her head, her eyes trained on her hands in her lap. Her fingers are interlaced, fidgeting within themselves, her same old nervous tick. *Macie has been planning the Christmas party; she's been telling me all about it.*

You always loved doing that. I lose her eye contact again to her fidgeting hands. She inhales a deep breath and lets it out slowly, so I cock my head down to get her eyes back on mine. *You still don't have your memories back?*

Her head shakes slowly. *Not really.*

Not really? That wasn't a hard no. *What do you mean, not really?*

A rush of air escapes her lips from a deep sigh. *When I'm awake, I don't have any old memories, only from when I woke from the coma. But...* she trails off.

But, what?

At night, I'm having dreams.

This is a good sign. Maybe. *Dreams about what?* I press.

Most often... you. Her eyes shy away from me again, but only for a moment. She stares at her hands, then mine, then her eyes trail slowly back up to meet mine. *I can't tell if the dreams are just dreams or if they're memories.*

She's dreaming about me? My heart is racing now at the confession, and I need to know more. *Tell me about one, please. Scar, I can help you.* I am beyond ecstatic. And also, a little terrified.

Tracey Gramajo

I don't know, they're hard to remember after I wake up. I just wake up and feel you.

Me? Just me? No one else? I don't even want to say his name, I don't want to bring him back to mind or back in the picture.

Sometimes Helen, sometimes my dad... mostly you.

Please, Scar, try to remember one. Coming across too desperately could scare her, but I *am* desperate to know her dreams.

There's one where we are both young, maybe ten years old, maybe a little older, she starts. I sit forward to engage. *We're at the beach, making a sandcastle. And once we've finished, you place a shell on top. Just then, a wave comes in hard and strong, it knocks me over and I fall right into the sandcastle. I start crying because it's ruined. But you hug me, pull me in tight, and tell me you'll build me another one. And if it gets knocked down, you'll build me another one after that.*

My heart is beating so hard and fast I fear it will beat right out of my chest. *Scar.* My eyes are wide as I slowly pull her name sign down across my chin. *That's a memory.*

Her eyes widen too, glistening with fresh tears that threaten to seep down her cheeks. *That actually happened?*

Yes, I built you three more sandcastles on that trip. We were in Myrtle Beach for spring break. The fresh tears brim over her eyelids and slide down her cheeks as she watches me sign. *You were eleven, I was thirteen. Our families went to the beach together every year until we both had gone off to college.*

Her hands are fidgeting again, so I reach over, grabbing hold of them. My eyes fixate on hers while her tears start flowing. She pulls one hand from mine, keeping hold of me with the other. With her one free hand she signs, *I can't wait for more dreams now.*

Chapter 44
Scarlett

The weight of his embrace is heavy as he pulls me into him. My ragged breathing is interrupted by heaving sobs. His arms envelop me, squeezing tighter, his breath hot in my ear as he breathes out a shushing sound. Inside, I feel gutted, I feel empty. Yet, as he attempts to console me, little bits of emotion swell back into me. Warm tears soak my cheeks, and my eyes burn from the running mascara. He pets my hair, stroking slowly up and down. No words are exchanged between us. Once my heaving sobs have drifted into quiet, slow breaths, he pulls away from me, locking his eyes with mine. The sight of his face, I know that face. It's so young, yet so familiar. How do I know this face?

  My body jolts awake, and my eyes snap open. Lorenzo? I dreamt of young Lorenzo again. There wasn't much more to the dream than him consoling me through tears. After seeing him in my new office at ENCSD the other day, I now question if this is more than a dream, if this too is a memory. The raw emotion felt eerily real, like I had experienced that emotion before. Could it have been him consoling me after my dad's passing? The young features of his face make me think he was a teenager, which was around the time my dad passed. There's a pull inside me, clenching my stomach, willing me to text him. I need to feel his embrace, I need to know if the way it felt in my dream is the way it feels in real life.

  Before I can reach for my phone, Binx jumps up on the bed, rubbing the side of his face against my cheek. He's hungry. It's Saturday morning, so I'm late for his morning feeding from sleeping in. "Ok, Binx, I'm coming." I give him a few head scratches before guiding him off my chest so I can get out of the bed. Tucking my phone into my pocket, I pad barefoot into the kitchen, Binx follows close behind me. He practically knocks me over as he weaves between my feet. I've been staying in my house for almost six months now and have become very familiar with it. So, I head straight for the pantry to get a can of food for Binx. After feeding him, I press the start button on the coffee grinder and empty the old grounds and filter from the machine. My phone vibrates in my pocket, and I reach in to retrieve it. It's a text from Lorenzo.

    ZO: GM, it was so great to see you the other day.

The smile that spreads across my face is involuntary. I wonder if, somehow, he knew I had dreamt of him before waking up this morning. I wonder if he woke up from a dream about me too. I text him back.

    Me: So great! What are you doing today?

    ZO: No plans, just woke up and thought about you. I haven't even gotten out of bed yet. LOL

    Me: Want to spend the day with me?

    ZO: On my way.

Lorenzo is knocking on my door within twenty minutes. In that time, I've cooked breakfast, French toast, and set the table for two.

    Smells amazing in here, he signs as soon as I open the door.

    I open the door wider and step back to allow him the space to come inside. *I made breakfast for us. Have you eaten?* He shakes his head, then snakes an arm around my waist and pulls me into his body, wrapping his other arm around me. Breathing in his scent, I almost melt against him, soaking in the familiarity of him. *Come on,* I sign after breaking away from the embrace.

    He follows me into the kitchen and takes a seat at the small table by the window where I had set plates and coffee. *Looks delicious, thanks, Scar.*

    I wasn't sure how you take your coffee, cream and sugar? I offer.

    Black coffee is perfect, thanks. His eyes sparkle behind the wide grin he flashes me.

Forget Me Not

The French toast is still in the pan on the stove, I carry it over and serve him three slices, two for me, then take the seat across from him. After we taste our breakfast, I set my fork down to sign. *I had a dream again this morning before I woke up.*

Really? Tell me about it, he signs with one hand while continuing to eat with his other.

There wasn't much action, just me crying and you consoling me. The emotion I felt in the dream was so strong, like I had been hollowed out inside. You were shushing in my ear and petting my hair, holding me tight. Before I woke up, I saw your face, you were young, like a teenager. I describe what I saw and felt as best as I can.

After your dad died, he says it so matter-of-factly without hesitation as if the memory for him is at the forefront of his mind. *I hated seeing you so broken, it killed me inside. We spent so much time together that week, mostly not saying anything. I just held you and let you escape with your emotions. I hated that you hurt, but I loved being there to help you through it.* Conflicting emotions cover his expression. There's sadness in the memory, but also a hint of something else, something happier.

So, you're saying that is a memory? I ask, hopeful that soon all my memories will come flooding back to me.

He nods. *Maybe we can't pinpoint the exact moment, but certainly that happened. Yes, I think it's a memory.*

The memories are still only coming in unconsciously. I close my eyes, squeezing them tightly together in an attempt to force my brain to remember consciously. It doesn't work. Lorenzo taps the table, making a light sound to pull my eyes back open. His eyes squint as his brows pull together, an incredulous expression. *I want more memories,* I confess.

Let me help you. He takes a deep breath and lets the air exhale slowly. *I know you needed space, but maybe now that you've had space, we can spend more time together. I can help you, Scar. I have almost all of your same memories.*

He's still hurt from when I walked away. He's holding back, not wanting to smother me and scare me away again. In all honesty, he's right. I've had my space, I'm ready to let him back in. *Help me, Lorenzo.*

A satisfied smile pulls from the corners of his mouth. *What do you want to do today?* he asks, subtly changing the subject.

I feel this urge to decorate for Christmas. Can we go shopping for a tree? I can't remember if I like Christmas, but even if I didn't before, I know I like it now.

You have a tree. He laughs.

I pout my face at him. *How am I supposed to know that?* We both laugh at that comment. *Where is it? Can we put it up today?*

It's in the attic, and of course.

We finish our breakfast and sip our coffee until the heat has subsided and the liquid runs cold. Before leaving the kitchen, he offers to help me with the dishes. Even though I have a dishwasher, we stand side by side, shoulder to shoulder, while he washes, and I dry. Each time our shoulders bump each other, electricity rushes through me. Once the dishes are done, I follow him to the spare bedroom where he shows me the attic access ladder that I didn't even know I had. Deep down, I'm very thankful that he and I were so close before, that he knows me so well still.

With his tall stature, he reaches up with ease, tugging the cord that pulls the ladder down from the ceiling. *Go up, I'll show you which boxes are Christmas decorations.*

It strikes me as odd– he could just pull them down for me. But I climb the ladder anyways, wanting to see what's up there for myself. He follows me up the ladder, and I stop at the top to reach for the light string. The light flickers on and he is now right behind me, one arm on either side of me, his breath near my ear, his body pressed against mine. In an instant, I feel like the same electricity that flowed through the light is now flowing through me. I suck in a deep breath.

His hand comes around my body and he signs in front of me as if my body is attached to his arm. *There are three tubs and a tree box.* He points to the plastic tubs that have 'Christmas decos' written on the side in sharpie.

I steady myself between him and the ladder and reach out for the tub closest to the opening, sliding it over to me. Lorenzo taps my lower back to get my attention. That's exactly what he got, my body goes into full attention, tension coursing through me as goosebumps take over my flesh. I turn my head to try and see what he has to say, but he pulls on my hips instead. When I'm nestled back against him, he signs in front of me again. *I will get them.* He climbs back down the ladder, and I follow.

His scent combined with the feel of his body pressed against me sparks this intense familiarity that ignites a fiery desire inside me. I watch him climb back up the ladder, bringing each tub and the tree down one by one. The way every nerve inside of me is electrified by his touch, his closeness, I question how the Scarlett I was before never fell for him. He is insanely sexy, and in this moment, I find myself fiercely wanting him. It could be because I haven't seen any action since before I woke from my coma. Or maybe, now that I'm not blinded by our memories, I am finally open to the innate attraction I have for him.

Once all the tubs are down from the attic, he lifts the ladder and eases it back into the ceiling. *Thanks,* I sign, unable to control the sheepish smile that has taken over my face.

He eyes me, a smirk now taking over his expression. His lips purse forward slightly, and he nods his head up. Instinctively, I know he's asking me 'what's up' without asking me what's up. I shake my head and shy my eyes away from him. He steps forward, his hand reaching into my line of sight and spells, *What?*

Slowly, my eyes trail up his body and meet his. I give him a subtle head shake, lifting my brows ever so slightly, and with one hand sign, *Nothing.* It begins to feel like all the air has been sucked out of the room and I can't breathe.

His head cocks to the side, his smirky grin still ever present, and ever so alluring. It's as though he can see right through me, as if he can read my mind. Before either one of us has a chance to think, he steps forward again. His hand whisks behind me, pulling me into him and his mouth comes down on mine. His other hand comes around to hold the back of my head, and my arms reach around his neck, fully embracing the kiss. My body tenses with desire, yet somehow relaxes with relief at the same time. His lips are soft on mine as they suckle my bottom lip between them. Under my shirt, my nipples pucker with excitement against the silk of my bra, the hardness of them rubbing against his chest. A deep groan rises up from his gut causing his lips to vibrate against mine. Then, without warning, he pulls away from me.

I'm sorry, he signs with one hand, wiping his mouth with the other. *I just... I'm sorry.*

I wave both hands in the air. *You don't have to apologize.* My eyes shy away from him, then I bring them back up to meet his again. *I liked it—* I confess with slow, intentional signs. *I wanted you to kiss me.*

His eyes widen at my confession. Then his face goes serious. *Scar, I've wanted you in so many ways for such a long time. Right now, I feel like it's best if we don't rush things. Let's focus on getting your memories back.*

I let out an exasperated sigh, my cheeks flushing hot with embarrassment. *You're probably right. It's just, you keep showing up in my dreams. And now that I'm around you, you affect me, physically.*

An ever so subtle cock of his eyebrow lets me know that he is pleased with that bit of insight. *I guess we'll just have to spend time together and allow things to develop naturally.*

I guess so. I'd be lying if I said I wasn't disappointed.

Chapter 45
Lorenzo

*T*hat was literally the hardest thing I've ever had to do. God, her lips taste just how she smells, like coconut and vanilla. When her nipples started to pebble against my chest... fuck me. I could feel the blood rushing straight to my... yeah, I had to back away. I didn't want to scare her away. But then she told me she wanted it, that I *affect* her physically. It's like my dreams coming true right before my eyes, and I am here for it. At the same time, I know we can't rush this. Her memories are coming back. Sure, she's only remembering in her dreams right now, but it's just a matter of time before she remembers everything. She'll remember Eli. She'll remember when she cut me out of her life. She'll remember the side of me she didn't like. And what I fear the most, she'll remember that to her, I am family.

    I'm spending the day at her house. We're putting up her Christmas tree. It reminds me of the night a year ago when I confessed my love for her and when I kissed her the first time. Except, this time we actually got the tree up and now we're working on hanging the ornaments. Going up the ladder behind her was a ploy to help trigger her memories, because it was just how it had been that night. That night, my hopes were lifted, only to be pulled back to reality the next morning. This time, I'm hopeful that she has developed a new connection with me that will help her move forward into a new direction with our relationship.

    I pick up another ornament from the coffee table where we have them all splayed out. It's very familiar to me because I made it for her in high school. The fact that she still has it blows my mind. I wave my hand at her to get her attention, she looks over her shoulder while still sliding an ornament onto one of the branches. *I can't believe you still have this,* I say, pointing to the ornament that dangles from my left hand.

Is it special? She turns to face me and strides over to the table. Taking the ornament from my hand, she inspects it with hers. It's simple really, we had rolled up little strips of wrapping paper and stuffed the rolls into clear plastic ornaments. Most of the kids in my class had thought it was stupid, but I knew how much Scar loved Christmas. I couldn't wait to give it to her.

Yeah, I made it for you when I was in high school, I say it nonchalantly, but inside I am beyond ecstatic that she's kept it all these years.

Her eyes start to glisten as her lips pull into a grin. *It's beautiful. I'm not surprised I kept it.* She turns back to the tree and hangs it front and center. *It's perfect.*

We spend the rest of the morning and early afternoon hanging her lights outside and placing her inside decorations throughout the living room and kitchen. Once the house has fully transformed into her personal Christmas wonderland, we order Chinese takeout and pull up Netflix to find a movie.

What kind of movie do you want to watch? she asks, flipping through the main screen on the tv.

Anything. You pick. We could stare at a blank screen, and I'd be thrilled just to be curled up next to her.

She thinks for a moment and then signs. *I don't really know what kind of movies I like,* she confesses. *Please, you pick something.*

I know exactly what to watch. I remember watching this movie with her when it first came out. She cried so much, and when it was over she said it was her new favorite movie. I switch to a different streaming platform and type CODA into the search bar.

CODA? she asks, still unfamiliar with the word. *What's that about?*

Basically? I sign with raised eyebrows in a rhetorical question. *You,* I say simply. She eyes me, her brows furrowed with questions. It's adorable and it makes me laugh. Finally, I ease her torture. *CODA means Child of a Deaf Adult. This movie is about a girl whose whole family is Deaf, she's the only hearing one. The first time we watched it, you told me it was your new favorite movie.*

Her lips curl into a perfect 'o,' showing that she recalls the term. *Right, I think you told me that word before, when I first woke up.* I nod. *Let's watch it.* Her face lights up with excitement.

I press play and as the opening credits come on the screen, I pull the throw blanket from behind us, settling it over our laps. She eases in closer to me, curling her legs up beside her and nestling her head on my chest. Welcoming the closeness, I lift my arm and drape it over her shoulder, allowing her to snuggle in even closer. We've watched many movies this way over the years, the closeness is always intense for me. Now I'm hoping it's just as intense for her.

The movie's opening scene comes onto the screen, the girl singing as she works on her father's fishing boat alongside her brother. To be honest, I like this movie too if only for the fact that it's one movie where through most of it I don't have to read captions the entire time. Scar turns to look up at me, a huge smile on her face. *I like it already,* she says, barely two minutes into the movie.

I could stay here in this position forever. Well, maybe I would want to try some other positions, some more intimate positions. But for now, being here snuggled up with my Scar feels like heaven. It feels like I never want to leave. My phone vibrates in my pocket, Scar barely flinches as I lift one of my hips to reach my hand in there and retrieve it. A banner lights up across the lock screen telling me that our Doordash order has been delivered. I flash the screen to Scar so she can see, and she lifts her head to allow me to stand.

After grabbing the bag of food from the front porch and closing the door behind me, I hold the bag up toward Scar who is still seated on the couch. *You want to make a plate?* The Scar I know would want to make a plate in the kitchen and bring that to the couch, because her fear of overeating never allowed her to eat from the cartons.

She nods and pads her bare feet toward the kitchen. She moves with ease through the kitchen, pulling plates from the cabinet and fishing forks from a drawer. I reach under the island and pull a bottle of wine from the built-in wine rack, holding it up along with my eyebrows to ask if she wants some. She nods again, this time with a mischievous grin. We don't talk as our hands are busy, hers dishing food onto a plate, mine opening and pouring the wine.

A bottle of wine later, and I'm uncorking a second bottle. We've finished eating and Scar picked out another movie for us to watch. I'm in absolute heaven. Handing a freshly filled glass to Scar, I settle back into our cozy position, then my phone vibrates again. It's a FaceTime call from Mom. Shit. I forgot about family dinner. I press the accept button and rest my phone against my knee so I can sign with my free hand, not wanting to move my arm from around Scar. She notices and looks over at my phone, but doesn't move away from me.

Hey, Mom. I sign once her face is on the screen. I can see in the self-view that Scar is somewhat visible on the screen as well. It's quite obvious that my arm is around her.

Zo? Are you coming to dinner? Your dad said you were coming, she asks, her expression a mix of panic and intrigue. *Is that Scar?* she asks her next question before I even have a chance to respond.

Yes, I say, unable to hide the huge grin on my face. In my peripheral, I can see that Scar is watching the phone, she can see my uncontrollable smile as well. *Yes, I'm with Scar. Sorry, Mom, time got away from me. I forgot about dinner.*

It's not too late, bring Scar, she says, her own face twisting into a smile at the sight of Scar in my arms. Her eyes turn to address Scar beside me. *Please, come to dinner, we'd love to have you.*

Forget Me Not

I turn the phone slightly to allow for both of us to be in view. Scar holds up her wine glass before responding. *I'm not sure either one of us can drive tonight. How about tomorrow? Invite Helen too, I'd love to come.*

Mom's face lights up. *Perfect, I will see you two tomorrow.* A sly expression takes over her face. *Have fun tonight.* She winks, then quickly adds, *Not too much.*

My eyes roll at her suggestive comment. *Later, Mom.* I give her a quick wink that goes unnoticed by Scar before pressing the button to end the call.

Scar turns her face up to me and smiles, saying nothing. We sit there for a beat, holding eye contact, and then our lips meet again. Everything inside me lights on fire. These lips are meant to be mine. Soft and sweet, they fit perfectly with my own. She shifts her body, placing her glass on the coffee table before turning into me. With my long arm, I move my own glass to the end table next to the couch before reaching it around to hold Scar's face. It's only been hours since I told her we should go slow, let things happen naturally. I know I need to be a man of my word and follow through. I know I need to stop this before it goes too far. But her lips... her damn delicious lips.

Giving in, I shift my body to stretch my leg across the back of the couch. With one knee bent, my foot firmly on the floor, she now blankets my body with hers. All the blood in my body has run to its central location and I'm hard as a rock. I know she can feel it, she knows I know she can feel it. She has one hand cupping my face, the other pressed to my chest, and her body squirms against me. My pelvis begins to press against her, I don't seem to have any control over this. The hand resting on my chest slides down my torso and up under my shirt. The warmth of her palm penetrates my skin, radiating through me and I let out a deep groan. Fuck. I desperately want to rip her clothes off and touch and kiss every inch of her. I have to fight it. I have to at least make the effort to be a gentleman.

Gently, I push her up, pulling our lips apart. She's straddling me now, making this even harder for me to attempt stopping. Her head cocks quizzically, a look of disappointment taking over her expression. With one hand still clutching desperately to her thick hip I sign, *Scar.*

She eyes me, waiting for me to say more. Begging me to let her have this moment with me. *I want this, Lorenzo. I want you,* she assures me.

Our eyes lock while my mind races, studying her for any doubt, any hesitation. All I see is desire. Shit, all I feel is desire. Deciding we both want this to happen, I reach my arm around her and flip us over in a swift swoop. Our first time, I will make love to her. She can be in charge next time. Her head tosses back with a giddy smile on her face, and I can only assume she's giggling in delight. It's that same smile she always has when she laughs, only this time it's even more special and beautiful than ever. My mouth plunges into hers and she paws at the hem of my shirt. I'm obliged to let her pull it up over my head, tossing it on the floor beside us. God dammit, this is it. This is the moment I've been waiting so many years for. I sit up again, I want to take this in, savor it. My hand is practically shaking as I reach down to grip the bottom of her shirt.

As I pull it up, she sits up to allow me to glide it over her head, tossing it on top of mine on the floor. Fuck me. She's not wearing a bra, her breasts bounce back into place, full and bottom heavy with perfectly pink nipples centered in the creamy flesh, just as I have always imagined. Without hesitation, my mouth devours one, then the other, leaving them hard and wet.

Grabbing her hips, I guide her farther up on the couch, slinking my fingers into the waistband of her pajama bottoms. As if I'm unwrapping a gift, which is exactly what she is to me, I take my time sliding the fabric over her ass and down her legs. She's fully naked now, completely exposed to me. We take another moment to lock our eyes, another moment to confirm we are taking this leap.

This version of Scar isn't as shy about her body, she doesn't remember that part of her. This version of Scar gives me a sly smile and presses her hips up, wanting to feel my mouth in her most intimate places. I, of course, oblige. Her body shivers when my lips meet her thick juicy lips. She's already soaking wet, her silky desire spilling out as my tongue parts her core. She writhes beneath me, and I cling to her hips, forcing her to stay still and endure the painful pleasure.

    She doesn't take long, and her body quickly shudders as she orgasms against my tongue. I kiss her clit lightly, teasing the swollen button, and she grabs hold of my head, pulling my face back up to hers. She kisses me deeply, our lips now slick from her wetness. My dick is throbbing, and the loose fabric of my joggers does nothing to conceal how ready I am. Scar reaches for the waistband, tugging downward. God, I'm aching to be inside her, to feel her warmth and wetness. I give in and decide to give her what she wants. Helping her release me, I sit up and wiggle out of my pants, now as naked as she is. Her eyes widen at the sight of me. She's seen me hard through my pajama bottoms before, I chuckle inwardly remembering her reaction. This time, I'm fully exposed, fully hard. Slowly, I drape my body back down onto her and settle myself between her thick thighs. The length of me folds forward, resting against her wet lips. Her chest and throat vibrate as a moan radiates through her body. I can't hear it, but her breath is hot as the moan escapes her mouth.

    She clutches my hair into her fists on either side of my head and studies my eyes, begging me to make this final decision, begging me to ease into her. So, I do. My hips press back allowing my hardness to fall into place, and as I press them back against her, the warm pool between her legs coats me. Her head falls back, her mouth is wide, and I feel that same vibration of her throaty moan.

    Neither one of us seems concerned with protection, only the raw desire that pulses between us. I feel confident she's good, and I know I would never do anything to hurt her. I plunge in and out as she rocks her hips up and down against me. Wanting to savor every moment of my first time inside of her, I keep my rhythm slow. My arms reach around her body, squeezing her up against me. We are so close that our faces are cheek to cheek, so I turn my head and kiss her neck, breathing in the scent of her hair. Fucking coconut and vanilla. She clutches my back so hard I can feel her nails dig into my skin. She's coming again, her core throbs around me, pulsating bits of pleasure and I have to focus hard on holding back my release. The pleasure is too much for me, and as I feel myself ready to explode, I quickly yank out of her, letting it spill out onto her stomach instead.

    She looks up at me, a sheepish, satisfied smile on her face. I'm supporting myself with one arm, so I unwrap my hand from around my dick and sign what I've felt in my heart for over sixteen years. *I love you, Scar. I love you with everything inside me.*

    She's not ready to say those words back to me. Right now, I'm perfectly fine with that. She will say them soon enough. She just smiles up at me before reaching her hands up to cup my face and pull it down to her. We share a sweet kiss, and without the words, her lips tell me what her hands couldn't. She loves me too.

Chapter 46
Scarlett

𝒜 montage of images and clips run through my mind. In a long silver, sequined dress, my arm stretching out as a pink corsage is slipped onto my wrist. Young Lorenzo smiling at me as he holds that same pink corsage. A sea of navy-blue graduation caps over a football field as I walk in a line across the stage, followed by an image of Mom, Alana, Corbin, and Lorenzo smiling in a sunny set of packed bleachers. My hand holding a single key, turning the lock on the front door of my house, and then Lorenzo carrying boxes from a U-Haul truck parked in the driveway. Me, nestled in Lorenzo's arms on the couch, a fuzzy blanket draped over us. Then, Eli. Eli's face comes in with a backdrop of Lake Wilson, his hand reaching up to brush hair from my face. Sitting around a bar table, Lorenzo on one side and Eli on the other. A green velvet dress. Eli, naked in front of a shower with steam swirling around the room. Lorenzo tilting me down and kissing me. Followed by Eli's fist slamming into Lorenzo's face. Lorenzo's face, with sad, tear-filled eyes. Walking into the bar full of faces I know shouting 'Surprise!' Eli, down on one knee, sliding a gorgeous diamond ring on my finger. A steering wheel, one hand holding a phone open to a text box screen. Slamming into a tree, my body flying through the air. Then my mind goes black.

    I jolt awake, sitting up straight in my bed. My heart is racing, and my hands are clammy with sweat. Lorenzo is next to me. He stirs at my movement and I'm suddenly aware that we are both naked. I snatch the blanket up to cover my exposed chest as his eyes open and he smiles up at me.

    His expression immediately twists into concern once he sees the state I'm in. *Scar? What's wrong?* He sits up just as quickly as his expression had changed.

I stare into his eyes, remembering the day we had yesterday. Remembering how intimate we were, how exposed I was to him. His eyebrow cocks and he tilts his head forward, urging me to respond. *I... I had more dreams.*

His face lights up at that. *More memories?* Both his brows lift with anticipated intrigue. *Tell me, what did you see? What did you dream about?*

Everything. That is all I can say. It's the truth too. As soon as my eyes open, all I have is the memory of the memory montage. The actual events still elude my conscious mind. But I know that these images and scenes that played through my mind are my experiences creeping their way out of the shadows and into the forefront.

There's a hint of fear in his eyes. He knows there is something I will soon remember that could damage the relationship we've developed. I'm sure it has something to do with the image of Eli punching him in the face. Still, deep down in my soul I know that he and I are meant to be together. Whatever held me back before the accident was erased along with my memories. Because without knowing our past, without being closed off by previous boundaries, I am able to open myself up to the natural pull between us. That was confirmed for me when we made love for the first time... and second... and third.

Breaking the silence, I curl my lips and smile at him, assuring him that he has nothing to worry about. *Don't worry, Lorenzo. Whatever memory you are afraid will come back, I'm sure we can work through it.*

He visibly relaxes, the tension in his shoulders easing away, the fear in his eyes replaced with a glistening hopefulness. *I hope so,* he signs slowly.

I bend down and kiss him, hoping that I can assure him with my lips, if not my hands. Then decide there's something I need to do today. *Dinner tonight, with your parents?* He nods. *I'm excited, I can't wait.* Then I hesitate a moment before asking for the day to myself. *There's something I need to do today. But I will meet you there, okay?*

His eyes shift back and forth between mine, the fear still hidden deep inside. *OK,* he finally says.

My hands are shaking as I stop in front of the door to Fire & Ice, feeling a little uneasy about going inside. It's been six months since I walked away from Eli. The last time I was in his bar, I had given him his ring back. There's a certain feeling of dread coursing through me, knowing he probably doesn't want to see me. I hesitate before finally slowly pushing the door open. It's still fairly early in the afternoon on a Sunday, so it's not busy.

Immediately, I notice Ana behind the bar, and she notices me. We share a look. I'm trying to communicate empathy and embarrassment. She is communicating surprise. After a moment, she smiles and waves at me, and I inch my way over to the bar. My eyes scan the room for Eli, though I don't see him by the time I've closed the distance to the bar.

"Scarlett, how are you?" she asks with a genuine smile.

"I'm good, really good." I can say that with confidence because life is actually quite good. "How about you?" I return the polite question, hoping to bide time and not have to ask for Eli.

"Pretty good, Diedre and I just bought a house." Her cheeks pull apart in a wide grin at the mention of her exciting news.

"Ana, that's amazing!" I'm assuming Diedre is her partner and I've met her at some point. Though I'm not sure Ana realizes that it would have been before my accident.

My eyes dart around the room again, hesitant to ask for him, though Ana knows who I am here to see. "He's in the office working, would you like me to tell him you're here?" she finally offers, breaking the awkward silence.

"Yes, please," I say with a sheepish tone.

Fierce thuds pound in my chest as my heart begins to race in anticipation. I don't want to give him the wrong idea. I don't want to hurt him again. But deep down, I feel this need to apologize. A need to make things right. Then I see him, walking down the hallway. He stops short and is just standing there with his eyes on me. His face is almost in disbelief.

The empathetic smile I give him urges his feet forward toward me. There's a gush of air I've been holding in that rushes out of my lungs. "Hi, Eli," I breathe.

He shakes his head before speaking as if shaking away the disbelief. "Scarlett, hi. How are you?" It looks like he's deciding whether to hug me, so I step forward with open arms to make the decision for him.

"I'm really good, how about you?" I say as we back away from the embrace.

To my surprise, a big smile spreads across his face. "Honestly, same." It's like he can't hold back some newfound happiness trying to escape him. "What brings you here, did you get your memories back?" His expression tells me he's optimistic about my answer.

"Not exactly." He gestures for me to sit on one of the barstools as he sits on the one next to it. We turn our chairs slightly, so we are facing each other. "I've been having dreams. The dreams feel so real, like déjà vu."

"Scarlett, that's amazing. Have you talked with the doctor about it?" He's different from the last time I saw him. The sadness is gone, and it makes me wonder what helped him through it.

"Not yet." I shake my head. "But I believe they are memories, not dreams. It's just that they only come when I'm sleeping, or half asleep. When I'm awake, I can't bring the memories back yet." I give him a little explanation without mentioning that Lorenzo was the one who confirmed that my dreams are actually memories.

"That's really great. I'm sure your memories will come back anytime now," he assures me, placing his hand on top of mine. The gesture is friendly, not romantic. "Hey, I'm glad you came by. Now that you're here, I want to tell you there's no hard feelings. I was very heartbroken for a long time, but I'm at peace now."

His words give me more hope than I've had since I woke from my coma. "Oh, Eli, thanks for telling me that. I've felt bad about how things ended up with us. Most of the images I've seen in my dreams are memories from before I met you. But you showed up in them last night."

One corner of his mouth curls up in a satisfied smile. "Hopefully all good things."

I nod, letting out an amused giggle. "I felt this pull to come and apologize to you for everything that happened."

His head quickly shakes back and forth. "Really, there's no need. We are good." His eye twinkles as he winks at me, assuring me that there truly are no hard feelings.

For a moment, I debate with telling him that I've reconnected with Lorenzo. Words play in my mind of how I can tell him without upsetting him. "Also..." the word slowly leaves my lips, "I ran into Lorenzo recently."

His jaw clinches ever so subtly that only someone who has spent their lifetime reading facial expressions would catch. I watch his Adam's apple slide down his throat as he swallows whatever emotions that name evokes inside of him.

"I wanted to let you know, he's helping me with bringing those memories back. And..." I clear my throat. He doesn't need to know we've slept together, but it's only fair he knows we are potentially involved. "There are feelings there. Feelings I think have always been there, but were just suppressed by my view of who he was to me."

His lips press together in a hard line, he swallows again, and then he smiles. "I'm glad you have someone, Scarlett. I hope he treats you well." There's a curtness to his tone, though he seems genuine in his words.

"Thank you, Eli. I hope you—"

His face turns away from me, his attention pulled to the front door. I turn to see who has his attention. "Excuse me, Scarlett." He stands, his face glowing as he makes his way to a redheaded woman who is standing just inside the door.

As they embrace, he kisses her, then takes her hand and leads her over to me. While they walk, he signs, *I want you to meet someone.* I gulp.

Scarlett, I want you to meet Rose. He spells her name first and then shows me her name sign. Then he spells my name to her. *Rose, this is Scarlett.*

Nice to meet you. I instinctively code switch into sign language, realizing that Rose is Deaf. A fact that digs down deep inside of me, warming my soul.

Scarlett, you seem familiar to me, she signs. Her smile is riveting. Not only is she gorgeous, she seems to be a genuinely sweet person too.

My parents are Deaf, we've probably met at some Deaf event in the area in the past, I explain. Then I turn to Eli and ask, *Are you two... dating?*

They both nod while staring into each other's eyes. *We met a couple of weeks ago, right here. She came in with friends and,* his smile grows wider, *thanks to you, I knew enough sign language to talk to her.*

I can feel the corners of my own mouth turn up at the revelation. *That's amazing, and Eli, wow, your signing has gotten really good!*

We practice often, Rose chimes in with an impish smile.

Watching them for a beat, I feel a sense of satisfaction. Eli has found love, maybe even his true love. It's all so clear to me now, Eli and I weren't meant to be forever, we weren't meant to be soul mates. We were meant to cross paths, to open his world to a new culture, a new language. I'm sure our time together was special, in many ways. Though now I can see it was to open his pathway to Rose, who from the looks of it, is his true soul mate. I get the strong sense that Eli has made this same revelation.

I'm glad you two found each other. I turn to Eli, *I'm glad you're doing so well.* We share a moment between us, an unspoken understanding of closure. It's the most intense and concrete closure, exactly what I needed.

Although I am using my phone's GPS to direct me to the Tate's house, it feels like there is some unconscious pull inside me that is actually directing me. When I pull into the driveway, I can see that Lorenzo and Helen are both here. Slinging my purse over my shoulder, I make my way to the front door. My hands fidget in front of me as I wait for the door to open. I'm not sure why I am so nervous, I know everyone inside cares deeply for me.

Corbin is the one to answer the door. I've seen him quite a few times over the past several months since he interprets at ENCSD regularly. "Scar! We are so glad you came tonight." He pulls me in for a hug then steps aside for me to come in.

"Thanks, it's good to see you, Corbin." I look around the room for Lorenzo or Helen, ready to turn my voice off and switch to sign.

"Everyone is in the kitchen," Corbin says, pointing toward a hallway across the room.

He leads me toward the kitchen, and as I pass by the Christmas tree in the corner, an image flashes in my mind. It comes as such a shock to me, making me stop in my tracks, pulling my hand to my forehead and squeezing my eyes closed. In the image, I'm a young teenager or preteen. Lorenzo, also a teenager, is sitting on the floor with his back up to the couch and I am next to him. Our parents, all four of them, are seated on the couch and loveseat around the room. There is a mess of gift wrapping on the floor.

"Scar? You OK?" Corbin asks. I'm sure I look like I've just been hit with a horrible migraine with the way my hand is pressed to my forehead and my eyes shut so tightly.

Without opening my eyes, I nod my head. "I just...I think I just had a memory."

"Oh my god, Scar! That's amazing! Let me get everyone." I hear him trot off to the kitchen to tell everyone else.

I'm willing the image to come back into my brain, but it has escaped me. So, I open my eyes and look at the tree again, then squeeze them back tight. Another image flashes through my mind. This time, there are only three parents, but Lorenzo and I are right there on the floor, side by side, leaned up against the couch. He has one arm tucked behind me, showing me how to use what looks like

Tracey Gramajo

a hand-held video game. The image flashes away as quickly as it came on.

My body collapses down to the floor, as I'm kneeling there, still holding my forehead, I hear the rush of footsteps from the other room. A hand rests softly on my shoulder, and I can smell Lorenzo. I know he wants me to look up at him. "Scar, I'm here." I hear Lorenzo's accented voice in my ear.

I just want more images to come back, so I keep my eyes closed and sign, *I need more memories.*

His body slides down next to mine, I can feel him next to me as one arm comes around to rub my back. That's when another image flashes through my mind. Much like one that came to me in my dream, Lorenzo hugging me. The image starts to move, and I can feel us rocking back and forth, I can feel his hand rubbing up and down my back. I'm suddenly overcome with the emotions that seem to connect with this memory. It's after my dad died, and Lorenzo was consoling me. Tears stream down my face both in the memory and real life. Lorenzo's other hand reaches around, and with one finger, he wipes a tear from my cheek.

On my other side, I feel a softer female presence. Helen... Mom. Breathing in her scent, I am able to conjure another memory. I'm seated in a chair, maybe ten years old, and she's standing behind me. I watch the reflection of her braiding my hair into two French braids in the mirror in front of us. As she ties the second braid at the end, I jump off the chair and run through the house, out into the front yard. There, I see Lorenzo standing next to a bike, one hand holding it steady. He grins at the sight of me and signs, *Ready?* Then we ride off on our bikes together.

I've let go of my forehead now, and reach one hand to hold Lorenzo's, the other to hold Mom's. I squeeze them tight, letting them know I need them there in this moment, thanking them for being there. They both squeeze back. Another memory comes, it starts with that same reflection in the mirror of Mom behind me, styling my hair. I'm older this time and wearing that same silver dress from my dream. Prom night. Mom smiles lovingly at me in the mirror, her eyes brimming with tears, then she signs, *You're so beautiful, my beautiful baby girl.* I sign back to her in the mirror,

Thanks, Mom. We walk down the stairs to see Lorenzo and his parents waiting in the living room of Mom's little bungalow. His face is positively glowing, I feel a flush of heat over my cheeks from nerves and embarrassment. No, those aren't the emotions I'm feeling. Love... it's love! Or at least a schoolgirl crush. I squeeze Lorenzo's hand tight again.

One by one, the memories come flooding back. Everything from learning to ride a bike up to the text message I sent to Lorenzo before looking up to see brake lights in front of me. There are ups and downs, highs and lows. My heart aches as each emotion I've experienced with these memories inundates me. I let the tears flow, and I breathe out heavy sobs, unable to hold them in. The good, the bad, the ugly, all of it is beautiful because it's me. It's us. Outside of Mom, there is one constant throughout my memories. Lorenzo. How could I never see it before? How did it take losing my memory to erase the block I had set for him? How is it I am only now realizing that Lorenzo is my soulmate, the love of my life? He's my rock. He always has been. Finally, I open my eyes.

All four of them surround me, Lorenzo on my right, Mom on my left, the Tates in front of me. They're waiting with rabid anticipation. *My memories... they're back,* I sign slowly. *I remember everything.*

Mom squeezes my hand. I turn to her, and we share a tearful smile. She pulls me in for a hug. Once she releases me, I turn to Lorenzo. Grabbing hold of his hands, I stand up, pulling him to his feet with me. Our eyes meet, both wet with tears. My hands let go of his and reach up to cup his face before I say what he's been waiting so long to see me say.

I'm sorry it took me so long to see it, but I've finally realized my missing piece. His eyes widen and his brows lift waiting for me to say it clearly. *It's you, Lorenzo, it's always been you.* I point to my chest, cross my fisted hands over it, squeezing them tight against me, then point to Lorenzo.

Instantly, without hesitation, he grabs my waist with one hand, and my face with the other. His lips plunge against mine without care for the company we have in the room with us. After a moment, he pulls away. *I love you so much, Scar. My Scar.*

Epilogue
Scarlett

Beep, beep, beep. A rhythmic tone pierces my mind, my eyes flinching tighter with each staccato punch. The throbbing pressure in my head begins to resonate with the high-pitched sound, almost harmoniously— if it wasn't so painful.

"Miss Reese? Scarlett?" An unfamiliar woman's voice hums gently, echoing my name. Her presence is perceptible next to me, yet I can't seem to open my eyes. "I think she's waking up."

Beep, beep, beep. The noise steadily increases, in time to the heavy thudding in my chest. Is that... my heartbeat? A gush of air blankets my face, sending shivers through me. Warm hands engulf mine, then cup my face, relieving the cold. I know those hands, I'd know them anywhere. Silently speaking to me, even with my eyes still seemingly glued shut.

Unable to pry my eyelids open, I slowly lift my hand to sign the two letters of his name. *Lorenzo, you're here.*

His hand slides away from my cheek, slipping under my palm. With his fisted hand, he flicks his wrist up and down. *Yes.*

Questions flood my mind. I desperately want to open my eyes, to ask my questions and fill in the blanks. Where am I? What day is it? Did we—? His warm breath closes in, and I feel his soft lips place a kiss on my forehead. Light as it is, the touch awakens a pain, reminding me of the throbbing pulse. I wince. It's enough to slit my eyes open.

Blurred by my lashes, the stark room slowly comes into view. It's bright and white. White walls, white tile floors, white bed sheet, white curtains drawn over the large window. Lorenzo stands there, one hand still cupping my face. I lean into the warmth, the familiarity.

He smiles at me, though his smile is hiding fear. There's something different about him too, he's grown out a beard and his hair seems a bit longer. *I'm so glad you're finally awake. How do you feel?*

Clearly, I'm in the hospital. How I got here, that's one of the many questions I have. *My head is pounding.*

I'm not surprised. You had a pretty bad head injury.

Just then a man in blue scrubs comes in with a nurse following closely behind him. A woman, who I imagine is an interpreter for Lorenzo, steps in the doorway as well. "Miss Reese, you're awake," the man states observantly. "I'm Dr. Harris, I've been your doctor since you came in. I'm going to check you over, if that's alright."

Lorenzo steps back to make room for Dr. Harris, who has started toying with the beeping machine next to the bed. "Since I came in? How long ago was that?"

Dr. Harris jots down something on the clipboard that had been hooked to the foot of my bed then slips the pen back into the pocket of his white coat. His eyes trail up to the ceiling, momentarily in thought. "Hmm, almost four weeks ago. You've been in a coma since you got out of surgery."

Panic stabs at my heart as all the blood seems to drain from it. "Surgery? Coma? Oh my god, what happened?" The beeping on the monitor speeds up again.

Lorenzo pats my foot to get my attention. *You were in an accident, a bad one.*

"You came in after an accident. A broken rib had punctured one of your lungs, and you had significant swelling in your brain from trauma to the head. I induced a coma after surgery to allow the swelling to come down," the doctor explains.

"Another accident?" I say the words out loud, but even my thoughts somehow feel contradictory.

Dr. Harris cocks an eyebrow at me. "Not as far as I know." He pulls the pen from his pocket again and holds it in front of my face. It's terribly familiar. "Follow this with your eyes, try not to move your head."

My eyes trail after the pen as he moves it up, down, and side to side. "You did that before too. Except, did you used to have a mustache?"

His eyebrow raises again and he jots a note on the clipboard. "This is a common test after a head injury, perhaps you've had it done before with another doctor."

"No, no, it was here. It was you, I had amnesia. How could you not remember that?" The throbbing in my chest quickens, sending a warmth through me. My palms feel clammy and the room starts spinning around me.

Lorenzo has been watching the conversation through the interpreter. He looks over at me, his brows clench and his eyes narrow in on me. *Scar, what are you talking about?*

What am I talking about? I pause, holding back my answer. My eyes flit back and forth between Lorenzo and Dr. Harris, both waiting for my response. But my mind races and somehow freezes all at once. Cloudy images of me waking up in a hospital bed, with the same throbbing in my head, clash with the scene before me. I shake my head, wanting this moment to pass.

"I think maybe you need to get some rest. Give yourself some time for your conscious mind to catch up. You've been unconscious for quite some time," Dr. Harris suggests before hooking the clipboard back to the end of the bed and heading out.

As the nurse takes down my vitals, the doctor's words sink in. *Allow time for my conscious mind to catch up.* Catch up with what? My unconscious mind?

Lorenzo doesn't let me off so easily. *Scar,* he presses, *what are you talking about? You think you've had two accidents?*

I don't know, I swear I woke up from a coma like... maybe six months ago? I had lost my memory. You were here, and Eli — Oh my god, Eli. My heart sinks thinking about how amazing he was, how terrible it was for him when I gave him back the ring. How heartbroken he was when I walked away.

Eli? The bartender? He tilts his head, pinching his brows together in confusion. *You only met him just before the accident, why would he be here?*

We were engaged, don't you remember? Full on panic sets in. My signs start to become erratic. *We started dating before the Christmas party last year, you had told me you loved me, but I chose him. Lorenzo, how do you not remember this?* My head is spinning. My thoughts blur between reality and faint whispers of mental images. *You took it really hard. Then I wrecked Eli's car, when I woke up right here, you both were here, said you never left my side. Lorenzo, how do you not remember?*

Lorenzo moves closer to me, touching his hand to my forehead. He winces, pulling his hand back quickly. *You are warm, Scar. I think maybe you should rest. I'm going to let Helen know you're awake.*

No. Lorenzo, don't leave me. I reach my hand out to him. *I'm so confused.* A heavy tear forms in the well of my eye, spilling over and sliding down my cheek. *Can you tell me what happened?*

You were in an accident. A tow truck ran a red light and T-boned your car. According to witnesses, your car spun out and flipped over. You were unconscious when the paramedics got there. They brought you straight to surgery. That was four weeks ago.

My eyes squeeze shut, searching the depths of my memories for anything from that accident. *What happened the day before the accident?*

He rakes a hand slowly through his hair, reluctant to respond. *We spent the night together.*

I swallow the dry lump that formed in my throat. *We watched my favorite movie and... made love.*

A sound chuffs from his lungs, I can't tell if it's a laugh or pure shock. *No, no. I told you that I've been in love with you since we were teenagers. But, no, we did not make love.*

Right, I remember the night he told me he loved me. The night we pulled Christmas decorations from the attic. The night after I met Eli at the bar. That was a year ago. Wasn't it? *I* remember that night, I asked you to hold me. Wasn't that last year? Then I went on a date with Eli and— I'm cut off by my own confusion.

You never made it to your date with Eli. I guess you were on your way to meet him when the accident happened.

Wait, so what is today?

It's Friday, December 15th,

What year?

2023.

My lungs are on fire. I can't breathe. If this is all true, then I spent the past four weeks in a *vivid* dream cycle. I think back over what I believe are memories of Eli. Flawlessly perfect Eli. Our first date where he kissed me overlooking Lake Wilson. The next Monday when he brought me lunch at work, a lunch that he cooked for me. How he dealt with a jealous Lorenzo patiently and gracefully. The way he respected me, waiting for the perfect moment to take our relationship to the next level. His fluent signing skills within six months of meeting me. His perfectly chiseled body standing stark naked in the hotel bathroom. The images become more and more fuzzy in my mind as I realize that everything about Eli had been everything I had dreamed my perfect man would be. I play through the fading images again. Our first date, I remember it so clearly, he was watching me instead of the ducks. I remember how I looked through his eyes— wait. How can *I* remember how I looked through *his* eyes? I close my eyes and look back over the reel of events cycling through my mind and realize there are scenes and images that I wasn't even present for. How is it I remember those?

My eyes meet Lorenzo's, I study them, conjuring the memories of him from this dream cycle. His jealous, erratic behavior. His desperate attempts to disrupt my budding relationship with Eli. His sad broken eyes when Eli and I got engaged. I can feel *his* emotions, the thoughts *he* had. How is *that* possible? That wasn't Lorenzo. Not my Lorenzo. He's always been so supportive of me, caring, concerned. He's always been like the sweet, patient Lorenzo I remember from after I woke from my coma. My *other* coma. My *fake* coma? Did I dream this whole thing?

With a subtle clinch of his brows and flick of his head, I know Lorenzo is asking me what is going through my mind. I can't answer him, not yet. I'm still deciphering what's real and what my unconscious mind fabricated in my dream. *I think I had a very elaborate dream while I was in the coma. It felt so real. I'm trying to make sense of it all.*

Must have been one heck of a dream.

It was. I debate whether to ask my next question, but curiosity takes over. *What happened to Eli?*

He checked in on you once, after he found out about the accident. He thought you had stood him up. But he barely knew you, so he didn't come back around after that.

I nod knowingly, then study Lorenzo again. My heart swells, sending a warmth through my body. Even though I know the memory of us together is fake, it opened my mind. This man in front of me, here with me now, he truly is my rock. He's everything I've wanted in a man. He may not be perfect. But somehow, I think he might just be perfect for me. *Is the Christmas party still happening?*

By the look on his face, Lorenzo thought it an odd topic change, but rolls with it. *Yeah, Macie stepped in and made sure everything was taken care of while you were here.*

I smile mischievously at him. *Will you be my date?*

Acknowledgements

Setting out to write a book is a scary thing. But when you're surrounded by people who geek out with you and show you all the love and support, it makes it just a little bit easier.

    First, I have to thank my husband, Ramon Gramajo. When I anxiously told him I wanted to write a book, and seriously pursue becoming a published author, he said, "What are you waiting for?" There was no judgment, no concerns with my writing ability. Only full-on support. Every day through the writing, and publishing process, he would say, "Chop, chop." Thank you, Mi Amor, hopefully soon you'll be the stay-at-home husband you've been waiting to be, working on building our dream skoolie!

    Next, I have to thank my coworkers who had to hear me talk about this book and these characters practically nonstop. Most especially, Emma Joynes, who not only listened to me go on and on, but also helped me talk through ideas and completely geeked out with me. I think she fell in love with these characters as much as I did. Thank you, my OG beta reader slash book coach! Oh, and Christine Mairer, thanks for nothing! I hope you read the next book.

    A special thank you to my developmental editor, Brandy Gibson, who I connected with through Fiverr. She did a phenomenal job of helping me bring my writing and story to the next level. I absolutely plan to work with her again on my next project.

    Also through Fiverr, I connected with a few beta readers who provided invaluable feedback. Kristin Fricke, Chris L, and Gina Karasek. Gina especially went above and beyond; she taught this amateur writer an important grammatical rule that will help me throughout my future writing career.

    Finally, thank you to those pre-publishing readers who had the opportunity to read the polished manuscript for final feedback. Octavia Earl, don't worry, I'm saving your spot in the made for TV movie! To hear comments like, "I started to forget you wrote it and realized I was reading a real book!" really helped keep me motivated through navigating the challenges of self-publishing. Can I just say, writing a book is the easy part of writing a book.

I'm thankful to have finally completed my debut novel after many years of feeling inadequate. This was perhaps the most enjoyable challenge of my life, and I cannot wait to dive headfirst into the next novel.

Forget Me Not

Discussion Questions

1) One common feature of American Sign Language is facial expression. Deaf people often use facial expressions that may commonly mean something else to the general public. One expression that shows up often in the story is Lorenzo's "signature expression," described as raised brows and pouty lips. Does this expression make you feel like he is upset or sad? Or does it read more as being nonchalant? Now knowing that ASL uses these expressions in a different context, does that change how his expression reads for you?

2) When reading from Lorenzo's perspective, he often comments on Scarlett's looks, feel, and scent. Do you think that his lack of one sense makes him place more emphasis on input from his other senses?

3) Throughout the book there are a few times where the concept of love is expressed in ASL. In chapter 2, Lorenzo says "love it," by kissing the back of his fist. At the end of chapter five, Scarlett describes the sign for "I love you" used by the community to express any and all types of love. Later in the book, that same sign is described as holding up the fingers for I, L, and Y. The last chapter describes crossing fists over the chest to say, "I love you." These do represent three different types of love, the love of things, friendship love, and romantic love. Which do you think applies to each type of love?

4) In chapter 3, Scarlett mentions that it is rude to use your voice when Deaf people are in the room, and everyone knows sign language. Why do you think that is?

5) It's obvious to everyone in the story except for Scarlett that Lorenzo has been in love with her for years. Why do you think she

was so blind to his affection? Could she have compartmentalized him, blocking any possibility of falling in love with him? Could she have, on some level, been avoiding having to spend the rest of her life interpreting for a Deaf partner as she had for her Deaf parents?

6) There were a few instances in the book where conversations are described in the intimate register for ASL. What did you notice about those scenes and how the production of ASL is different from a more casual or formal register?

7) Think about the first five chapters. Scarlett has two potential love interests, as the reader, which character do you root for in the beginning? Are you team Lorenzo, or team Eli?

8) Despite telling Lorenzo she needs time to consider a shift in their relationship, Scarlett falls hard and fast for Eli. Why do you think that is?

9) Lorenzo begins to behave somewhat erratically once he realizes that he is rapidly losing his chance with Scarlett. He shows a clear distaste for Eli, his competitor. Do you think he is taking his frustration out on Eli when he could actually be mad at himself for waiting too long to confess his feelings for Scarlett?

10) Eli seems too good to be true. He's open, honest, protective, and behaves like a gentleman. Do you think he is actually that secure, or is he too good to be true?

11) When Lorenzo and James are in the office chatting, James says to Lorenzo that he's in a Hallmark movie and that his character always gets the girl in the end. Do you think this was foreshadowing?

12) The morning of the Christmas party, Scarlett woke with a nagging feeling that something was going to go wrong during the party. She wrote her unease off as nerves surrounding the fact that she knew she would be spending the night with Eli for the first

time. In fact, quite a few things went wrong that night, what were they?

13) At the party, Lorenzo gets his dance with Scarlett. With alcohol and other substances involved, Lorenzo kisses Scarlett in the lobby hallway. He later says he misread signals. Do you think he believed she wanted to kiss him or was he so desperate he would try anything?

14) Eli suspects that Lorenzo drugged Scarlett. He does mention the CBD he put in his own wine. Do you believe Lorenzo was so desperate that he would have drugged Scarlett or that she drank his wine by accident?

15) How do you feel about the male love interests now? Are you still on the same team? Have you switched sides?

16) Ultimately, Scarlett decides to walk away from her friendship with Lorenzo, choosing to focus on her relationship with Eli. Six months go by and we learn that Lorenzo is still pining after Scarlett. What do you think is holding him back from moving on?

17) After having the most amazing birthday, including getting engaged to Eli, Scarlett has a terrible accident. While she's in surgery, Lorenzo and Eli's dispositions almost flip flop. Lorenzo becomes calm while Eli begins to spiral. Why do you think they both experienced this shift?

18) When Scarlett wakes from her coma, she has lost all of her memories. Because language and memories are functions of different parts of the brain, she still knows sign language but has lost all knowledge of Deaf culture. Does this seem believable? Why or why not?

19) Without her memories, Scarlett has a sense of connection to Lorenzo, but not Eli. Could this be because she has known him her whole life? If so, then why doesn't she feel that connection with Helen?

20) While Scarlett begins to navigate life without her memories, she develops her connection with Lorenzo into feelings. Do you think that by forgetting who she used to believe he was, she could open herself up to accepting the feelings she'd had for him all along?

21) Eli struggles with how to handle Scarlett losing her memories. For him, they are very much in love and just got engaged. For her, he's a perfect stranger. How does he manage these feelings within himself?

22) Macie quickly becomes a source of comfort for Scarlett after losing her memories. Macie has been team Eli since he came into the picture and continues to be after the accident. Do you think her suggestion for Eli to pretend like they were meeting for the first time helped?

23) After spending time with both Lorenzo and Eli (and kissing both of them!) Macie helps Scarlett remember why she never dated Lorenzo in the past. She reminded her that she would have never dated two guys at once. Scarlett chooses to walk away from both men. Do you think this was a smart decision?

24) In part three, Lorenzo runs into Scarlett after not seeing her for six months. She is happy to see him and confesses that she's been having dreams about him. We learn that these dreams are actually memories. Do you think when memories come back after amnesia that they would first manifest as dreams? Would they come slowly overtime, or all come rushing back at once?

25) Scarlett and Lorenzo immediately spend time together. She is clearly attracted to him and quite aroused around him. Is this because he's been in her dreams? Could it just be a natural human need for intimacy after a lack of intimacy?

26) Lorenzo recreates the intimate moment he and Scarlett shared on the attic ladder in an attempt to help jog some

memories. It creates intense sexual tension instead. Even though he tries to resist, ultimately, they both give in to their desires. As the reader, does this feel too quick? Does their long history and strong connection excuse their rush to intimacy?

27) At the end of the story, Scarlett realizes that Lorenzo has been there for her the entire time. She realizes that she actually is in love with him too. You might even say they are soul mates. How do you feel about the fact that in this romance novel, the main character has an intimate relationship with someone else through most of the novel, but ends up with another man in the end?

28) After reading the epilogue, we learn that everything after chapter five was just a figment of Scarlett's unconscious mind. She discovers that everything she "knows" about Eli was just a dream. What conclusion does she come to?

29) Now that you know Scarlett dreamt everything, does it change your view of Lorenzo or Eli?

30) What is the overall message you got from reading this story?

Tracey Gramajo

About the Author

Tracey Gramajo works full time as an educational interpreter for the Deaf. She has always been an avid reader and has a passion for writing complicated love stories in her free time. She toyed with writing for decades, and finally took the leap into publishing her debut novel. After many years of being a single mom to her one son, Malachi, Tracey met the love of her life during her favorite class at the gym. She lives with her husband, Ramon, they share a love of the outdoors via hiking and camping, cats, the beach, and pairing wine with food. Tracey and Ramon dream of retiring on the beach, or on a converted school bus going on adventures with their six cats, while she continues to work on authoring more stories of life, love, and laughter.